Helens-of-Troy

Janine McCaw

What Readers have Said About

Helens-of-Troy

"My daughter said this rocks which, presumably, is a good thing." - Jim Darcy

"Awesome! Girls who kick ass and not a sparkle in sight."- Joanna

"Thank God! Real by-golly power-chicks fighting the supernatural fight, instead of the usual "fake" ones serving as props for pretty boys. Thanks for this and your brilliant dialogue. This one I'll keep coming back to."-Mephisgirl

"How witty and modern!" -Elizabeth Wolfe

"You know, we've been thinking about your work and wondered why you never used the phrase "KILLmore Girls"? - @necropology - The Madore Brothers.

Dedication

*For my Mom, Delphine — who made me bacon on a bun every morning before school.
The fine-dining establishment in Troy is named for her.*

This book is also written for my friends, who keep pushing me for another.

Acknowledgments

The big thanks go to:
Paul Busch, for his encouragement, love and understanding,
Shelley Grainger for her endless reading,
Melva McLean, for her endless knowledge,
Cosmic Debris and Karen Powell for a couple of great lines,
Randy Eustace-Walden, for finding the house,
Nick Orchard, for letting me use his house,
Tom McCaw, for the book cover,
Debbie Walker at Translucent Publicity.

This book is a work of fiction. All characters are figments of my imagination. Sometimes they can't type, or spell or form proper grammatical sentences. Go figure.

Chapter 1

*H*elena LaRose dragged the body out of the house and rolled it up and across the canopied swing on her front porch. First went the feet, then the torso. By the time she got to its flailing head, the rules of motion took over, and the corpse moved itself. Its weight caused the creaky three-seater bench with the weathered cushions to rock, hitting Helena straight in the kneecaps as it swung forward.

"Easy there, Sport," she said, reaching forward and slowing the swing to a halt. "There will be no swingers on the porch tonight. I've got a reputation to maintain." If the corpse was trying to get one more kick at her, it would have to do better than that.

Taking a step back to observe her handiwork, Helena knew that something wasn't quite right in Deadville. "I should have thought more about this," she said to herself, struggling to prop the body upright. "He's just not a looker." His lifeless arms flopped around her, hitting her in the head. "Son of a bitch," she sighed.

She brushed back a strand of dark hair that had fallen in front of her eyes, and put her hands on her hips in exasperation. Moving cadavers around had certainly been a lot easier when she was younger.

"Do you need some help there, Helena?" asked the old man who had been silently viewing the entire scene from the sidewalk. "I don't think he's obeying the laws of physics. I'm pretty sure dead weight isn't supposed to move around."

She jumped. There was nothing worse than being caught in the act. She had hoped to keep things undercover a little longer. Timing never had been her thing.

She turned and gave her neighbor a wary smile. "I'm afraid you're going to have to sit in the rocker today, Mr. Wagner. I know you'd prefer to stretch out on the swing for a bit of a rest on your afternoon walk, but it's occupied at the moment."

"So I see," Mr. Wagner said, taking it all in stride. He sat down in the pine rocking chair next to his usual spot. "I guess I could break from my routine just for today."

"Thank you," Helena replied.

Mr. Wagner glanced at the body and pouted. "You've covered him with my blanket. The one you always give me to use. Do you think you can get me another one? I'd take it from him, but there's just something unsettling about using a blanket that has covered a dead guy."

"I've got another blanket ready for you, Mr. Wagner. It's in the front hall. Cotton. I know wool makes you itch. The newspaper is there, too. I'll get them both for you."

"Helena, don't get old," he sighed. "It's a bitch. Stay young and beautiful like you are."

Helena laughed. At fifty-eight, she was hardly young, but there was some kind of ageless beauty about her that was hard to dismiss.

"Young is a relative thing, but thanks, Mr. Wagner. How about I put the kettle on for us while I'm inside?"

"Can I have regular orange pekoe today?" he pleaded. "None of that herbal stuff?"

"Do you really think you should? The anti-oxidant level is so much higher in the rooibos I blended for you."

"Helena, stop being the naturopath that you are and give an old man a decent cup of tea. I'll sign a waiver if you like. I rely on a little caffeine to keep my eighty-three-year-old heart pumping. I like coffee in the morning, tea in the afternoon and a stiff shot of scotch at night. Write that down in case your doctor books don't cover the real secret to a long life."

"That won't be necessary," she laughed. "Just don't let it get around. It's bad for my business. I spend a lot of time telling my clients that peppermint tea is the elixir of life. You're right though, peppermint schnapps may be closer to the truth."

"Absinthe makes the heart grow fonder," he winked wryly, smirking at his pun. There was nothing wrong with Mr. Wagner's mind. He was sharp as a tack.

Helena watched him stretch his age-spotted finger in the direction of the body.

"Your man there, he's got a problem," he announced. "His leg has slid down to the floor. They're the first things to go, you know. Legs. For me it was the knees. Do you want me to make him sit up so the kids don't trip over him later tonight?"

Helena didn't hear him. She was staring towards the house, her mind evidently elsewhere.

"Hello? Earth to HEL-EY-NAH..." he said slowly, emphasizing each syllable of her name. "I SAID, do you want me to fix him? Are you going deaf? Do I have to shake you senseless? That's what people do to me when I have my hearing aid turned down too low."

He tugged at her skirt. A very short skirt that showed off her magnificently toned legs. He knew that would get her attention. It certainly got his. He might be an octogenarian, but certain things still worked. As much as that thought may have bothered some women... hell, it might have downright creeped them out... he often flirted with Helena and she didn't seem to mind it in the least.

Helena turned her head back towards him. "I'm so sorry, Mr. Wagner. Honestly, I don't know where my head is today. I guess I tired myself out, putting up all the Halloween decorations. I had all this running around to do this morning, even before I got started getting the house spooked-out for tonight. If you could help me with the body, that would be wonderful."

"I like the cobwebs you put up. You didn't have to buy them though. I have plenty at home I could have lent you."

Expecting a witty comeback from her, Mr. Wagner was concerned when he didn't get one. "Is everything okay, Helena?"

She cocked her head slightly and took a slow look around her front property. "Yes, although the hairs on the back of my neck seem to be a little overactive today. I can't put my finger on why that is. It must just be the occasion. I love Halloween, don't you, Mr. Wagner?"

"It's a lot more fun since you moved onto the street," he admitted.

"The house is really going to look spooky this year. I've rented some strobe lights and a fog machine from a special-FX place in the city. You'll have to come by and see it tonight. I think it will be quite something."

"I'm sure it will be. I'm a big fan of your Halloween house, you know that," Mr. Wagner said. "I wouldn't miss it for the world."

"Thanks, Mr. Wagner. I'm just a little worried. Most of the neighborhood kids are getting older now. They're harder to impress." She looked at her watch. "I thought I'd be done setting up by now, but Mr. Death-warmed-over, he's just not co-operating."

"Dead men are like that," Mr. Wagner said.

"It's not just the dead men," Helena laughed.

"That's better. I thought for a moment you were losing your sense of humor. If there's anything else I can do to help, besides fixing his leg, you just let me know. I'm not totally feeble. I can still tape up a decoration or two."

He stood up and walked over to the body. The rubber mask that Helena had stuffed for the head was pretty realistic. Under the shadow of the night it was going to be more so. He noticed the male clothing that she had stuffed to make the body. It seemed somehow familiar. A twinge of jealousy ran through his veins. He didn't like to think about Helena having a boyfriend.

"Thank you so much," Helena sighed. "I don't know what I'd do without you. See if you can prop him up a bit while you're at it. Maybe you can make it look like he's watching the kids coming up the stairs. That would be kind of scary, don't you think?"

"Oh, I'm sure it will be very scary tonight," he agreed.

"I think so too. Now, if you don't mind," she said, walking towards the front door, "I've got to go upstairs and get the rooms ready for my girls. Oh, I haven't told you, have I? My daughter and granddaughter are coming tonight to stay with me for a while. They called late last night and told me. That's probably why

I'm in such a tizzy. It's all so sudden. I haven't even gotten around to making up their beds yet. Aren't I terrible? But don't worry, I'll bring you out some sweets in a few minutes, I promise. You just make yourself at home."

"The blanket and the paper?" he reminded her, shaking his head. "I'd actually prefer that to sweets if you have too many things to remember today." He started to move the body on the swing. "I think it looks better lying down," he said. "But I'm going to turn him around like you said, so he can watch the kids coming up the walkway."

"You are now officially in charge of the dead guy, Mr. Wagner. That's one less thing for me to worry about today. I will entrust you to make it look real."

"When you're in your eighties, you get to be a bit of an expert on dead guys," he shrugged. "It's nice that you're going to be having some company. I don't want you to be lonely."

"How can I be lonely with you around, Mr. Wagner?" She sensed a note of sorrow in his voice. "You're like family to me. Telling me all the who's who and what's what when I first moved here, to Troy. I never would have guessed that Burt McGee was the preacher's illegitimate son. Not in a million years."

"Well, I still don't know how you figured out that Liz Delaney and Stacey Freeman were two sisters who were separated at birth. They don't even look alike. One's a redhead and one's a blonde. That might be close enough to call, I suppose, but one is a lot uglier than the other."

"Call it woman's intuition," Helena laughed.

"Girlie, you've got more than your fair share of that," Mr. Wagner winked. "I sometimes wonder whether you've got that E.S.P. thing going on. I really hope you don't, because if you really could read my mind, we probably wouldn't be friends."

"I'm afraid I'm not very good at reading people's minds, Mr. Wagner. Although I know a few people who can." She paused for a moment, her lips coming together tightly in a grimace. "You'd think they'd be happy with that gift, but no. Me, I'd love to be able to do it."

Mr. Wagner looked at her, unconvinced.

"Rest assured, your deep dark secrets are safe from me," she admitted.

A look of relief crossed the old man's face.

"But," Helena said, leaning in to him so close that he could smell her sandal-wood perfume, "if you swear to take it to your grave, or at least lie and say you saw them both on the beach, I'll tell you how I figured it out. The sisters have the same birthmark on their left shoulder. Identical. Shaped like a pineapple. I put two and two together when they came to my practice complaining about shoulder tension. That's where we women carry our stress."

"If you say so," he said, still intoxicated by her presence. She was wearing a tight, striped sweater that was cut low both in the back, and in the front. He couldn't take his eyes off her. She had a magnificent set of ta-tas.

"It's true, Mr. Wagner. You take a look at them next summer."

He coughed, and she realized where his gaze was aimed.

"The sisters, Mr. Wagner. They both spend hours in the sun and they've got the leathered skin to prove it. I've got them on a vitamin E regimen."

"If you say that's how you figured it out, I'll pretend I believe it," he winked. "But I still think there's more to you than the lovely picture you present to the world."

"You're always great for my ego, Mr. Wagner. I guess I do have a way with people. Well, with men anyway. Women can be a little standoffish."

"They're just jealous. You just ignore what Betty Lachey is saying."

"Why? What is Mrs. Lachey saying?"

Mr. Wagner changed the subject. "Tell you what, I won't visit for the next little while. I'll let you enjoy your company all by yourself. You won't need an old man hanging around your house."

Helena put her arm around her friend. "Nonsense. I'm sure my granddaughter Ellie will love to hear your gossip just as much as I do. She's quite the talker herself, our Ellie. She loves Halloween, as I recall. You'll be able to laugh about all the kids who were afraid to come up the steps. I'm sure you'll both find that amusing."

"Children aren't much for stories from old folks these days," he lamented.

"Well, Ellie's not exactly a child. I haven't seen her myself for a few years. She was eleven then and she's fifteen now. I suspect she's grown up quite a bit. I don't know how much she remembers about me. I wouldn't be surprised if she makes a little strange in the beginning, although I hope that it's not strained for long. I don't know if I remember how to talk to a teenager. It's been a while."

"That's what happens," he said sadly. "They grow up and they have no time for you."

"They do get busy," Helena agreed, knowing in her heart that the old man was right. Her only daughter Helen rarely even phoned her. Just a card on her birthday and a cheese tray at Christmas.

"That's probably why the hairs on my neck are standing up," she thought to herself. "Why did Helen call and ask if she and Ellie could come and stay for a while? Why now?"

Her relationship with Helen was awkward at best. It had been that way since Helen was a teenager. That's why the phone call last night had been disturbing. There was something in her daughter's voice that hinted there was more to the story than she was initially letting on. Something that intuitively told Helena that "Ellie wants to get to know you," really meant "Ellie's in danger and you've got to help us." Helen never was a good liar.

"Don't be upset if my daughter Helen doesn't seem friendly," Helena explained to Mr. Wagner. "She's like that with everybody. I don't know where she gets it from. I've lost track of how many languages she can speak… French, Spanish, Italian… but try and communicate on a human level? Well, that is a whole other ball game with her. I dare you to ask her wassup!"

"A little uptight is she? Okay, I won't take it personally. Thanks for letting me know." He looked at the dead man and sighed. The legs had fallen down again. "Are you sure this stubborn old coot isn't supposed to be me? I'm starting to see a resemblance."

"Take it easy, Mr. Wagner. Don't let him give you a fight. I can always ask one of the Lachey boys to help me with him later."

"Never you mind," Mr. Wagner said. "You put me in charge of him, and come hell or high water, in charge I will be. Mr. Corpse here would frighten the bejeezies out of young Stanley. I know he just had his eighth birthday, but he's still a bit of a baby if you ask me. You just go about your business. I'll tend to our friend here. I'll be fine. It takes me a while longer to do things, but I have no plans for the rest of the afternoon. Especially since it looks like I won't be doing any newspaper reading anytime soon."

"Maybe I didn't make the legs right," Helena said, oblivious to his remark. "Anatomy wasn't my strong subject. I probably spent too much time on the head. Did you notice the wound I made?"

"You mean the slit eyeball?"

"I spent a lot of time getting the blood on it just right."

"I can see that. Wonderful job. Brian De Palma would be proud. Now go and make the beds or do whatever you need to do. Leave him to the master. I'll set those legs straight. I'll make the man look like rigor mortis has set in."

Helena laughed. "Oh Mr. Wagner, you kill me. Well, not really, but you know what I mean. You've got quite the funny bone. Tell you what, I'll take you up on that offer and leave you to it. I'll be back in just a bit. If you need anything, just holler."

"Maybe there's another blanket up there in one of the bedrooms?" Mr. Wagner asked hopefully, but Helena had already turned away, leaving him alone on the porch.

"I might as well join you on the swing," he said to the body, "for all the attention I'm getting around here today."

Helena walked into the house and headed straight for the family-sized kitchen. She quickly filled the tea kettle with water, placed it on the stove burner and turned it on. The water would take a few minutes to boil, allowing her time to rush upstairs and check the bedrooms.

She ran up the staircase faster than she had ever done before. It winded her slightly, and she made a mental note to bring the exercise bicycle out of storage for the winter.

Standing inside the converted attic bedroom on what was the third floor of the old house, she took a look around the normally unused room. It was a good size, with plenty of closet space that could be used for a teenager's endless wardrobe. As an added feature, there was a door opening to a little balcony above the second floor. Helena knew Helen would be envious, but she wanted Ellie to have this room. It would offer the teenaged girl the privacy Helena knew Ellie would covet at that age. It would also put a floor between Ellie and her mother, and that was probably also a good thing at this point in all their lives. But it needed a good dusting before nightfall.

"So much to do, so little time," Helena sighed. She closed her eyes and drew in a deep breath. She could hear the swing creaking on the porch, but soon tuned it out. She was listening for non-earthly sounds. "You're not fooling me," she said aloud. "I can feel it. The winds of change are blowing around me, and I can tell they are not fair weather winds. So help me, if you mess with my family, I will kick your ass."

Her green eyes opened slowly and she looked around the room. There was no sign that anyone else was there, or that anyone else had heard her. "I need to get this room ready for Ellie," she said, not convinced. "So don't even start."

Shaking off the shiver that was running down her spine, she walked over to the old oak mirror hanging on the wall. She was overwhelmed with the need to look over her own shoulder. "Not that you'd show up anyway," she acknowledged, gazing into the reflection. "At least not during the day."

She paused as if she were waiting for an answer. The room offered her none. "I hope I've made myself perfectly clear."

Taking some sheets from the closet, Helena made up the bed. Ellie's bed. That thrilled her. Never in a million years did she think her granddaughter would ever be under her roof.

She spread out a handmade quilt that some Amish friends had painstakingly made for her years ago. The design was constructed from several pieces of patterned fabric laid out like stained-glass windows, all on an off-white background. It wasn't the most modern of bedspreads, but it would be warm. The room at the top of the stairs got quite chilly at night. Besides, if Ellie didn't like the bedspread, they could always take a trip together into the city for a bed-in-a-bag. Helena wouldn't take it personally. It was a teenager's prerogative to hate things. In the meantime, the covert religious symbolism might not be such a bad thing… the crosses in the pattern covering her granddaughter at night. It most likely wouldn't mean anything to Ellie, but it would make Helena sleep better, given the foreboding sensations of doom she was having.

Helen, though… Helen would be another story. Helen was smart. She'd figure out the symbolism of the bed covering in about thirty seconds and there would be hell to pay. Hell that would go on forever. "Not good," Helena said, deciding to roll back the bedspread to the foot of the bed. "What Helen doesn't know won't hurt her. At least for now," she said, opening the balcony door to let some fresh air into Ellie's room.

Leaving the door open behind her, Helena went down the flight of stairs to the second floor and headed for the room at the back of the house that would become Helen's.

That decision would have its own problems. Having her daughter sleeping down the hall meant Helena was going to have to behave herself. But other than banishing her daughter to the cottage in the backyard... the space she used as her medical office... where was Helen to sleep? She laughed. There were only three bedrooms in the house. The room with the gaudy peony-covered wall-paper that had been left by the previous owner really *was* the only answer. Her daughter Helen would hate it. That thought made Helena laugh a little harder.

"I'll be nice when she gets here," Helena promised herself. "Okay, at least I'll try to be nice."

She gave the room a once-over. She regularly vacuumed the entire second floor, so there were no cob-webs in the corners of the windows, or dust bunnies under the bed. She knew Helen would check.

Satisfied, she went down the hall and peeked in to her own bedroom, the master. It was tidy enough for company. She looked around for telltale signs of her personal life. Everything that needed to be hidden was.

Low whistles from somewhere outside the room interrupted her train of thought and made her feel afraid. "No," she whispered, turning at the noise. "Not now. The girls are coming."

She listened intently for more telltale sounds. Then she remembered... the tea! She gave her head a shake. A sense of relief warmed her veins. The sound was coming from the kitchen. She had completely forgotten about the orange pekoe. Poor Mr. Wagner!

She ran downstairs and threw a couple of teabags directly into the whistling kettle. There wasn't much point trying to be fancy. She hoped he would forgive her. "Tea, paper, blanket," she said as she gathered everything up and headed outside to the front porch.

It was too late. Mr. Wagner had left.

Helena put the tea down on the seat of the now empty rocking chair. Across from it was a perfectly positioned stuffed dead body lying across the swing. Apparently the corpse had won that battle and remained supine despite Mr. Wagner's best intentions. The blanket had thoughtfully been placed over it so the neighborhood kids wouldn't see it too early.

"Nice job, Mr. Wagner. I guess I'll see you later," she sighed.

Chapter 2

"*D*o you have to bring that?" Helen Bocelli pleaded with her daughter. "Yes I do," Ellie replied, holding the yellow ragged teddy bear under her arm. "It's my continuity. You may have moved me several times in my life, city-to-city, uncle-to-uncle, dad-to-dad, wherever… but Beastie Bear here, he always comes with me. Taking away my security so early in life could cause irreparable damage. I would have thought that was covered in those parenting magazines you've subscribed to over the years."

"Ellie, you're fifteen," Helen sighed, "so I'll ask you again, nicely. Isn't it time you let go of that ragged old bear?"

Ellie looked at her mother in mocked horror, her newly applied black lipstick adding forced drama to the dropped-jaw look she was trying hard to pull off. She flicked her long black hair over her shoulder in defiance before assuming a stance of implied superiority.

"Do you have to bring THAT?" she asked her mother, pointing to a van in the driveway. "I mean, I'm glad you're dumping him, but don't you think it's time you let go yourself? By law I think he gets fifty-percent of your communal property, and I'm thinking the stupid van is a good place to start. Put it on his side of the equation."

Helen studied the white vehicle. It *was* an eyesore. "I'm just borrowing it," she said. "Our stuff won't fit in the back of the BMW. I have to get us to your Nan's somehow."

"In a van marked 'TONY'S EXTERMINATING SERVICE'? I'm sure Nan will be impressed. I can hear her neighbors now. 'Do you have cockroaches, Mrs. LaRose'? No, that's just my daughter and granddaughter coming to live with me for a while. They like to travel in style."

Helen sighed.

"Mom, think about this," Ellie continued. "Do you actually think it will be easy for me to make friends when my mother makes me show up in a bug-mobile? Like, hello?"

Helen looked for the slightest sign of compassion in her daughter's make-up blackened eyes. There was none.

"What?" Ellie asked. "Is there something wrong with my thought process or something? I'm a straight-A student, so that would be a bit questionable, but I suppose it could happen."

Helen admitted to herself that her daughter had a point.

"I know, I know. Just get in the van, Ellie," she sighed. "I'll be bringing it back to Tony once we've settled in." She felt a loose strand of hair fall down across her neck. She reached back and placed it back into the bun at the back of her head.

There is nothing worse, Helen thought to herself, than having a fifteen-year-old daughter who is more together than you are.

Helen had agonized about leaving her husband Tony and moving Ellie to a new home for weeks, but Ellie had packed her bags in less than an hour when she had told her the news. In fact, Helen realized, it was almost as if Ellie had been expecting it.

"Don't your feel just a little bit sad, Ellie?" she asked, throwing the last suitcase into the van.

Ellie could barely contain herself. "Mom, he's a loser," she said. "Always was, always will be. I don't know what you ever saw in him. He's not good looking, he's not rich, he's just… hairy. But I'll pretend to be sad if you want me to be."

Ellie pouted, pulling her blackened bottom lip out as far as she could, just for effect.

Helen thought for a moment before answering her daughter. Tony *was* ungodly hairy. "What did I see in him? I don't know. I suppose I was looking for a protector for us. Tony is big and strong. He's really a nice man, Ellie. You just never gave him a chance."

"Do you have one of those fun-house mirrors in your bedroom or something? Tony? Big and strong?" Ellie snapped back. "Mom, the man has a complex.

He likes to kill things for a living. He keeps referring to himself in the third person as "The Exterminator," in this weird Schwarzenegger-type voice. That alone should have been your first clue. Is he Austrian? No. Should he really have an accent of any kind? No. He was born here. Has he ever even been to a foreign country? No. He's a suburban-pest-controller-hit-man-wanna-be and I'm glad we're leaving."

"How do you really feel, Ellie?" Helen commented, opening the passenger door angrily. Ellie had pushed her too far. "Get in the van. Enough of the lip for a little while, okay? I want to get to Nan's before it gets too late. And for your information, Tony and I went to an exterminator conference once, in Mexico. So he has been out of the country. For a day or two."

"There's really such a thing as an exterminator conference?" Ellie rolled her eyes at her mother. "I stand corrected."

"Grow up," Helen said, hopping into the driver's seat and fastening her seat-belt. She started the van up. The muffler made a huge racket.

"So much for sneaking into town," Ellie said. "I guess I'll just have to be satisfied with making a grand entrance. It's a good thing I'm flexible. Be proud that you've raised a daughter that isn't frightened by change. I'll go far in life."

As Helen put the van into gear, Beastie Bear did a face-plant from his spot on the dashboard.

"It's probably from the fumes in this van," Ellie commented. "Can't you smell it, Mom? It's disgusting in here. It's kind of a mix of powdered insecticide, dead bugs, an old gym bag and a hint of pepperoni. There may even be notes of alcohol on the nose, and that's not good for a scent. Eau-de-knock-off." She reached down and pulled a beer bottle out from under her seat. "Ah ha! The nose never lies."

Rolling down the window, Ellie tossed the bottle onto the lawn, much to her mother's dismay. "We wouldn't want to be pulled over with it in the car, would we?" Ellie asked with mocked innocence. "That muffler is like a magnet for the cops. Come ticket me, I'm noisy. Hmm… maybe I'd better check under your seat too, Mom."

Helen took a sniff of the air. There *was* an odd chemical smell in the vehicle, but that was pretty much an occupational hazard. "Okay, you're right about the van. I'll get it back here and make the swap for the convertible as soon as I can." She looked over at Beastie Bear. He looked like he had passed out. "I'll tell you what," she said, reaching over and propping him back up, "I'll let you out around the block from Nan's if you'd like, okay? So you won't have to show up in the van. I'd walk with you, but you know, we've got all this baggage we're carrying. I mean luggage. Wrong choice of noun."

Ellie laughed. "Thanks Mom, but you'll need my smart mouth around to protect you when the neighbors see the van. You haven't stood up to verbal abuse very well lately."

Right again, Helen thought. There was a time when she could joust with her daughter for hours, quite impressed with the vocabulary of her young child. But now Ellie was a teenager and that same vocabulary was thrown at her in a whole new way. And even though her daughter probably needed her more than ever, lately Helen's own words of wisdom had been coming out all wrong, or worse yet, not at all.

"I could follow you in the Beemer. I know how to drive," Ellie pleaded hopefully.

"How do you know how to drive?" Helen screeched, without realizing she was doing so. "Never mind. I don't want to know. No, you can't drive the coupe. Tony bought it for me, and I will not have you smashing it up. It took a lot of dead cockroaches to pay for that car, I'll have you know." She adjusted the rear view mirror. The sun was beginning to set behind them. "Wait, maybe I do want to know. Who taught you to drive? Did Tony teach you how to drive? Because he's a really bad driver, so don't listen to him."

"Tony's bad at a lot of things, so I don't ever listen to him. What happened to Dave?" Ellie asked, changing the subject. "I liked Dave."

"You were five and Dave liked you a little too much. You're not much of a judge of character."

"Tony doesn't like me at all. So much for your own character assessing abilities. I would have thought that would have mattered to you, you know, that your new husband at least be civil to your daughter. What makes you think we need a protector anyway? We were doing fine with Bill. Remember Bill? Bill was great.

People used to say I looked like him, even though he wasn't my dad. Why would you leave Bill for Tony?"

"It's complicated," Helen answered. As much as she tried to be open with her daughter, there were some things she just couldn't tell her.

"That's your answer to everything."

"Well everything *is* complicated."

"Fine," Ellie sighed, and began to chew her black, polished fingernails. She avoided looking at her mother.

"Are you nervous about something, Ellie?" Helen finally asked. "This nail-biting thing is relatively new for you. There's some gum in the glove compartment, if you'd prefer to chew on lovely mint flavor rather than old nail varnish." It seemed like only a few months ago that she had argued with Ellie about cutting the very same fingernails. They had grown so long they were starting to curl downward on their own.

"You're taking me to live with a woman I hardly know, in a town I've never heard of, where I have no friends. What's there to be nervous about?" Ellie asked sarcastically, reaching for the glove compartment door. She opened and closed it quickly. "Don't even ask what's in there," she said, her eyes opened wide in shock.

"Ah, so underneath that cool Goth exterior you've personified for yourself, the old, sweet, apprehensive Ellie, still exists," Helen smiled to herself.

"Something like that. It's complicated."

Her daughter was a bright one, Helen knew. Sometimes it made dealing with her all the more difficult. "I know you think I'm the most un-cool mother on the face of the earth..."

"Don't flatter yourself, Mom. You're at least the third," Ellie smirked, the corners of her mouth curling up goofily like some character on MAD TV.

That was it. No more late night television for her, Helen decided. "As I was trying to tell you before you immaturely made that face at me... and I hope it stays that way just to teach you a lesson... I know a little about the Goth look myself, you know. It's not exactly a new fashion statement you're making here. It's been around for generations. It's a very old European style, dating back centuries. As in, ancient. You don't want to look ancient, do you?"

"I don't know about ancient, but nineteen would be good. What are you trying to say, Mom?"

"Ellie, do you think maybe you could take off the Goth make-up before we get to Nan's?"

Ellie looked at her mother as if she had lost her mind. "It's my style."

"Look!" Helen said, pointing out the van window. "There's a Biggie Mart. Maybe we can find you a new style."

"Mom, we've discussed this before. There's nothing wrong with how I dress. Nothing's too short, nothing's hanging out… nothing. If you think about what I could be wearing, I think you'll find you've got it made. I could dress like a slutty, schoolgirl/pop-star and maybe somebody like Dave would come along and…"

"Okay, okay, I get the picture. But Ellie, look at it from my perspective. We're going to your Nan's, and today is Halloween. She's going to think it's a costume. She'll say, 'Ellie, you look so cute!' But the joke will be on her when she realizes you dress like this all the time. Not just for pagan festivals, but at Christmas, and Mother's Day, and whatever other three hundred and sixty-two days of the year there are."

"Mom, you're exaggerating. I take the make-up off at night. So you can take Christmas Eve out of the scenario and revise your count. Which is a little off, I might add, given that there is probably more than one pagan festival a year."

"That will be a relief to her, I'm sure."

"I'm her granddaughter. She'll love me no matter what."

"You think so, do you? Try calling her 'Grandma'. She'll claim you belong to the neighbors." Helen ran her finger across her throat execution style "Or kill you, so you'll never utter those words again."

"She will not."

"Give it a try. Let's see what happens," Helen shrugged.

Ellie sadly watched in the side mirror as every familiar landmark became smaller in the distance. She tried to remember what her grandmother was like, but it had been a long time since she had seen her. She remembered liking her, and she remembered that her mother didn't. Which made her wonder why they were going there in the first place?

"Do you think I'm going to embarrass her or something?" Ellie asked pensively.

"The thought had crossed my mind."

"And parking a van in front of her house, a van that's side-painted with a dead cockroach lying on its back… won't? Thanks a lot."

"So we're back to the van again. I hate it when you're right. Look, when we get to Nan's, let's pretend we like each other, at least tonight. Okay?"

Ellie looked at her mom, bewilderedly. "I do like you, Mom. Except when you treat me like a child. What did you mean by that anyway? Don't you like me? You said 'pretend we'."

The remark stung Helen. "Nothing. I'm sorry, Ellie. Of course I like you. I love you. This has just been an emotional day for me, that's all."

"You can like someone without loving them, and you can love someone without liking them," Ellie said thoughtfully.

Maybe she was growing up after all, Helen admitted to herself. She reached over and flipped Ellie's long black hair over her shoulder so she could see her daughter's face. "I like and love you, Ellie. That's also possible."

Helen thought for a moment she saw the slightest beginning of a smile on her daughter's face. It didn't last long.

"Then why are we moving to Nan's anyway? To this Troy place? Why don't we just move around the block or something? That way I can still be friends with Dina and go to the same school. We don't have to move miles away just because you've dumped your latest husband."

Helen knew the tender mother-daughter moment had passed. "I'm not sure being friends with Dina is such a good thing for you. I think she's going to get herself pregnant. It will do you good to meet some new friends. Country friends."

"She already is pregnant."

Helen sighed. "Okay, see that's what I mean. This move is going to be so good for us."

"It's not contagious or anything, being pregnant."

"It kind of is, Ellie. Sure, you won't get it from her, but if it's going around, it's going around. And don't pretend you don't know what I mean, because I know you do."

"Is that what happened to you? Didn't Nan move you to a small town in time?"

Ellie had wanted to hit a nerve in her mother, and she did. A big one.

"Ellie, you're driving me crazy. Can we change the subject please?" Helen yelled, her voice hitting decibels her daughter had never heard.

"Then let's go back to the real subject, which was, before we segued, why are we moving to Nan's?"

Ellie saw her mother panic and let go of the steering wheel, if only for a moment.

"Mom? Are you okay? I mean, if it's some deep dark secret you don't want to tell me, you don't have to. I don't have a huge issue with the unknown. If you need to keep a secret, keep a secret. I know this may come as a big surprise to you but there are some things I don't tell you. I have some secrets too."

"Oh God, I don't know if I even want to begin that conversation," Helen thought to herself.

She knew she had become too upset to drive. Looking out the window towards the right, she saw some fast food outlets coming up, off the highway. "Are you hungry, Ellie?" she asked. Not waiting for Ellie's answer, she pulled onto the off-ramp.

"Well, I kind of had some pizza at Dina's earlier," Ellie began, watching her mother's erratic behavior. She could see her mother was trembling. "Mom?"

Helen pulled into the nearest drive-through and put the van in park. "I just feel safer at Nan's."

"Why? Are we in danger or something? You're acting really weird. Did Tony threaten you? Because if he did, I can take him."

Helen smiled. If it came right down to it, Ellie probably could take him. "No, Tony didn't threaten me. Or you."

"Then what's wrong?"

Helen hesitated. "Won't it just be nice to live in a small town? Where everyone knows your name? Where all the neighbors say hello? I want the best for you, Ellie."

Tears were beginning to well up her in eyes. Not now, she told herself.

"The hookers outside of Tony's office say hello to me all the time."

Helen rolled her eyes.

"You know I get my eye-rolling thing from you," Ellie offered.

Again, Ellie was right. She was right about a lot of things, but still so wrong about others. It was all part of growing up, Helen knew, but Ellie was special. Not special like every mother's daughter is, but special in a way that only Helen and her own mother could ever possibly attempt to understand. Sooner or later, and lately it was looking like sooner, Helen was going to have to figure out a way to let Ellie understand how special she was without scaring the shit out of her. For that, she needed Helena.

"Look, let's just give it a chance, okay?" she pleaded. "Your Nan is so excited that we're coming. I know you don't know her very well, but people say she's really nice."

"People? She's your mother. Don't you think she's nice? Everyone else seems nice to you. You still think Tony is nice, and you're leaving him." She paused for a moment. "I've heard you tell Tony that Nan is nuts."

"Did I?" Helen winced. "I was exaggerating. She's just a little eccentric."

"So, is she nuts in the way I think you're nuts sometimes? Just because you're my mom?"

"Yes. Exactly like that. She drives me crazy. Even more than I do you."

"Impossible. Like what? Tell me, what does she do?" Ellie begged.

"Well, for example, I know you hate the way I dress as much as I hate the way you do. I'm much too conservative for your taste. You think I'm stuck in the eighties with big shoulder pads and big hair. I'll have you know I have let go of the shoulder pads."

"You still have a lot of hair."

"Which is why I wear it up or pulled back. Having said all that, the way you dress is too deep, dark and depressing for me. I would rather see you in something a little less funeral-esque. But I try to live with it. Your Nan however, well she's just in a world of her own."

Ellie was suddenly enthralled. There was something about her grandmother that drove her mother batty. "What about her? Is she muumuu-ville or something?"

"How on earth do you know what a muumuu is? That's way before your time."

"I sometimes watch reruns of Three's Company. They're those curtain-like dresses that Mrs. Roper wore, right?"

"Yes, but no. Your Nan is definitely not muumuu-ville. You really don't remember much about her do you?" Helen asked. "She's more like…"

"Like what?" she asked excitedly.

"Like the slutty schoolgirl/pop star."

Ellie howled. "I love her already."

"And that, my darling," Helen said, reaching across Ellie's seat to tussle her hair, "is exactly what I am afraid of."

Chapter 3

*B*y evening, a cold wind from the north began to blow through Troy. The autumn leaves, neatly raked and piled only a few hours earlier, were now whirling around in the air. Neither the cold nor the leaves seemed to bother the little ghosts and goblins out trick or treating. For them the night was full of adventure.

Most parents in the city preferred to bring their costumed kids to a supervised Biggie Mart party down at the mall. This wasn't the case in Troy. Every house on the block had the porch light on, awaiting cries of "shell out, shell out, the witches are out." The small town streets were safe enough for the excited ghouls to scamper door to door uninhibited. A few of Troy's teenagers could be counted on to get out of hand later on in the evening, but it was only seven o'clock and there not a burning leaf bag in sight.

One thing was for certain that night; everyone, no matter how old they were, paused to look at the LaRose house. The full moon cast an eerie shadow through the branches of Helena's now leafless maple tree, the barren limbs forming an effigy of a hunchbacked crone. Every thirty seconds or so, Helena's rented strobe light added to the illusion, making the shadow figure appear to boogie to a danse macabre. "Step on a crack, break the old hag's back," the children sang, as they hopped over the walkway to avoid stepping on the silhouette.

"I can't believe it's the same house," Wendy Robinson remarked, holding her young daughter Annie by the hand. "All summer long the porch had the most amazing display of pink and purple fuchsias, hanging down from moss-covered baskets. Helena won a blue ribbon for them from the horticultural society. What on earth is hanging there now?"

"I think they're spider webs," her husband said. "It looks like the stretched cotton batting we use down at the mill. The dead guy on the porch looks pretty real. Let's go take a closer look."

"How about if we just move along to the next house?" Wendy replied. "If you think I've forgotten the skimpy cat outfit Helena LaRose wore last year, you're wrong."

As the family moved on to the neighbor's house, a little girl dressed in blue gingham ran behind their backs. She disappeared around the corner as fast as her little feet would take her.

"Where'd she go?" a young boy dressed up like a cowboy asked his friend. They had just come around the corner themselves and the little girl had almost knocked them over in her rush to get away.

"Brooke runs pretty fast for a girl," his ghostly companion said. He adjusted the huge sack of candy he was lugging over his shoulder. They had been to almost every house on the street and his bag was getting heavy.

"Yeah, but…"

"Forget her," the ghost said to his lasso-laden friend.

They appeared to be about the same age, but the ghost was a little bit taller and quite a bit pudgier than the cowboy.

"Let's see what Mrs. LaRose is giving out this year," the bigger kid said. "Last year I reached into that big cauldron on the porch and pulled out a roll of dimes. Five bucks!"

"I only got a chocolate bar," the cowboy lamented.

"Everybody knows she puts the good stuff at the bottom, Stan. I dare you to do it this year. Put your arm all the way into the pot."

Stan Lachey was not so eager. "Something might happen to it. You don't know this house like I do, Kevin. I heard a kid went missing here last year. Somebody dared him to go into the back yard and he's never been seen alive since. I'm not taking any dares, that's for sure. A chocolate bar's not so bad. If that's what's on top."

Stan pulled the string under his chin a little tighter, ensuring his black faux-Stetson wouldn't fall off. His hand reached down to the toy gun in his plastic holster, like he had seen many an officer did on *COPS*. It did little to comfort him. Taking a deep breath as he gazed at the house, he wished he had brought his inhaler. He could feel his chest tighten and wasn't sure if it was his asthma acting up or whether he was truly going to be scared to death, right there on Maple Street.

"Don't be such a wussy," Kevin complained. "If the story was true, the place would have been crawling with cops. Mrs. LaRose would be in jail, not treating my mom for her sciatica, whatever that is. I'm going up to the porch. Remember last year she had that awesome scarecrow propped up in the rocking chair? There was blood coming out of his nose and his ears and white frothy stuff gagging out of his mouth… it was totally wicked."

Stan shuddered. He wasn't much for blood and gore. "Shut up, Kevin. Maybe I'll just give it a miss this year."

Stan's older brother Ryan, who had been casually observing the situation from his spot behind a hydro pole, approached his younger sibling. Being sixteen and too old for trick or treating, Ryan Lachey and his friend Tom Williams found themselves babysitting Stan on the annual candy raid. It would only take an hour or so, and besides, Ryan's mom had slipped them a twenty for their troubles. They weren't quite sure how they had gotten stuck with Kevin, but Kevin was an okay kid and Stan's only friend, so they had let it slide.

"We'll use the money to get Old Man Wagner to get us some beer," Ryan assured Tom. "And we can prowl for chicks while we're out here. It's like a job with benefits. That's how I see it."

"Old Man Wagner's a beer scalper," Tom complained. "That twenty will barely get us a six-pack if we ask him to get it. He'll make us throw in another five. He's been ripping us off all summer."

"What are ya gonna do?" Ryan shrugged. "No one else believes we're twenty-one."

"He doesn't believe we're twenty-one," Tom replied. "He just does it. He says he's too old to worry about jail, but not too old to make a buck or two. Cheap bastard."

It took a while for Tom's assessment to register with Ryan, and even then, Ryan didn't want to believe it.

"He's okay though, for a guy who's almost dead," he assured his friend. "My mom said he was a fucking sly dude when he was younger. The cops were always hauling his ass off for something. They ripped out his whole garden one summer in the sixties, or so my granny told her." He took an imaginary toke and shrugged. "He probably figures... what the hell? Give the dudes some brew. Tell you what, if my mom knew he bought us beer, he would be fucking dead. So he's okay by me. Even if he is a cheap bastard."

"Yeah, I guess so," Tom said. Sometimes it was easier just to agree with Ryan than try to explain things to him.

"Fuck. I wish I had worn a coat tonight," Ryan admitted. He pulled down the sleeves of the jersey he wore beneath his black number twelve football jersey, but it didn't help. He shivered. The nylon pants he wore hanging down below his crotch gangsta-style, didn't offer much protection from the wind.

"Fashion alert," Tom taunted. "You can wear hoodies after September. Even jocks like you."

"Why don't you tell me stuff like that before I leave the house? Shit," he complained.

Ryan stood six feet tall and weighed in at a bone-crunching two hundred and ten pounds. "What? What are you gawking at?" he asked Tom rhetorically. He knew damn well what Tom was staring at. He had shaved his head earlier in the afternoon in preparation for the upcoming football game.

"The 'do' dude," Tom replied, shaking his head. "I can't get used to it. It's a little Smallville." He didn't know if the evil-son/bad-guy look was quite what Ryan was aiming for. "They killed him off, you know."

"Reborn, my friend, reborn. Anyway, I was aiming for a scary wrestling dude," Ryan corrected him. "A lean, mean, fighting machine. I mean, would you want to run into me on the field? Like, fuck no. I thought about this a lot before I did it. It's all part of my master plan for total territorial dominance. Besides, I'll save on haircuts."

He wished he had thought about how his hairless head would handle a Troy winter. He pulled a ski-band out of his pant pocket and placed it over his ears. They were starting to numb in the cold.

"What's the matter, Stan?" he asked, moving closer to hover over his brother. "Scared?"

"No," Stan answered. "I'm not scared. But I'm not stupid either."

Stan watched as Kevin, who had recently turned nine and was full of bravado, made his way up the walkway towards the front porch. "How come," Stan asked his brother, "there's lightning all around this house when it's not raining? Don't you think that's a little weird?"

Ryan looked at Stan in disbelief as the special effects worked their magic. "You're a little weird. You might want to re-think that stupid remark."

"Stan, come on," Kevin begged. "It's awesome. I can see a dead body on the swing. The hand is sticking up like it's stuck or something." Kevin kept going up the stairs until he reached the dead guy. Daring to touch the arm, he was amused by its stiffness. "Look, when I push it down, it doesn't move. Awesome!"

Feeling the chill of the night air himself, Tom Williams did up the zipper on his brown leather jacket. He put his hands deep in his pockets and struck a pose of indifference. Tom was the total opposite of Ryan. His tight jeans clung to his slightly shorter, lean body in a manner only a sixteen year-old could pull off. He casually ran his hand through his blond, spiked hair, pausing to look at his reflection in the side-mirror of a car parked on the street. Liking what he saw, he nodded, and turned his gaze to the house. "Didn't your mom teach you to respect the dead, Kevin?" he asked, taking note of the Halloween prop. "Leave it alone."

"Whatever!" Kevin said, holding his arms out zombie style, his fingers rigid, towards Stan. "I am a creature of the night," Kevin claimed. "I come to suck your blood."

"You're seriously mixing up your monsters there," Tom corrected him.

"Like they've got rules?" Kevin laughed.

Stan's eyes went wide as his whole body froze in fear. "That's not funny, Kevin. This house is really haunted, no lies. You shouldn't make fun of them like that."

Ryan tapped Stan lightly on the shoulder from behind, causing Stan to jump about a foot. "Boo."

"Cut it out, Ryan. I'm telling Mom."

Ryan could see tears forming in Stan's eyes. "It's just the LaRose house, you big suck. The same house you raked the leaves at yesterday. What the hell is wrong with you tonight?"

"Tonight?" Tom jeered. Ryan's little snot-nosed brother was being a royal snot-nosed jerk.

"It's freaking Halloween, Ryan. Don't you know anything?" Stan stammered.

Ryan could see the strain on his brother's face. For an eight-year-old, Stan was already starting to look old. The deep furrow in his brow was going to be with him for life. He slapped his brother across the head. "Don't swear. Don't even pretend to swear. You'll fuck it up, and I'll get in shit. So, no swearing, you got it?"

Stan nodded.

"What do you mean, anyway?" Ryan asked. "What don't I know? Just stop blubbering and tell me."

"Everybody knows Halloween is the one night a year they can make their move because everyone else looks just like them," Stan whispered, his voice cracking with fright.

"Who's them?" Ryan asked, throwing his hands into the air. "Booger people? Who?"

"You are so dumb, Ryan! T.H.E.M! The-Human-Eating-Monsters!"

"Stan..."

"Okay," Stan began slowly, trying to get his point across to his brother. "Explain to me how come five seconds after I bagged all the leaves in the backyard yesterday, they were all over the ground again? I'm telling you, cross my heart, all the leaves moved. It's like someone else was there, tossing them all around. Only I couldn't see him."

"I don't know, Stan," Ryan sighed. "Maybe there are some kick-ass *Man from Glad* ghosts in the neighborhood hiding behind the trees just waiting to jump out and make you shit your pants. That's the only other explanation I have. Yesterday was not Halloween, so there goes your theory." There was a look of exasperation on Ryan's face as he looked to Tom for help.

"Sorry, Ryan. He's right," Tom admitted reluctantly. "I've heard about it before. There's this force that can move all around you, even touch you, without you seeing it. But usually you can feel it. It makes your body cold."

"See," Stan said. "Tom knows what I am talking about."

Tom laughed, putting his hands on Stan's shoulders and shaking them. "I'm talking about the wind, Stan. Chill buddy."

Ryan grabbed his brother by his six-shooter belt, pulling him closer to his own body. He put his massive hand over Stan's cowboy hat and shook his brother's head up and down a couple of times, forcing him to nod in agreement. "Okay, Stan. It's time to wrap this up. Make this the last house. Tom and I want to get home and Mom doesn't want you out on the streets alone." He looked slyly at Tom. It was time to toughen Stan up, one way or another. "Not after that kid went missing last year," he added. "You remember me telling you about that, right? I heard that Mrs. LaRose has got the body buried behind the house. Did you notice any patches in the backyard when you were over there? Something that looks like a grave? You did, didn't you?"

Stan nodded his head slowly. "Uh huh."

"You probably even raked over some of his hair poking out from the ground. News flash. That wasn't a new rake she got you to use last week, Stan. It's a corpse-o-matic 500 styling comb." He ran his hand across his bald head, shaking imaginary hairs from his fingers in front of Stan's eyes. "Psyche," he said, looking back at Tom and nodding with satisfaction.

"See, Kev," Stan yelled. "I told you." He turned to Ryan. "Maybe we should go home now. I don't need any more candy. I think I'm going to barf."

"Stan. We're only messing with your head. There's no missing kid. There's no body. There's no grave, there's nothing. I swear. You've got to loosen-up bro. I'm not always going to fucking be here to hold your hand."

"You wait until Kevin goes missing and winds up on the news. Then we'll see."

"Stan's already got a bag full of candy, Ryan. Let's just go," Tom said impatiently. "Maybe Jacey knows where there's a party going on. We can call her from your place. Maple Street isn't exactly a prowl party."

"Hang on," Ryan said, reaching into Stan's bag and pulling out a couple of chocolate bars. He handed one to Tom. "This is the last house, I promise. I want to see what Mrs. LaRose is wearing tonight. Maybe she'll be dressed in a long, black, silky thing. Or a short, black, silky thing." He grinned lasciviously. "Whatever."

"You worry me, buddy," Tom said, shaking his head. "Mrs. LaRose, she's like a grandmother. Why don't you ever go after someone our age?"

"Grandmother or not, Mrs. LaRose is hot. You find me someone our age that looks like her and I'll make my move. Until then, I don't mind hanging around here for a few more minutes." He turned towards Kevin. "Kev. Don't just stand there. Ring the bell."

Kevin was too busy digging through the candy in the cauldron to pay any attention to Ryan.

"I guess I'm going have to do it myself," he said. "Come on, Stan. Get on my back. I'll take you up there."

He began to lower his massive frame so his brother could piggyback on him. But his plans were interrupted as his attention turned to the sound of a loud van coming down the road. "What a piece of shit," he said, as it pulled to the curb in front of the LaRose house.

Tom noticed the corporate logo on the side. "It's the city death squad."

"There's chicks inside it," Ryan noticed, standing back up without his brother on his back. "Why would chicks be riding around in a roach mobile? It's got to be part of Mrs. LaRose's Halloween thing. The show's getting better every year." He nodded for Tom to join him back in the shadows of the tree. They silently watched the passengers get out of the vehicle.

Ellie took a good look at the LaRose home. "I didn't know Nan decorated her house up every year," she said to her mother. "It's pretty cool. It looks like the Addams Family house. I'll fit right in."

Helen came and stood on the sidewalk beside Ellie. "Hmm..." she pondered, looking at the decorations. "I just hope she takes it down before Christmas."

"You know, you sounded just like Marge Simpson when you said that," Ellie commented. "Not to mention your hair's looking a little bouffant."

Helen patted her windblown bangs down. "I would have kept the window up but I was getting a little car sick," she admitted. "I am definitely bringing the van back as soon as I can."

"Check it out," Ryan whispered to Tom. "They could be Mrs. LaRose's sisters, they look so much like her."

"I guess they kind of look like her," Tom shrugged. "I don't spend as much time looking at grandmothers as some people around here do."

"Dude, they're babes."

"Ryan, the one on the right is like forty."

"Really? My dick can't tell them apart." His eyes became as intimate with the female forms as their bulky autumn clothing would allow.

Tom took a long look at Ellie. "Are you on crack? Goth-Chic is our age. She's got a math book under her arm. Look familiar? I guess not to you."

"Not Goth-Chic. I meant the preppie babe. Her and Mrs. LaRose. I'd do 'em. You can have Goth-Chic."

"Isn't there some polygamy law against that?" Tom asked. "You haven't joined some fundamentalist religious sect on me, have you?"

"It's only illegal if you marry them," Ryan shrugged. "I don't make the laws, dude. And like you said, I don't have to worry about the age thing."

"I find it disturbing that you've thought about it," Tom admitted.

Kevin, bound and determined to find money at the bottom of the cauldron whether there was any or not, was starting to get impatient. "Stan, are you coming or what?" he asked, his arm buried deep in the candy. "Should I just throw you something?"

"Stan," Ryan yelled, giving his brother a push. "Get the FUCK up the stairs. I want to go home."

Helen turned, noticing the boys for the first time. She did a ten-second sum up. Two of them looked to be Ellie's age. The bald-headed kid with the foul mouth was trouble, no doubt about it. He had a look only a mother could love. Maybe. The other boy wasn't much better in her eyes. He was too good looking for his own good. He'd also be trouble. Two minutes in Troy and there were already two reasons to leave.

"Lovely language they speak here," Helen commented to Ellie. "Don't be in a rush to learn the local dialect."

A flash of the strobe caught Ellie, illuminating her in slow motion. The unflattering light outlined her mascara-laden eyes and made her complexion eerily pale.

She looked at the boys. Trash-mouth, well she could teach him a few choice words of her own if only her mother weren't around. The other one... the cute one... left her momentarily speechless.

Tom looked at Ryan. "Oh yeah. Goth-Chic's a hottie," he said sarcastically. "Thanks for giving her to me."

"My name is not Goth-Chic," Ellie snarled back at them.

"Fuck, she's got bat hearing or something," Ryan whispered to Tom.

"I guess we were being kind of loud," Tom offered. "We'd better cool it if we want to make a good impression."

"Too late for that. The Mom's already got the 'lock-up-her-daughter' look going on," Ryan sighed. "I know it well."

Ellie noticed Stan standing by himself on the sidewalk. She offered her hand to him. "Come on, kid. You want candy? I'll take you up there. This is my house now."

Her dark demeanor was not assuring to Stan in the least. He noticed the chipped black nail polish on her fingers. He also noticed a spider tattoo peeking out from under her sleeve. "Thanks, Cruella," he said nervously, "but I'm not supposed to go anywhere with strangers."

"Suit yourself," Ellie shrugged.

The front door of the LaRose home opened, framing Helena in a long, sexy, slit-to–the-navel, black dress.

Helen rolled her eyes. "I knew it."

"Sweet," Ryan smiled.

"I thought I heard a car door slam!" Helena squealed, slinking down the stairs in six-inch stilettos.

Stan looked towards her and froze in fear. He could have sworn he saw something pass swiftly behind her on the walkway, then turn and head into her backyard. It was only there for a moment, and it looked right at him. Whatever it was.

"What's the matter, Stan? Cat got your tongue?" Helena asked. "You're awfully quiet tonight. Don't let my outfit scare you. It's just a little ensemble I threw together for the occasion. I couldn't decide whether I wanted be a witch or a vampire queen. I went for both."

Stan grabbed at his throat, choking as he gasped for air.

"For heaven's sake, Stan. It's just a figure of speech!" Helena said. "There's not a cat in sight." She looked at Ryan for help. "Did he swallow a gumball whole? Do I need to do the Heimlich maneuver on him?"

"It's okay, Mrs. LaRose," Ryan assured her. "He's just scared. I have his inhaler in my pocket." Ryan pulled it out and gave it to Stan, who promptly filled his lungs in hurried puffs. "He's always forgetting it. I figured he'd need it sometime tonight."

"He's lucky he's got you to look out for him, Ryan. Is he going to be okay?"

"He'll be fine," Ryan assured her. "Just give it a minute."

"A boy Stan's age shouldn't have shock-related asthma. You tell your mother to bring him around to my office one day this week. I'd like to see if I can help. I think a lavender elixir would work wonders for him."

"I'll ask her, Mrs. LaRose. But I wouldn't hold your breath."

Helena turned and reached her arms out towards the girls. "My darlings! I didn't mean to ignore you. Come give me a hug. This is the most wonderful visit I've had all year. Go inside and make yourselves comfortable. I'll be about another half an hour with the kiddies, so that will give you some time to settle in. Helen, you can have the room down the hall from mine on the second floor. Mine would be the big room. Ellie, the room at the top of the peak with the little balcony there is all yours." She pointed at it from the walkway. The light was on awaiting Ellie's arrival. "You must be tired. We can catch up in the morning."

"Thanks, Gram!" Ellie said, looking up at the house. "Wow. I've never had my own private balcony."

Helena shuddered, and then waved her manicured finger at her granddaughter. "Uh, uh, uh, enough of that, Ellie. If you choose to let the odd expletive loose in this household, it will be overlooked. But utter THAT four letter word again, and believe me, hell hath no fury, as they say."

"I warned you," Helen reminded her daughter, repeating the neck slashing gesture she had made in the van. "Ix-nay on the gram-nay."

"Sorry, Nan?" Ellie said apprehensively.

"Much better," Helena said, giving Ellie a big hug.

Ellie's arms gave her a big squeeze in return.

"That's what I've missed," Helena said to her granddaughter. She then stepped towards Helen, hoping for the same reaction, but her daughter pulled back from her. "Is everything okay, Helen?" she asked.

"Really, Mother," Helen began, "are you telling me, that in all the closets in that big old house of yours, you couldn't find something a little less revealing to wear into the middle of the street than a flimsy evening gown? It looks so... cheap."

"Helen," Helena sighed. "Don't be such a stick in the mud. It's Victoria's Secret, dear. I can assure you it wasn't cheap. Now give me a proper hug." She threw her arms around her daughter and gave her a big kiss.

Helen wiped her face with her glove. Even as a child she had hated when her mother left lipstick on her cheek. "How come Ellie gets the room with the balcony?" she pouted.

"Because she is young and beautiful and will probably have a wilder sex life than either of us can dream about. She'll need to get by you somehow."

"She is only fifteen. She doesn't have a sex life. At least she better not have. I'm counting on you to set an example."

"Another conversation for another day," Helena said knowingly.

"Don't go putting ideas into her head, Mother."

"Can we help you, Mrs. LaRose?" Ryan asked.

"No, you cannot help," Helen stated. "Why are you still here?"

"Helen, don't be rude to the boys. They can help bring the luggage in," Helena answered. "Just the things they'll need for the night please, boys. We can unload the rest in the morning. The van will be safe enough." She looked at the exterminator logo on the vehicle parked in front of her house. "Really, Helen. And you have the nerve to question *my* style."

"I told you," Ellie echoed to her mother. "We should have come by bus."

Ryan followed Helen as she walked to the rear of the van. "Can I carry something for you, Mrs. LaRose? I mean you, the other Mrs. LaRose. Or whatever your name is. I figure you probably don't want me calling you Helen. Or do you?"

"It's Bocelli, actually," Helen replied, irritated. "On second thought I'll probably be switching it back to LaRose. Ms. LaRose is fine. Helen is not." She opened the rear doors and pointed at a suitcase. "Take the heavy blue one, will you? Thank you. Ryan, is it?"

He nodded. "I live next door. Nice and handy, in case you need anything. Anytime."

"Great," Helen muttered, under her breath. Just what she needed. A swearing, sex-crazed behemoth living a stone's throw away from her impressionable daughter.

"So... it's Ms. LaRose. I take it you're single?"

The look she threw him said it all.

"Okay then, I'll just take these into the house," Ryan said, giving her the same look back.

Tom walked over to the side of the van and opened the sliding door for Goth-Chic. "So you'd be Ellie Bocelli?" he smirked.

Ellie stared him down, having heard that one before. "You can rhyme. Very good. You must be the smart one." She pulled her duffle bag from the car seat and threw it on the ground.

"Nice to meet you too," Tom said sarcastically, unsure what had set her off.

"I'm not Ellie Bocelli. I am a LaRose. I'm technically a bastard. But that's more information than I usually give somebody I don't know. Happy now?"

"Working the 'Miss Congeniality' thing are you? Why do I get the feeling that's not a costume for you? I'm surprised you can stand there under the streetlight. Doesn't that hurt you people?" he sassed back.

Ellie grinned, appreciating the quick comeback. She took a lingering look at Tom. There had been plenty of good-looking boys at home, but Tom, he was definitely worth the move.

"We took that into consideration when 'my people' designed energy effi-cient bulbs. You'll notice the soft-pink light they produce reduces glare. Not only does it not make me want to immediately crawl into a coffin," she paused, suddenly losing her icy edge without wanting to do so, "it's easy on the eyes." She felt her heart begin to beat faster. Just looking at him did that. She desper-ately hoped her voice had not just given her feelings away.

Tom, upon closer inspection of Ellie, saw that Ryan was right. They all did look alike, which meant that Ellie was also a babe. Her hair was long, dark and silkily beautiful. His eyes lowered to her chest, where he guessed that under-neath the baggy black sweater she was wearing, she was built a lot like her grandmother. It was hard to tell. He smiled at Ellie, slightly embarrassed.

"Easy on the eyes," he repeated, a sexy smile coming across his face. "Okay, Goth-Chic. Let's start again. I'm Tom. Tom Williams. I live two streets down on Pine Crescent. I'm a straight-A student and I work part time at my dad's hardware store down on Main. I couldn't throw a football if my life depended on it. That makes me a loser in this football crazy town. Tossing a pigskin would be my buddy Ryan's job. He's the all-star. And a letterman. That last part might surprise your mom. Of course he got it for football, but apparently it still counts."

Ellie smiled back shyly. He was beyond cute. Her shoulders raised and her fists tightened uncontrollably as she tried to prevent herself from gushing right in front of him. "My name's really Helen, like my mom, but everyone calls me Ellie. Ellie LaRose. It gets too confusing otherwise. I'm athletic, but I'd never get a letter for sports. I like the javelin. Weird huh? I like to pierce things."

Tom noticed her ears held several earrings. His mind began to wonder about what else might be pierced. Nothing would surprise him.

"And I like to dress in black," she summed up.

"So I see," he said, subconsciously running his hand through his hair, mak-ing sure every one was still in place.

"Anything else you want to know?"

"Helena, Helen and Ellie?" Tom asked quizzically.

"You've got it. You *are* the smart one."

"It's kind of ironic then..."

Ellie looked at him bewilderedly.

"The two of you moving to Troy," Tom said. "Population 3,000 and well, two."

Ellie suddenly got it. "Oh my God," she said, slapping her forehead with her hand. "That makes us the Helens of Troy. Please don't point that out to anyone else."

"See. You are smarter than a fifth grader. Don't worry, I won't."

Ellie laughed. Tom took it as a sign their verbal jousting had come to an end. He relaxed a little. There was something unusual about her, he thought. And it wasn't just the outfit. Maybe it was her big green eyes, framed by lashes that were longer than any he had seen on a girl in his life. Maybe it was just that she was hot, like Ryan said. Maybe it was the fact that for the first time in his life, he was actually seeing an aura around someone.

"I heard your grandmother ask you to call her Nan. Nan, Gran, what's the difference?" he asked, his head tilting from side to side looking at her, following the patterns of light around her that only he seemed to be able to see.

"A big one, apparently. She doesn't like to be reminded of her age. She thinks people will think Nan's short for Nancy or something. I guess I could call her Helena. I don't know. Whatever makes her happy. What are you looking at?"

"Nothing," he said, trying not to look at her glow. "Ryan's in love with her, just so you know. Ryan's pretty much in love with anything that's female and alive."

Alone on the sidewalk, Stan was feeling abandoned. "Hello? I'm over here. Remember me? The kid who wants to go up the stairs before next year," he yelled, finally finding his voice. "What? Am I invisible or something?"

"Stan. Will you just go up the..." Ryan started?

"Could you please not drop an f-bomb?" Helen interrupted.

"Stan, go up the stupid stairs," Ryan continued, looking at Helen defiantly. "You little wimp-ass," he added.

Stan thought it over. He didn't want to go down in history as the only kid who was afraid to go up Mrs. LaRose's porch. Especially now that these new people had arrived. Kevin, Ryan, Tom and even Mrs. LaRose pretty much knew he was afraid of the littlest things, but he still had a chance with the strangers. He slowly walked up the stairs, onto the porch and reached into the cauldron. Fearing to look inside, in case something truly evil lurked there, he turned towards the swing. He screamed. He could feel his head swirling, and he knew no matter how much he didn't want to do it, he was going to faint.

Ellie darted to the porch. As Stan spun around, she held out her arms, catching him.

"Well! This has never happened before," Helena exclaimed.

"Kid," Ellie said, easing him to the ground. She slapped him across the face. "Kid, wake up."

"Don't do that," Ryan yelled, running up behind her. "His name's Stan. He'll come to in a second. He always does this. He has a short synapse or something. It makes him pass out when his adrenalin gets charged."

"You mean thanks, right?" she asked him. "For catching him so he didn't split his head open when he fell?"

Ryan nodded sheepishly.

"How'd you know he was going to do that?" Tom asked, joining them on the porch. "You were running up to him before he even turned to look at the dead guy." The aura about her had changed. It was dimmer, as if some of its power had been lost.

She thought about it. "I don't know. I just had this feeling."

Stan began to stir. He tried to open his eyes, but his pupils were stuck somewhere up in his head.

"Do you want your inhaler, Stan?" Ryan asked.

Stan shook his head. His speech was slurred, but the color was starting to return to his face. He tried to focus. "There's a dead body on the swing."

"Yes dear, I know," Helena said, feeling his forehead. He was a little clammy. She reached for his wrist and felt his pulse. It had returned to a normal rate and he seemed to be breathing easier. She heaved a sigh of relief. "Maybe this one's a little too realistic this year."

Tom looked at the dead guy on the swing. He pulled the blanket down from his face, wanting to get a closer look at him "Um, Mrs. LaRose?"

"Cover his face up again, Tom. I don't want him scaring any more children."

Tom didn't move.

"Tom? Are you okay?"

Tom, like Stan before him, was turning ashen before her eyes. It was only a moment before he too, passed out on her porch.

"Well, I didn't see that one coming," Ellie said.

"What is going on here?" Helen asked. "Mother?"

Helena had no idea.

"I can't take them anywhere," Ryan joked, but even he was feeling uneasy. "I'm used to Stan visiting Neverland, but that was a first for Tom." He turned and looked at the swing. An odd look crossed his face. "Mrs. LaRose?"

"Ryan, you stay firmly planted there," Helena stated, pointing at his feet. "There will be no more fainting tonight. Three's a crowd."

"I don't know how to tell you this," Ryan said, his voice suddenly becoming solemn. "There really is a dead body on the swing. It's Old Man Wagner."

Chapter 4

*P*icking up and moving wasn't so bad this time, Ellie thought.

In the past, she and her mother would wind up renting a tiny, run-down apartment on the west side of the city. Bits and pieces of her life would be carelessly thrown into her mother's car, to be unloaded in a cramped little bedroom she and Helen would have to share. If they were lucky, the flat would be semi-furnished with other people's castoffs; mismatched chairs around a kitchen table that looked like it had been salvaged from a restaurant makeover. The table would serve double-duty as her homework center. Eventually, a new man would enter her mother's life and there would be another move. It was always to a bigger place, and she always got her own room, but it was always temporary.

This time she hadn't wanted to bring many of her personal things along. As she had glanced around her room at Tony's one last time, it dawned on her... this room is a girlie room. It was pink and perky, and she just wasn't anymore. Even her favorite posters on the wall seemed juvenile. There was no accounting for her musical taste when she was twelve. In her heart she knew she no longer belonged in the room that said "Ellie" on a ceramic nameplate on the door. She had half expected her banged-up skateboard to flip up and hit her on the ass on her way out.

Her Nan's house, she was delighted to discover, was fully furnished. It had a welcoming feeling about it... lifeless human on the porch swing aside. There was a big, solid oak table in the dining room. It was big enough for eight people to sit at, their butts held firmly on chairs that actually matched. In the living room she found a well-worn beanbag chair that she was pretty sure her Nan didn't sit in anymore. It was an avocado color that screamed "I was made before you were born," and it was amazingly comfy. Ellie dragged it from the corner of the room and settled down in front of the fireplace. It was a real fireplace with real wood burning in it. She could have stared at it for hours. She had a craving for a soda, but she heard her mother arguing with her Nan in the kitchen, and she just didn't want to go there. Instead, she watched the fire until the burning embers lost all of their color and the crackling noise stopped. It was time then, she decided, to make her way up to the room at the top of the stairs for the night. Her room.

Once inside, she started to unpack her suitcase, tossing her clothes wildly across the room. She laughed when her jacket caught itself on the hook on the bedroom door, as if it knew instinctively where it belonged.

"I finally have a real bed," she squealed. "A double bed. It might even be a queen-sized bed." She jumped on top and began to make snow angels upon the mattress. "I've got room to roll over. What a concept." She sat up and propped some pillows against the headboard. "And... I have room for somebody else," she smiled saucily.

Her cell phone was in her pants pocket. She reached into it, pulled it out and called her friend.

"Hello, this is Dina. Leave a message. I'm out," said the teenaged voice on the other end of the line.

Ellie sat up on the bed. She could barely hide the disappointment in her voice. "Hey Dina. It's Ellie. Sorry to call you so late. You'll never guess what happened tonight. We got here to this stupid Troy place, and I met the cutest guy. His name's Tom and he is tall and blond and oh-my-god-gorgeous. You just have to see him. I'll try to get a celly-pic of him and send it to you. And there was a dead body on my Nan's porch. Mom totally freaked. She kept sending death stares to my Nan like it was her fault or something. It was the weirdest night. Call me back."

She hung up and looked around for an electrical socket to recharge the phone. Her eyes followed a lamp cord until it led her to an outlet near where she had earlier dropped her duffle bag. The big t-shirt she liked to sleep in was poking out from where the pull-ties of the bag had come loose. She went over to the bag and pulled the top out and smelled it. The scent of the fabric softener her mother always used lingered on the cotton and she found it oddly comforting.

"At least it doesn't smell like bug death," she said to herself, taking off the clothes she had worn during the day and putting on the shirt. She found her phone charger in the front pocket of the bag, and plugged it in, placing the phone on the nightstand.

She plopped back down on the bed. As she stared at the stucco ceiling above her, she thought again about the warning look she had seen her mom flash at Nan when they first entered the house. What was up with that? It wasn't like Helen hadn't seen a dead body before. Dead bodies seemed to follow her mother around. Like the time when Ellie was five and an ice storm snapped the overhead wires on the street where they lived. They whipped around for what seemed like minutes before finally falling and electrocuting the garbage man before their very eyes. Her mother didn't seem very upset about it. She told her the man in the dirty coveralls was very, very bad and got what he deserved. Ellie never found what he had done. Her mother had told her to never speak of it again.

She was also to remain mum about the time they were canoeing and they accidentally hit a lump of seaweed that turned out to be a lump of torso. She had heard her mother drop an f-bomb herself that time. "Fuck, Frankie," Helen had said, and Ellie never learned who Frankie was or how her mother could recognize him or her without a head. That conversation was also always met with what Ellie referred to as "the death stare."

Ellie turned out the lights and tried to settle down but something wasn't right. She tried to put her finger on it. It wasn't the bed. It wasn't the room. It was... Beastie Bear. She needed him and he was still in the van. That wouldn't do.

Throwing the bedspread back in a huff, she got out of the bed and headed into the hallway. She passed her mother on the way down the stairs.

"You're still awake, Ellie?" Helen questioned. "It's after midnight."

"Yes. I left something in the van. I'll be right back."

"Do you really need it now? Can't it wait until the morning?"

"Beastie Boy," Ellie said firmly. She was ready to cause a scene if she had to. "I want him."

"Okay, be quick about it though, it's cold outside. Put a coat on. The keys to the van are on the table by the front door." Helen was too exhausted from the long day to fight with her daughter again.

Ellie nodded and continued down the stairs. She noticed Helena in the living room, looking outside through the paneled glass aside the front door.

"Are you okay, Nan?" Ellie asked.

"I'm fine," Helena replied, her gaze not moving from the window. "I just thought I heard something outside." She shrugged. "It was probably a stray cat. Can I get you something?"

"I'm just running to the van. I forgot... something. I'll be back in a minute. Can I borrow your shawl?" she asked, picking Helena's wrap from the chair it rested on. She paused only long enough to acknowledge her Nan's nod of permission. Shoving her feet in her sneakers without actually putting her heels into her shoes, she grabbed the car keys from the table and flip-flopped her way outside, her bare heels sliding and hitting the damp ground every other step.

The wind had died down, revealing a strange scent in the still night air. It smelled like dirt. It smelled like a stinky gym bag. It smelled like a wet dog. She wrinkled her nose. Something was definitely up with her sense of smell tonight. "Mom must have left a window open in the van," she mused, as she headed around to the driver's side of the vehicle to check. "We are polluting the neighborhood with eau-de-cockroach."

Inside the house, Helena had moved to the dining room window. Her face grew grave as she watched her granddaughter outside. "Ellie, come back around where I can see you," she whispered, sliding the window open so she could call to her granddaughter if she needed to. As the smell of the night air filled the room, Helena's hands motioned the scent towards her nostrils, much like one would sample the aroma of a fine French perfume. The smell was disturbing. It smelled like danger. It smelled like hunger. It smelled a wet dog. She walked back to the front door and opened it. "You are polluting my neighborhood with eau-de-fear," she whispered into the darkness.

The interior van light went on as Ellie opened the driver's side door and hopped inside. Reaching across the dashboard to pick up Beastie Bear, she could see through the passenger side window that Helena was now standing on the porch watching her every move.

"What? Does she think I'm a baby or something?" she asked aloud. "If I'm going to have both Mom and Nan watching me day and night, I might as well roll over and die a virgin."

She checked the windows. They were all rolled up. "Hmm," she thought. "That's weird. It smells worse outside the van than inside. What is that smell?" She plugged her nose with one hand and slid over to the passenger side to get out. As she reached for the door with her free hand, she heard a low, rumbling growl. She jumped back in the seat. With the edge of the shawl she rubbed away the fog that was forming on the inside of the window. Through the condensation streaks she could see a wet, mangy dog circling the van, marking its territory as it did so.

"Okay, I'm a baby!" she gasped, rolling down the window the tiniest bit. "Nan!" she screamed. "Help me! I'm trapped by *Cujo*!"

Ellie saw the ears on the animal twitch as it raised itself up on its hind legs and placed its front paws against the van's window. Its brown fur was matted, and the dried blood around its mouth suggested it had just feasted on some poor animal that wasn't quick enough to get away. Its hollow eyes, one blue and one brown, stared at Ellie like a wolf stalking its prey. As if sensing the fear within her, it began to emit a blood-curling howl.

"I'm trapped and it knows it," she gasped. "Nan, get it away from me," she begged, banging on the window with her fist.

Helena tried to creep up behind the animal, but its hearing was insanely keen. As it turned to look at her, its claws slid down the passenger door, putting deep scratches into the van's white enamel. It barred its teeth, the elongated canine's dripping with an unsightly mix of what Helena hoped were only rodent guts and saliva. It looked at her with an expression that was almost human. "Take me on, bitch," it seemed to taunt her, licking its snout in anticipation of the feast.

"Don't even think of it," Helena said, coming menacingly close to it, a wooden rake in her hand. "I'll have you burning in a bonfire before the animal control people get a whiff of you."

Ellie's eyes widened as she saw Helena take the end of the rake and smash it on the cement sidewalk, just inches from the dog. The rake had snapped like a toothpick.

Helena pointed the sharp broken handle right between the animal's eyes. "Listen up, pup. You're not Lassie. There's no happy ending here. Run along home. If you want me to destroy you, I will. The choice is yours."

The animal put its tail between his legs and dropped its head in defeat. Helena watched as it slunk down the road.

"Damn coyotes," Helena said. "Come on love, it's safe to come out now. Let's get you back inside the house."

Ellie quickly opened the door and scrambled out, tucking Beastie Boy under the shawl.

"You," she gasped, giving Helena a big hug, "are totally awesome. I swear you broke that rake with superhuman strength. Weren't you scared?"

"Maybe a little," Helena admitted. "But I'm going to be more afraid of your mother when she sees what that animal did to the door of the van." She put her arms on Ellie's shoulder. "Let's not tell her about this, all right? You know how she gets. I'll tell her some kids stole the rake out of the garage and scratched the truck. Kids gone wild. This being hell night, that sounds plausible."

"You're going to lie to my mom?" Ellie questioned, somewhat wide-eyed.

"Do you want to be locked up for the rest of your life?"

"A plausibility it is," Ellie agreed.

Pushing her granddaughter slightly ahead, Helena looked down the street. The cur was at the end of the road, watching them. His eyes had turned to a single shade of red, the same shade of red Helena's own eyes, unbeknownst to Ellie, had turned as she angrily glared back at it.

She took a moment to compose herself. "Well, you have to admit it hasn't been a boring day, Ellie," Helena mused as they went back inside the house.

"It doesn't even register on the boring day chart," Ellie said emphatically.

"Ellie, I love you," Helena smiled.

"I love you too… Nancy," Ellie laughed. She turned to Helena and gave her another hug. "Nan, you really kicked butt out there. Thanks for saving me."

"I wish I could always be there for you," Helena said wistfully, leading her granddaughter back into the security of the house.

Upstairs, safely tucked in her bed with Beastie Boy by her side, Ellie grabbed her phone from the nightstand and checked to see if Dina had called her back. There were no messages. Saddened, she put the phone back and turned out the light. She couldn't believe how tired she suddenly was. Within minutes she had fallen into a deep slumber.

Across the room, the door leading to the balcony opened by itself, bringing a rush of cold air inside. Ellie subconsciously tried to pull the quilt tight around her, but her actions were met with an unidentifiable resistance. She woke up and glanced at the foot of the bed. What her half-awake mind could only describe as a shadowman was now standing before her, beckoning her to follow him outside. She tried to resist, but she was no longer in control of her own body.

If she had taken some hallucinogenic drug, there might have been an explanation for how she suddenly found herself transported from the safety of the attic bedroom to standing alone in the middle of a country side road. But Ellie didn't take drugs, which made the situation all the more baffling.

"Nan," she said to herself, "come up with something plausible for this."

The mist rolling on the ground was cold on Ellie's feet. "Where the hell am I?" she wondered. She could see an old wooden bridge over a creek, and beyond that, a three story brick building that was desperately in need of repair. "You know," she whispered breathlessly, "eight hours of sleep is so overrated. Let's wake up now, please."

Hearing someone whistling in the distance, she turned towards the sound.

"Frère Jacques?" Ellie asked. "Is somebody whistling Frère Jacques? I can't stand that stupid song. This nightmare is getting worse and worse by the minute."

She listened intently. The notes were slow and methodical, more like a funeral march than a lullaby. The tempo began to lull her into a trance-like state, her body moving towards the sound under no will of her own. "Oh no, not again," she pleaded. She tried to dig her heels into the earth to stop moving, but she could no longer feel her feet. "I'm floating," she discovered. "This is crazy."

She could see the outline of a man on the other side of the bridge. He was tall and lanky and oddly beguiling. He leaned against the wooden structure with a devil-may-care slouch. As he turned his profile into the moonlight she could see that he was handsome in a rugged sort of way. But there was something unnatural about him just the same. He was there, but he wasn't. "You're the shadowman," she said. "You were just in my bedroom. Did you bring me here?"

He lifted his black cowboy hat from his brow and looked long and hard at Ellie.

"Frère Jacques, Frère Jacques. Dormez vous? Dormez vous?" he sang. He beckoned for Ellie to come nearer. "I know you hate that that song. You always did. But maybe we can sing it in a round. For old time's sake."

"Do I know you?" Ellie asked.

"Maybe. I know you. That's all that's important. Sonnez les matines, sonnez les matines, din dan don. Isn't that how it goes?"

"Who are you?" Ellie asked. "Why did you bring me here to the little swamp on the prairie?"

He smirked. "Don't worry. You're not in any immediate danger." He pointed down the road. "Though I can't say the same about her. She's got a big problem."

Ellie could see a figure running towards them with incredible speed. "Somebody ought to sign that person up to endorse running shoes," she quipped.

"I'd get out of his way," the cowboy suggested, "unless you want to draw attention to yourself before you have a plan." The shadowman grabbed the back of her T-shirt collar and drew her towards himself.

"Watch it buddy. Do that again and I'll drop kick you in your shadow-crotch," she said, yanking herself free. "I don't need a plan. I need an alarm clock."

"Quiet. Don't let him hear you."

"He? I thought you said *she* was in danger. If you can't tell the difference, let me educate you. Never mind. Forget I said that."

"Stay inside the bridge, Ellie. Don't let him see you." The shadowman pulled her away from the wooden archway.

"Do you mind?" Ellie commented, bringing her fingers to her nose. "It stinks in here. Like skunk cabbage. It makes me want to puke."

The runner was now approaching the creek. He had a blanket around him hiding his face and he was carrying something bulky in his arms. Something hidden, that was emitting a horrible cry.

"What the hell is that?" Ellie gasped.

"Do something," the shadowman said, distancing himself from Ellie and the apparition. "You're the only one who can. The problem is also yours."

"What's my problem?" Ellie asked. "Other than my REM stage lasting way too long." She turned towards the shadowman but he had vanished. "Great. Thanks a lot for your support. Am I supposed to solve the mystery or am I supposed to hide? I am so confused." She turned to leave, trying to remember the direction she had come from.

The figure was now at the end of the bridge staring at her, his eyes poking out from a hole between the blanket layers.

So much for hiding, Ellie realized.

"What's the matter?" she taunted. "Didn't the other little kids in the neighborhood want to play with you? You're supposed to say 'ollie-ollie-oxen-free' before you come to find me. Now turn around and count to one hundred."

He hissed at her.

"You have GOT to be kidding," she laughed. "I'm sorry, dream from hell or not, nobody hisses anymore. Speak in tongues or something if you're just trying to be scary."

He slowly removed the blanket from around his head. His long dark hair hung in sweaty strands over an unusually angular face. He had high cheekbones, model type cheekbones, that framed his long and slender nose magnificently.

"Okay," Ellie said cautiously, fascinated by his appearance. His features reminded her somewhat of an afghan hound. He didn't look much older than she was. "Apparently you and I were meant to be. Acquaintances anyway. So... do you want to tell me what are you hiding under that blanket of yours? Or do you really want to play 'I'll show you mine?' Because as you can see, I haven't got anything to counter with." She held her empty arms up and waved her hands in the air. "Nada."

His feet shuffled uncomfortably. He lowered his head and turned to peer at the water momentarily. As his body moved, parts of the blanket draping his body became loosened.

Ellie could see a tiny patch of blue gingham poking out from beneath the bundle he was holding in his arms. It moved in the opposite direction of the twist of his torso, as if trying to get away. She took a step closer to him.

He growled.

"Now that's just rude," she said.

"Go away," he urged.

"Look, I don't want to hurt you," she said, softening her voice. "I just want to know what you've got in your little bundle of joy there, and then I'll be on my way." She remembered the courage her Nan had shown facing the coyote earlier. She desperately wanted to summon up some of that courage for herself. "Oh hi, Nan," she lied, waving. "Am I ever glad to see you."

The fake-out worked. The teenager immediately turned around to see if there was someone behind him, giving Ellie the opportunity she needed. She darted towards him and pulled the blanket down from his shoulder in one fell swoop, her hand brushing against his exposed neck as she did so. He was cold. Icy cold.

The sudden human touch startled him and he accidentally released his grip on the bundle he was holding.

Ellie watched in horror as a young girl tumbled from the blanket. She landed on the ground with a thud so hard, Ellie wondered if she was still alive.

The child let out a weak moan. Her little gingham-covered arms reached out towards Ellie. "Help me, Ellie. Find me."

"I'm here," Ellie assured her. "I'll help you."

The teenager turned towards Ellie, his red eyes glaring at her intently. He snarled at her again, and this time Ellie could see two sharp fangs beneath his blood red lips.

"You bastard," Ellie shouted, reaching for the child. "Keep away from her."

"Leave my kiddie meal alone," the teenager screeched in an ear-shattering octave. He dragged the girl out of Ellie's reach.

"What?" Ellie screamed in disbelief. "You are sick, do you know that?"

"A little salt, maybe a shake of pepper. She doesn't have as much meat on the bone as I like, but she'll do." He looked at Ellie and licked his lips. "For starters." He continued to drag the girl to the edge of the foul smelling water.

"Nighty-night," he taunted, as like the biblical parting of the sea, the waters separated and the teenager disappeared into its muddy bottom with the little girl.

Ellie ran to the edge of the creek. It was really too shallow for them to have disappeared, but they were definitely gone. The only reflection Ellie could see in the moonlit water was her own. She shivered.

"He left the blanket behind," the shadowman said, startling her as he reappeared beside her. "You might as well keep warm."

"You've got a lousy sense of timing," she said to him, refusing to pick it up. "I'd rather freeze to death, thanks."

"Your choice," the shadowman shrugged. "You're as stubborn as the rest of them."

"What do you want from me?" Ellie asked, perplexed.

"Sonnez les matines, sonnez les matines, din-dan-don, din-dan-don," he sang, leaning forward to sweep a dark strand of hair from Ellie's face. "You have been summoned Ellie. The bell that tolls, it tolls for thee."

In the attic room on the third floor of the old Victorian house, Ellie awoke from her slumber, sat up, and let out a silent scream.

Chapter 5

Always an early riser, Helena left her bedroom and crept down the stairs towards the front door, trying not to awaken Helen or Ellie.

"That was a night and a half," she said to herself, pausing in front of the mirror in the hallway to look at her reflection. She gently fingered her hair, pushing her bangs away from her eyes. "All things considered, I think I look presentable enough to greet the world. The Maple Street portion of the world anyway."

Morning was her favorite time of the day. She felt everything was so peaceful before the rest of the world woke up. Stepping out into the quietness of her front porch, she looked down the paved walkway that ran through the middle of her lawn. The streetlight was casting enough light to confirm what she had already suspected. The weekly local paper was not where it should have been.

"Now where did it go?" she wondered.

"How ya doing, Mrs. LaRose?" Ryan asked, pulling his beat-up black Toyota in front of her house. His mother had given him the car when he turned sixteen last year. It was old and dilapidated, but he loved it, despite the engine that constantly backfired. The neighbors on Maple Street had a slightly different opinion of it.

"Just fine thank you," Helena replied, taking a few steps towards him. "That was quite the bit of excitement we had last night, wasn't it?"

Ryan shrugged. "Beats the hell out of watching videos."

"I guess that's one way to look at it," she agreed. She was somewhat surprised by his nonchalance. "How's Stan?"

"He was pretty quiet this morning. I don't know if he'll be around to finish cutting your grass this afternoon. I might have to stop by and do it for you tomorrow."

Helena looked at the decaying leaves on the lawn. The grass, once lush and green, was now turning a rusty shade of brown. "It's okay," she sighed. "I think it can wait, Ryan. Everything around the house seems to be dying off."

Ryan laughed. "You're hilarious, Mrs. LaRose."

"I was talking about the lawn, not Mr. Wagner," she informed him. "You're not the least bit disturbed by what happened last night?"

"Well, it's not like he didn't have it coming," Ryan began. "I mean, you know, he was old. It'd be different if he was some hot chick stabbed to death by a guy in a mask... being Halloween and all... but, you know... it was just Old Man Wagner, taking his last snooze."

"That almost sounded poetic, Ryan. I didn't think you had it in you."

"Well, don't go telling Tom or anyone, but yeah, I guess deep down inside, part of me knows that somebody, somewhere, loved the old guy. I don't exactly know who, because I never saw anyone visiting him or anything, but he sure liked sitting on your porch. I think he had a bit of a thing for you, Mrs. LaRose. He did have a smile on his face, before the cops covered it with the blanket one last time. Maybe that's not such a bad way to go."

Helena couldn't help but smile. She liked Ryan despite all the negative things the neighbors said about him. He definitely had a knack for rubbing people the wrong way. Her daughter Helen wasn't the first person to take an instant disliking to him. She wouldn't be the last either. But when the snowstorm hit last year, it was Ryan who went door to door making sure everyone on the street was okay. It had been Ryan who shoveled Mr. Wagner's driveway and then drove him to his doctor so he wouldn't miss an appointment he had waited months for. And it would be Ryan, she knew, carrying a good share of the load as one of Mr. Wagner's pallbearers. For Helena, Ryan's actions spoke louder than Ryan's words. Most of the time.

"All the same, you handled yourself well last night, Ryan. Keeping calm under pressure is a talent."

"Well, I play ball," he boasted. "I just put myself into the zone. When I'm there, you can come at me with all you've got." He tightened his face muscles and gave her a stare that sent shivers down her spine. His skin turned red. His eyes began to bulge. He began to froth at the mouth with saliva. Then he stopped.

"Like that," he explained to a mystified Helena. "When I do that, nothing can intimidate me. Not even death. Remember that, Mrs. LaRose."

"That's a little disconcerting, Ryan. But I suppose it does come in handy. Just keep it on the field, okay?" She knew that if Helen saw him make that face, she'd have him tested for rabies.

He nodded.

"I get the feeling Stan hadn't seen a dead body before?" she asked apprehensively.

"I don't think it was on his to-do list."

She wanted to laugh, but the look on Ryan's face was serious. "Really? He has a to-do list?"

"What can I say, Mrs. LaRose? Stan doesn't like surprises. Mr. Wagner pretty much freaked him out," he admitted. "I know he's my brother, but he's a little weird. This will haunt him for months."

"That's terrible, Ryan. Should I go have a word with your mother?"

"That's probably not a good idea. My mom thinks that... well, never mind what my mom thinks. She's messed up."

"But maybe I can help," Helena offered.

"She hates you, Mrs. LaRose."

"Oh... well, since you put it that way, tell Stan I hope he feels better soon." She thought about him for a moment. "He doesn't hate me, does he?"

Ryan shook his head. "No. He just thinks you've got a body buried in your backyard."

Helena took a deep breath. Keep calm, she told herself. "Why does he think there are bodies buried in my backyard?" She could feel her heart beginning to beat a little faster.

"Body. Singular. I told you he's a little weird. I have no idea why he thinks that. But he does. He seems to think it's under the grass just off your back porch, if you really want to know."

Helena laughed nervously. "That's ridiculous. I can assure you there is no body by the back porch."

"Like I said," Ryan shrugged. "He's just a weird little kid."

Helena listened carefully to what Ryan was telling her. She was going to have to make some changes at the back of the house if the neighbors were feeling uncomfortable. She couldn't have Stan being afraid to go into the yard when spring rolled around. Lawn seed. Colorado Blue. She'd have to order some in for the dead patch.

"I know the spot he's talking about. I'm afraid a coyote has taken a liking to letting it all flow there. I've tried just about everything to get the grass to grow back. You don't have a magic solution hidden away in your garden shed do you? Your lawn doesn't seem to have the same problem."

"No," Ryan replied. "I think Betty puts down mothballs." He leaned out the window and pointed towards the side of Helena's house. "I can see the newspaper under the bush, if that's what you're looking for."

"It is," Helena sighed, walking across the lawn. "Good help is hard to find. I certainly miss the days when you had the paper route. At least you could throw."

As she reached down to pick up the paper, her silk housecoat came untied. She looked up to find Ryan staring at her ample breasts, proudly displayed within the bodice of her nightgown.

"You're squinting, Ryan. You don't need glasses, do you?" she asked coyly, taking her time doing up her robe. "Although, I guess football players prefer contacts these days."

"I can see everything just fine, Mrs. LaRose." He winked at her. "I have 20-20 vision. And that's not the only thing that's perfect about me."

Raunchy little beggar, Helena thought to herself. "Ryan, if I were several decades younger than I am, I might entertain the notion of determining what is and isn't perfection with you. But as it happens I'm not, and besides, my daughter Helen would have a fit, so let's just put a lid on the innuendos for now, okay? You're an incredibly muscular young man and I'm a rather well-endowed... what's the word... cougar?" The natural yet somewhat seedy attraction that causes, should probably be our little secret."

Ryan was silent for a moment. "Oh, I get you. Your daughter's the jealous type."

"Something like that."

"So what's up? Is Ellie going to be coming to our school?" he asked innocuously. Rejection wasn't a big problem with Ryan. He had clearly moved on.

Helena honestly didn't know how long the girls were planning to stay, or whether Troy Tech was going to be in Ellie's future. "Your guess is as good as mine, Ryan."

"I was only asking because it's Friday night football tonight," he said with excitement. "She could come with Tom and Jacey and me and check it out if she's hanging around that long. It's a pretty big game for us. The coach is expecting a sell-out."

Helena smiled. "I'll let her know."

"Tell her if she wants to come, to be out by the curb around five and we'll pick her up. If we don't see her, we'll just keep going, no sweat." He glanced at his watch. "Whoa. I've got to go now. I promised Mr. Czewzinski I'd show up early today. He said he'd show me how to tune the engine. I don't think you've noticed, but my car's been sounding like shit lately." He waved, honked his horn twice, and started to pull away from the curb.

Thank God, Helena thought. If you only make it to school one day this year, make it today. "I'll tell her. And Ryan, no drinking and driving, do you hear me?"

"I never drink until after the game, Mrs. LaRose. I promise. The coach would have a fit."

"That's not what I meant. You're still underage."

He squealed away in as much of a squeal as the old Toyota could muster.

"Ryan," she said to herself, "I have a feeling you are going to be my granddaughter's best friend and my daughter's worst nightmare. And you live right next door! How conveniently Shakespearean."

Helena headed back into the house and wandered into the breakfast nook. As she began to unroll the newspaper onto the kitchen table, she noticed some dirt falling from between the damp pages. At least she hoped it was dirt.

"Ew," she said, taking a napkin from the holder on the table's Lazy Susan and wiping the debris off. "Environment or not, I miss the plastic bag the paper used to come in."

She picked up the paper and studied the weather page. "It's supposed to be a gorgeous day," she said as she stood and waited for the coffee to finish brewing.

Below the advertisement for Williams Hardware she saw a tiny story about the streetlights being shattered on Main Street again.

"You'd think they would know better than to fix them before Halloween," she sighed as she put the paper on the counter and poured herself a cup of java. Her eyes skimmed down to the bottom of the page. There was a report that a coyote was on the loose and it had been dining on a few gourmet selections, specifically a Siamese feline and a purebred miniature poodle. The owners had discovered their half-mutilated remains deposited outside their back doors. "Sucked the guts right out of him," Warren Curtis had been quoted in the article as saying.

"Coyote my ass," Helena thought aloud, walking over to the back door. She turned on the porch light to survey her own back stoop from the window. Thankfully the coast was clear. There were no dead animals to have to remove before the girls came down. None that she could see, anyway. She thought again about the encounter Ellie had with the wild dog last night.

"He's getting too big for his britches," Helena said, walking back over to the counter.

"What's that, Mother?" Helen asked, entering the kitchen in her blue flannel pajamas.

Helena started to tell her daughter about the news item, and then thought the better of it. "I was just talking about my ass. It's getting too big for my britches. Coffee dear?" Helena asked, taking another mug from the cupboard and turning towards her daughter.

"God no. I don't want anything that might keep me up tonight," Helen replied. "I was so tired yesterday, but I couldn't sleep a wink." She leaned against the counter. "I kept thinking I heard something howling at the moon. I hate Halloween."

Helena put the mug back. "I guess you were still a little wound up. Moves can be a bit unsettling."

Helen looked at her mother in disbelief. "It wasn't the move that was unsettling. It might have started out that way, but somewhere between stuffing all our earthly possessions in a van, leaving the home and relationship I've known for the past five years and arriving here in Amityville, the day got even worse."

"It's not always so crazy around here, I can assure you," Helena said.

"Oh, that's a relief. You act as if it's normal, the police showing up and taking a dead man from your home. I still can't believe we weren't all taken away for questioning."

Helena folded her arms across her chest. "Darling, Chief Cohen was fine with it all. What did you expect? If we had murdered Mr. Wagner, I'm certain he would have handled things differently."

"And what was up with that?" Helen asked, throwing her hands up in the air questioningly. "The Chief of Police shows up at your door and acts like this happens here all the time. 'Oh, okay Helena, it's a suicide. I'm sure the note will be in the pocket just like you say it will. Barney Fife and I have to get back to the station now. We'll wrap this up in the morning. Or not'."

"Your point being?" Helena said tersely. "And for your information, Barney Fife's name is Rick Purdy."

"What kind of cops do you have in this town" her daughter grilled. "Do they find their badges inside cereal boxes?"

Helena took offense. "Well, they didn't come back did they? Obviously the note was there just like I said it was going to be."

"And how did you know that? Are you mind reading these days?"

"Don't go there, Helen. You'll be sorry you did. Mr. Wagner had been diagnosed with terminal cancer. He was beyond chemo, so I was doing what I could for him from a holistic approach. He was my patient. All summer long he would come and sit on my porch and drink the herbal tea I would leave out for him. He told me once that's where he wanted to die, sipping tea on my porch. He said he wouldn't bother me with the details, but when it was time, it was time, and I would find a note in his shirt pocket. I should have left some tea out for him yesterday. I meant to. I just got busy." She paused for a moment, a look of puzzlement crossing her face. "I wonder what he did with the other dead body?"

"What other dead body? Do you mean there's more than one?"

Helena took her housecoat off, fully revealing the matching silk negligee underneath. "Oh relax, Helen. I meant the stuffed shirt and pants I put out there on the veranda earlier in the day as a Halloween prop. Honestly, you're letting your imagination get the better of you." She picked up the cereal box and peered inside it. "Nope. No police badges inside. Satisfied?"

"This is why I moved away from home the first chance I got. You're like a tornado. Anything in your path that's the least bit unbalanced, spins around and winds up dead on your doorstep."

"Are you saying that *you're* unbalanced?" Helena said tersely as she sat down at the table. "Are *you* about to die on my doorstep?"

"Of course not."

"Then that statement is a bit extreme, don't you think? So what if we have a gust of bizzaro from time to time around here? Every household does. Mr. Wagner wasn't unbalanced. He was just lonely. So stop your nonsense, take some of the iced tea out of the fridge and sit down. Don't worry, it's not going to kill you. There's no eye-of-newt in it. It's decaf."

"That's not funny. Where do you keep your drinking glasses?"

"It wasn't meant to be. Top right cupboard." Helena noticed the look of anger on her daughter's face as she passed by her. "All right then, we'll change the subject. Ellie looks lovely."

Helen's face turned a deep shade of crimson. "I am so sorry about that. I don't know what's gotten into her. She won't leave the house without her 'dawn-of-the-dead' make-up. I tried to get her to take it off before she came here yesterday, but she wouldn't." She walked over and opened the refrigerator. "I don't see it. The tea, I mean."

"Top shelf, behind the milk. I wasn't being sarcastic. She really does look lovely. I haven't seen her in ages. Those eyes of hers are gorgeous... that piercing green stare she has beneath those killer long eyelashes... she must send the boys wild. You didn't actually think I'd be offended by her appearance did you? It's nothing to be embarrassed about."

Helen poured herself a drink. "The thought had crossed my mind."

"For heaven's sake, Helen. She's not the only one who dresses like that. There are quite a few non-confirming gothic teenagers conforming in this town, let me tell you. It's just a phase she's going through. And you do too know what's gotten into her. You just weren't that clever when it happened to you."

"When what happened to me?" Helen asked, sitting down at the table.

"When you appeared to be twelve and you were really fifteen. It can't be easy for her. It wasn't easy for you. You stuffed your top."

"I did not!"

Helena choked on her coffee. "You went from a 32a to a 34c overnight."

"I was a quick blossomer," Helen replied, putting her head in her hands. "Oh God. I did do that, didn't I?"

"I still have the pictures. Maybe that's why you're so insistent on covering your boobs up to this day."

Helen pulled her flannels closer to her chest. "Not everyone has the uncontrollable urge to expose their mammary glands to perfect strangers like you do, Mother."

"Well it's an icebreaker, that's for sure. Do I need to remind you of your short-lived punk rock period? You used to buy your belts extra-long so you could wrap them around your leg and then up around your waist. Now that was a look a mother could be proud of. Bondage. You may recall I chose to ignore your fashion experimentations at the time. Thankfully you seem to have been able to make the jump to Armani. I'm sure in time, Ellie will too."

"Please don't tell her about that. I'm trying to instill her with a sense of what it means to be a successful career woman, and if she gets even the slightest hint that I wasn't always so conventional, it'll be game over. It's not easy, you know, trying to get her focused on what she wants to be. She's got it into her head that she wants to be a plumber."

"Maybe she should be a plumber. Your PhD in medieval history hasn't done you that well in the long run. Or should I say mid-evil?"

"That's not fair. There's just not a lot of demand for my particular expertise right now."

"You should have listened to me and majored in Archeology. Archeology/grave digging, what's the difference, really? You'd always have a job."

"Nice to see you too, Mother."

Helena looked at her daughter, wishing she could break down Helen's hard exterior. "Where is your sense of humor, Helen? I was kidding. Of course it's nice to see you. Is everything okay?"

"Not exactly. I've left him."

"So everything's fine then. I warned you not to marry that man. He reminds me of Napoleon."

"Napoleon was French."

"He was a mouthy little dictator. End of story. You know you and Ellie are always welcome here. How long are you staying?"

"Thanks for your concern, Mother. What time is check out?"

"That's not what I meant," Helena insisted.

"I know you didn't like Tony," Helen admitted, "but I thought I'd at least get some empathy from you. I know sympathy would be out of the question."

"He's not dead and that's not why you're here. I wasn't born yesterday, Helen. If you just wanted to move away from Tony, you could have moved anywhere, anytime. Like perhaps before school started this September. I don't think here in Troy, with me, at the end of October, would be first on your list if that were truly the case. What's really going on?"

Helen stood up and began to pace in the kitchen. "Ellie's having nightmares," she finally said, her voice trembling.

"What kind of nightmares? Have you had a talk with her yet?"

"I don't even know how to begin that talk."

"Well darling, don't you think it's time you figured that out? It's not like the sex talk. She's not going to figure it out on her own."

Helen glared at her mother, her eyes revealing the anger her lips failed to emote. Was her mother being difficult on purpose?

"Calm down, Helen," her mother warned. "You're going to give yourself an aneurysm."

"I'm sorry, Mother," Helen protested. "I haven't seen the talk show episode yet where the psychologist says, 'Helen, you need to look your daughter in the eye and tell her she's never going to look her age. Her blood contains proteins that slow down the aging process by oh, a century or two. She's eventually going to have to move every five years so people don't get suspicious and start sticking needles into her to get some of her DNA'." She took a deep breath. "I must have been grave digging the day he covered that topic."

"Ten." Helena said indignantly.

"What?"

"Ten. I move every ten years. People aren't that quick. Hereditary youth is a wonderful thing, Helen. At least when you're older. I'm willing to bet that to this day you don't mind running into your old friends. I'm surprised you're not head of the reunion committee. What are you telling them these days? That you are still thirty-nine? I tell everyone I'm fifty-eight, just so you don't blow it for me."

Her mother had a point there. People were starting to talk about how Tony was looking older and she wasn't. It was another reason it was time for her to leave him. But not the most important reason.

"Mother, I'm serious. I'm worried about Ellie. She sleep walks."

"So did you."

"When I was four."

"I see what you mean," Helena acknowledged. Ellie was a little old to be doing that. "Does she do anything else odd?"

"Define odd. She's a teenager."

"Does she scream out in the middle of the night for no reason?"

"Sometimes," Helen admitted. She had gone running into Ellie's room several times only to find her sound asleep in her bed.

"That's okay. Most people do. I blame it on jalapenos. Don't eat them before bedtime. Does she have visions?"

"You mean like knowing that kid was going to faint before he did? Things like that happen all the time around her."

"Well, Stan's a bit nervous. It was bound to happen. She didn't foresee Tom collapsing. Mind you, she was probably blinded by that smile of his. If I was fifteen and Tom was around, my mind might not be focused either." She chuckled then became serious again. "Tell me more."

"She whistles in her sleep. Not happy little lullabies, either. They're these low, haunting little melodies. She never whistles when she's awake. Ever."

"Oh dear. That's not good. That could mean it's starting."

The two women ended their conversation abruptly as Ellie walked into the kitchen, ignored both of them, and headed toward the fridge.

"She's not much of a talker in the morning," Helena commented.

"No, wait…" Helen replied, raising her hand alarmingly to her mother.

They watched as Ellie crashed head first into the-side by-side panel door of the refrigerator.

"Do you see what I mean?" Helen whispered. "She's asleep."

"She made it sleepily all the way downstairs, in a house she hardly knows. What's a little navigational issue like a fridge? She's fine." Helena assured her. "Although she does look like she's twelve without all the make-up."

"Mother! She is not fine. Look at her feet. They're covered in mud."

"She went outside last night to the van and her runners fell off her feet. I was watching from the front window. Darling, you really should have taught her how to put her shoes on properly."

Helen walked over to her daughter, placed her hands on Ellie's shoulders and shook her. "Ellie. Ellie, wake up." She clapped her hands loudly in front of Ellie's face, awakening the teenager from her slumber.

Ellie shook her head dizzily as she tried to recognize her surroundings. "Sorry," she said bleary-eyed. "I don't know why I keep doing this."

"You're over-tired," Helena offered. "You had too much excitement last night. Apparently so did your mother."

"I guess so. Maybe that and too much sugar. I snuck some of your left over chocolate bars into my room. They were really good," Ellie said, rubbing her head.

"Headache, dear?" Helena asked. "There's some pain killers in the bathroom cupboard if you want some."

"No. I'll be okay. I'm just a little groggy. I had the weirdest dream. There was this whistling man… you know those wooden cowboy cutouts some people have on their fences… he sort of looked like that. And he took me out to the country to this little girl who was wearing a blue checkered dress like you'd see in Oz. The whistling dude, he kept telling me I had to save her, that it was my manifest destiny or something. And she kept saying 'Ellie, find me. Save me." She took a deep breath. "It was totally scary."

"And then what happened, dear?" Helena asked, entranced.

"Then I hit my head on the fridge."

Helen anxiously turned to her mother. "What do you think?"

"I think that would hurt," Helena replied. "I still think she needs a pain tablet."

"No," Helen sighed, with exasperation. "Do you think… you know?"

"Willie?" Helena asked. "I suppose it's possible. I haven't seen him in years."

"Will he, won't he, what? Hello?" Ellie waved, "I'm right here in front of you. It's not nice to keep secrets. I am awake now. I can hear you. Were either of you whistling Frère Jacques earlier? Because that would be a big help."

Helena looked at her granddaughter gravely. "Ellie, sit down dear. We need to have a little talk."

"I hate little talks," Ellie sighed, pulling a chair up beside Helena.

"I hate little talks with your mother too. But this one's different." She looked at Helen for some assistance, but Helen only shrugged, helpless. "Ellie, there's no easy way to tell you this. We're not normal, we LaRose's."

"Well, that explains Mom. But you and me? Not normal how?"

"You know how your Nan was dressed as a witch last night," Helen interjected. "That wasn't a big stretch for her. For any of us."

"Helen, don't be so simplistic. We are not witches," Helena stated.

Ellie looked from Helena to Helen looking for an answer. There was none. "Well that sucks. First I am, then I'm not. A witch. Talk about parental cruelty. You've taken away a possible career choice and any supernatural powers I may have in less than a minute."

"What your mother is trying to say is we're more like…"

"Ghostbusters," Helen again interrupted. She could see Helena hang her head in desperation.

"Come on, you guys," Ellie pleaded. "Halloween's over and it's a little early for April Fool's day."

"That's not the word I'd use, Helen. They're not always dead. We're more like…"

"Buffy the Vampire Slayer?" Ellie suggested.

"Why yes!" Helena said excitedly. "I like that analogy. She had such a sense of style. Not to mention she could kick-ass kill anything that got in her way. I loved that show. And that Angel fellow! He was certainly worth a hickey or two."

Ellie looked at her mother and her grandmother hoping one of them would burst out laughing. Neither did. "I think when I hit my head I gave myself a concussion. With any luck, in another few moments I may even forget your names. What is with you two?"

"We're see'ers," Helena continued. "We dream things. We feel things. We know things. From time to time we get called upon to handle things other people can't."

"Right...let me get this straight..." Ellie's voice did not sound convinced, "...a rational adult, and a woman known to the world as my mom, are sitting here telling me that I'm living in some episode of Sabrina the Teenage Witch?"

Before Helena could answer, the back door opened and Chief Cohen came walking into the kitchen. He took off his hat and nodded to the women. For a man his age, he still had quite the head of hair.

Helena smiled.

It was the kind of smile that men noticed.

Helen noticed it too. "Don't you knock? We're in the middle of an important family conversation here," she said with exasperation.

The Chief bit his tongue. "Nice to see you again, Helen. I'm sorry we had to meet under those circumstances last night. I hope you and your daughter's stay in Troy is a happy one. I can appreciate it didn't get off to a great start." He turned to Helena. "I don't mean to be rude, but could I see you outside for a moment? Alone?" He motioned for her to follow him to the back stoop.

Helena stood up and went towards the door. "Of course, Roy. Is something wrong? I didn't tell you the wrong pocket or anything? Mr. Wagner was a little vague. At least he wasn't as hard to remove as Mrs. Harbinger, thank God. She wrecked my shovel." Her voice trailed off as she followed him outside.

"Roy?" Helen noted, jabbing Ellie in the ribs. "Did you hear that? Your grandmother is on a first name basis with the police force. That's probably not a good sign."

Ellie took a handful of dry cereal from the box on the table and began munching slowly. "Well, maybe it's not the whole police force. Maybe it's good that she knows them. Did you notice Nan didn't lock her doors last night before we all went to bed? Is it just a small town thing? Or is she losing it?"

"I did notice. In fact, I locked it. But about ten minutes later I walked by and it was unlocked again."

"What did she mean about Mrs. Harbinger? Who's she? And why did Nan need a shovel?"

"I don't know, and I don't want to know. And neither do you."

"I'm thinking I do," Ellie said in defiance.

Helen moved to the side of the window, to get a better look at her mother and Chief Cohen outside. She shook her head in disbelief. "You may be right, Ellie. Your grandmother is on her back steps, talking to a policeman, in her negligee. And apparently she doesn't think there's anything wrong with that. She *is* losing it."

Outside, Chief Cohen held up a photo for Helena to examine.

"I need your help, Helena. A young girl has gone missing. You might know her, she's Dr. Quinlan's little girl, Brooke. She was supposed to go over to her friend Annie Robinson's to go trick or treating and then stay overnight. Or so the Quinlan's thought. They watched her walk across the street to Annie's like she had a hundred times before. But what happened next no one knows. She never made it inside the Robinson's home. Never rang the doorbell. Annie's parents thought there had just been a change in plans and didn't think much about it. They took their daughter out alone. They said they remembered seeing Brooke run by your house, but assumed her parents were waiting for her around the corner. It was this morning before it all got pieced together. Dr. Quinlan took this photo just before Brooke left the house. She was all dressed up for trick or treating."

The girl in the picture was about six years of age, dressed in a blue checkered dress, carrying a toy dog in a cloth-lined basket. Roy Cohen studied Helena's reaction as she looked at it. He could see the color draining from her face. "What is it, Helena? Do you remember seeing her?"

"Oh my goodness, Roy. No. She didn't come to my door. I'm sure I'd remember her. It's just such a shock. I do know the little girl. Her family must be beside themselves with worry."

"We're going door to door asking people if they know anything of her whereabouts. Give me a call if you hear anything. There are some off-duty officers coming in from the city to help. If Brooke hasn't returned home by this afternoon, we'll need to expand the search tomorrow morning. I know I can count on you to help."

"Of course, Roy."

Chief Cohen turned and headed across the grass to knock on the Lachey's back door. Helena watched him, taking a moment to gather her thoughts. This was all too much of a coincidence... the little girl, the dream. But there was nothing concrete she could tell him about.

She started to open the door, and then stopped, turning towards the back-yard. "You are no longer welcome in my home," she whispered.

The leaves in her yard blew into a mini cyclone in response.

"If you want a temper tantrum, I'll give you a temper tantrum," she promised the leaf pile. She glanced quickly towards the Lachey home. "I hope Stan didn't see that," she thought. "What the hell am I going to tell the girls?"

"Nan, who's Mrs. Harbinger?" Ellie asked as soon as Helena entered the kitchen.

"Ellie dear, you look tired, why don't you go lie down," Helena said, her voice taking an unusually stern tone.

"I'm not really tired, Nan. I just woke up, remember? I'm going to go put on my make-up and go for a walk."

"There's some melatonin in the bathroom, why don't you take some? Oh hell, just take a sleeping pill. A growing girl needs her beauty sleep."

"Mother! Are you trying to drug my daughter? What is with you?" Helen demanded. "She said she's not tired."

Helena sat down. There was really no easy way to break the news to them. "A little girl from town has gone missing. Her name is Brooke Quinlan, she's six. Roy... I mean Chief Cohen... showed me a picture that her parents had taken of her. She was dressed in her Halloween costume, Dorothy from The Wizard of Oz."

"Oh my God," Helen cried, putting her hand over her mouth.

Ellie could barely contain the shivers running up her spine. "That is just too creepy."

"Ellie, do you remember anything else from your dream? It's important," Helena begged.

"Ellie. Go upstairs and take the sleeping pill like your Nan says. Maybe you'll start dreaming again." As much as Helen wanted this to mean absolutely nothing, she couldn't shake the churning feeling in her stomach.

"Have you both lost it?" Ellie questioned. "It's a co-incidence, that's all. Quit looking at me like that." Feeling uncomfortable, she reached for a piece of fruit on the counter. "Don't bother with breakfast for me. I'm going to eat this when I'm out. I can't digest properly when I'm stressed," she said as she walked out of the room. The last thing she felt like doing was remembering that dream.

Helen lowered her voice. "What are we going to do?"

"Let's hope it is just all a big coincidence. And if it's not, let's hope to hell that Ellie tires out early tonight and that the mysterious cowboy makes another appearance. This is going to be a long day's journey into night."

Chapter 6

Ellie sat on the front porch, her knees pulled up inside her ski jacket, trying to keep her body warm. Nan had said the boys would be there by five. It was now a quarter after, and they hadn't shown up yet. Maybe Nan got it wrong. Maybe they didn't want her to go to the game with them. Maybe it was all a big joke.

She looked down at her feet. Earlier she had polished the left toe cap of her heavy black boot with a black magic marker she found in a kitchen drawer, and she was quite pleased with her handiwork until she looked at the other foot and realized she should have done the same to it. In retrospect, it would have been easier to leave it alone, but her boots were looking rather worn and she didn't want to appear like someone who couldn't afford new ones, even if it were true.

"If we stay here," she told herself, "I'm going to have to get a part-time job to pay for some new clothes."

She was thanking her lucky stars she had remembered to pack her black skinny jeans. They had been getting a little tight so she almost left them behind, but she thought she looked hot in them, and thankfully she managed to squeeze herself in one more time.

"I hope Tom likes them," she said. "I hope Tom likes me."

Tom was the reason it had taken her ten minutes to pick out a top. The choice between sexy or warm was not normally a brain drainer, but it was freezing out today. She eventually caved into the weather and threw on her favorite bulky black sweater. Picking out earrings to go with the outfit had not been any easier. Not if you have as many holes in your ears as she did. She finally settled on two silver hoops. The other holes would just have to be naked tonight.

The day had gone by slowly, as she had spent most of it alone on the front porch, imagining how the evening would unfold. Ryan would be conveniently playing ball on the field and she would have Tom all alone in the bleachers. As alone as you could be at a high school football game. The other girls would be staring at her of course, but with looks of envy rather than looks of "who the hell are you?" It would be chilly, and Tom would put his arms around her. Then after the game they would ditch Ryan and go somewhere. Just the two of them. They'd share a passionate kiss under the moonlight, and there might even be a thundercloud when it happened because the world would be so damn jealous.

"No sign of them yet?" Helena asked, peeking through the door.

Ellie shook her head.

"Hang in there. It's not like Ryan to be late," she comforted. "You mother and I will be walking over to the game a bit later, if they don't come by. Not that they won't," she added quickly.

"You and Mom are coming?" she asked, trying to hide the disappointment in her voice. They had not been a part of her perfect date scenario.

"She doesn't know it yet, but yes," she said. "Don't worry, we'll sit down in front with the rest of the parents. You won't even know we're there. It'll do Helen some good to get out of the house. It will do us all good." She watched as her granddaughter's face turned pensive. "What's wrong, Ellie? Is it something I can help you with? I'm sorry about this morning."

"That's okay, it's not you. Or Mom. I'm just feeling a little lost, that's all."

"Lost as in I'm fifteen? Or lost as in I'm someplace new?"

"Can you read my mind?"

Helena laughed. "No. My talents lie in another direction."

"I was kidding, Nan."

If only she knew, Helena thought. "You'll never be fifteen again, Ellie. Don't be too hard on yourself. They'll show up."

"Maybe Ryan didn't really mean it," Ellie said glumly. "Why would they want to be nice to me? They hate me. They call me Goth-Chic."

"Goth-Chic?" Helena smiled. "It could be worse. Your mother's nickname when she was your age was Pumpkin Butt."

The unmistakable sound of Ryan's car coming around the corner interrupted their conversation.

"See, there you go," Helena said, "that noise you hear is your finely tuned limousine approaching. Apparently Ryan never made it to class on time."

"They're coming?" Ellie squealed, as all the insecurities that were weighing heavy on her mind suddenly vanished.

"I'll leave you alone to enjoy the moment," Helena said, heading back inside. "Have fun. We'll see you later, Goth-Chic."

Ellie forced a weak smile. Maybe the nickname wasn't so bad.

"Black-Chic!" Ryan yelled through the open window, as the Toyota squealed up to the curb. "Hurry up. Tom took too long trying to be perfect. We're going to be late if we don't move it."

"Huh?" Ellie questioned.

"Try again, Lachey," Tom said from the backseat. "He hasn't thought that nickname through, Ellie. I'll explain it to him later."

"Well, she didn't want us calling her Goth-Chic," Ryan shrugged. "She's always in black. That's all I meant. I am a man of irony. I'll just call her GC. Come on up front with me, GC."

Sitting in the front with Ryan was not what Ellie had been thinking about all afternoon. She was hoping that Tom would come to her rescue and insist she sit in the back with him.

"GC is too much like Jacey," Tom said. "We can't have two Jacey's. I'll go mental. Ow! Watch where you're elbowing me."

Ellie looked at Tom and then at Ryan. Ryan's hands were firmly on the steering wheel. He couldn't have elbowed Tom even if he had wanted to.

"Erm, and what is wrong with the name Jacey?" a new voice said.

"No, no, no," Ellie said to herself. There couldn't be a female voice in the car. There couldn't be a female with a perfect little British accent, sitting in the back with Tom. Her Tom. Nan hadn't mentioned anything about a girl. Nan had mentioned some other guy, "J.C." somebody or other.

"Right," the voice said. "So this is the new girl you've been talking about." The girl reached around Tom, and looked out the window at Ellie. "Hello El," she said, her voice sounding softer and sexier than Ellie had ever heard someone her age sound. Not that Ellie spent a lot of time thinking about the sexiness of a female voice. She did however, spend a lot of time sizing up her competition when necessary. This would be one of those times.

"I'm Jacey Sumner. It's nice to meet you. I'm getting rather tired of having to keep these two in line all by myself," she smiled. The perfect little smile. The perfect little smile to go with her perfect blonde hair.

Ellie wanted to rip her perfect little face off.

"Would you be comfier sitting back here with me?" she asked. "Tom, go sit in the front with Ryan."

Was she out of her perfect little mind? Apparently not. Apparently she had Tom wrapped around her perfect little thumb. He was already half way out of the car.

"You know, it's really okay," Ellie insisted, her stomach knotting the whole time, "I can get in the front with Ryan. It's no big deal."

Tom didn't help. With what could only be described as an awkward expression of chivalry he held the rear door open for Ellie. It would have almost been romantic if she hadn't almost wanted to throw up. Her dream boy, was holding the car door open so she could sit beside what could only be described as *his* dream girl.

"Ellie, get in the car," he said. He sounded eerily like her mom. She walked around to the front passenger side of the car and got in beside Ryan instead. Tom shrugged and went back to his original spot.

"Are we done with the musical chairs?" Ryan demanded. "I'm going to be late for the game." He threw the car into gear and hit the accelerator. His three passengers immediately fastened their seatbelts as he took the corner a little too fast.

"If I look straight ahead," Ellie thought to herself, "I'll get a last glimpse of life if we crash, and better yet, I'm not going to have to look at *her*."

Jacey leaned forward and tapped her on the shoulder, forcing Ellie to turn around. Some people just didn't pull their lap belts tight enough.

"Erm, I was just wondering," Jacey began, "if you are a devil worshiper. Because you're really, really pretty, but really… I can't put my finger on it." She gazed at Ellie intently.

Tom and Ryan burst out laughing.

"I was just wondering," Ellie began, "if you were a cheerleader. Because you're really, really pretty, but your rah-rahs are really...I can't put my finger on it." Ellie turned her head away from Jacey.

"Chick fight!" Ryan said delightedly.

"Sorry, El," Jacey tried to explain, "I didn't mean to tick you off. It's just that there were some boys from Manchester, where I'm from, who were into that sort of thing and they turned out to be very scary lads. That's all. Not that you're scary. You're not. I think you're really fit."

If this girl could put her foot any further into her own mouth, she'd be choking, Ellie thought. "Look, for the record, I'm not a devil worshipper. I'm not a worshipper at all."

Jacey sat back in her seat, playing with the cross that hung from her necklace. The five-minute drive to the high school suddenly became very, very quiet.

"This is it, Goth." Ryan finally declared, as they arrived at the school. "All you need to know about this place is there is one kick-ass football team here. Look around. Do you see this many people here on a regular school day? No. I rest my case."

The parking lot was already full but that didn't pose too much of a problem for Ryan, as he calmly pulled the Toyota up beside the garbage dumpster. "Reserved parking," he said, as he got out, moved the dumpster onto the lawn single handedly, returned to the car and parked it where the dumpster had been. "Works every time," he said with a smirk.

"Just once I'd like to get here early and smell, oh, I don't know, fresh air?" Jacey complained as they all got out of the Toyota.

"I'll catch ya all later," Ryan said, ignoring her. "You just look for the guy making all the plays, Goth. That'll be me. Number 12. The last of the dozen."

Ellie started to roll her eyes.

"Easy, Goth," Tom assured her. "The scary part is he really will be guy making all the plays. He's a demon on the field."

The bleachers were almost full by the time the three spectators wished Ryan a good game and headed for their seats. Ellie saw empty spots in the first row, but as she turned towards them Jacey gave her sweater a tug from behind.

"It's kind of like church," Jacey explained. "We want to sit at the back. The front rows are where the parents sit." She started up the stairs with Tom following, puppy-dog like, behind her.

"How about there?" Ellie asked, pointing to empty seats beside another girl who was also dressed in black from head to toe. Thank God there was at least one other girl in Troy that didn't look like she had stepped out of a photo shoot for Prom Queens-R-Us.

"Erm, no. Let's keep on going, shall we?" Jacey replied, dragging Tom by the hand. "I see some empty seats up at the back."

Ellie reluctantly followed as Jacey found a spot big enough for two and a half people. True, it was the only other available spot, but Ellie already knew how this was going to play out. Jacey would be forced to cuddle with Tom, or even worse, sit on his lap, and there wasn't a whole lot she could do about it. This night was beginning to really suck.

"Why can't we sit down there with that other girl, what's her name?" Ellie asked Tom. "I thought you were friends."

"Tara. Jacey and her don't always get along," he whispered to Ellie. "They've got this love-hate thing going. Tonight it's hate. I'll tell you about it some time."

"Is there a problem?" Jacey asked, sitting down on the metal bench.

Tom slunk beside Jacey and patted the seat beside him, motioning for Ellie to sit down. "Not when I'm sitting with the hottest girls in town," he said, putting his arms around both of them.

Jacey grinned.

Ellie wanted to die.

Football was not her thing to begin with. To her, it was right up there with golf under the Jeopardy category "stupid games you play in the rain." So to divert her attention away from Jacey, and unbelievably from Tom, she turned and studied the crowd.

Ryan had been right about the turnout. It looked like half of the town had shown up to watch the game, if her quick math count had been right. Either there wasn't much else to do in Troy on a Friday night, or football was a really big deal here.

"Is it always this crowded?" she asked.

"They're on a winning streak," Tom told her. "As long as that continues, everybody will show up no matter how cold it gets. Everyone loves a winner, and I don't think these guys are planning on loosing anytime soon."

"Unfortunately," Jacey sighed. "You might want to bring a blanket next time, El. And ask for some hand warmers for Christmas. It'll be spring before the season is over and we get our Friday nights back."

"Weather is part of the game," Tom insisted.

Ellie saw Helena and her mom arriving at the field. Helen would never have gone to a football game at her old school, she knew. She wondered what secret power Helena had over her to get her mom to do things she didn't enjoy.

"Look," Tom noticed, "the Helens have shown up." He watched as the LaRose women took the empty seats down front. "It's like your Nan has season tickets. She always sits at the 30-yard line."

"Really?" Ellie pondered as the teams took to the field. She was learning something new about her grandmother every day.

A minute later the starting whistle blew, sending a hush over the crowd. Troy had won the coin toss, and elected to receive. Ellie saw Ryan taking his position. He was a linebacker. She knew that much.

"Did you hear about the girl that's missing?" Jacey asked innocently.

"Ellie wouldn't know her," Tom reminded Jacey, momentarily letting Ellie off the hook. "My Dad said there might be a town-wide search tomorrow. Do you want to come if there is one?"

"Erm, I don't know," Jacey hesitated. "I'll think about it."

"What about you, Ellie?" Tom asked. "Are you up for a little search and rescue?"

"Maybe," Ellie offered up. Her head was beginning to pound. She wished they'd get off the subject. She was trying as hard as she could to get the image of the little girl out of her head, not in it. She turned her attention back to the game. Ryan, she couldn't help but notice, was pretty agile for his size. That surprised her.

She wasn't the only one noticing him. She could see a man in the front row videotaping his every move. She watched as his camera followed Ryan up and down the field.

"What's going on?" she asked Tom, pointing to the videographer.

"Scout," Tom replied. "Ryan's up for a ticket out of town."

"That's pretty cool," she said. She could hear the tone of the crowd change as the other team took possession of the ball.

"Get 'em," Tom screamed, following the play. "Run, Lachey run. Yeeeee..... sss!" He threw his arms into the air, accidentally smacking Ellie across the head. "Sacked!"

"Ow!"

"Sorry," Tom apologized. "I got a little carried away."

"You should see him when there's a touchdown," Jacey laughed. "He does a little thing with his booty."

"You know," Ellie said, thinking this might be a good time for the third-wheel to bail. "As much as I would love to see him do that, I think he's going to need a little more room, so I'm going to move." She grabbed her purse and stood up. "I'll catch up with you guys later."

"Don't go, Ellie."

It had been Jacey who said that, not Tom, Ellie noted with disappointment.

"It's okay. I'll meet you by the car after the game," Ellie tried to say like it was no big deal. She glanced around and noticed that a seat beside that other girl, Tara, was still unoccupied. She gave Tom and Jacey a half-hearted adios wave as she turned into the aisle.

"Tom, you hurt her feelings. Go after her and apologize," Jacey said.

"Let her go," Tom said, putting his arm around Jacey.

She removed his arm from her shoulder. She had a pretty good idea where Ellie was going. "Tom Williams, look what you have done. You've forced her to go to the dark side."

Ellie made her way down the rows until she reached the seat beside the girl Jacey apparently hated. She was lucky to find that it was still unoccupied.

"Do you mind?" Ellie asked politely.

"Actually, I do," the girl snipped.

"Sorry?" Ellie queried in disbelief.

"Yes, you are," the girl said.

"Do you have an issue with me or something?" Ellie prodded. "I mean the seat is empty, and I thought, judged on your clothing, that maybe we'd have something in common. I almost bought that jacket at the Undercurrent. That's such a hot store, don't you think?"

The girl glared at her. "Oh, we have issues all right. Lay off my boyfriend, for starters."

"Your boyfriend?"

"Ryan Lachey. The football star. He's mine."

The picture started to become clearer for Ellie. "Um, okay...I'm not quite sure how we got off to a bad start, but I'm willing to try again. My name is Ellie LaRose. I'm Ryan's next door neighbor. That's all. He gave me a ride over here tonight because I'm new, and I don't know my way around."

"I know your type," the girl snarled. "You know your way around better than anyone."

"Excuse me?"

"There is no excuse for you."

"Okay, then..." Ellie said, moving away from the girl. She now had something in common with Jacey. She didn't want to sit with this girl either.

Ellie weighed her options. She could go back up with Tom and Jacey... no option there as far as she was concerned... or she could admit defeat and go sit with the Helens. That made her head hurt even more.

"At the risk of being branded a dork for life," she thought to herself, "I think I'll just say I have a stomach ache and call it a night." She made her way over to where her mother was sitting. "Mom," she said, her back to the field, "I think I'm coming down with something, I'm going to head back to the house."

"Do you remember how to get there?" Helen asked.

Before Ellie had a chance to answer, a shock wave went through the crowd, and the fans were suddenly on their feet.

"Did you see that?" Helena asked. "That goon hit Ryan, and he didn't even have the ball."

Ellie turned around. The home team had gathered around their fallen player.

"That's going to hurt for a while," Helena said. "He took it on the shoulder."

"He's a big boy," Helen said. "I'm sure he can take it."

The crowd gave Ryan a standing ovation as he picked himself up. They could see he was holding his right shoulder as he walked over to the bench and had words with the coach. He left the field shortly thereafter.

Ellie thought Ryan would probably stay until the game ended, but waiting alone for him by his car was the lesser of all evils at the moment. She wasn't certain if she could find her way home herself or not. Night time was probably not the best time to try to find out.

She made her way outside to the garbage area and tied her scarf around her nose. It wasn't so much the smell that made her do this. The night had gotten colder and the tip of her nose was beginning to go numb. She sat on the hood of the car and tried to call Dina, getting only her voicemail once again.

"Out of sight, out of mind, I guess," Ellie said disappointedly, putting her phone back into her pocket.

Five minutes later, Ellie heard the big metal school door open. She turned and saw Ryan making his way over to the car. He actually looked happy to see her. "Can you drive, Goth?" Ryan asked, throwing her the keys.

"Yes," Ellie lied.

"I think I'm okay, but I don't know how long it's going to take for the pain-killers to kick in." He tried to rotate his shoulder but had difficulty doing so. "It hurts so much I don't even want to hang in until the end of the game."

"How'd you get painkillers? You haven't even seen a doctor."

"No doctor tonight, Goth. He's looking for his kid. I keep a few in my gym bag for just such an emergency."

"What about Tom and Jacey? Maybe Tom can drive your car. I'll go back in and get them."

"Tom is the worst driver in Troy. There's no way I'd let him behind the wheel. And Jacey's just learning to drive a stick." He studied Ellie. "You really can't drive, can you?" he asked, snatching the keys back from her hand.

"I can drive. Stick or auto. But the license is a bit of a technicality."

"It's okay to say that, Goth. I'll still respect you in the morning."

"Then... is it okay to point out that having taken painkillers, you probably shouldn't drive either?"

"True enough. Maybe we could walk home together. You can make sure I don't stumble into a ditch. Tom and Jacey will figure it out. I can pick up the car tomorrow."

"But what about your girlfriend?" Ellie questioned hesitantly. "Shouldn't you walk home with her?"

"What girlfriend?" Ryan laughed. "What are you so nervous about all of a sudden Goth?"

"This girl just totally dissed me when I went to sit with her. She made it rather clear that there would be a voodoo doll with my name on it if I even glanced in your direction."

"What were you doing sitting with some freak? How come you didn't sit with Tom and Jacey?"

"It's complicated."

Ryan laughed harder. "Jacey has a way of doing that. What's wrong Goth? Have you got a thing for Tom?"

"No..." Ellie said. She could feel her face getting warm.

"You DO have a thing for Tom. I know the look. I've seen it a hundred times," Ryan laughed. "You're a blusher, GC," he added.

"Please don't tell him," Ellie begged.

"What's it worth to you, Goth? Will you carry my gym bag for me? I can't lift it with my shoulder the way it is. If you don't tell anyone about that, I'll keep quiet about your little high school sweetheart fantasies. Deal?"

"What's wrong with your other arm?" Ellie asked him.

"I took that TV into your room for Helena. That's a big bed you've got in there," he teased. "Do you think about Tom when you're lying there naked?"

Ellie grabbed his bag. "Deal. I'd also appreciate you calling off the Doberman with the short black hair and the nose ring."

"Tara? Tara Wildman? Is that who you sat with? She's not my girlfriend. Tara and I have an understanding that she doesn't quite understand, is all."

"You think?"

Ryan laughed. "See Goth, you're picking the wrong guy. All the ladies, they go after Tom. They don't see the potential in me. They probably will in a few years when I'm on Monday Night Football, but for now, I've got to coast. I take what I can get. I can get Tara. Life works in mysterious ways."

"That's not very nice," Ellie replied, smacking his sore shoulder. "Your eventual superstardom does not give you the right to act like a pig right now."

"Ow! Take it easy Goth. I hurt like a girl."

"That's probably the only no-bull thing you've said to me since we left the school," Ellie noted. "There was some guy following you with a camera tonight. Is this injury going to ruin your scholarship chances?"

"I doubt it. I've got scouts coming out of my ass. And look at my ass, Goth. It's a wide one. I'll kill the fucker who did this to me next time we play. It was a cheap shot. I'm on a hit list."

"Like a gang or something?"

"No. Like someone else wants my college scholarship."

"My Nan could probably help you with your shoulder," Ellie offered kindly.

Ryan turned and studied Ellie. He had known all the girls in his school most of his life, so it was nice to have someone new in town to talk to. Maybe that was part of the attraction. Ellie was someone who wouldn't know about things he had done in the past, or not done in the past, and therefore wouldn't judge him the way most of the other girls did. It seemed too good to be true.

"Why are you here, Goth?" Ryan asked, stopping in the street. "Why is a nice, hot, city-chic like you gracing us Troy-mongers with your presence? Are you preggers?"

"You've got more in common with my mom than she thinks," Ellie assessed. "Why does everyone assume I'm going to get pregnant? And why do they think Troy is the answer? Did a condom factory move out of town or something?" She shrugged. "I really don't know why we're here. My Mom just decided to leave her dead-beat husband all of a sudden, so here we are."

"Sorry to hear that," Ryan offered. "I know what it's like when people split up." He cleared his throat uncomfortably.

"It's okay. Sometimes 'all of a sudden' takes about five years too long. It was bound to happen. You sound like you're talking from experience."

Ryan didn't answer.

"Okay, I'll change the subject," Ellie said diplomatically. "What kind of music do you like? Are you a rocker or are you into the whole gangsta-rap thing?"

"Both," Ryan laughed. "But since we're bonding here Goth, I'll tell you something not even Tommy-boy knows. When I'm all alone, down in my basement... "

"Ryan..." she said nervously.

"I sing country."

"What?" Ellie laughed. She tried to picture him in a Stetson hat and a blue denim shirt, with a guitar strung over his back. It somehow didn't flow with the sweaty athlete image standing beside her.

"Maybe I'll serenade you outside your window one night. I'll sing you a hurtin' song and I'll steal your heart away." He laughed and started back down the road. "There are lots of things we need to get to know about each other, Goth. Consider me a sheep in wolf's clothing."

"Don't you have that backwards?"

"That's for me to know, and you to find out," he said, howling at the moon for effect.

Ellie stared at his face.

"Goth," Ryan stammered, "I was only joking around."

"You don't have two different colored eyes, do you?" she asked.

"What?"

"Never mind."

Saturday...

Chapter 7

*R*oy Cohen picked up the megaphone and prepared to address the crowd of a hundred or so people that had gathered outside the town hall. During the nearly three decades that he had served on the Troy police force, he had his share of tragedies to contend with. None of them prepared him for today.

"On behalf of the Quinlan family," he began solemnly, "I would like to thank everyone for coming down here. If you'll all just give me a few minutes to get organized, I'll be able to brief you on what we need to do today. If we divide it up, we should have most of the town covered before dark."

There was a grumble from the crowd, prompting Roy to raise his hand. "Before you say anything, I know most of you won't be able to stay the whole day. I appreciate the time you can spare. I'd rather you do a thorough job for a short period of time, than rush this. As more people show up, we'll have them sub in for those of you that have to leave. The Topaz Cafe has donated some coffee, juice and pastries this morning, so please help yourselves."

He put the loud speaker down and reached into his pocket for his leather gloves, wishing Colin and Cody Dayton, his two scheduled day officers, were there to help. As luck would have it, they had called to say their radiator had blown on the way into town and they were being towed. There was no sense calling in Rick Purdy. That would leave him short on the night shift. He was going to have to handle this himself.

Flory Neuberg, the manager of Neuberg's Drug Store, approached him carrying a box full of photocopier paper. He took it from her and placed it on the folding table the town council had thoughtfully provided for his use. Inside the box were hundreds of copies of Brooke's photo. He barely glanced at them. Her image was hauntingly embedded in his mind.

"Ellie," he called, noticing Helena's granddaughter in the assembled group. "Can you help me for a few minutes and hand these out?" He lifted a bundle of pages from the cardboard box.

"Um, okay," Ellie grunted, as she tried to suppress a yawn. She was surprised the cop remembered her name.

"Are we keeping you up?" the Chief of Police asked her.

"Somebody did," Ellie snapped, glancing back towards the Helens. "My parental unit is well practiced in ancient forms of sleep deprivation."

Having raised three children of his own to adulthood, Roy knew teenage sarcasm when he heard it.

"Good. If you've learned anything from the experience, you'll be able to teach my officers a thing or two. Their interrogation skills need work." He smiled at her. He could see the family resemblance between the teenager and her grandmother.

Her nose up in the air, Ellie turned to her mother and shoved a poster into her hand without saying a word. She headed off into the crowd without so much as a see-ya-later.

"Do you think she's still mad at us for waking her up last night?" Helena asked.

"Well, every hour on the hour might have been a bit much," Helen admitted. They had hoped that Ellie would have been pulled back into a dreamscape during the night. But every time the Helens thought she had finished a deep sleep cycle and woke her up, Ellie had nothing new to offer them... aside from a few choice words about a lack of beauty sleep normally being their problem, not hers.

Helena was certain Ellie had flipped them the finger beneath her covers at least once during the night. She was prepared to forgive her under the circumstances.

"It's odd that he didn't reappear though," she commented to Helen. "Willie, I mean. He's usually a keener for a repeat performance."

Although the man in the dream was just an anonymous antagonist to Ellie, her description of him had led the older LaRose women to the same conclusion about his identity. He was "Whistling" Willie, so named for his annoying habit of whistling to announce his unwelcomed arrival.

"Maybe Willie got it all wrong and he's gone off to haunt some other family," Helen shrugged. "It wouldn't be the first time he was confused."

"Confused, yes. Wrong, no." Helena corrected her. "He'll be back. He knows where the little girl is. You mark my words."

"If you're so sure, why are we here? I have other things to do. I should be taking the van back to Tony."

"We all have other things to do," Helena told her. "We're here to keep up appearances. How would it look if we were the only family in town not looking for the little girl?"

"I suppose. But what does this all have to do with Ellie? Maybe our imaginations are running away with us and it is just what everyone else thinks it is... something humanly criminal?" Helen offered.

"Willie doesn't do humanly criminal. He's not human. Not anymore, anyway." She paused for a moment, considering what she was about to say. "I don't think Ellie has told us everything. If this were a child who simply ran away and met misfortune, Willie wouldn't be this interested. There has to be something else going on." She bit her lip as she thought this over. "Maybe I should call him."

"You can't just call Willie," Helen reminded her. "He's on the other side. What are you going to do? Use your long distance calling card?"

"Oh, he'll come if I call him," Helena threatened.

"Don't you dare," Helen snarled, trying to keep her voice down. "He is a bad, bad, man."

"Willie himself is not the problem," Helena protested. "You know that."

"But he's connected to the problem. He always is. We'll solve this on our own. I do not want that man near my daughter ever again."

"You may not have a choice. Helen, you have got to sit that girl down and tell her who Willie is."

"He is a nightmare. That's it. No further explanation necessary."

Helena started to reply, but Helen cut her off abruptly. "The discussion is over. You just watch your friend Roy solve the big mystery. That ought to keep you entertained."

Helena's face turned red as she turned her eyes to Chief Cohen, who was in turn, looking at her.

In Roy's eyes, Helena was a welcomed sight. He wouldn't say that she was unflappable, because he knew that wasn't true. But he knew she was good in a crisis. He needed a dozen more people like her to help out today. He was more concerned about the other inexperienced volunteers. Most of them were dressed for a day at the mall, not winter dumpster diving. When this was all over, he was going to have to form a proper search-and-rescue group in the community.

Ralph Wildman showing up this morning was a mixed blessing. He was a dairy farmer, and Roy knew he had spent hours on end in the barn with the calves, getting them through their first winter. Ralph wouldn't get cold being outside all day, and he wouldn't give up easily. That had to count for something, Roy hoped, because Ralph was normally a major pain in the ass.

Forming a group to Ralph's left were the students from Troy Tech. Roy was somewhat surprised they were here, given the altercation he had with a few of them after the game last night. They weren't too happy when he confiscated their beer and poured it down the sewer. He knew they probably didn't care about the lecture he had given them, but at least they cared about a lost little girl, and no one told them they had to.

"Just a couple more minutes," Roy assured everyone. "I want to make sure we've got all the sections covered." He disappeared inside the town hall to get a map.

"I don't envy him," Helen said to Helena as she tightened a fuchsia-hued scarf around her neck. It clashed with her coat, but it was the only one she could find while scrounging through Helena's hall closet. "Having to tell a parent you can't find their child," she continued, "that would be a horrible thing to have to do." She thought about all the times Ellie had threatened to run away when she was younger.

"It makes finding the odd body on a porch swing seem like a walk in the park, doesn't it?" Helena said sarcastically. "I'm sure our bad days don't even compare to theirs. I have to clean up snot all the time when I'm teaching someone how to use a neti pot. They scrape brains off of windshields after a head-on collision. Neither are pleasant, but really…"

"Okay. Don't get so defensive. Or descriptive. I take back what I said about the police and the cereal box," Helen said. "Neti pot?"

"Think nose bidet. And thank you. But it doesn't get you off the hook. You still need to tell Ellie about Willie."

"Who's that plump, curly-haired woman who's glaring at us?" Helen asked, in an attempt to distract her mother. "I'm not getting a love vibe from her."

"You mean the one dressed in the neon pink tracksuit?"

"Yes. She's got to be cold in that outfit. Not to mention embarrassed. Never wear neon after Labor Day. Or ever, really."

"That's Betty Lachey, Ryan and Stan's mom and our illustrious neighbor. With any luck she'll be hibernating soon and we won't see her until spring."

"That's not very nice."

"Nor is she," Helena laughed. "She hates us."

"Us? How can she hate me? She doesn't even know me."

"Hate by association," Helena said, forcing a smile and giving her neighbor a wave. "There's a small town attitude in Troy, I'm afraid. You'll get used to it. I did."

"Is there a Mr. Lachey?" Helen asked, nodding politely to the woman.

"That subject is strictly verboten if you happen to want to keep the peace. Betty got sick of him constantly hanging around the house and told him to get a hobby. Well he did. A five-foot-six Texan named Traci. She was a brassy woman with guns from the double D ranch, if you get my drift. He ran off with her two summers ago."

"Well, that explains why she hates you."

Helena looked at her daughter. "For the record, I never even looked at her husband."

"Hate by association," Helen answered. "Listen, don't say anything to Ellie about Ryan's father running off. The less those two have in common, the better."

"She's going to find out eventually. What's the big deal? Oh...oh, Helen. Haven't you told her yet? About her father? Really, Helen. When are you going to have *that* talk with her? When are you going to have that talk with me?"

"Well, not right now. Maybe in thirty years."

"Helen, your denial of who you are and what it all means is going to put Ellie in danger. You have to get over it," she said sternly.

Betty Lachey began to walk towards them, and Helen sighed with relief. She didn't want to talk to Helena... or Ellie, about any of that. Not now. Not ever.

"Is Stan feeling any better?" Helena asked, genuinely concerned. "It's not like him to miss one of Ryan's games. I noticed he wasn't there last night."

"Stan was just getting over the death of poor Mr. Wagner," Betty began, "and now there's all this terrible business with little Brooke. I swear, I don't know what to tell him anymore. This town is going crazy." She paused for a moment and pulled an orange winter vest from the bag she was carrying. She noticed Helen wince as she zipped it over her jacket. "What? Like that scarf matches your coat, Miss Hoity-Toity?"

Perhaps her mother was right about Betty Lachey, Helen thought.

Helena smiled. "Well, she's got you there. You should have taken the black one. No fuchsia after Labor Day. Fuchsia is another word for neon."

Suddenly self-conscious, Helen began to tuck the scarf under her coat to hide it. "It was in *your* closet."

"I'm not happy about what happened at your house the other night," Betty continued. "But I at least I know Stan's alive and safe at his piano lesson. That is a darn sight more than the Quinlan's know about their child. So it makes you stop and think."

"I'm not totally batty, Betty. I can assure you that if I knew Mr. Wagner was dead on the swing, I would have taken care of it."

"Humph," she said. "Like you took care of Mrs. Harbinger? Never mind Stan, I'm having a hard time getting over that one."

"There's that Mrs. Harbinger thing again," Helen said, poking her mother. "Do tell."

It was Helena's turn to change the subject. "Betty, I don't think you've been properly introduced. This is Helen, my daughter."

"I know who she is," Betty snorted, as she turned her back on them and headed towards the pastry table. "And I know who her daughter of darkness is too."

"Bitch," Helena said. "I think she needs a good tongue-lashing."

"Mother," Helen cautioned, "get that look out of your eyes, and harness all that negative energy. The Chief is coming back outside."

Chief Cohen faced the crowd. Tell them just what they need to know, he reminded himself. "Okay everyone, let's begin. We've got a lot of ground to cover."

"What's going to happen at the school on Monday?" Ralph asked. "Are we going to have to worry about some nutcase roaming the halls, trying to snatch another kid?"

Roy could sense the mood of the crowd changing. Most of the parents probably hadn't thought that far ahead until Ralph mentioned it.

"Ralph, I understand your concerns, but let's just try to focus on right now," the Chief replied. "We'll have security in place Monday morning if we need to."

"Shouldn't you set up some roadblocks or something?" Ralph insisted.

"Ralph, there isn't really much point doing that now," Roy said calmly.

That one got Betty Lachey going. "He would have had all night to get away. You should have set up one of those spike lines across the highway yesterday."

"Ralph, Betty..." Chief Cohen began, "I appreciate your insights, as always. But you're all just a step or two ahead of your favorite cop show. Things don't work that way on Troy time. The only person we're looking for right this moment, is Brooke Quinlan. That's it. That's our job today."

"Why don't you use some dogs?" Ralph Wildman asked.

Roy wanted to stuff a sock in Ralph's mouth. "I need everyone to look with all of your senses. For example, use your eyes. If you were around Brooke's neighborhood yesterday you'd know that we did bring a canine unit in from the city. The dogs were using their eyes and their nose. Unfortunately, they were unable to track the scent beyond the end of the street." He lied. The truth was that the dogs had refused to follow the scent past Helena's corner. The German shepherd had dug its claws into the pavement and no command given to him would make him go further. The town didn't need to know that part.

"Use your ears. She hasn't had any food or water and she might be hurt, so any sound she makes may be slight. Pay attention. If you have a blanket in your car, it would be a good idea to get it and take it along. She may be hypothermic, or in shock," Roy added, noting that their faces had grown grim.

The town also didn't need to know that the dog heard something… something in a pitch so high, no human could hear it. Roy had seen the dog get down on its belly, cover his ears with his paws and howl in agony. In all the years Roy had been around dogs, both fully trained working dogs and those of the house pet variety, he had never seen a dog do that.

"You should have called me to bring my dogs," Ralph insisted. "They can track a rabbit in wet grass. They'd have Brooke home by now."

"Those dogs are so old they can't even smell each other's butts," Ryan said aloud, looking at Ralph Wildman with contempt.

"Okay, okay, settle down," Roy commanded. He knew had to get everyone grouped and on the road before they got more restless. "Does anyone have any other information on the whereabouts of Brooke Quinlan? I didn't get a chance to talk to everyone in town over the last twenty-four hours, so if you have anything to tell me, this would be a good time to do it."

"I saw her," Ryan offered. "She ran by Stan and Kev just before they went up to Mrs. LaRose's house. It was about seven o'clock."

Tom looked at him. "Are you sure? I didn't see her."

"Well, I notice girls more than you do," he laughed good-naturedly, giving Tom a body nudge. He winced. "Crap. I really wrecked my shoulder last night. It's still not sitting right in the rotator."

"You notice girls when they're six?" Ralph Wildman asked, sneering at Ryan. "What's wrong with you, Lachey?" He raised his voice so others could hear what he was saying. "Maybe we should be checking your house first, since you seem notice little girls more than the rest of us."

"Fuck you, Wildman. That's not what I said."

"You got a girlfriend, Lachey? One that's your age?"

"I don't need a girlfriend, Wildman. I do your daughter."

Tara Wildman, who had been staying behind her father, moved even further away. "Lachey, stay away from my daughter," he said loudly. "You're a pervert."

"I'll see what I can do, Fuckwad." He turned to Tom. "I have no time for that asshole."

"Ryan, maybe you should just cool it," Tom said. "People are looking at you like you're psychotic."

"People always look at me like I'm psychotic."

"Yeah, well you calling him that... it just makes him more psycho. It's like you two are in some demented ping-pong game. You know he wants to smash the ball down your throat, so you call him a name, just so he'll lose his edge for a second."

"Exactly. My serve," Ryan smirked.

"Why don't you give it a rest? Just walk away from him," Tom asked.

"Maybe I keep him amused. Maybe he's so fucking bored with his own sorry life that I keep him from shooting himself in the head," Ryan said, unnecessarily loudly.

"Lachey, you're a hopped up loser," Wildman sneered. "They ought to test you for hyper-steroids before they sign you to any college team."

Mrs. Lachey walked towards Ralph. "You say anything else about my boy, and I'll have you up for slander." She turned to her son. "Shut the hell up, Ryan."

"Ryan, shut up," Roy Cohen agreed, then added, "Ralph, shut-up. Betty, shut-up. We don't need any accusations flying around. This isn't a vigilante force. It's a search party. We need facts. Think, Ryan. Did you see which way she went?"

"I don't know. Tom and I were watching Stan and Kev, so I didn't pay a whole lot of attention to her."

"That's what you say now," Ralph said.

Chief Cohen looked directly at him. "Not that it is any concern of yours, but I can confirm that Ryan, and Tom here, had an alibi that night. I was with them at Helena's until well after eleven. So don't go there, Ralph. We've got to all work together. I need everyone to get into groups. I'll give each of you a photocopy of this map of the town. Each one has a different highlighted area. That's your territory. I need you to go there and look around. Look in the alleys. Look in the trash bins. Knock on every door. Make sure everyone in Troy sees the picture of Brooke. Come back here as soon as you've cleared your area. Groups of two, no more than three, please. I don't want anyone going alone, but we don't want to spread ourselves too thin. There's a lot of ground to cover."

Ryan stepped forward and took a map from Roy Cohen and motioned for Ellie to come over. "Tom and I'll take Goth over there as our number three. You're on your own, Wildman."

Standing alone in a crowd, Tara Wildman looked at Ryan with fire burning in her eyes. He may as well have been talking about her, not her father, with that last remark. How dare Ryan take the new girl along with Tom, when he knew damn well she was here, wanting to spend the day with him. Things were not going as she had planned ever since this new Goth-Slut had moved into Troy. Ryan and this new girl were getting far too cozy for her liking.

Ralph Wildman moved within inches of Ryan's face. "You're trouble, Lachey. You've got an un-natural preoccupation with any girl that isn't your own age. I don't know how you did it, but I'd put money on the line saying you did it."

"Yeah. And you've got an unnatural preoccupation with jerkin' your right hand. It is what it is, Wildman. Did you hear what the Chief said? I have an alibi."

"Where were you before and after, boy? That's what I want to know." He turned to Ellie and pointed his tobacco stained finger at her. "I'd think twice before I went anywhere with him, missy. Don't say I didn't warn you. That boy ain't right."

Chapter 8

The map that Ryan received had an area on the outskirts of town highlighted in yellow, indicating the streets they were to travel to get to their destination. The twenty-minute walk from the town hall would take the three of them out past the new subdivision and down a dirt road to the abandoned gravel pit.

"Could you have picked a map that takes us any further away?" Tom asked.

"We could take my car," Ryan offered. "I have to go back to the school and get it anyway."

"I think the idea is to look along the way," Ellie reminded him. "The car would kind of defeat the purpose."

"Don't get lippy with me, Goth," he teased. "I don't think I pinky swore to secrecy last night." He leaned over and gave her air kisses.

"Keep it up and I'll start giving you a reason to sing a hurtin' song," Ellie threatened, looking sternly at him.

Ryan howled in laughter. "Is that your poker face, Goth? You could make me some money, Loser." He flashed a finger "L" in front of her face. "Ellie's got a royal blush," he said in a sing-song voice.

"What the hell is up with you two?" Tom asked. "You're giggling like a couple of girls." He eyed the two of them suspiciously. Something had passed between them last night. Something he wasn't a part of.

"Me 'n' Goth were just talking," Ryan shrugged, sensing he was crossing the line with Tom. Why should Tom care, he wondered? Unless Tom had a hard-on for Ellie. That would figure. Tom always went after the new girl in town. It had been the same with Jacey.

Ryan grew quiet and avoided Tom's gaze as they continued down the road.

Their silence gave Ellie plenty of time to re-think what that evil girl had said. Evil-Girl. If she was destined to be Goth-Chic, Tara Wildman would forever be Evil-Girl in Ellie's eyes. Evil-Girl and her Psycho-Dad. The whole hyphenated family. Maybe the Wildman's hated everybody. Maybe they hated the whole-wide-world. Maybe it wasn't personal after all.

"Where's Jacey?" Ellie asked. She was trying to come to terms with the fact that if Tom and Ryan were destined to be her new best friends forever, then she was going to have to get used to the Jacey creature, like it or not.

"I don't know," Tom said. "She probably broke a nail or something and is waiting for elective surgery. How's your stomach?"

"My stomach?"

"From last night. Are you feeling okay now?" he asked. "We looked for you after the game and your Mom said you left early."

"Yes, thanks." Ellie had forgotten all about the little excuse she had come up with to leave quickly. "I'm probably just getting used to the water here in Troy. The water is softer. I have a delicate stomach. And my head was pounding. How's your shoulder, Ryan?"

"He's fine," Tom answered.

"She asked me," Ryan was quick to point out. "And it's still sore. I can't fully extend my arm yet."

"You can throw a pass if you want to," Tom snapped, moving ahead of Ryan and Ellie.

"Glad you're feeling better, Goth. I get the Jacey flu from time to time myself," Ryan confessed, giving Ellie a nod.

"What's wrong with Jacey?" Tom asked, turning around and facing them.

"Nothing," Ryan said. "That's the problem."

Ellie laughed. Either Ryan knew of hidden flaws in the girl that she would pry out of him later, or her perfection bugged the crap out of him too. Either way, she couldn't help but smile.

"Then let's get off the Jacey subject," Tom said irritably.

"Okay, okay," Ryan said. "Anything to get you to morph back into Mr. Personality."

"What's up with him?" Ellie asked Ryan. All the guessing going around in her head was starting to drive her mental. "Do we need to take him to a chick-flick so he can cry?"

"Some people are put out, some people are not putting out," Ryan answered. "Troy's a town full of Trojans with no place to go."

"Will you shut up, Ryan?" Tom begged. He turned and looked at Ellie.

She could sense he wanted to say something but couldn't. "What?" Ellie asked. "What's wrong? If she doesn't want to hang around me, you can tell me. Tara didn't seem to have a problem telling me."

"No, it's nothing like that," Tom tried to explain. "Jacey says she likes you. And Tara Wildman is as loony as her old man. Don't pay any attention to her."

"Leave Tara out of this," Ryan warned Tom. "Tara hasn't done anything to you or Jacey."

"I don't know if Jacey would agree," Tom argued.

Ellie stepped between them. "Okay, okay...let's play nice. Tell me the truth. Why didn't Jacey want to come, Tom?" she asked.

"Look... I didn't want to say anything, but you guys just won't let it drop. Jacey's not mad at me and she's not mad at Ellie. Okay, she's kind of mad at me, but that's got nothing to do with it. She said she didn't want to come today in case we found a dead body." He paused. "Happy?"

Ellie and Ryan gave each other looks that started off as fear and changed to disgust.

"Ew!" Ellie gasped.

"What did you say that for?" Ryan asked.

"That's what she said," Tom explained. "You wanted to know. Now you know."

"Cohen didn't tell us to look for a dead body," Ryan said. "That would change things. Big time. He gets paid for that kind of shit, we don't." He looked at Ellie. "We should have taken the car so we can get the hell out of there if we need to."

"I don't think she's dead," Ellie said. "So don't even go there."

"How do you know?" Tom asked. "I hate to break it to you but there is that possibility."

"I'm operating under the assumption we've had our quota of dead bodies this week," Ellie offered uneasily. "Let me see the map, Ryan. I don't know north from south in this town yet."

Ryan handed it to her. "I'm not an expert on these things or anything, but we're supposed to go search the gravel yard." He pointed to a spot on the map Ellie was holding. "There, at the end of the yellow line. That's the yard. Tom's right, there are definite dead body possibilities there."

"Gravel yards. They're right up there with cement factories," Tom explained.

"We are not going to find a dead body," Ellie insisted. Brooke hadn't been dead in her dream, but she couldn't tell them that. "Trust me."

"Seriously, Ellie," Ryan said pensively. "What happens if we do find her, you know, hanging from a tree with her skipping rope around her neck or something? Do we cut her down? Do we leave her hanging there? What do we do?"

Ellie had no answer for him.

"You almost sound excited," Tom noted. "Maybe Wildman's right about you."

"With Old Man Wagner," Ryan continued, ignoring Tom, "I only had to pull the blanket back up over his face. He was ready to be taken away. Stiff, but ready. Touching a dead little girl would be..."

"Do you have to be so graphic?" Ellie asked, cutting him off. She looked to Tom for help.

"You're lucky you missed the summer camp stories with him when we were kids," Tom told her. "I still have nightmares from the ghost stories he made up. Especially the one about the axe murderer."

"It could happen," Ryan insisted. "What if..."

"Stop," Tom interrupted. "Let's say for the sake of argument that we do find her, and she's not happily picking buttercups in a meadow. We'd have to take her pulse to see if she's alive or dead. That much I know for sure. Other than that, we probably shouldn't touch her. Cohen wouldn't want us disturbing the scene."

"Quit talking like you're going to be conscious," Ryan said testily. "I've seen you in a similar situation and I can tell you now, you'll be out cold and it'll be Goth and me taking care of 'the scene, Mr. Dead-Man-Fainting."

"Fuck you," Tom replied.

"Fuck you," Ryan echoed back to him.

"You two are talking like your Trojans are intimate," Ellie said. "Kiss and make up already."

"So you got that earlier reference?" Ryan asked sheepishly.

"I'm not twelve, Ryan. I'm fifteen. Jacey didn't put out and Tom's pissed off. Yes. I got that reference." She looked over at Tom who was avoiding her gaze. "Now will you two knock it off and get serious about this?" She hesitated. There was something she needed to know, but she was unsure if this was the right time to ask. "Have you guys lived here all your lives?"

"Yes," Tom said. "Are you going to make that a good thing or a bad thing?"

"Good. Do you know if there is a bridge by this gravel yard we're headed to?" She tried to look at the map as she walked, but the motion was making her ill.

"No bridge. Why?" Tom questioned.

"Just curious. Is that the yard at the end of this road?"

"Destination dead body yard is indeed in our sight," Ryan said.

Ellie paused for a moment and looked at the landscape. While they had left the residential area of town and she could see farm pastures up ahead, the area didn't bear any resemblance to the location in her dream. As they reached the yard, all she could see around her were piles of rock. No bridge. No schoolhouse. Just rocks. She felt relieved and disappointed at the same time.

"Watch your step," Tom cautioned, as he stomped over a 'no trespassing' sign. There was a hole in the wire fence as big as a bulldozer. Gaining entry to the area was not going to be a problem. "There's rusted scrap all over the place. Every one up on their tetanus? Be careful what you pick up. It could be nasty."

"Story of my life," Ryan said. "I guess we're looking for a ruby slipper sticking out of a rock pile. That ought to narrow it down from whoever else we find here."

"You really can't help it, can you?" Ellie asked sarcastically, her stomach beginning to churn at the thought of what they might really find.

"Easy, Goth. I'm just playing the odds. The more we talk about it, the less likely it is to happen."

"Mr. Tough-Guy-Folding," Tom said under his breath.

"I'm not folding. That's not part of my game plan," Ryan insisted.

"Game plan?" Tom asked.

"I've been running possible plays over in my head. If this were a ball game, I would see the opponent coming at me. I'd have to make a split second decision how to get by him. And if that didn't pan out, I'd measure the amount of pain I'd have to take when he hit me, and get ready to suck it up. Right now, I don't know if there's some maniacal serial killer lurking behind that porta-shitter up ahead, waiting to kill us. If there is, I don't know how much he weighs. So the pain is questionable. I do know it's about a hundred yards away. I can run that in 15 seconds. How about you guys?"

Tom and Ellie looked at each other and shrugged.

"I'm a goner," Tom admitted.

"This is why you need me, in case there was ever any doubt," Ryan told them.

"We should have brought shovels," Ellie said, looking around the yard. There were piles of stones ranging from pebbles to boulders all around them.

"Negative, Goth," Ryan continued. "Again you need me. Here's what we do. We take a look around and apply the rule of bird shit."

"The rule of bird shit?" She glanced at Tom for a clue.

"Don't look at me," Tom replied. "I don't know where's he's going with this."

"Listen and try to keep up. As you can see, all the rocks in here are covered in bird shit. If anyone had come in here and dug an area up, say to bury something, they would have had to disturb the rocks. Clean rocks equal dead body. Bird shit equals we can go home."

"That actually makes sense," Ellie admitted.

"Okay," Tom said, "but what if he just dumped the body and ran?"

"If he didn't bury her and she's just lying there, she'll reek," Ryan offered. I know it's cold but it even if she froze solid last night, this winter sun would be giving her a little defrost factor. Thawing rotten meat still stinks."

"Are you trying to make me barf?" Ellie asked. "Maybe we'd be better off keeping our opinions to ourselves."

The three teenagers combed the dusty yard for almost an hour before giving up. In the end, the only sign of death they had found was what appeared to be the remains of a large bird.

"Well, that was useless. We found squat," Ryan summed up. "Let's head back, give them the good news and then grab some grub at the Topaz. I could murder a burger."

"I'm kind of hungry myself," Ellie admitted. "Now that I've got my appetite back."

"What do you think really happened to her?" Tom asked, as they slipped back out through the hole in the fence.

"Some perv. It happens all the time," Ryan said. "I mean; what else could it be? No kid strays far from home on Halloween. It goes against the ritual. Stan was right about that."

"What do you mean?" Tom asked.

"It's a total freak show out on the streets. Kids don't want to put up with all that bullshit. The objective is to get the candy and go home."

"Your theory is sound," Tom agreed. "Greed over gore."

Ellie hesitated. "Okay listen, don't think I'm weird or anything, I know this is going to sound really strange. I had a dream about her the other night. That's why I asked you guys about the bridge. In my dream, I saw this old wooden one over a small brook, no pun intended. It was one of those covered ones like you'd see on the cover of an old Western novel."

"You had a dream about Brooke? That's weird. You don't even know her," Tom said.

"You should be dreaming about what I look like naked in the shower," Ryan teased.

Ellie gave Ryan a pained look.

"Or not," he offered.

"I said the dream was strange, not totally out of the question," Ellie snapped back. She turned to Tom, hoping for a sympathetic ear. "I saw her. Out there somewhere." She paused for a moment. "I think there was some sort of old school or something off in the distance. It wasn't in town. It was out in the country somewhere. At first I thought it might be around here, but nothing looks familiar."

Tom stared at her. He could see the aura back around her, turning a purple shade as she told her story. It turned deeper as she became more agitated and lightened up when she was collecting her thoughts. It mesmerized him. He wanted to ask Ryan if he saw it as well, but then again, he didn't want Ryan thinking he had totally lost it over her. Maybe he and Ellie were connecting in a way Ryan could never understand. He secretly hoped they were.

"I saw her wearing that costume even before the cops had the picture of her," Ellie informed them. "She was calling my name, asking me to find her and then poof, they were gone."

"Poof?" Ryan laughed, and then howled like a wolf to add a bit of drama to the tale. "Oh, Goth. Save me. I don't want to die," he teased in a falsetto voice. "POOF me already."

Ellie's face grew grim. She was tiring of Ryan's wolf impersonations. They reminded her of the wild dog she met in front of her grandmother's house. "That's not funny. I'm serious, Ryan."

"You said 'they'," Tom pointed out.

Ellie nodded her head. "There was this kid... well not a kid exactly... some guy about our age. He was really, really, pale, and he had these fangs."

Ryan laughed even harder. "Are you trying to tell us he was like a vampire or something? Goth, what have you been smokin'?"

Tom hit one side of Ryan, hoping he would lighten up. Ellie hit the other side of him, hoping he would shut-up.

"Damn it. Watch the shoulder, people." Ryan cried, rubbing it.

"I'll give you something to howl about," Ellie promised.

"Ignore him, Ellie. He's just being an ass." Tom tried to put his arm around Ellie in a feeble attempt to calm her down. He felt a static shock as he touched her, and immediately pulled back. "Ow! Man, the air is dry today."

Ryan had heard the snap. "Stop shuffling your feet, dude."

Tom looked down. "It shouldn't have happened. I'm wearing rubbers."

The boys looked at each other and laughed.

"Dude. One will do," Ryan snickered.

Ellie groaned. While under different circumstances Tom's attempted touch might have made her warm and fuzzy, i.e., before she met Jacey, it certainly didn't now. It had been a stressful morning, and she knew they were being juvenile to blow off steam, but they weren't taking her seriously and it was really starting to annoy her.

"Please," Ellie pleaded with them. "You guys are the only friends I have here. I know this sounds crazy, but I swear I'm not making it up. There really was a vampire, or someone who looked like a vampire, in my dream. That's all I'm saying."

"Okay. I really was being an ass." Ryan admitted. "Goth, there are no such things as vampires. Not in Troy. Reality check time. You'd have to have to be living in a town with blood pulsing through its veins to attract them. You're not. This ain't New York, New York." He posed for her, snapping his fingers as he began to croon "We go to sleep in a city, that doesn't wake up."

Tom laughed. "Dude, you do have the pipes."

"Fine. Forget it. I knew I shouldn't have told you. I knew you wouldn't understand." She looked at the two of them and wondered why she had even attempted to tell them her story in the first place. "Thanks for your support," she added sarcastically. "I'm out of here."

"You don't know where out of here is," Ryan laughed.

Ellie turned and glared at him. "I have the map, Brainchild. That is why I DON'T NEED YOU. I can find my own way back." Her pace quickened as she headed back down the road.

Tom and Ryan looked at each other.

"What do you make of that?" Tom asked.

"She's a chick," Ryan shrugged. "I don't try to understand them."

"No, I mean the dream thing. Do you think she's for real?" He noticed that the aura around Ellie had disappeared.

They started to follow her, keeping their distance.

"You know I want to love them all, and it goes against every throb in my cajones to have to say this, but dude, some of them are just whacko," Ryan said. "If you need one for whacko-sex, fine. But I have Tara for that."

"Ellie might be wacko, the jury's still out... but maybe we should pretend to believe her and see how far it gets us," Tom offered.

"You mean, you. How far it gets *you*. Leave me out of your little love-sca-pade. I'll be the dude who comes back to pick up the pieces of her broken heart."

"I thought you didn't care."

"Never underestimate the emotions of a grateful family," Ryan smirked.

"It'll never happen. This fantasy thing you have with the LaRose women," Tom tried to tell him.

"Maybe. But while we're referencing images on the weird radar, check this out. I think I know the bridge Goth was talking about. It sounded like the one out on county road three. The one over Stillman's Creek. There's that old abandoned Amish schoolhouse out past the pasture. I took Alison Fuller there once."

"Get out!" Tom questioned. "Alison Fuller is way out of your league."

"Okay. I tried to take Alison Fuller there once. She spent the night asking me to hook her up with somebody else."

"What did you want to go there for? That's by Tara's place."

"Moonlight. Water. Isolation. Stillman's Creek is the perfect make-out spot. You have to admit it sounds like the place she described. Maybe Goth's onto something."

Tom stopped in the middle of the street. "Vampires, dude?"

"I'm just sayin'... if you haven't lived in Troy all your life, there's no way you'd know about that bridge. You've got to hike around through Wildman's property to get to it since they blocked off the old highway road, but it's still there. Let's do it, man. Let's go and check it out. Maybe we'll knock down Ralph Wildman's mailbox while we're at it."

"I think you're more whacked than Ellie is. What's your beef with Wildman, anyway? If you're going to marry his daughter someday, you've got to bury the hatchet."

Ryan faced Tom and raised his fist. "Ugh. I am not going to marry Tara Wildman. I'm not going to marry anybody," he said seriously. "I am going to my grave a single dude. But since you asked, my current beef with Wildman is simple. It's about this missing kid. He told half the town that he thinks I did it."

"Dude. Let it go," Tom demanded, surprised that Ryan had threatened him. "I was just joking around."

The "zone" look that Ryan had shown Helena yesterday morning had now reappeared on his face as his attempts to contain his inner rage failed.

"Yeah? Well, Wildman wasn't."

Chapter 9

*R*yan had just turned the corner onto Main Street when he noticed Tara coming out of the Scissors Salon. She was strolling towards the Topaz listening to her iPod with her headphones, and didn't hear the roar of the Toyota's engine.

Ryan reviewed his options. This might be his chance to kill two birds with one stone. First of all, if Tara felt like hanging out with him, he'd have a reason to go out to Stillman's Creek without saying a word about any vampire hunting. The less said about that, the better. Second, he might even get lucky.

He pulled the Toyota into the vacant parking space just before the restaurant.

He leaned on the horn to get her attention. "Tara, do you want a ride somewhere?" he asked.

Tara turned towards the noise, revealing the results of her newly shorn hair. Seeing Ryan, she smiled and walked back towards his car.

"You got your hair cut again," he commented, trying to hide the disappointment in his voice.

"Do you like it?" Tara asked hopefully. The hairdresser had cut it shorter than she had wanted, but had definitely delivered on the punk look she was after.

"At least you left your bangs alone," he shrugged, secretly wondering what army barber reject they had recently hired at Scissors. To him, her hair looked like it had been buzzed.

"I guess that's a no," Tara pouted.

"Give me a break, Tara. I'm just a long hair fan," Ryan tried to explain.

"You?" Tara said indignantly. "You have no hair."

"I'm a guy with a family history of receding hairlines," Ryan shrugged. "I'm just speeding up the process."

Sensing he had hurt her feelings, he tried to think of something to say to make her feel better.

"I like your earrings."

Tara remained sullen.

"What's up, Tara?" Ryan asked, knowing those three words could lead him into dangerous territory. Tara would either go mental on him and be done with it, or she might drag the inevitable fight out all night long. Sometimes it was best just to get it over with.

"Thanks a lot."

"This isn't about your hair," he sensed. He had been through several styles with her, and several emotions because of them. Sometimes it took until things began to grow back before their relationship began to settle down. If that was true, this one might take a while. "The search group," she whined. "Why didn't you pick me to join your group of three this morning? Jacey wasn't there. Why did you pick that new girl?"

Ryan winced. At the time he hadn't thought about that choice coming back to bite him. "Oh that. You know Tom. He's a player. He wanted to get to know Goth."

"Tom didn't pick her. You did. I heard you."

Ryan had to think quickly. "We had it pre-arranged."

"Liar."

He knew he was caught. "Okay, you got me. But I couldn't ask you to come with us. Your dad was standing right there. You must have heard him telling every-one what a deranged piece of society I was. I'm personal non gratis with him."

True, Tara knew. Ralph would have had a fit if she had gone with Ryan, Still...

"You mean persona non grata," she corrected him.

"Whatever. Hop in the car and I'll take you for a drive." He leaned over to the passenger door and opened it from the inside.

"A drive?" Tara smiled. The stars were aligning perfectly. It was a rare Saturday night when Ryan didn't want to hang out with Tom and Jacey. Finally, she thought, a chance to get some alone time with him. "That'd be great! Where do you want to go?"

"I was thinking we could drive around for a little while and then go get romantic down by Stillman's Creek. How does that sound?"

"Stillman's Creek is a cesspool, and it happens to back onto our farm. We can't go there. If my dad catches us, he'll kill you." She looked at him like he had completely lost his mind. "Why would you want to take me there?"

"Well, Goth said..."

The switch in Ryan's brain that should have told him to shut up, had just malfunctioned.

Tara slammed the car door shut. "You, Ryan Lachey, can go to hell. Or you can take Goth to Stillman's Creek. I really don't give a shit."

"It sure seems like you do. You keep mentioning her. Why is she up your ass? Are you worried I'm going to ask her out or something? Because I'm not. Goth's a little out there, you know."

Ryan didn't know if he could save the situation, but he was going to try. Tara being this jealous of another girl was something new to him. An interesting turn of events. He could have told her not to worry, that Ellie had a thing for Tom, but he was finding it all kind of amusing.

"What do you mean?" Tara asked.

"Well, she thinks a vampire took Brooke Quinlan." He used his index finger to make a loony signal around his head. "How's that for starters? She's checking out the seat-sales to Mars as we speak, trust me."

"Why? What did she say?" Tara re-opened the door of the Toyota herself and slipped into the passenger seat. If the new girl really was as crazy as Ryan was making out she was, then she maybe she didn't have anything to worry about after all. This little tidbit of news intrigued her.

"She said she had a dream where she saw this vampire-dude take Brooke Quinlan off into the night."

"A vampire? She told you this?" Tara laughed. She might have found it hysterical except when she waited for Ryan's laughter in return, it didn't happen. "Wait a minute. If you really think she's crazy, then why do I get the feeling your sudden need to visit the swamp at the back of our farm has something to do with her? Did she say the vampire was at my place?"

"Maybe," he admitted sheepishly.

"Ryan, you are so gullible. She's just messing with your head. Girls like her are like that."

"All I know is, she's not talking to Tom or me right now," he shrugged.

"There's some good news. So why don't you just forget about it? I can think of plenty of things we can do that don't involve her," Tara suggested hopefully.

"Because it's been my experience that when chicks give you the silent treatment after they tell you something, they weren't joking around."

Tara tried to read Ryan's face. She couldn't get an accurate read on whether he was making this whole story up or not. At the moment, Ryan just looked perplexed. Did Goth really have a crazy dream complete with a blood sucker living at the edge of the Wildman farm? "Why do I get the impression that as much as you're sitting there telling me that you don't believe her, you actually do?" she questioned.

"I don't. I mean, I think I don't," Ryan sighed. "Okay, I really don't know what I think. Here's the problem. Goth, she's new here, right? She couldn't make her way to the park without someone having to show her where it is. But in this dream she had, she talked about that old wooden bridge out by your place. The one over Stillman's Creek. She even saw the crappy old schoolhouse down the side road. You have to admit that's kind of freaky."

"So, let me see if I have this right. You want to take ME on a romantic drive to my OWN backyard to see if we can find Goth's vampire?"

"It doesn't sound so good when you say it that way, but yeah. That and some other stuff. I thought maybe we could finish off what we started last weekend."

"Does it not register in that thick, bald head of yours, that I can't stand the new bitch?" Tara asked angrily. "Maybe I don't want to have anything to do with her, or her dream."

"Goth's not a bitch, she's just...."

"Drop dead, Ryan."

Tara threw the car door open again and climbed out. Ryan had been thick-headed before, but this time he was going too far. She might not have had any plans for Saturday night, but even if she did, there was no way they'd involve that new girl.

She stormed off down the sidewalk, without a glance back to Ryan.

"What? What did I say?" he yelled, as he threw the car into gear and spun out onto the road. "Chicks," he screamed out the window to startled passersby. "One's as nutty as the next."

He reached over and turned on the car radio. He had left it on the country station. Somehow, listening to the top-ten countdown didn't fit the mood he was in. Despite what other people might think, it wasn't the best music to listen to when you're about to go looking for a body in a swamp. He switched it over to the oldies station, knowing it wouldn't be long before something moody hit the airwaves.

"Next up, Jan and Dean with Dead Man's Curve," the deejay promised. Ryan liked that song. He found it ironic, how Dean Torrence was killed in a car crash after writing the tune. Not that it was a good thing. It wasn't. But it got him thinking about what would happen if every song a songwriter made up, wound up coming true.

"It'd probably wipe out every blues singer on the planet," he realized as he thought about the ballads he had written himself. The ones that no one had ever heard. Like the song he wrote about Betty. He laughed. "Won't come back from Stillman's Creek," Ryan sang in falsetto as the station went to a commercial.

There was surprisingly little traffic in town for a Saturday night. It was as if a curfew had been put in place keeping everyone at home behind locked doors. All because of the missing girl.

Ryan stopped for an orange super guzzler then headed out the highway towards Tara's farm. Other people might have been afraid of whatever sinister thing had taken up residence in Troy, but he wasn't going to let it get to him. If luck was on his side, Ralph had gone home, got into some of the homemade hooch Tara said he made, and was now passed out in the barn with the heifers. He didn't really feel like another confrontation with the crazy old fart tonight.

His own plan was to get to the creek, check it out for vampires and go home. Just to ease his mind about the whole crazy story. It was a simple plan, but a plan all the same. He liked plans. Tom always let him do the planning when they hung out, because as smart as Tom was, he over-thought things and as a result, his plans were lame. Someday the chicks would figure that out. Someday they'd learn that Tom's good looks were as useful as an unloaded gun. But probably not until they were forty.

He turned onto the county road that led past the Wildman's farm and out towards the old covered bridge, dimming the headlights on his car as he did so. There was no sense drawing attention to the fact that he was heading out towards the water. Having just experienced his own ridicule with Tara over the whole "is there or isn't there a vampire out there", he knew why Ellie had been so upset with the jokes he had made earlier. This was something that had to be done alone.

"Lachey, just keep your mouth shut," he said to himself.

Within the boundaries of the isolated area he could hear what he thought were a million bullfrogs, croaking in the background. Weird, he thought.

"It's a fucking frog-fest. The coyotes that are eating all the stray cats around town should just head out here," he surmised. "Frogs taste like chicken. You'd think that'd be pretty appealing to a canine."

With the bridge now a few feet ahead of him, Ryan slowed down and drove the Toyota slowly onto the wooden slats. They creaked as he edged his car across them.

"Creepy," he said, as he noticed how dark the darkness really was inside the old structure. The walls were restricting the reach of his headlights, and throwing the high beams on only made it worse. They bounced back and blinded him. He decided to park right where he was.

"Where's the flashlight?" he asked himself, exiting the car and heading towards his trunk. Thankfully it was in its usual spot in the hub over the left wheel.

A small brown bat swooped down from the rafters, startling him. He shone the light in the direction from where it came.

"Looks like I've got company," he said, as three more of the mammals darted down towards him before their internal radar sent them flying out into the night. "What are you guys still doing here in November? You should be down in Cabo by now sipping tequila from half-empty tourist's glasses."

A foul smell wafted through his nostrils, forcing him to plug his nose with one hand and hold the flashlight with the other. He shone it around the floorboards until he found the source of the smell. At his current vantage point, he could only tell that whatever it was, it was about half the size of him and definitely dead. He needed to get closer to identify it. He suppressed an involuntary gag by moving his hand from his nose to his mouth as he cautiously took a few steps towards whatever the hell it was. The flashlight's beam soon revealed to him the half-mangled head of a bear cub. Judging from the pile of bat feces and maggots in and around it, Ryan figured it wasn't a fresh kill.

"Okay," he gasped. "I didn't need to see that. All the same, I hope mama bear's not going to put in a guest appearance around here anytime soon." He took a deep breath before taking another look at the carcass. "The skull's all in one piece, so it probably wasn't shot. What the fuck happened?" he wondered.

While the head looked like it had been partially devoured, the body of the bear was mainly intact.

"Maybe the bear got hit by a truck and crawled away to the corner of the bridge to die. And then the coyotes came along and mangled his brains," Ryan pondered. "Or maybe it was some bear-ball nut job who killed him, panicked and ran."

He couldn't tell from the position of the bear whether this was what happened or not. Either way, he didn't feel like sticking around any longer to figure it out.

He exited the other side of the bridge into what he hoped would be fresh air, but the smell by the creek was nothing short of skanky. He couldn't take a deep breath even if he wanted to. Something seemed to be sucking the oxygen from his every breath. He found himself wheezing, just like Stan often did. His heart began to beat rapidly.

"This is whacked," he acknowledged. "It's like I stepped through a time portal into the dead zone."

The story Ellie had told him began to replay itself over and over in his mind, with the vampire getting bigger and nastier each time the scene played out.

He stood still for a moment to calm himself down, wishing he had a sports drink chocked full of electrolytes to put his metabolism back together. The area was suddenly eerily quiet. No bullfrogs croaking. No bats flapping their wings overhead. The creepy animal convention had packed up and gone home in less than five minutes. He wanted to do the same. "Lachey, get a grip," he told himself.

"Find the girl. Be a hero. Get laid. What the hell was I thinking?" he wondered. "This was a bad idea. I'd be having a better time at home with Betty and Stan." It struck him how true that statement really was.

He had parked the car at the far end of the bridge. To get back to it, he either had to go back past the bear, the mere thought of which was making him nauseous, or wade through the water to approach the Toyota from the other side.

"Betty always told me to stay away from bears," he said. "No coin toss necessary."

He grabbed a broken tree branch from the bank of the creek and measured the depth of the water. It was about waist deep, and he knew he had a pair of old track pants in the car trunk that he could change into after he crossed through the algae infested liquid. He figured it would take about five minutes to get from the creek to the Toyota. There was no current to contend with to slow him down.

He stepped in and moved through the cold, murky water, taking the stick with him in case he needed it.

"Falling in is not part of the plan," he said, deciding to use the stick much like a blind person would, to feel what was before his feet in the uneven creek bed.

The stick hit something small, and he used it to knock whatever it was out of the way. A dead fish rose to the surface.

The more Ryan poked around, the more dead fish floated towards him. "I never did like bobbin' for apples," Ryan sassed, his stomach beginning to churn.

He was almost across the water when his right foot hit something that the stick had missed. A sunken tree limb?

He used the stick to feel its width. It was about two inches thick, he surmised. He straddled the object, trying to step over it, but it was wider than he had initially thought, and he inadvertently knocked it loose from the bottom of the creek. It rose up between his legs.

The heel of a little red shoe floated to the surface first.

"Oh my God. Oh. My. God. It's a fucking leg."

The rising human limb startled him, causing him to lose his balance. He fell backwards into the water, barely managing to keep the flashlight above his head. He wiped his face with his slime soaked sleeve as he strained to see the body in the water. It was now rising, floating face up, right beside him. He shone the light across it.

A water spider ran across the little bloated face. Brooke's face.

"Fuck me," he said, turning his gaze from her and scrambling up the adjacent edge of the water.

The urge to vomit overwhelmed him, and he spewed his downed super guzzler over the creek bank. For once in his life he didn't care if anyone saw him puking his guts out. This was way worse than any story he could have dreamed up on a camping trip with Tom.

He reached for his cell phone and attempted to turn it on. No such luck. The water had shorted out the battery.

"Now what do I do?" he wondered.

He sat on a rotted tree stump, put his hands in his hoodie pockets, and tried to figure something out. He was unaware that he was being watched.

A pair of eyes, one blue and one brown, were tracking him from the edge of the tree line that backed onto the Wildman's farm.

"I can't just leave her there," Ryan thought. He slowly stood up and turned back in the direction of the water.

The silence surrounding him was broken by a deep-throated snarl from behind.

Ryan turned and shone the flashlight into the direction the noise had come from. He saw nothing.

"Who's there?" he shouted into the darkness.

"Don't touch her," he heard someone hiss.

Ryan looked around nervously. "Tom?" he questioned.

Tom must have followed him out there. That was the only explanation available, because the voice sure as hell didn't sound like Tara's, and nobody else would know he had come out to the bridge. "Quit pissin' around. Get over here and help me. I've found Brooke."

He waited for Tom's voice to answer him.

"Seriously, dude. This is no time to try to get me back for anything stupid I did to you in the past. How do we get her out of here? I don't want to touch her. Do you have your cell phone, so we can call the cops?"

The hiss grew louder. "I said, don't touch."

Ryan turned around. Before him stood a teenager, about his age, but slighter in build and a few inches shorter. His dark hair hung over his face, hiding his features.

"Who the fuck are you?" Ryan asked. "My mother? Nobody tells a Lachey what he can and can't do."

"Lachey," the teenager said. "French, no? You're all stubborn pricks, boy band members, or both. Go home," he snarled, showing his fangs to Ryan. "And don't talk about yourself in the third person. It's just wrong."

"Dude. Really. You should call my barber."

Ryan's cocky demeanor was short-lived as he watched the teenager walk upon the water, and pick Brooke's body up into his arms.

"Give her to me," Ryan demanded. In his head, he could hear Tom telling him not to touch the body, but there was no longer much hope of keeping the crime scene intact. "Good trick with the water walking, Incisor-Boy. But I'm guessing you're not a man of the cloth."

"She's mine," the teenager warned. "Go get your own girl."

"Like I haven't heard that one before. I know who you are. You're the dude in Goth's dream. Sorry to take away your meal ticket, Funshine. Hand her over before I..."

"Before you what?" the teenager laughed. "Before you kill me? Sorry. That film ended. We're onto the sequel now. Mortal."

"Didn't you ever listen to Journey?" Ryan sneered. "The movie never ends, it goes on and on and on."

He rushed back into the water, throwing all his weight towards the vampire. The ratio of weight to bone was in Ryan's favor, forcing the stranger to lose his grip on the girl's body.

"Tumbling dice," Ryan said as he grabbed the vampire by the collar of his jacket.

"I told you to leave her alone," the teenager said as he turned and positioned his fangs within biting distance of Ryan's left hand.

"That's my throwing arm, asshole," Ryan commented, taking his right fist and pummeling it into the teenager's nasal cavity. "Ambidextrous. Look it up."

"Don't you know what I am?" the teenager hissed. "You can't kill me. I'll feed later tonight and then I'll come back for you."

"Feed on this," Ryan said, grabbing his own crotch. "Now, are you going to leave her with me, or am I going to have to make you even uglier?"

"There's only a half-quart left in this half-pint anyway," the vampire sighed. "Keep her. But you owe me," he warned Ryan, shaking his finger at him.

"Ooh, I'm shakin'. Tell you what. Next time I'm in the neighborhood of 666 Hadesarootin' Drive, I'll stop in for a bite. Or is that your line?"

A strong wind blew in from the west, forming a mist upon the water. Ryan's view of the teenager was now non-existent. When it had passed, Ryan saw that the vampire had vanished into the night, leaving him alone with the little body.

"This has got to be the part where the aliens come," Ryan laughed aloud. The laugh was full of nervous emotion, and even to Ryan's own ears, it sounded like one only a raging lunatic would let out.

He walked back to the creek and pulled Brooke gently onto the grass.

"Now I know why Tom fainted when he saw Old Man Wagner. Sometimes there's only so much a guy can take."

His own consciousness left him, and he collapsed to the ground.

Across the water, Ralph Wildman was listening to a story his daughter was telling him. She was upset. That Lachey kid had insulted her new haircut, and he hadn't stopped there. He had wanted to do things with her. Down by Stillman's Creek. She was pretty sure he went there anyway and was probably waiting by the bridge, hoping she would change her mind. But she wouldn't, because Ryan had said Brooke's body was down there, and she wasn't having anything to do with that.

Ralph went for his rifle.

Five minutes later, the long barrel of Ralph's firearm was jabbing into the good shoulder of Ryan Lachey, who was lying next to the body of Brooke Quinlan.

"Get up," Wildman said angrily. "I'm not going to say it twice, you warped little prick."

Ryan regained consciousness and flinched.

"Wildman? Fuck, I never thought I'd say this, but am I ever glad to see you."

"Tara told me what you tried to do to her tonight. She told me you knew where the body was."

"Wildman. This is not what it looks like. Brooke was already dead when I got here. And that little girl of yours is bi. As in polar. I want you, I don't want you. She can't make up her mind. Is Mrs. Wildman like that?"

He tried to stand up, but Wildman pushed him back to the ground.

"What was it you said earlier? About me being bored and wanting to shoot something in the head?" Wildman raised the barrel dangerously close to Ryan's face. "Give me one reason why I shouldn't unload this rifle into that sick, demented brain you have, Lachey. It would save us taxpayers the cost of a trial."

This wasn't good, Ryan knew. Of all the people that had to stumble across him and the body he himself stumbled upon, it would have to be Ralph Wildman. Someone who really couldn't give a shit whether he lived or died under the best of circumstances. Ryan had to think fast. One wrong word and it could be lights out forever. Then he remembered. Ping-pong.

"Because seeing me in the electric chair would give you an orgasm," Ryan sneered "Fuckwad."

Chapter 10

om walked nervously down the Maple Street lane past Ryan's house and over to Ellie's place next door. The thought of having to tell Ryan he wanted to talk to Goth alone made beads of sweat form on his forehead. He still wasn't sure what had gone on between Ryan and Ellie the night before. Had Ryan tried to make a move on Ellie? The idea was making Tom's ego take a bruising. He had never lost a girl to Ryan, and the mere thought that maybe this time he might, was preying on his self-confidence.

What Tom did know, was that somehow, in the past twenty-four hours, he had managed to get two totally hot girls mad at him. This was not good. He tried running the scenarios over in his head, searching for an answer that might get him out of at least one doghouse.

Jacey, he knew, would get over it. She'd give him the silent treatment for a few days, maybe even a week, but eventually she would crack and they would be friends again. He would try to score with her once more, and he would be turned down again, and the pattern would continue until it drove him to a wet dream.

Ellie, on the other hand, was a wild card. He had no history with her to rely on. She might be one of those girls who remained pissed off at him and never looked his way again. "That would suck," he admitted, taking a deep breath as he reached for the doorbell. There was just no way to read girls, to know in advance if they were the forgiving kind. "Come to think of it, none of them are the forgiving kind," he said to himself. He braved the spiky rosebush pathway at the far side of the LaRose house to get to the front door without being seen.

Helena opened the door a few moments later. She couldn't help noticing that Tom looked disappointed. "I know the feeling, Tom Williams. I was expecting someone else myself. But for the record, it isn't good for a woman's ego to have that smile of yours fade so fast. I take it you want to see Ellie?"

Tom nodded. He noticed that Helena had changed from the blue jeans she was wearing earlier in the day into something slightly dressier. A little too dressy for lounging around the house, he thought. More like something he imagined she'd wear out for dinner at Chez Delphine if his own mother were any sort of guideline. This could be good. This could mean the two Helens were going out somewhere and he'd have Ellie all alone tonight.

"She's upstairs. Come on through to the kitchen and I'll get her," Helena said. She motioned for Tom to follow her. "Where's your partner in crime?"

"I don't know where he is," Tom answered. His guilt eased up somewhat. That much was true. Ryan's car hadn't been in the Lachey driveway.

Unlike Ryan, he had never been inside the big white LaRose home before. It smelled of fresh-baked pie. Not "company-is-coming-over-and-let's-spray-some-air-freshener" scent, but real homemade pie. He hadn't smelled it in his own home since his mother went back to work at the hardware store.

As he walked through the hallway, he noticed pictures of Ellie and Helen, taken years ago, hanging on the wall. He wanted to stop and look at them, but Helena was moving too fast. He took a quick glance at a larger portrait. Ellie hadn't changed much. Her eyes were big as saucers when she was a kid, just like they were now. He smiled, knowing the size of the human eye never changes from birth to death.

"Ryan was a bit of a jerk to Ellie this afternoon. I'm leaving him alone to think about it," he finally answered Helena.

Sure you are, Helena thought, but she gave no indication that she was any the wiser.

"So that's why Ellie has been in a foul mood since she got home," she offered, holding the kitchen door open for him. "I wondered what was up. Go on, do tell. Do I have to box his ears?" She propped herself up against the island in the kitchen and waited for his answer.

"Huh?"

"It's an expression my own mother used to say. Let me translate. Do I have to smack Ryan up the side of his head?"

Tom looked uncomfortably at Helena. He didn't really want to talk about it, but she had him cornered. "He just said some stuff. He didn't mean it. You know how he is. He thinks he's being funny. He is kind of funny... to me, but to girls..."

"Girls not so much, hmm?" She pulled a chair out for Tom. "Sit." She waited for him to do so before continuing. "Would he have said it to me? I appreciate a good stand-up routine. Was it that kind of funny?"

Tom squirmed uncomfortably in the chair.

"I take it that's a no." She moved and took a seat across from him at the table. "Relax, Tom. I know Ryan's harmless. His libido and his mouth just work faster than his brain. There's nothing so strange about that in a sixteen-year-old. Male or female. I'm sure Ellie's heard it all before. A simple apology can go a long way. Tell him to try it."

"Well," Tom confessed. "We were both kind of jerks."

"I kind of figured that," Helena said. "Do you want to tell me about it?"

"No," he laughed nervously.

Helena leaned forward, her green eyes gazing intently into Tom's. "Once upon a time I was a teenager myself. There's not much that you can get up to that I haven't seen or done." She sat back and smiled knowingly at him.

Tom found himself in the peculiar position of thinking that Ryan was right about at least two of the LaRose women. Helena was having an effect on his emotions, and if he weren't careful, those emotions would become visible in his tight jeans. He was pretty sure she knew that. And he wasn't sure whether she was doing it on purpose or not.

Helena rose slowly from the table. "Keep that in mind, Tom Williams," she said, in a breathy voice that reminded Tom of a late-night Playboy Channel vixen. "And remember, I will always be one step ahead of you. Watching. You hurt my Ellie, you answer to me."

"Did you just give me 'the lecture' in four sentences?" he asked, not wanting to look her directly in the eye.

"I believe I did," she agreed.

"Well thanks for that. It took Jacey's foster parents an hour. Their English isn't so good. Not that I'm two-timing Jacey or anything. Or Ellie. Jacey and

I are just friends. Just like Ellie and me. No two-timing here," he tried to assure Helena.

"That does make things less complicated," Helena agreed. "Jacey lives with foster parents?"

"She lives with the Kim's. They're the Koreans who own the landscaping business above my dad's store."

"Oh, that's right. The Kim's. I heard something about that, come to think of it. Jacey's father was in some kind of accident back in England wasn't he?"

"Yeah. She doesn't like to talk about it though."

"There's a lot of that going around. People talking about things that are superficial and not talking about things that matter. They say it's a defense mechanism, but I'm not so sure it's effective in the end. A lot of my patients wind up with ulcers. How did she wind up with the Kim's?"

Tom, relieved the conversation topic had changed to something other than himself, was more than willing to fill Helena in on as many of the details as he knew. "Mr. Kim and Jacey's dad were in the war together. Mr. Kim saved her father's life. He's her godfather or something. So when her father died and there was no one to take care of her, Mr. Kim got Jacey a plane ticket over here. She's been with them almost a year now."

"Where's her mother?"

"She doesn't know. It was a messy divorce or something."

"Ooh, I know how that can go. Still, it's odd she'd totally abandon her own daughter."

She thought about that. Helen hadn't been much older than the teenagers when she left home and refused to keep in contact with her. People sometimes had their own reasons for non-communication.

"I guess they moved around a lot, what with her dad being in the service. She doesn't have any other relatives that she knows of. The Kim's have become her family."

"Well then, I'll be extra nice when I finally meet her. I'm sure she and Ellie will get along just fine. Speaking of Ellie, I guess I'd better get her for you. I've held you captive here long enough."

She opened the kitchen door and yelled upstairs. "Ellie. There's a hot guy down in the kitchen waiting for you and if you don't come down right now, I'll send him up to your mother's room." She looked at Tom and winked. "That ought to get her down here. She'll come through that door and give me a look that could boil water, just you watch. Or Helen will. There are fifty-fifty odds on that one if you'd care to make a bet."

Tom laughed.

As if on cue, Ellie's face turned beet red when she walked into the kitchen and saw Tom sitting there.

"Looks like the lobster's already in the water," Helena quipped.

"Nan..." Ellie pleaded. "Please don't embarrass me. That's Mom's job. It's the only one she has. Taking that away from her might push her over the edge."

"It got you down here, didn't it?" Helena said. "And as I am an equal opportunity embarrasser, Tom has something he wants to say to you. Go ahead Tom. Spit it out. Don't just sit there like a goof. It doesn't become you."

Tom's eyebrows rose in surprise. This wasn't how he had pictured giving Ellie an apology. "Um, okay... listen, Ellie, I'm sorry about this afternoon. Ryan and I making fun of you, I mean."

"Ellie, accept his apology so I can leave you two alone. If you need me to kick him out, I can do that, but I should really change my shoes. The six-inch heels would poke him in the ass much better, if that's the way you want to go on this."

Ellie rolled her eyes. "No, Nan. It's okay."

"Good." She turned to Tom. "The four sentences. Remember them. If I have to cut them down to one, you're a dead man," Helena said, heading into the hallway.

"Gotcha, Mrs. LaRose," he said.

"What was that all about?" Ellie asked.

Tom shrugged. "Never mind. It'll take me more than four sentences to explain."

An awkward silence fell between the two as Ellie waited for Tom to say something. She hoped he'd make it quick. She could hear the toilet flush upstairs, followed by the sound of her mother's feet thundering down the staircase.

In the hallway, Helena blocked Helen from entering the kitchen. "Uh-uh, leave them alone."

"Them?" Helen asked. She glanced nervously towards the door.

"Ellie and Tom."

"Tom's the 'hot guy'? Then I'm definitely going in there."

"No, you're not. He's not the demon seed. You don't have to go in there like some religious nutcase to save her from his evil spawn," Helena said, her voice getting louder. "Give them some space."

"You don't know what they'll get up to in there."

"I know exactly what they'll get up to," she insisted. Her voice was now quite loud. "That's why we're staying out here. Hellsbelles, Helen. Must you be omnipresent?"

"I beg your pardon?"

"Well, you don't really want to watch them try to control their raging hormones do you? I didn't peg you as that kind of a voyeur."

"Mother, really!"

Ellie poked her head momentarily into the hallways. "Control your own raging hormones. The demon seed and I can hear you in here!"

Helena pointed her finger angrily at Helen. "That's your fault."

"Trust me, she's only beginning to find out what it's like living under your roof," Helen growled back.

"Tom, I'm so sorry you had to hear that," Ellie said as she returned to the kitchen. If nothing else, the Helens outburst had cleared the air between the teenagers. "Separately they're bearable, but you put them together in the same room and..."

Tom laughed. "It's okay. I like them. Your mom seems a little uptight, but your Nan's actually... (don't say hot)... pretty cool. She calls it as she sees it, that's for sure."

"I guess so."

"Okay then," he said, patting the seat next to him at the table, indicating Ellie should sit down. "Forget about them. Come over here."

Ellie was apprehensive. "Why are you here, Tom? Have you come to see whether they keep Goth-Chic in a padded room?" She sat in the seat Helena had occupied earlier and studied him. The blue in his sweater perfectly matched the deep blue of his eyes. That wasn't making it any easier to stay mad at him. She wondered whether he had agonized about what to wear before coming over. Probably not. Guys weren't like that.

"You're looking at my sweater. Do you like it?"

"Uh huh," she sighed.

Tom inched his chair closer to her. "El," he began, "I'm really sorry about this afternoon. "We shouldn't have made fun of your dream. We were all a little spooked-out down at the gravel pit. It's not every day we talk about finding a dead body when, you know, there actually might be one." He moved his chair closer to her. "Ryan can be an insensitive jerk at times. It's not his fault. He plays defense. He's not supposed to be nice. It goes against his nature. In fact, they spend hours out there on the field, training him to desensitize from humankind. Sometimes he just forgets that the field has boundaries. Somebody has to call foul on him. Which you did."

"I guess so," Ellie contemplated. She found herself wondering whether Tom's hair was streaked naturally, or had a little help. Not that it mattered.

Tom noticed the dimmer switch on the wall behind him. With one arm, he reached up and lowered the light. Following through with a well-practiced move, he began to put his arm around Ellie with the other.

"Um... what are you doing?" Ellie asked, her voice quivering. She knew what he was doing. She just wasn't sure why he was doing it. She raised her hand between them.

"Please don't shock me this time, Ellie. I like you. Electricity between us is supposed to be figurative."

Ellie blushed and looked deep into his baby blues. She had spent a lot of time earlier hoping and dreaming that this new guy she met would say something sweet and wonderful to her, but now that it was actually happening, she found herself full of reservation. Part of her wanted to say, in a husky, sexy voice, "you are the finest thing I have seen in my life, take me now," but barely audibly out came "I um, I like you too."

"Does your Nan have any bandages? I think I scraped my knee when I fell for you."

That was enough to give Ellie her voice back. She couldn't contain her laughter. "Oh puh-lease. That is the worst line I have ever heard."

"I swear it worked for Ryan once."

"Who'd he say it to? Another de-sensitized football player?"

They both laughed.

"How come you hang around with him?" Ellie asked.

"What do you mean?"

"Well, if I had seen both your pictures in a yearbook. I wouldn't have thought the two of you were friends. I would have thought you were a 'Prom King' and he was more of a 'Burger King.'"

"Now who's being insensitive?" Tom pointed out. His ego was starting to sigh in relief. 'Burger' was probably not the adjective you'd use to describe someone you were hot for. Whatever had happened between Ellie and Ryan last night was most likely innocent.

"It's not like he's my only friend, but he is my best friend. He's a 'go-to' guy. I can't really say any more about that. You'll just have to come to your own conclusions about him. Just give him a chance. A lot of people write Ryan off way too quickly."

He reached up and took some of Ellie's hair into his hand. "Your hair is so soft," he said, waving the strand under his nose. "And it smells so good."

Ellie bit her lip nervously. This wasn't the first time a guy had come on to her, but it was safe to say it was the first time one of them looked as 'oh-my-God-I-can't-breathe' to her as this one did.

"I'm also sorry about that fainting thing the other night," Tom said, his voice dropping as he put his chin on her shoulder, and looked up at her.

"It's nothing to be embarrassed about. I hear it happens to perfectly healthy males from time to time. If it gets to be a problem, you can take a pill for it," Ellie said before the 'don't say something stupid' part of her brain could kick in. She could feel his breath on her neck, and it was sending her heartbeat straight to the heavens. It was hard to be witty when you were trying not to gasp in sheer passion.

"I think you're talking about something else, El."

He began to pull her hand up his leg, but Ellie took his hand in hers, and laughed shyly.

Tom sensed that Ellie was slowing him down, but not rejecting him. He decided to try another approach. "You know, you have killer eyes," he continued, "they sparkle when you laugh."

"Tom..."

He had her, he sensed. This would be the time to move in for the kiss. "Maybe some time I could see them without all the make-up. Maybe some time I could..."

"What did you have to say that for?" Ellie freaked, throwing her hands up in the air.

"What?" Tom stammered, immediately pulling back from her.

Every bone in Ellie's body tensed up. If she took off her make-up, he would see that she really looked years younger. Jailbait younger. More than anything else in the world, Ellie didn't want him to see that.

"What did I say?" he asked again.

"Would you ask Jacey to take off her make-up?" Ellie asked defensively.

"That wouldn't be the first thing I'd ask her to take off... I mean NO, no I wouldn't. I would not ask Jacey to take off her make-up. That would be wrong."

"YOU, Tom, are the insensitive jerk. Go away and leave me alone."

"Wait a minute, Ellie... " Tom pleaded. "If I moved too fast, I'm sorry. I got the message. I'll back off. Just don't get so mad at me."

Ellie didn't want him to back off. But she didn't know how to handle the situation either. She got up and opened the back door. "I think it's time for you to go now."

"El, listen... "

"I thought you wanted Jacey. What am I? The fallback girl?"

"No. But I don't think you were all too concerned about Jacey a couple of minutes ago. If I read you wrong, I'm sorry." He could see her aura begin to appear again. He took a moment to embrace it. Ellie might be loony as hell, but he couldn't keep his eyes of her. He didn't want to leave, but he knew he wasn't welcome. Not right now.

"Ellie, I'll call you tomorrow," he said, as he left her standing alone in the kitchen. "And that's not just a line." He meant that. He knew that even in the morning, when he had time to digest everything that had happened today, he would still want to call. He glanced nervously at the Lachey driveway as he headed out the back door, but Ryan's Toyota thankfully had not yet come home.

Ellie burst into tears and ran upstairs, past her mother and Helena who were both watching television in the living room, in chairs moved as far apart as possible. Helena was slumped in the beanbag. Helen sat upright in the arm chair. The empty, comfortable couch between them was a sign of their ongoing standoff.

"I told you it was a bad idea to leave them alone," Helen pointed out. "I guess we're not going to be able to go and have a quiet dinner together."

"They've had a fight, that's all. It's a part of growing up. She's not a child anymore. She's going to have to learn to take it when love hits you with a tire iron."

"She's my baby," Helen sighed.

"Please. She's a pint-sized Lara Croft waiting to happen."

"Ellie," Helen called. "Ellie come down here. We want to talk to you."

"I am never coming down there as long as I live," Ellie screamed from the top of the stairs.

"Child," Helen sighed.

"Raging hormonal teenager," Helena countered. "Borderline woman. I wish I had tape recorded you when you were her age."

"Will you stop that please, Mom?" Helen asked.

"Mom? You never call me Mom."

"Mother," Helen sighed. "Can we call a truce on this one? I really need your help. I've never had a teenaged daughter before. I've never had a teenaged anything before. I know I'm holding on to her too tight. But with all the other stuff coming into the picture, it's making it even harder to let her loose on the world."

Helena was moved. "Well, I have raised a teenager as you recall. And at the time she yelled and screamed at me daily. I gave her all the freedom she wanted. And she bolted the first chance she got."

"I didn't bolt because of you."

"I know that. But it's taken you sixteen years to admit it."

"I was barely older than Ellie, pregnant and scared. I thought the early appearance of a grandchild for you would be more than you could handle."

"Oh Helen," Helena sighed, "I was still young enough then to have called her my own." She waited for Helen's pained reaction. "Darling, I am just kidding. I would have opened my arms to you both, just like I'm doing now. I tried to tell you that. But you, Helen, are not a listener."

Helen though about what her mother was telling her. Helena wasn't the only person in her life who had told her that. They were all wrong.

"You did manage to take care of Ellie and get a university education. That shows if nothing else, you have tenacity," Helena offered.

"If I haven't already thanked you for your help with that, thank-you. That nanny you sent along was a godsend. What was her name again? It was something peculiar..."

"Marita," Helena answered.

"That's right. Marita. Only she pronounced it with a pause between syllables. Mah-Rita. I wonder what ever happened to her. For two years she was there and then without a word she was gone. I had to get a husband to replace her," she laughed.

"I'm sure I don't know," Helena said uncomfortably. "Life goes on."

"Hmm. I wonder if Ellie remembers her," Helen paused. "I'll have to ask her sometime. She was only about six years old then."

"Ellie," Helena shouted. "Come on downstairs. We're not done embarrassing you tonight. We're going out for dinner and then we'll take in a movie at the Roxy."

"She'll never come with us," Helen said. "She's supposed to show up with a boy, not her female guardians. I remember that much from my teenage years."

"I don't want to go see some stupid love story," Ellie cried down the hall.

"See," Helen said, "what did I tell you?"

"Well then, you're in luck. It's a horror festival. This is the last night it's playing. I'd really like to see it. It'll give me some ideas for next Halloween,"

Helena shouted back. "You can watch a bunch of guys getting ripped to shreds. It'll make you feel better. We'll just stay for the first show."

"That's not going to work. But if you want to waste your breath, go right ahead," Helen insisted.

"Ellie, darling," Helena said, with a note of anger in her voice. "If you think for one second that any granddaughter of mine is going to wallow away in her room because some wanna-be poster-boy made her cry, you've got another thing coming."

Helen's jaw dropped as Helena continued.

"We LaRose women pick ourselves up, dust ourselves off, and go strut our stuff. That's the way it has always been and that's the way it will always be as long as I'm alive. So unless you're thinking of snuffing me out in the next ten minutes, get your ass down here."

Ellie came slowly down the stairs. "You called me your granddaughter," she whispered.

"It's time to stop all this denial," Helena said, looking at Helen. "At least within these four walls." She pointed at Helen. "You are my daughter." She looked at Ellie. "You are my granddaughter. And we are united in ways others can only dream of. Someday we'll figure it all out. But right now, I'm hungry and I want to see a movie. Come on, or we'll wind up with a table by the restrooms."

Helena walked to the front closet and handed the girls their coats. "Even superheroes need some down time."

"Are we taking the van?" Ellie sighed.

"Not in this life," Helena replied. "We'll take my car. I parked it in the back lane." She watched as Helen ensured the front door was locked. "Expecting a problem?"

"Just being cautious," Helen replied.

As they headed down the driveway, they were met by a very upset Betty Lachey, coming out the side door of her house. Her over-sized body wobbled with nerves as she made her way towards the LaRose women.

"You!" she screeched at Helena. "I don't know how you did it, or why you did it, but I know this is all because of you." She fumbled with the zipper on her bright orange vest. The concentration needed to pull a bit of fabric from its teeth was more than she could handle at the moment, so she left it undone.

"Well, at least this time it's your fault," Helen noted.

"Why is the pumpkin yelling at us?" Ellie asked.

"I haven't the foggiest," Helena answered. "Just ignore her and get in the car."

"You are evil, Helena LaRose," Betty shrieked. "EVIL. I'm going to tell everyone what you did, and you're going to be run out of town."

"Nan?" Ellie questioned.

"Ellie, we all have to make choices in life," Helena sighed. "Sometimes they're not easy, but they need to be made. This one however, is a no-brainer. Wave goodbye to the lady who forgot to take her meds." She opened the rear door of her black Ford Mustang and motioned for Ellie to get in the car.

"I am so glad you live on the corner," Helen said, getting into the passenger seat beside her mother. "One nutty neighbor is enough."

Helena nodded.

"They've got him," Betty screamed down the driveway.

"Mother?"

"I swear Helen; I don't know what she's talking about." As Helena reached to adjust the rearview mirror, she glanced at Betty Lachey's figure in the background, and she instinctively knew that their lives were about to be changed forever.

"Girls, here we go," she said, as she pulled out into the back lane. "Here. We. Go."

Chapter 11

*R*yan sat on the edge of the single bed, eating some giant sunflower seeds that Officer Purdy had slipped him through the bars of his jail cell. He was trying to spit them into the toilet but they were a little too big, and by the time he had licked the salt off, a little too soggy, to work well as a projectile.

This wasn't Ryan's first time in the town jail... there had been the broken window incident at Old Man Wagner's when he was ten and Betty wanted to teach him a lesson... but this was a whole different thing. The police were taking the situation much more seriously.

Purdy had taken Ryan's wrist watch from him, along with his belt and his shoelaces, when the teenager first arrived. Ryan supposed Purdy was making sure he wasn't going to try to commit suicide.

"If I really wanted to kill myself," he argued with the officer, "I could give myself a death wedgie with my tightie-whities. Did ya ever think of that?"

Purdy evidently didn't find this funny. "I'd wipe that smile off your face, Lachey. You've got nothing to smirk about. Shorts off."

"I didn't know you wanted to see my ass," Ryan pushed back. "Should I be nervous?"

"Why don't you spend some time thinking about what you're going to tell your mother when Chief Cohen brings her here. Maybe you can come up with something better than the vampire story you were babbling about when we brought you in."

Ryan's face turned red. "I didn't do anything. I apologized for the broken window when I was here half a decade ago, and I'll apologize to the Quinlan's for being at the wrong place at the wrong time. I had nothing to do with Brooke's death."

"You had the body in your arms. You were caught 'flagrante delicto,' as they say."

"That sounds... just wrong."

"It's a Latin legal term. Get used to it. You're going to be hearing a lot of it."

"De-lickto my butt. What's with all the Latin today? Did everyone wake up and think, hey... let's talk a language nobody knows? I'm not into doing it with a dead anything. And she was already dead when I got there." Ryan insisted. "It was... what do you call it? Circumstantial."

"Good luck with that one," Purdy replied, leaving the police station. "How old are you now, Ryan? Murder automatically ages you in the court system."

Ryan shuffled his feet and ran his hands across his bald head. The hair was beginning to grow back, forming a rough layer of stubble, but he knew asking for a razor was out of the question. "You can't fucking believe I really killed her?" he stammered.

"It doesn't matter what I do or don't believe at this point," Purdy said, taking his winter coat off the hook by the front door, barely glancing at Ryan as he did so. "I'll be back in a half an hour. I hope you like toaster strudel, because that's what you're getting for breakfast," he said, letting the front door to the station slam behind him.

Ryan glanced at the television above Purdy's desk. It had been left on, and Ryan was happy that the last station Purdy had watched had been the sports network. With any luck, the nightly highlights would keep him occupied until he got back. He didn't like the places his imagination was beginning to take him. Boredom in jail, he realized, was depressing.

He swaggered over to the stainless steel toilet to take a whiz. He was glad there was no one else around. The cell didn't offer any privacy and he wasn't looking forward to the time he was going to have to take a shit. He hoped it wouldn't be when Betty was around.

He sat on the edge of the bed and contemplated what he was going to say to her. There was no good way he could tell her about the events that had happened earlier in the evening.

"See Ma," he practiced "I went there to try and save the girl, but I got into a fight with this vampire... who I could have taken any other night if I hadn't wrecked my shoulder during the game… and things just kind of got out of hand."

"I am so fucked," he admitted, realizing that wasn't going to work. He stretched himself out on the bed and watched some television. The freedom of being able to change the channel whenever he wanted to was now a thing of the past, and it was just one more thing making him irritable.

Forty-five minutes later he heard the police cruiser pull up on the gravel driveway next to the jail. It was Chief Cohen who came into the building first. He stood in front of Ryan and began to say something, then reconsidered. It was a little late to try to knock some sense into the teen. They were both probably too tired to listen to reason.

A few moments later, Officer Purdy led Betty Lachey into the cell area. "Lucky for us, your mother says you like toaster strudel. I got you four flavors. Take your pick." He offered the brown bag to Ryan, who shook his head negatively.

"Prick," Ryan wanted to say aloud, but instead he looked sheepishly at Betty. She had been crying, he knew, because her black mascara was running down her cheeks. Ryan couldn't remember the last time he had seen his mother cry. Now she stood before him, looking at him in a bleary-eyed way, as if she was sedated. Zombie sedated. Ryan chuckled nervously at that thought. He was starting to sound like Stan.

"Ma, I didn't do it," he finally blurted out. That was all he could think of to say that made any sense. She looked at him with a sullen look which told him that for her, this was way too much to handle.

"What am I going to tell your brother?" she whimpered. "He's in the back of the police car scared out of his wits. Getting dragged down to the police station at this hour of the night. What were you thinking? He looks up to you."

"What did you bring him here for?" Ryan asked.

"Because there was no one to leave him with. Mr. Wagner's dead. He won't go to the LaRose's. I couldn't just leave him alone. I thought there was a child killer on the loose." She looked forlornly at him and said softly "I didn't know it was you."

Ryan felt like he had been stabbed in the heart.

"Alleged child killer," Purdy pointed out. "Just so we're all clear here."

"Betty," Roy Cohen said, giving Purdy a look of disapproval, "to be fair, we haven't gotten to the bottom of the story yet. I have to tell you though; it's not looking too good."

"What happened, Roy?" she asked quietly, afraid to hear the answer.

He told her the events as they had unfolded earlier at Stillman's Creek, without telling her Ryan's version of the story.

"We're waiting for Ryan here, to get his facts straight before we take his statement. He seems a little confused by the ordeal."

Betty felt sick to her stomach. "You have done some stupid things in your life, Ryan Lachey, but never in a million years would I have thought you were capable of something like this."

"I'm not capable. I'm never capable, except at football. You always tell me that. This isn't any different," Ryan pleaded. "I just had a feeling I knew where she was."

"Shut-up until I can get you a good lawyer," Betty managed to whimper. "I'm going to have to mortgage the house for this."

"You might consider legal aid," Purdy offered. "Murder trials can drag on."

Betty's knees began to buckle. "I think I need to sit down," she said, grasping her chest with her right hand.

"Betty, you need to see a doctor," Cohen said as comfortingly as he could. Her doctor was most likely Dr. Quinlan, the dead girl's father. That was now out of the question.

"I'll take her to the hospital," Purdy told Chief Cohen, as if reading his mind. "I'll drop Stan off at my house along the way. I'm sure Donna won't mind looking after him under the circumstances."

"Thanks," the Chief said, watching his officer lead the emotion-wracked woman out the door. He turned to his prisoner.

"You have left your mother speechless," Chief Cohen said sarcastically. "I've known her all her life, and I can honestly say I have never seen that before."

"What was I supposed to say?" Ryan asked. "Was I supposed to tell her that Wacko-the-teenaged-vampire did the nasty deed? Do you think that would have made her have more faith in me?" He shook the cell bars angrily. "I am not a violent person."

The irony wasn't wasted on the Chief. "I can't begin to help you if you don't tell me the truth," Cohen sighed. Ryan's version of the events leading up to having a dead body in his arms hadn't been the weirdest story Roy had heard in all his years of policing, but it sure as hell came close. He hoped that in the morning, Ryan would come to his senses.

"I'm sticking to my story," Ryan insisted.

"Son, unless you're trying to cop an insanity plea, I'd spend some time thinking about what really happened."

"I don't have to tell you anything until I get a lawyer," Ryan argued. "That's what's really happening."

"You're beginning to annoy the hell out of me," Cohen snapped. "Are you forgetting that when Officer Purdy and I arrived at the scene, Wildman was standing with a rifle pointed at your head? You're lucky he was in a good mood and didn't blow your brains out. He's not a friend of yours on your best day. As it stands now, he's a witness for the prosecution."

"So?"

"So... I'd start thinking about the events that led you to Stillman's Creek tonight and come up with something a jury will believe."

"I didn't kill her," Ryan said, his voice filled with rage. "I found her. I told you that. You know Wildman has it in for me. He was pretty much calling me a pervert in front of the whole town Saturday morning. He knows more than he's telling."

"Are you saying Wildman somehow framed you?" The Chief looked Ryan straight in the eyes. He was hoping that Ryan was about to shed new light on the crime.

"No, I'm not saying that. I'm not a liar. Well, maybe sometimes I stretch the truth around Tara, but not about something like this."

Cohen thought about that. In all the years he had known the teenager, Ryan had been boorish, intimidating and often stupid, but never much of a liar.

"Then why did you go there, Ryan? Can you tell me that much? Were you planning to meet someone else?

"Ellie had a dream," Ryan said. "I told Tara, and Tara sent her old man after me."

"Slow down," Roy demanded. "Why would Tara send her dad after you? Were you planning to have a little rendezvous with Tara out by the water? Was that why Wildman went to the bridge?"

"How the hell should I know? Maybe he's stalking me. Go ask Ellie LaRose. Ask her about her dream."

It was disturbing to the Chief to know that Helena LaRose's granddaughter might also be involved in this. She had been in town less than a week and already she was pinging on his radar.

"What exactly did Ellie LaRose tell you?" he asked.

"Just forget it," Ryan said, putting his head in his hands. "Right now, I'm pretty much wishing I had never met Ellie LaRose. Or her mom." He glanced at the Chief and stopped short of adding Helena to the list. "Go ask Tom. Tom was there."

"At the creek?"

"No. When Ellie told me about the dream. Tom was there then. I talked about it later, with Tara. Go talk to them."

"Why don't you just tell me about this dream?"

"Because you already don't believe my story. See if they back it up. I'm not trying to tell you how to do your job or anything, but don't you want some collaboration?"

"You mean corroboration?"

"Maybe."

"I'll be doing that," the Chief assured him. "It is a little suspicious that Ralph Wildman just happened upon you when he did."

Ryan looked hopefully at the Chief. "So, you believe me?"

"No. You were right the first time. I don't believe your cockamamie story. But," he hesitated, "I've arrested hundreds of criminals, and a few murderers in my time, and I have to say that something is off. I'm not sure you did it. If you took some drugs... blue tabs or four-ways or whatever else you want to call it... before you found her, now would be a good time to tell me. It would somewhat explain your story."

"My scholarship is on the line," Ryan replied, "I've got a physical coming up and I'm subject to random drug testing. I never did mushrooms. I don't do crack. I'm not going to blow my pro ball career for a few hours of induced happiness. I want to make the pros and get out of this hellhole town. Things happened just like I said they did," he insisted. "I maybe had a couple of beers before I had the argument with Tara. I got them from Betty's fridge, but I'd appreciate it if you didn't tell her about it, because I've got other problems right now."

Cohen sighed. "The one thing I am sure of, is that the only place you are safe is here behind bars. Because by morning, once the news starts to spread, half the town is going to want you dead. You're not just a murderer in their eyes, you're a child killer. So think about that for a while, and then decide if you want to remember what actually happened."

The Chief's cell phone went off, and he immediately pulled it from its belt holder.

"You should download a ring-tone like the theme song from Hawaii Five-O," Ryan commented. "Da-da-da-da-da-dah-, da-da-da-da-dah…, he sang. "What? I have the Ventures version on vinyl. They weren't big on words."

"Troy Police. Cohen here," he said, ignoring him.

The voice on the other end of the line was talking in such an animated tone that Ryan almost overheard the Chief's conversation.

Cohen realized this and turned his back on him. "Calm down, Tara."

Ryan, hearing Tara's name, tried to listen more closely, but the Chief was already walking towards the door. "I'll be there as fast as I can." He turned to Ryan. "Stay put. I don't know what's going on in this town. But you'd better be here when I get back."

"How the hell am I supposed to do anything else?" Ryan asked, perplexed. "I'm locked behind bars." He shook his head. Had the whole town gone insane?

He heard the Chief start the car and turn on the siren.

"Dude's in a hurry," Ryan thought to himself. He could see the cruiser lights began to flash through the station window, drawing his attention to an outside world that at least for the moment, he was no longer a part of.

A dark form moved stealthily past the window. The sight of it forced an uncontrollable shudder down Ryan's spine.

"Not you again. Come in here, you fucker," Ryan yelled. "Let me finish you off."

As soon the words had left Ryan's mouth, he felt the room grow cold. A mouse that had been eyeing the strudel bag on Purdy's desk aborted the mission and made a quick dash back into the safety of a hole in the baseboard.

"Bright lights, say goodnight," the voice said, as the jail lights were dimmed, and the television turned itself off. "Haven't you heard? Too much TV rots your brain."

"What the hell?" Ryan asked, turning around to see the teenaged vampire standing before him once again.

He held the remote control in his pasty-white hand. "I'm super-dead, not super-human," he shrugged, tossing the remote out of Ryan's reach. "Thanks for inviting me in. I like what you've done with the space."

"How about I stuff something in your mouth?" Ryan taunted, throwing a right hook in the vampire's direction.

The night creature spun around on his heels and blocked Ryan's fist, following through with a left upper cut to Ryan's cheek, which left the football player momentarily stunned and bleeding profusely.

"Aw, shoulder still hurting you? Isn't that the excuse you're using?" his adversary mocked.

"Fuck," Ryan cried out, his hand going to his face to move the flow of blood away from his mouth. He cowered as the vampire moved towards him, running his icy finger under Ryan's chin to collect the run-off of fresh blood as it trickled down his profile. "What do you want with me?"

The vampire dripped the dark red fluid down his own finger and into his mouth. The taste was unpleasant to him, and he immediately spat it out. "Vintage Lachey has corked."

"Fuck you."

"What is this obsession you have with that word?" he asked amused. "If I don't want to drink you, I certainly don't want to fuck with you. Not in that sense, anyway."

"Get out of my cell you blood-sucking pervert, before I take you down."

"You're hardly in a position to take me down. Look at you, all caged up like some animal in a zoo," he sneered. "Are you hungry, Ryan? Is that why you're cranky? He patted his own stomach. "In case you haven't noticed," he teased, his voice rising up an octave, "I've got that 'stuffed myself with turkey' feeling. Like I drank a gallon of tryptophan. I almost need a nap."

Ryan swallowed hard. The vampire did look a little less gaunt than the last time he had run into him. Not that he cared about his health. He sensed his visitor was not there to make idle conversation with him. "What are you talking about?"

"The Nouveau Beaujolais I had an hour ago," he said, laughing to himself. "I had your little nerdy brother's friend. Don't look so disgusted. He was tasty for a nine-year-old."

Stan only had one friend. "Kevin? You have Kevin?" Ryan stammered.

"I'm starting to get a taste for children," he explained, as if it were no big deal. "Oh get that look off your face. I don't do anything with them sexually. What do you think I am? A monster?" He laughed demonically at his own joke.

"You're a fucking nut case."

"We're all murderers in some fashion," he contemplated. "Meat eaters are murderers, vegetarians are murderers. Something has to die for every living being to live. Mother Nature is the original serial killer."

"You're a cannibal."

"That's a bit harsh."

"You're a fucking nut-case cannibal."

"I'm not the one in jail, Ryan," the vampire said calmly, removing some dirt from his beneath his thumb with the nail of his pinky finger of the other hand. "I really need a manicure."

His nonchalance made Ryan lose control again. He gathered his strength and took another swing at him. "I don't believe you, you oversized mosquito," he said as he threw the punch.

"Missed me, missed me," the vampire sang. "Now you have to... oh, forget that part. You're definitely not my type. Blood type I mean. I would have brought a photo, so you could see Kevin's sorry little ass, but you know us vampires, not big on cameras."

"What exactly is your problem?" Ryan asked.

"You're not very bright, are you, Ryan? I'm a vampire. Most people would consider that enough of a reason to not dwell on what is or isn't my problem." He gave Ryan a look of distain.

"Leave Kevin alone," Ryan warned.

"I will. I promise. He's already dead."

"What?"

"Careful now, Ryan. How much do you really want to know about the death of Kevin? Aren't you already in enough trouble for knowing too much about my 'leftovers'?"

Ryan paused. The vampire had a point. Having to explain how he knew about another murder was probably not in his own best interest.

The vampire laughed. "Oh all right, if you insist. I'll tell you. We're just like buddies now, aren't we, Ryan? Sharing secrets. See... Kevin, was it? Kevin was walking home alone from the orthodontist... kind of a waste of money, under the circumstances... and I was feeling a little peckish, so I snuck up behind him and took him." He raised his arms in the air and shrugged, indicating, "what else could I do?"

"Why the fuck would you do that?" Ryan demanded.

"Why? I'm following the hundred-mile rule for my food. Everyone has to be green these days, Ryan. Happy planet and all that." He looked at the stainless steel toilet. "That looks cold."

Ryan looked away. There was a lump forming in his throat the size of a baseball. He almost wanted to cry. But he hadn't done that since he was Stan's age, and he sure as hell wasn't going to do that now.

"He was a scrapper, Ryan. You should see the nail marks on my back. He fought me tooth and nail as they say, but in the end he was no match for my prowess," he bragged, licking his lips in remembrance.

"You really fucking killed him?"

"I didn't mean to. I wanted to keep him just barely alive so I could have a food supply for a few days. But let's just say refrigeration isn't all it's cracked up to be. I forgot he couldn't breathe locked up in one."

"You locked him in a fridge?"

135

"Well, my mom always said not to play in them. I guess now I know why," the vampire smirked.

"Your mother is a bitch," Ryan snarled.

"See, that's what you and I have in common," the vampire snapped back. "We both have issues with our mothers. Betty's no bucket of daisies, is she? But at least she's still alive. That's why you're going to help me. You understand my position."

"I'll never fucking help you."

"I'm thinking you will, Ryan. Not that I'm a physic or anything." He shook his head. "I'm not. That would just be a little too much, wouldn't it? Having to deal with a vampire that could see the future?"

"Okay, I'll bite. What's your mother got to do with all this?"

"My mother," he replied, "is dead. Dead-dead. No living for eternity for her. She was murdered. Oh, some say she was killed in self-defense, but from my point of view, which is the only one that matters to me, she was murdered. I need to avenge her death. And that's where you come in. And by the way, never say 'bite' to a vampire. It gets us all excited." He stared down at the floor. "They keep this place pretty clean, don't they?"

"Not that I ever would help you," Ryan protested, "but as you've pointed out, I'm in jail. A lot of good that will do you. And by the way, you've got the attention span of a gnat."

"You really, really, aren't that bright, are you?"

"You really, really, are pissing me off," Ryan retorted.

"Let me explain how things work," the vampire said with mock indifference. "You're in jail because that poor excuse for a farmer… Haystack Wildman… found you with the little girl's body. Now, I can't have my new best friend in jail for a crime he didn't commit. That would just be wrong. So in a way, I've done you a favor by killing again. This time I left the body where someone else would find it. And you see, Ryan, I killed Kevin when you were already in jail. They'll have no choice but to let you out. And then you'll owe me one."

"I told you I would never help you. Whatever your sad story is."

The vampire became irate. "That's where you're wrong, Ryan. You *will* help me. You'll help me because by the time you do get out, I'll have your nerdy little brother. I've been watching him. I've been watching your whole damn family, your whole damn street. And you know what the really demented part is? I don't even really want him. He'll just keep me amused until I get what I really want."

"And that would be...?"

"Revenge, Ryan. You might think you understand that emotion, but it's really something you need to experience first-hand. That's why your brother is going to be my little pawn. And when you bring me my treasure, we'll make a little trade."

"For what?"

"For the girl. It's always about the girl."

"Why don't you just go get whoever you really want yourself?"

"Because they'll know. They'll know if I'm tracking her down," the vampire sighed. "They took something from me, so I need to take something from them. But they're stronger than me, so you'll have to find a way to get me what I want. A queen for your pawn. Bring me the girl you call Goth-Chic."

"But..."

"That's all," the vampire said. "I don't care how you do it. If you want to see your brother alive again, you'll find a way."

His message delivered, the vampire shifted through the bars on the open window above Purdy's desk, leaving Ryan alone in the cell to contemplate what had just transpired.

As hard as it was for Ryan to believe that Kevin was dead, he couldn't help but recall the words that Stan had said on Halloween. "You wait until Kevin goes missing and winds up on the news, then we'll see," he had said.

"Shit," he thought. "What if the little squirt has been right all along? What if there is evil lurking in the LaRose backyard?" He shook the bars ferociously. "I have to get out of here."

Again he saw a shadow cross by the window above Purdy's desk and for a moment Ryan thought the vampire was coming back. He was relieved to see it was Tom peering at him through the iron bars that crossed the window frame.

"What the hell's going on, Ryan?" Tom asked. "Jacey just called. She said Tara's going around shooting her mouth off that her old man caught you with Brooke's body. You didn't really kill her, did you?"

Ryan detected a note of uncertainty in his friend's voice. "What the fuck? You know I didn't kill her. You were with me Halloween night."

"What made you go down to Stillman's Creek?"

"Because I'm a fucking moron. I DON'T KNOW. I was just thinking about what Ellie said. Her stupid dream. It seemed so real to me then, the places she was describing. I couldn't get it out of my head, and I thought I could help. Well fuck, Tom. She was right. The body was right where she said it would be. In the dirty, slimy cesspool that is Stillman's Creek. You'd have known that if you had come with me."

"I'd be in jail if I had gone with you."

"At least I'd have someone to talk to. Where the hell have you been tonight? You have no idea what I have been through."

"I too, have been fishing in shark infested waters," Tom insisted.

"What the fuck does that mean?"

"I can't explain it in four sentences, so I'm not even going to try."

"Well, could you try to get me out of here? Go tell Cohen what happened. Tell him about the dream. Tell him I didn't do it."

"Okay, okay," Tom said, trying to calm Ryan down. He noticed the large sweat stains beneath Ryan's armpits, a certain sign that Ryan was more worried than he was letting on.

"And go get Ellie."

"Uh, Ellie...why?" Tom cringed.

"Tell her I know. Tell her I saw him," Ryan urged.

"Saw who?"

"Jacob who-who and the sharpened fang. Tell her I saw her fucking vampire."

Chapter 12

Helen raised her fingers to her temples as she got out of Helena's car. Ever since they had left the house earlier, she had been struggling with a headache that started at the front of her forehead and worked its way to the base of her neck. She had spent most of the movie with her eyes closed, just wishing it would end and so she could go home and deal with it.

"What's wrong, Mom?" Ellie asked. "Was the movie too loud for you? I thought that part when they blew up the whole werewolf factory was awesome!"

"Are you getting one of your rain headaches again?" Helena asked. "I've got some magnesium powder in my office that will help take care of that."

"No, I don't think that's it," Helen said quietly.

"I'll try to keep it quiet and do a little reading in my room before I go to bed," Ellie said, running towards the door. "I'm reading Jane Eyre. It's on my curriculum Mom, and it's pretty titillating given its era. So don't get mad at me. I have to read it."

"Wait!" Helen cried, suddenly running after her, stopping her from entering the house.

Ellie gasped. "Seriously Mom, you can phone the school if you don't believe me. The Brontes. English Lit is all over them."

"No," Helen protested. "The house... let me go first."

"Mom?"

Helen reached towards the doorknob and gave it a turn. It was still locked. She heaved a sigh of relief.

"I will get keys cut for you girls next week," Helena sighed. "If you can wait until then." She took her keys from her purse, opened the door and turned on the hallway light. "See Helen, no bogeyman. It's safe to go in."

"I don't know what came over me," Helen said, cautiously crossing the threshold. "I'll be glad when you take those Halloween decorations down and start planning for Christmas. The stores will be doing it by Monday."

"I guess we'll put that on Sunday's agenda," Helena replied. "We can move the swing down to the other end of the porch so you don't get a reminder of Mr. Wagner every time you come up the steps."

"That might help," Helen agreed.

"Night Nan," Ellie said, giving Helena a kiss on the cheek. "Thanks for the movie. You were right. It was a big help. I feel better now."

"Never underestimate the power of popcorn therapy," Helena replied as she watched her granddaughter head upstairs. She hung her coat up in the hallway closet then turned and looked at Helen.

"Don't say it," Helen pleaded.

"I don't have to say it. Ellie already said it. Something about me being right about the movie. But she's gone upstairs now, so do you want to tell me what was going on with you and the front door?"

"I was just checking that it was still locked. I've noticed you don't normally do that yourself."

"Maybe I want someone to come over," she shrugged.

"I don't think I want to go there," Helen replied.

"I'll keep it locked just for you, if it makes you feel better," she said, putting her arm around her daughter. "But I think you'll find that nobody locks their doors in Troy. Except maybe the Lachey's. Betty, as you have seen, is a bit nervous. And poor Stan..."

Helen abruptly pulled herself away from her mother. Her body began to rock back and forth uncontrollably.

Helena studied her daughter. "What's going on, Helen? Are you okay?" She could hear her daughters breathing becoming irregular. "Is it a full-blown migraine? I'll get you some tomato juice to go with the magnesium. That ought to help."

Helen reached out to the wall for support. A wave of nausea had suddenly come over her. "I think I'm going to faint."

"Not you too? Do I need to call an ambulance?" Helena asked, taking her cell phone from her pocket. "Maybe I need to call someone to check this house for a gas leak."

"No," Helen gasped. "Forget the ambulance. Call a priest." She had now slumped as low to the floor as she could without physically lying down.

Helena shut the cell phone off and put it back in her pocket. It was now clear to her that medical help was not what her daughter needed. She turned her back to Helen and lowered her own body to the floor as well.

"Climb up," she said.

"You want to piggyback me?" Helen asked in astonishment. "You can't carry me. I'll throw your back out." She tried to stand up. "It's okay. I think I'm coming around now... wooo... maybe not."

"Either you climb on my back so I can lift you, or I drag you across the floor. Your choice."

Helen reluctantly put her legs around her mother's hips and stretched her arms around her neck. It was the last thing she did before losing consciousness.

"It's probably just as well," Helena thought, as she prayed for some inner strength. "Isis," she said, lowering her head "Mother Goddess, send me the strength to protect my family."

She took a deep breath, stood up, and carried Helen's limp body into the living room, gently laying her down on the sofa. Perhaps it wasn't so gentle. Perhaps it was more like rolling a sack of potatoes off her back onto the couch. No matter. She got her to the couch as best she could under the circumstances.

"I'm changing your treatment plan. I think I need some fresh mint from the garden to bring you back to your senses," she told her sleeping daughter. "I'll be back in a few minutes."

Helen was in a deep slumber and didn't even notice her mother leaving the room.

Helena went into the kitchen and headed to the backdoor. She laughed as she realized she had left it unlocked. Helen would kill her if she knew it had been open the whole time they were out.

Outside, a bullfrog began to croak as she stepped onto the back landing. That was a good sign. If the amphibian was there, then he wasn't. She didn't know why that was, but it had always seemed to be the case. They didn't like to be around each other. Food for thought. In retrospect, that was probably why.

She stopped just before the herb garden, at what was the second dead grass spot on her property. Stan always seemed to miss mowing that part, probably because he had once trimmed a little too close to the fragrant plants and she had warned him not to do it again.

"Stan, you've got it wrong," she whispered, "the body's not by the back porch when he's here. He's by the garden."

She reached down and scratched at the area with her fingers, putting a quarter-sized sample of the grass and dirt into her hand. She sniffed it. It smelled earthy, but not musky.

"He hasn't been her for a couple of days," she told herself, now brushing the dirt from her hands. "The scary part is, I'm not so sure if that's a good thing or a bad one."

Helena pondered this as she reached over to the mint patch. She took leaves from several stems and rubbed them between her palms, releasing their natural oils. "At least it will wake up Helen's consciousness," she sighed as she inhaled the aroma. "I still need something to wake up her psyche. What I need to do, is call Willie."

She readied herself to summon him, but was distracted by the sounds of sirens wailing off into the night. There had been too many of those lately; her peaceful little town was changing. Even the Lachey house didn't look quite right. It was in total darkness.

"That's strange for a Saturday," she thought. Betty was normally in her upstairs bedroom at this hour, with the glare from her television casting shadows upon the window.

She glanced down the mutual driveway. The Lachey side door light was off, also an irregularity. Betty had always left the light on for Ryan ever since Stan had left his skateboard out one night and Ryan had tripped over it. Betty didn't want Ryan breaking his leg and ruining his football career. So unless Ryan had stayed in for the night... which was highly unlikely...there was something amiss at the neighbors.

Then it dawned on Helena.

"My little bitch," she said, dumping the mint from her hand. "She knows exactly what's going on. Forget a gentle awakening. I'm going to slap her silly until she wakes up."

She stormed back into the living room and did just that. She slapped Helen. Not hard enough to leave a mark, but hard enough to wake her up and annoy the hell out of her.

"Ow! Stop it!" Helen said, putting her hands up to protect her face.

"YOU stop it, Helen."

"What? I just passed out. I know it's not healthy but..."

"Passed out my ass. You fell into a trance. I thought you were just exaggerating when you asked me to get you a priest. What's going on, Helen? Do you know something about what's going on with Ellie and..."

"And who mother?" She glared at Helena. "Ellie and who?"

Helena ignored her. "Tell me what you know. What have you envisioned?"

"I don't want to know or see anything, Mother. I can put people on ignore too."

"You're making a big mistake," Helena warned.

"No. The big mistake was in coming here. Tomorrow night I am packing up that van and taking Ellie back to the city. She'll be back in class with her pregnant friend by Monday and everything will be fine because everything will be back to normal."

"There is no normal. Not for us. Do you really think Tony, or anyone aside from a LaRose, can really be of any help to you or Ellie? Come on, out with it."

"I can keep a secret too, Mother. Do you know what I remembered when I was passed out? I remembered more about the nanny who came and disappeared. Marita."

"So you remembered the nanny? Helen, that was years ago."

"Was it? Because I have a funny feeling it wasn't so many years ago that you last talked to her. Tell you what, why don't you tell me your story and then I'll tell you mine?"

"So help me, Helen... you are being impossible. I've had enough of you today. I'm going to bed," Helena argued.

"See, I knew if push came to shove that you'd find an excuse to avoid the issue. And you say I'm the one who's in denial."

Helen watched as her mother went up the stairs. If her mother was going to play silly-buggers, then she would as well.

"Good night, Mother. And say good night to Marita too. Marita Harbinger," she yelled angrily.

Chapter 13

*R*oy Cohen turned on the siren briefly, trying to get the car ahead of him to pull over. He didn't really want to wake-up the whole neighborhood, but the flashing lights on the roof of the police cruiser were not doing the job on their own.

"I don't want to stop you, idiot. I just want to pass," he sighed, referring to the driver in front of him. "I should pull your license until you remember how to respond to an emergency vehicle," he said aloud, his voice full of frustration.

It was times like this Roy wished he could exercise some road-rage of his own and flip the annoying driver the finger. When the driver finally did pull over, he saw it was Jacey Sumner behind the wheel of the sporty little blue Mazda. He gave her a stern look as he drove by, killing the noise and the flashers. What the hell was she doing driving around by herself at this time of night?

Hitting a yellow light at the Main and Queen intersection, he took advantage of the stop time to call Officer Purdy.

"What's up?" Purdy asked, answering the call immediately.

Roy fiddled with the volume on his earpiece. He was all for the hand-free cell phone law, but lately he had been having problems with the wireless signal, especially at night. There were times he wished he could just put his cell phone directly to his ear like he used to be able to do.

"Get on over to the Wildman's farm out on county road three as fast as you can. I'm already on my way," he answered.

"Roger that," Purdy replied. "But I've still got Stan Lachey with me. Long story."

From the back seat of the cruiser, Stan Lachey uttered a scream so loud that the Chief could hear him over the phone. "Is everything under control?"

Purdy glanced over his right shoulder into the back of the police car. "Oh for crying out loud. The kid's got his tongue stuck through the wire partition behind the front seat," he sighed. "Lachey... I told you to sit still and keep your seat belt on. Do I have to stop this car, get out and cuff you?"

"He's okay, right?" the Chief asked.

"Yeah. He's just bored. I think the excitement of riding in a police cruiser wore off when he realized all the cool gadgets were in the front of the car with me."

The Chief could hear a hollow echo emitting from Purdy's end of the phone line and he knew that meant he was on the speakerphone. "Purd, pull over to the side of the road and take the phone off broadcast," the Chief instructed.

"We're solo," Purdy said momentarily, confirming he had done so. "What's going on?"

"You go first."

"I left Betty Lachey at the hospital. They're going to keep her overnight for observation and see if she's calmed down any in the morning. Then I took Stan over to my place, but Donna wasn't home. Her sister's baby had decided it was time to enter the world, and she left a note saying she was headed to the city to be with her. That left me nowhere to leave Stan, so I told him I was taking him on a ride-along. He was pretty stoked about it at first. I didn't know what else to do. I thought he would have fallen asleep back there by now, but he must have caffeine in that puffer he carries. I guess I'll take him back home with me after my shift ends."

"I'll try to get through to Helena and ask her to come and get him."

"Betty's not going to like that," Purdy reminded him.

"Betty's not got a whole lot of choice. We've got another dead body on our hands."

"What?" Purdy asked in disbelief.

"Tara Wildman called it in. She was hysterical. I've tried calling Colin Dayton, but he's got his damn phone off and Cody is apparently out of town. So it looks like it's you and me again, at least until the morning. I saw Jacey Sumner driving around on Main. She's driving a brand new baby blue Mazda 3. You'll probably have to crash into her to get her to stop, but if you see her, give her

Stan. I know she's babysat for Betty before when Ryan was out of town playing ball. I had to break into the house for them once when Stan accidentally locked them both out."

"10-4. And if I don't run into her, and I mean that figuratively, I'll park on the side road by the entrance to Wildman's lane and leave Stan in the car with Country-FM on. He likes that station. I've had it on all night to keep him happy. Darned if the kid didn't to know all the words to that Carrie Underwood song. He says Ryan listens to it all the time, but I find that kind of hard to believe."

"I think our current prisoner is not what he seems to be," the Chief agreed. "Just make sure Stan's locked in. All the hairs on the back of my neck are standing up on this one. That's never a good sign. I'll see you there."

Roy hung up and hit autodial but the phone dropped the signal.

"Helena, where the hell are you?"

The cruiser turned onto the highway and Roy hit the accelerator. There were some line haul trailers heading south to the city, but not much other traffic. Within five minutes he had reached the turnoff. He turned his high beams on and headed slowly down the dirt road leading to the Wildman's farm. The country road was pitch black at this time of night.

As he pulled the cruiser into the long driveway leading up to the house, he was met by two of Ralph's dogs, who barked noisily at his arrival.

"Yeah, now you make noise. Where were you when the trouble started?" he thought to himself.

Roy slowly got out of the cruiser, and not knowing what he was about to face, had his hand ready on the butt of his pistol. He quickly surveyed his surroundings. No voices. No screams. No cries for help. Just the damn dogs.

Tara Wildman came running from around the back of the house to meet him. Her sweater was covered in what appeared to be vomit. He could smell her before she got three feet in front of him. "Wolfie, Max... shut up," she directed the dogs. "Get back inside the house."

The dogs stopped barking and wandered off, content that their job was done.

"Been drinking tonight, Tara?" Roy asked.

"No. I swear," she said, gasping for breath. She glanced down at her clothes. "I'm sorry. The puke. It happened when I saw him."

"Saw who, Tara?" Roy asked. He could see that the girl was extremely upset. Her knees were trembling, and he knew it wasn't just because she was cold.

"That kid." Tears ran down her cheeks, and she used her sleeve to wipe them away, her gloves also having traces of her stomach contents on them. "The one Ryan's brother hangs around with. "I think his name is Kevin."

Roy knew who Tara meant. The two boys had been together on Halloween when he had been called to the LaRose house after Mr. Wagner died. "Okay Tara, I need you to take a deep breath," he told the shaking teenager. "Is there anyone else here? Anyone with a weapon? A gun? Maybe a knife?"

"No," she insisted. "I haven't seen anyone else."

"Okay," Roy said hesitantly, still trying to get a sense of what had happened. "Walk with me. Talk to me. Take me to what you saw."

Tara moved slowly. Although she was relieved the Chief had arrived, she wasn't anxious to go back down her driveway towards the shed. It was unavoidable, she realized, but she would have preferred to let Roy go down there by himself.

"I met Jacey downtown and we were hanging around for a while at the Topaz," she began. "It got late and I needed a ride home, so she drove me back here. She dropped me off at the end of the driveway because she didn't want to run into my dad. She says he scares her. Dad left the shed lights on, so I went around to the back of the house to turn them off. That's when I saw the fridge turned over in the middle of the path between the shed and the barn. It's not supposed to be there."

Roy looked down the path. There was what appeared to be a fridge lying in the middle of the dirt walkway, between the house and a small wooden structure.

"It's the one my dad has in the shed. He keeps his home-brew in it for when he's fixing the tractor and stuff."

"I see the fridge."

"I could see the coils on the back when I got closer to it, and then I saw my dad lying under it."

"Is he dead Tara? Is that who you meant?"

She looked at him like he was crazy. "No, it's Kevin who's dead. I told you that. My dad's arm is just pinned under the fridge. I think it's broken. He's wearing dark clothes, but you'll see him when we get nearer. He's pretty much out of it."

Roy could now see Ralph's form on the ground towards what would have been the back of the appliance. Tara was probably right, he thought. Ralph was most likely out of it or he would have been able to pull himself free, judging from the angle of his body and its position to the top of the fridge, which had partially landed on an old tree stump.

"I can hear him moan every once and a while," Tara continued. "Yesterday he was talking about moving the fridge inside the root cellar so the animals wouldn't try to open it in the winter. The raccoons got into his beer one night last winter and it made him really mad. So that's what I thought had happened. I thought he had tried to move the fridge all by himself and it toppled over. I went around the other side of it to see if I could push it off him. That's when I saw..." She couldn't finish her sentence without gagging.

"Kevin Clark?"

Tara nodded, her body trembling. "I grabbed the door handle to try to get my weight behind it so I could push the fridge off my dad, but it didn't work because the door wouldn't close. I looked inside to see what was blocking it, and..."

She let out a long sob before continuing. "I saw him. I got so scared I let go of the door handle and I think I hit the kid in the head. I'm so sorry."

"Did you check if he was breathing? Kevin, I mean." Roy asked. He knew that if Ralph had been moaning, he had been breathing. At least at that point in time.

"I live on a farm, Chief Cohen. We have a lot of animals. I know dead when I see it."

She would, Roy acknowledged. "Have you called an ambulance?"

"No. I just called you. There wasn't much point."

"For your dad, Tara."

"Oh."

149

Her father was pinned under a fridge and she never called for medical aid? Roy shook his head. Things were not right in the Wildman household.

"Where's your mother?"

"She's in Vegas with Liz Delaney and Stacey Freeman. She's not coming back until Tuesday."

The fridge was now only a few feet away from them and Roy could see Ralph's breath visible in the cold night air. The air puffs emitting from his wide-open mouth were steady, and he was snoring.

"Ralph, this is Chief Cohen. Can you hear me?"

Ralph moaned in response.

"Okay, don't move. Stay flat on your back." The Chief lowered himself to Ralph's level, pulling some latex gloves from his pocket as he did so. He rapidly felt over Ralph's frame, but there did not seem to be any limbs in distress aside from his right arm, the one partially pinned between the fridge and the tree stump.

"Tara, I want you to stay here by your dad," the Chief said, removing the gloves, stuffing them in his right pocket and reaching for his cell phone.

He quickly dialed 9-1-1.

"This is Chief Cohen. I need a couple of ambulances to come out to the Wildman farm on county three. Hang a left from the highway. It's the last farm on the right, just before you get to Stillman's Creek. You'll see my police cruiser in the driveway. We're out back, between the house and the barn. I've got one male, in his 50's, possible broken arm, and one male child, status to be updated," he looked at Tara, "presumed critical, possibly deceased."

He disconnected from emergency services and started to walk to the front of the fridge.

"Oh God, don't go around there," Tara pleaded.

"Tara, I need you to watch your Dad, or turn around and watch for Officer Purdy. Don't watch me," the Chief directed. He could see a little leg poking out from behind the half-opened refrigerator door. He took a new pair of latex gloves from his left pocket and put them on, pausing to take a deep breath before opening the door further.

Roy knew then why Tara had thrown up. She was right. Kevin was deader than a stillborn calf. His little legs had been scrunched up into the area above the cold meat compartment. The egg tray had put a dent in his temple. It might have happened when Tara accidentally let go of the door, but maybe not. It wouldn't have mattered. Kevin was long past feeling any pain. Cyanosis had set it, staining his little lips an unnatural shade of blue. Roy took Kevin's pulse only because protocol said he had to.

"Dead." Tara said. "I told you."

Roy shone his flashlight around the ground. Frost had formed, and the only footprints Roy could immediately see were Tara's, the ones made by his own boots, and a third set of tracks, most likely a man's and even more likely, Ralph's.

"Did you touch anything inside the fridge, Tara?" he asked.

"No," Tara insisted. "I just wanted to shut it because... because nobody should have to see what I saw."

The Chief turned towards Tara and looked at her hands. "Were your mitts on the whole time you were out here?"

She nodded.

So forensics shouldn't find her prints anywhere on the fridge, the Chief thought. "What time did you say you left home today?" he asked.

"I didn't say. But I left about five."

Smart-ass, the Chief thought. "Where did you go? Did you go straight to the Roxy?"

"No."

"Were you by yourself?"

"I told you. Jacey was with me."

"Actually, you said you met Jacey. Did you meet anyone else?"

"Am I in trouble or something?"

Somebody's in trouble, Roy thought. He just didn't know who. "A lot went on in this town tonight, Tara. I'm just trying to piece it all together."

Tara's feet began to shuffle on the ground. Roy could tell she was trying to decide whether she wanted to talk to him or not.

"You might as well spill it Tara," Roy said, "because I already know who you were with earlier in the evening. What happened? Did you and Ryan have a fight? Was it about your dad?"

"I was only with Ryan for about fifteen minutes," she said. "He wanted to come out here, but… like I want to spend my Saturday night at home." She turned to look at Ralph, preferring not to look at the Chief.

So that much of Ryan's story was true, Roy thought. The two teenagers had been together earlier in the evening. "What did the two of you talk about?"

"What does that have to do with anything?" she asked.

"Kevin Clark died tonight," the Chief said patiently. "And I'm trying to establish a time line. Did you and Ryan talk about Brooke Quinlan? Is that why he came out here earlier tonight?"

He waited for her to answer. She was taking her sweet time about it, but damned if a sixteen-year-old was going to get the better of him. It would take more than a frosty night in November for that to happen.

"Maybe," she finally offered. "Are we done here?"

"Not by a long shot."

Roy wondered whether she was scared or just playing him. His instincts told him the latter was most likely. She was as ballsy as her father was. "If I know Ralph, he got on the phone and told half the town about what happened out here earlier. You know Ryan's in jail, don't you?"

Tara shrugged. "The new girl, the one Ryan calls Goth-Chic, she's the one who told him where the body was," she said coyly.

"Elaborate."

"Ryan told me that she told him to come out to the old bridge."

"Just like that? She told him to look in the water and he'd find Brooke's body?"

"Pretty much."

"Really? Why is it I find that a little hard to believe?"

"If you already know, why are you asking?" she said flatly.

"Maybe I want to hear your version of the story."

"I don't know what happened. Maybe Ryan killed Kevin before he found Brooke. Maybe he stuffed him in the fridge while he was out here."

"You certainly seem to want to land Ryan right in thick of things, Tara. Why is that? I've seen you two together before. I have the impression you're more than nodding acquaintances."

Tara paused. Again, the Chief could see she was hesitating before answering. The delay suggested to him that she was plotting an answer, not freely offering up one.

"I can't remember," she said. "Maybe I'll remember more in the morning."

"We'll both be a little cold standing out here until then, don't you think?"

"I didn't do anything. He's the one in jail."

"If you're as smart as you want me to think you are Tara, consider this. We'll have to wait for the pathologist's report of course, but I've seen a few dead bodies from time to time. I've seen everything from what you might call a 'fresh kill' right on up to the maggot infested remains of torso's blown apart and left to rot in the Gulf. I'm pretty damn sure that Kevin here died well within the time frame Ryan Lachey had his wide-end planted within the confines my jail."

"Oh."

"So..."

"Okay," she relented. "I thought Ryan just wanted to come down here to fool around. So I blew him off."

Roy looked at her.

"No! I mean I told him to get lost. But obviously he was more interested in what he'd find here than what he wanted to do with me. Ryan told me Goth-Chic had a dream the night Brooke Quinlan disappeared. He said her dream told her where Brooke's body could be found. Ryan thought it was spooky because Goth-Chic described the bridge even though she had never been here before. He wanted to check it out, but like I said, I didn't want to come back here, so I got mad at him and I left. Ryan thinks maybe Goth Chic's psychic or something. Personally, I think she's just sick. I don't like her. I don't like the way she looks at Ryan. So that's it. I ran into Jacey and we went to the movie at the Roxy, and then to the Topaz. We saw Goth-Chic at the movie, but we ignored her. Can I change out of these pukey clothes now?"

Roy could hear Purdy's cruiser arriving on the scene. He wondered what had happened with the Stan situation.

It was an unfortunate circumstance to be certain, but Purdy had no choice but to keep Stan with him as he headed out to assist Chief Cohen. He hadn't run into Jacey Sumner or anyone else he would have trusted with the boy. Luckily, about a mile out of town the country station had faded. "Say goodnight to Carrie," he told Stan, who immediately went out like a light. Purdy wished he had thought of turning the radio off earlier.

He parked the car far enough away from the farm that the boy couldn't see what was happening if he happened to wake up. The row of cedars Ralph had planted decades ago as a wind barrier screened the driveway from the side road. He tested the rear doors. Stan was safely in lock-down. He took an investigation kit from the trunk and went to meet Roy.

"How bad is it?" Purdy asked.

"Bag Tara's jacket and gloves," the Chief said without answering his question.

"All right."

Tara gladly threw the soiled clothes into the bag that Purdy held open. He marked it as evidence.

"Can I go now?" she asked.

"Not until we check the house," Roy said.

"But I'll freeze my ass off," she whined. "I'll be okay. Dad's other dogs are in there."

Purdy pulled a tiny foil emergency blanket from his bag. "Throw this on. It'll keep you warm enough."

"I left the back door of my cruiser unlocked," the Chief offered. "Go sit in it until we come to get you."

"All right," Tara sighed, secretly welcoming any chance to escape the scene.

He motioned for Purdy to move towards the fridge. "Don't worry about Wildman. The ambulance is on the way. He's passed out again, but his injuries are the least of our problems here. I need you to take pictures of the fridge and its contents."

"Gotcha," the officer said, as he walked over to the toppled appliance. He let out a low whistle. "Christ, it's Kevin Clark. I play poker with his dad once a month. What the hell happened?"

"Tara says she found them like this. Kevin dead in the fridge and Ralph pinned underneath it," Roy answered.

"Do the Clark's even know he's missing? We never got a call."

"We never initially got a call about Brooke either, strangely enough."

Purdy began to carefully take pictures of the fridge, Ralph Wildman and the surrounding area. Meticulously, he photographed every inch of the crime scene, reciting a few prayers under his breath as he did so.

"What did you say, Purd?" the Chief asked. Before his officer had a chance to answer, Roy's cell phone interrupted their conversation. "Cohen," he said. He listened for a moment. "Are you serious?" He rubbed his forehead with his fist as he tried to digest the information he was hearing. He put the phone back in his pocket. "This gets stranger by the minute. Purd, do me a favor. Make sure you've got few shots of Kevin's neck."

"I already did. Why is his neck of particular interest?"

Roy looked at him solemnly, "that was the Coroner on the line. He says he did a preliminary on Brooke and her body has been completely drained of blood."

"What?"

"There was a slight mishap with it when the paramedics unloaded it from the ambulance. He didn't elaborate, but apparently she didn't bleed. Whatever happened, it made him take a closer look at her before he went home for the night. He said he saw two puncture marks on the left side of her neck. That's it. No severed artery, no major contusion. Nothing that would cause blood loss of the magnitude that has occurred. They'll do a complete autopsy tomorrow but so far he thinks she hadn't been beaten, and she hadn't been sexually molested. She had however, for all intents and purposes been partially embalmed."

The look on Purdy's face said it all. "You can't be serious."

"That's what I said to him," Roy shrugged. "But that's what the chop man found."

Purdy looked at his commanding officer. "This still doesn't mean the older Lachey kid's story has an ounce of truth to it."

"Tara confirmed that Ryan went to the creek because of a dream Ellie LaRose had," the Chief said as he walked back over to Kevin's body for another look. "So he might have just happened upon her like he said."

He looked at the boy, hoping for some clue as to what had happened, as if Kevin was going to get out of the fridge and tell him. "Work with me for a moment, Purd... did you notice anything strange?"

"Stranger than Kevin Clark dead in a fridge?"

"See, that's the first problem for me. I might have bought it as an accident if it had been someone Brooke's age and they crawled inside the old fridge, the door shut and the death was due to asphyxiation. Kevin is... was... seemed to be... a smart kid. I remember that about him. He was full of questions about Mr. Wagner's sudden passing on Helena's porch the other night. He wouldn't have climbed into the fridge. Someone put him there."

"Agreed."

"I also think someone brought him here. It's nine miles into town. Bit of a stretch for a nine-year-old to bike ride, wouldn't you say?"

"I'm following you so far."

"Another thing I don't get is this... Kevin was a fat little kid. But I ask you... the boy in the fridge... does he look fat?"

Purdy studied the torso. "I don't know about fat... a little pudgy maybe."

"So how does a fat kid become just kind of pudgy?"

"There is no politically correct way to answer that."

The Chief knelt down beside the fridge to take a closer look. The initial shock of seeing the dead boy had worn off, and now he was able to view the body more objectively. "Look at his face. It looks drained."

"Well, it's safe to say he's been through a lot," Purdy offered.

"Not drained emotionally, I mean drained as in missing fluid. Kevin had pinch-able cheeks the last time I saw him. There's nothing to pinch now."

Purdy took a closer look at Kevin's face. "You've lost me. What are you getting at?"

"How much blood does a human body hold?" Roy asked.

"Seven or eight percent of its total body weight."

The Chief looked at Purdy. "I didn't expect you to actually know that. I was throwing it out as a rhetorical question."

"I watch a lot of cable," Purdy shrugged. "If you're wondering if the coroner is going to find Kevin's body missing all his blood, I doubt it. His face may be appearing gaunt because of his position at the time of death. Fluids tend to run south."

The chief put on gloves and reached for Kevin's hand. He pressed the child's fingernail, hoping to see his nail bed flush with blood.

"That won't work," Purdy said. "He doesn't have any blood pressure anymore."

"Exactly how much cable do you watch, Doctor Purdy?"

"Apparently more than you do."

"I know he has no pulse. I was just trying to confirm my suspicions about how long he's been dead. His muscles are still relaxed. There's no sign of rigor mortis. That leads me to think his heart stopped beating within the hour." He pushed Kevin's hair back from his neck. No marks were evident.

"That could mean the killer is still hanging around. Even watching us," Purdy noted. He looked uneasily at the farmland between himself and the creek.

"Maybe. Ralph's pegged under the fridge. It's possible that he killed Kevin, stuffed the boy inside it and then got himself caught underneath trying to make his getaway. But it's not very likely."

The ambulances could now be heard in the distance. The Chief put their e.t.a. at a less than five minutes.

"Are you going to leave Tara here or do you want me to bring her to the station after the paramedics are done?" Purdy asked.

"No, I'd rather keep her away from Ryan right now. I don't want the two of them talking and coming up with a different version of this situation."

"Go home, get some sleep. I can finish this up."

Cohen laughed uneasily. "There's not much chance of sleeping tonight. I'll tell you what. I'll take Stan over to Helena's. He'll be as safe there as anywhere. Can you head over to the Clarks? It might be easier coming from you."

"It's never easy," Purdy sighed. "And it might be a bit late for you to go over to Helena's."

"Some things can't wait," Roy said. "I've got a few questions for her granddaughter," he said as he started down the driveway towards his car.

"Do you think she has something to do with this?" Purdy asked, walking with him.

"Ellie LaRose, Tara Wildman, Ryan Lachey, Jacey Sumner, Tom Williams... they all have something to do with this. I just don't know what."

Roy opened the rear door of his cruiser. "Tara, the ambulance is here. I want you to ride with your dad to the hospital. I know it's late, but I don't want you here at the house alone."

"Surprisingly, I don't have a problem with that," Tara answered. "I'll go over to my aunt's afterwards."

"I just remembered I've got a sweatshirt in the back of the trunk," Roy said, opening it. He handed her his police sponsored softball hoodie. "It's clean. The game was cancelled. It'll do you for now. Throw it on. Keep warm."

"Thanks," Tara said sincerely, accepting the sweater.

It was another ten minutes before the police felt confident enough to leave the paramedics on their own. They made sure Tara was safely inside the transport vehicle and Ralph and Kevin had gone their separate ways before they were finally able to check inside the house. There was no sign of a struggle within the Wildman home, and they were confident the dogs would have scared off any stranger hiding within it.

"Okay," Roy said, locking up the house. "Let's get out of here."

"Stan's got to be wondering what the hell the commotion was," Purdy commented. "He couldn't have slept through all this."

"I'll come with you in case he asks too many questions," the Chief said. "My kids were young once. I've had practice lying to them about what goes on in our job."

The two officers turned out onto the side road and immediately reached for their firearms. In the darkness they could see a figure attempting to open the locked rear passenger door of Purdy's police cruiser. The car that held Stan Lachey.

Purdy pulled his gun from his holster.

"Freeze," he commanded. "Police."

The figure turned towards them and laughed.

"It's a freaking' teenager," Purdy noted, as he released the safety on his pistol. Given the murder scene he had just left, he was taking no chances.

"Step away from the vehicle," the Chief said, also aiming his gun towards the teen. "I won't ask you twice."

"What makes you think I'm going to listen to you now?" the voice said.

"Do we know this kid?" Purdy asked.

The Chief thought about it. The voice could have been one of thousand voices he heard any given week. But the way he laughed, mocking them with a depraved chuckle, well… the Chief knew he had heard that chuckle before. He was trying to remember where. The brief second he contemplated that thought was enough for the teenager to vanish.

"Did you see that?" Purdy asked. "He's gone. He was standing in front of us one second and gone the next."

"I *did* see that," the Chief said, bewildered.

The kept their firearms in front of them as they slowly approached the vehicle, Cohen taking the left side, Purdy the right.

Stan Lachey was in the back seat, wide-awake and crying.

"Get out of the car, Stan," the Chief said. "You're coming with me." He reached in and took the boy first into his arms, then took his hand as he put him down to the ground. "Are you okay?"

"He said he was going to get me," Stan said. "He said he was going to take me away and eat me."

"Stan, nobody is going to eat you," Purdy tried to assure him.

"He said he killed Kevin and he was going to kill me next."

Cohen looked at Purdy. While there was a chance Stan Lachey could have figured out that something bad happened at Wildman's farm, there was no chance he could have known it was Kevin's body they had just found. "Did he tell you his name, Stan? Can you describe him close-up? Could you help us draw a picture of what he looked like?"

"He said he was my nightmare. He was dark and scary," Stan said. "And he smelled bad. He always smells bad."

"Always? You've seen him before?" the Chief asked.

"Yes," the boy replied. "He's a vampire and he lives next door to me. In Mrs. LaRose's backyard."

Purdy looked at Cohen. "So... I'm thinking Helena's house is out of the question for Stan. I guess I'll be taking him home tonight?"

"Under the circumstances," Cohen agreed, "that's probably a good idea." He gave Stan's hand to Purdy.

"Are you still going over to Helena's? In case I need to get hold of you later?" Purdy asked.

Roy nodded. "Some things just can't wait until morning."

Chapter 14

Helen slipped her naked body into the old-fashioned pedestal bathtub. Its depth allowed her to slide her shoulders below the waterline without having to raise her legs too much to compensate for her height. She had poured some of Helena's Epsom salts into the water while it was running, and the muscle soothing effect was beginning to loosen the tension knots in her back. She closed her eyes and breathed in the steam rising from the water. It was like a mini-sauna and she was enjoying every minute of it.

For a few moments, she forgot about the situation in Troy. For a few minutes, she imagined she was floating in the aquamarine waters off Cozumel. She had been there once, on spring break with her high school class. It was a carefree time in her life; away from her mother and not yet a mother herself.

She took a sip of the Pinot Blanc wine from the glass she had rested on the soap holder on the wall. That was the bad thing about the design of old-fashioned tubs, no ledge to put anything on. The wine was room temperature, not really the way she liked it, but she wasn't going to follow Helena's suggestion and throw an ice cube into it. That would be uncouth. She also vetoed using a plastic wineglass, despite Helena's protest that she'd be sorry if it went crashing on the mosaic tile floor.

She imagined feeling the waves of the Atlantic Ocean rolling over her chest with her every breath. For a moment she almost thought she could hear the hired resort musicians playing wooden flutes in the background, their tropical notes lulling her to sleep.

But it wasn't the beginning of a wonderful fantasy. There really was water smacking her in the face. She sneezed as the salted water went up her nose. The melodic wind instrument was actually a wind of a different sort. It was more of a whistle. And it was off-key.

She tried to scream, but a hand reached around from behind her neck and covered her mouth, muffling her attempt.

"Helen, I'm going to remove my hand now," the voice said. "Do me a favor and keep quiet. We don't need to go and wake the dead."

She nodded in agreement, tricking him into thinking she was submissive, just before sinking her teeth into him, hard enough to break the skin. "You bastard!" she gasped, after releasing his hand from her jaws.

"Don't go there Helen," he sighed, "we all know who is and isn't a bastard in this house." He looked at the puncture mark on the fleshy part of his palm. "Do you know how many germs are in your mouth? That was borderline barbaric of you."

Helen took what was left of the wine in her glass and flung it at him. "Here, pour a little alcohol on the wound if you're so concerned."

"I see you're still a firecracker," he laughed. He reached for a hand towel and wiped the wine from his black jacket. "If you're in the mood to share your booze, I could murder a double malt scotch," he said, putting the lid of the toilet seat down so he could sit next to her.

"Willie!" she said, her throat holding back a quiver as she uttered his name. "What the hell are you doing here?" She had hoped she would never see this man again in her life, and here he was, making himself at home in her mother's bathroom.

"Oh, so now you're talking to me," he said. "I tried calling, I tried emailing... really Helen, you're not very good at keeping in touch. How long has it been? Five? Six years?"

"I don't know."

"Liar."

"What were you doing with Ellie?"

"I'm fine, Helen. Thanks for asking. And you?" he smiled. "She's a lovely girl. A lot like you in so many ways. Stubborn as hell, yet somehow beguiling."

Helen's eyes were burning with fury.

"Oh, don't look at me like that. I didn't lay a hand on her. I just took her on a little road trip."

"So I heard. You scared the hell out of her. You are such an asshole."

"That depends on how you look at it. I did what I had to do. She needed to see her destiny."

"No one needs to see his or her destiny, Willie." She felt his eyes peeping below the bath water.

"You still look pretty good," he said. "You've been working out."

Helen immediately stood up in the tub and reached for the towel she had placed on the floor. Her modesty seemed somewhat unimportant to her at the moment. "Willie, so help me God, if you lay a hand on her..."

"I'm not here to harm her. The danger she faces is far more evil than I am. I know that's hard for you to believe, but it's true. I am not the bad guy here. I'm just a guy stuck in a purgatory time warp. I have a thousand souls to save before I get out. I'm not even close, if you're curious. I can only see far enough into the future to see the Reaper hovering, and I can try to guide the mortals away from him, but they never listen." He shook his head. "Little lost lambs, they've been a problem since the Bible."

"Who are you kidding? You're never on time. An innocent child is already dead. Couldn't you have stopped it? Doesn't a child's soul count for you?"

"If the truth were known, her soul wasn't even on my radar." He moved to the edge of the tub and pulled the stopper out. The water started to swirl against the gravitational pull. "I don't know why that always happens," Willie said, perplexed. "I've never been able to wear a watch either. The hands go counter-clockwise."

"Quit changing the subject, Willie."

"Why? Isn't that what you do, Helen? Don't you change the subject every time paranormal conversations start around you? I love this floor tile. It reminds me of Grecian bathhouses." He glanced at Helen with the devil in his eyes. "Sorry, my bad. I'm not supposed to save lives, Helen. I'm to save souls. Not the same thing, unfortunately. The lifesaving I leave to you."

"Don't be ridiculous. I couldn't have done anything."

"How's your head, Helen? Does it still hurt? You should ask Helena for a diagnosis. Are you mildly schizophrenic with these voices in your head, or is it more like a massive high-pressure system causing a storm on your psyche every time you try to shut one of your visions out?"

"I don't know what you're talking about."

"Mendax, mendax, tuum braccare flagare," he insisted, waving his finger in front of her face. "Latin good enough for you, Miss Pants-On-Fire, or do you need it in Italian?"

"Shut-up."

"What did you see in that vision of yours, Helen? Did you see another innocent child being killed tonight? I think you did. Are you going to do anything about the actual life, Helen? I didn't think so. Can you live with that if your vision turns out to be true? At least Ellie wanted to find the little girl before it was too late. You're washing your hands of the whole thing. Maybe I need to pull you out of your bathwater and take you on a night-journey? I thought we were past all that."

"You have a peculiar sense of justice, Willie."

"Moi? Do you know anything about your next door neighbor being in jail for a crime he didn't commit? What is his name? Ryan? Well, he is."

Helen smiled.

"See that?" Willie laughed. "You're glad he's behind bars and away from Ellie. Is that why you haven't done anything about it, little Miss 'Scales of Justice'? Girl, you are going to get psoriasis, washing your hands of so much."

"Why don't you just go."

"I can't, Helen. I'm after a soul. Not just an ordinary run of the mill human spirit, but something a little more... enriched."

Helen's hand went to her mouth. "Ellie?"

"Ellie is safe in her bed right now. But mark my words Helen, that sweet slumber she's enjoying right now is going to be the last one she has for a while."

"Don't threaten me," Helen snarled. "You know damn well if Helena gets a whiff of this, or a whiff of you, there will be hell to pay."

"Maybe," Willie said, turning to look in the mirror hanging above the sink. "That woman can do some damage when she puts her mind to it. But Helena's powers aren't yours." He wiped the steam off the glass and looked at Helen's reflection. She was as beautiful as he remembered. "Helena will destroy anything in her sight that threatens you or your daughter," he continued, "but here's the problem... those darn lost lambs. What if Helena can't find Ellie? What if only you can do that?"

Helen lunged towards Willie, her hands reaching for his neck.

He grabbed her. "You need me, Helen. You need me more than ever."

"How could you do this to me?" she asked. "You know I vowed a long time ago, never to use my gift of seeing. I shouldn't have to remind you that for every reaction there is an equal and opposite reaction. Hell, you were probably there when Isaac Newton figured that out. You know the price I pay every time I listen to one of those voices."

"But is it worth Ellie's life, Helen? Ignorance is not bliss. Let me spell it out for you as much as I'm allowed, because evidently you're not listening to what I am trying to tell you. This chapter of Ellie's life began the moment she was born. Like you, and your mother before you, and her mother before that, she is a gatekeeper. It's in her blood. But let's face it. The girl hasn't a clue about what to do. So unless she gets some help fighting this... demon, the chances of her survival are slim. Newton's theory is already in motion. He had more than one theory, as you may recall."

"Demon? What demon? What do you know that I don't?"

"Didn't she tell you, Helen? Is Ellie keeping secrets like you do?"

Helen remained silent.

"We weren't alone in our dream, Helen. We had a visitor."

"I know, the little girl. She told us about that."

"But did she tell you about the boy? Of course not. Girls never tell their mothers about the boys," he sighed.

"What boy? Does this have something to do with Ryan? With Tom?"

"You should be so lucky," Willie said. "You could ask Helena," he teased, "but no, I've said too much already. I really have to be going. Let's do lunch sometime. Call me." He held his thumb to his ear and poised his baby finger by his mouth before exiting the room.

Helen paused at the bathroom door, debating whether she should follow him or not. At least he was being polite. At least he used the door. Or did he do that just for effect?

"He wants to drive me crazy," she sighed. "He wants me to follow him down the hallway and up to Ellie's room, just to show me he still has power over me. Well, I'm not going to do it. I'm not going to let that man run my life."

She heard a moan rumble through the hallway.

"Okay. Maybe I am," she reluctantly admitted.

Helen opened the bathroom door slowly, peeking around the opened frame, giving her eyes time to adjust to the darkness of the corridor. "So far so good," she noted. "There's no tall, dark and slightly handsome, in an evil-kind-of-way man, lurking in the hallway. Hmm, where the hell did he go?"

She began making her way down the hall, taking care not to step too hard on the cold, old floorboards. She didn't want to give away her approach.

"I'll have to talk to my mother about getting some wall-to-wall carpeting," Helen thought to herself. Carpeting… practical in so many ways, helping her sneak around being one of them.

She had only seconds to formulate a plan. She needed to creep by Helena's room without disturbing her, and on up to Ellie's floor to ensure her daughter was safely asleep in her room. There was no sense bringing her mother into this if there was no danger. Willie could have just been yanking her chain. It wouldn't be the first time.

Her thoughts were interrupted by another lengthy moan. This time it was closer to where she was standing. The voice didn't belong to Willie, it belonged to a female.

"My God," she gasped, not knowing what to do. "He's in Mother's room. He's not after Ellie, he's after her."

She ran to Helena's room, leaving slippery wet footprints behind her as she made her way down the hall. She reached for Helena's doorknob. The door was locked. "Sure, this door she locks," Helen said in frustration.

Then she heard Helena moan again.

"Willie, if you think a lock on a century-old door is going to stop me from saving my Mother, you are sadly mistaken."

Helen stepped back as far as she could from the door, pushing her back up against the wall across from it. There wasn't much room to take a running shot at it, but she was going to have to do the best she could within the confines of the tiny hallway to break the damn thing down. She turned her right shoulder towards it and charged at it with all her might.

The weight of her shoulder against the old door actually managed to break one of the decorative panels. Helen slid her hand through the splintered wood and released the lock from inside Helena's room.

"Helen, noooo..." she heard Helena scream.

"It's okay," Helen assured her "I'll be right there to help you. That bastard doesn't know who he is dealing with."

She entered the room and immediately the adrenalin in her body began to pump. Her vision quickly adjusted to the candlelight in the room, and she saw him, illuminated by a flicker of light on the wall. He had straddled Helena's body like a deranged killer about to snuff the life from her.

"Get off her," Helen screamed, leaping onto his back.

Before he could turn around, she hit him with an uppercut to the head that knocked the senses out of him. She rolled him on to his back, ready to deliver a left to his jaw, just to keep him from uttering any useless pleas of mercy. She couldn't wait to see the stunned look on that smug face of his when he finally realized who his attacker was.

"Uh-oh," she said, pulling back on her follow-up punch.

"Hellsbelles!" her mother shrieked. "What in the name of Hades did you do that for?"

"I thought it was Willie," Helen gasped, her hand going over her mouth.

"Willie? What would Willie be doing in my bedroom? That's Roy!"

"I can see that now," Helen sighed. "What's he doing here? Oh... oh..."

"Roy... are you all right?" Helena asked, giving him a gentle shake. "Helen, go get me some water and some ice. Don't just stand there gawking at us."

Helen sheepishly headed back towards the bathroom. How was she to know her mother was entertaining in the boudoir?

She took a facecloth from the towel rack and rinsed it in cold water. What if it really had been Willie? Did Helena stop for a minute to consider that? She had only been trying to protect her. And speaking of consideration, did Helena stop for a minute to consider that there was a teenaged girl in the house? Obviously not! What if Ellie had walked in on the two of them? Seeing your own mother with her legs apart waiting for her man was bad enough. Imagine if it were your grandmother.

"We are sooo going to talk about this," Helen seethed. She reached for the plastic cup on the sink and poured water into it before storming back down the hall. Helena could have got him some water herself. She still had to check on Ellie, and the two lovers had already caused her an unnecessary delay. All the commotion probably woke Ellie up.

Helena gently lifted Roy up and cradled him in her arms. "I am so sorry, Roy. You would have thought she'd gotten the hint when the door was locked."

"What hit me?" he asked.

"You were belted by one hundred and forty pounds of Hurricane Helen."

"Who taught her how to fight? She should become a pro-wrestler."

"I did," Helena said. "But I'm not particularly proud of her right now. We are sooo going to talk about this," she echoed.

Sunday...

Chapter 15

It was only 5:30 in the morning, but already people were starting to gather outside the police station. They were waiting for Roy Cohen to show up. To show up with answers. You couldn't hush up the murder of a child in a small town, particularly if it wasn't the only one that had happened. It now looked like Troy had a serial killer on its hands.

The jail at the police station was minimum security at best. It had been designed as a temporary holding station, not a permanent address. Serious offenders were normally transported by the paddy wagon to the jail in the city. Everyone knew that. So why was the man they had elected as Chief of Police, keeping Ryan Lachey... pervert that Ralph Wildman had always said he was... still within Troy's town limits? This was hard for them to understand.

Small towns being what they are, a good percentage of the gathered crowd had been in the police station at some point in their life. It didn't take them long to remember which side of the building the lone jail cell stood. They began to hurl rocks at the south wall.

"Fuck," Ryan said. He had a sleepless night, tossing and turning and wondering if the vampire was going to pay him another visit. "I guess it's wake-up time."

"You crazy bastard," a voice outside said loudly. "We don't take kindly to child murders in Troy. We don't care if you molested them or not. We're going to castrate you, cut your femoral artery and hang you by your feet until you bleed to death, you son-of-a-bitch."

"Great," Ryan sighed. They had said murders, plural. That meant the vampire had been true to his words and Kevin was dead. It also meant Stan was in serious danger.

He sat up and reached for the box of toaster strudel. It would have been nice if Purdy had left him a toaster to put them in, but that hadn't happened. Maybe it was a safety measure or maybe Purdy was just being a prick. He wasn't sure. He bit into the cold blueberry pastry anyway. It was rather dry, but the sweet filling gave him an instant sugar rush.

The front door of the police station opened and Ryan was somewhat relived to see Purdy standing before him with a bag from the 24-hour convenience store.

"What are you doing back here this early?" Ryan asked. "Don't they ever give you any time off?"

"Not under the circumstances," Purdy said, handing Ryan a hot breakfast burrito. "Here. I thought you might like something a little more substantial."

Ryan was puzzled by Purdy's sudden random act of kindness.

"Thanks," he said, reaching for the paper wrapped meal. "That's decent of you, dude."

Purdy nodded. The events of the past twenty-four hours had not totally exonerated Ryan's guilt in his mind, but he had to acknowledge there was now room for a margin of error. He might be guilty of one murder, but not two.

"Isn't there some law against leaving me alone in here?" Ryan asked. "What if there was a fire or something?"

Purdy pointed at the massive sprinklers above Ryan's head.

"What if I had a medical emergency?"

"Then I would have had three bodies to contend with. It gets to the point when you start to lose count," Purdy snapped. "You weren't totally on your own. I had the alarm company monitoring you."

"The police station has an alarm company?"

"We live in trying times."

"They can't see me take a whiz, can they?"

"No."

"Where are the Dayton boys?" Ryan asked. He hadn't seen hide nor hair of the twin constables since he had been confined. "Don't they work here anymore?"

"I've been wondering the same thing," Purdy admitted, tossing Ryan a carton of juice from the same bag.

"Cohen should fire their asses."

"That's kind of hard to do right now. We're a little busy."

"What happened to Betty and my brother?" Ryan asked between bites.

"Betty's still at the hospital. Stan stayed on my couch last night. I woke Jacey Sumner up at the crack of dawn and she's watching him over at your house now. I didn't think that seeing you locked up was going to foster any tender sibling moments between the two of you."

"Dude, you can't leave him with Jacey."

"Why not? Roy said she's looked after him before."

"We're talking about supermodel Jacey, right? She's not going to be able to help him if some nutcase tries to grab him. She's not going to scuff her shoes for nobody."

"She's just watching him for a few hours. He'll be safe."

"Safe?"

"He'll be okay."

"You said 'safe'."

Ryan studied Purdy's body language. His hands were on his hips in a stance that was too girly for the hard-assed cop Ryan knew Purdy was. It was the same stance his mother often took when the truth wasn't particularly convenient.

"Holy shit," Ryan exclaimed. "You believe me, don't you?"

"No. I don't."

"Yeah, you do. You don't want to believe me, but you're starting to. What happened after you left here?"

"That's classified information."

"Not if it involves Stan it's not. If my Ma's in the hospital, I'm his next of kin."

"You're in jail," Purdy reminded him. "This isn't a country club despite your private residence. And as far as I know your dad is still alive. You're not his next of kin."

"But my dad's not here. I'm here," Ryan reminded Purdy. "Are you going to formally charge me with something, or not? You're going to have to let me go soon if you don't."

A rock smashed through the large office window. It had a note attached to it with string. Purdy picked it up off the floor, unraveled it and showed Ryan the picture that had been drawn on the back of a paper trash bag. It showed an effigy of a football player hanging from a tree.

The artwork angered Ryan. "They got my jersey number wrong. How could they fucking get my number wrong? I'm the star of the team. Shit."

Purdy forced a smile. "Understand now? Even if we were to let you out, I'm thinking you wouldn't get very far. In case you haven't heard, there's a mob out there waiting to kill you."

"Well... shouldn't you go out there and tell them to fuck-off or something?"

"My job is to stay in here and protect you, oddly enough."

"You have to let me out."

"That's not going to happen."

"I have to protect my brother."

"I said I had it covered," Purdy insisted, turning on his computer and checking his email. The logical part of his brain was still trying to process what he had seen last night, everything from the horrific discovery of the child's body to the teenager who vanished into thin air.

"He was here yesterday," Ryan blurted out. "The dude of darkness. He said he was going after Stan."

That got Purdy's attention. "What do you mean, here?"

"In my fucking cell," Ryan began. "He said he killed Kevin and he was going after Stan next."

"Who the hell have you been talking to?" Purdy asked. Up until that point, he assumed Ryan believed the mob outside only wanted to lynch him for the girl's murder. But it was clear now that Ryan knew about both killings.

"I just fucking told you. The dude of darkness."

"He was here? In your cell?" Purdy asked. "Let's say I believe you for a nano-second. Every piece of vampire lore I have ever read, or watched on television says you have to invite them in. Would you have been stupid enough to do that? Invite him into the jail?"

Ryan thought back. "Maybe."

"Well smarten up next time. Ask him to leave."

Purdy checked the answering service for messages. There were none that demanded his immediate attention. He had hoped the Clarks would have checked in. They hadn't been home last night so he hadn't been able to tell them about the death of their son. That loomed heavily on his mind. Where the hell were they, and why weren't they wondering where Kevin was?

He then read through a few of the emails that had come in overnight. "How can I have over three-hundred messages?" he remarked. "Maybe I should just delete the ones with your name in the header followed by variations of the verb 'dismember'." He minimized the program on his computer screen and looked pensively at his prisoner. "So, what did he look like, this dude of darkness?"

"Skinny. My age. Long black hair. Black jean jacket."

Another rock came crashing through the window, landing on the floor beside the officer's left foot.

"Okay. I've had enough of this bullshit," Purdy said, picking it up and removing the note attached to it. He opened it, read it, and stood up. "You hold that thought," he said to Ryan, "while I go outside and find the guy who drew me a picture of your mid-range anatomy with a grenade attached to it."

As he opened the front door, Purdy saw Tom Williams trying to decide whether to come in or not.

"Can I talk to Ryan?" Tom asked.

"Can you draw a grenade?" Purdy asked.

"Uh, no."

"Then go on in," Purdy said. "But make it a short conversation and stay by the door where I can see you. I don't have time to frisk you." He surveyed the crowd. "You! Michael McMann. Stay put. You can't draw stick people any better now than you could in grade one. I'd know your crappy art anywhere."

Tom walked in and looked at Ryan. "Is he for real?"

"Pretty much. What the fuck happened last night?"

"It's been a busy one. Kevin Clark was found dead over at Tara's place. Somebody stuffed him in a fridge. Wildman's in the hospital with a couple of broken bones. Tara's gone to her aunt's. Jacey's over at your place babysitting Stan until your mom gets home."

So it had happened like the vampire had said it would, Ryan thought. "You've got to go to my place and help Jacey watch Stan."

Tom glanced at the door to see whether Purdy was watching him. Not seeing him, he moved closer towards Ryan's cell. "Jacey's not exactly talking to me. We had another fight after your game. Same old, same old."

"I don't give a shit. Fix it."

"What's going on, dude?" his friend asked.

Ryan rested his forehead on the bars of the cell and closed his eyes. What he had to say to Tom was not easy to say. "The killer... I think Stan's next on his death list."

Tom could tell from the tone of his voice that Ryan truly believed that Stan was in danger. "Why?"

"Look. Don't ask me to explain. He doesn't even really want the kids. He wants something more. The kids are only practice for him. Until he's better at his game."

"It's going to get worse?"

"Way worse. We've got to try to stop it. But I can't do anything while I'm locked up in here. Whatever you did to Jacey, I need you to work it out. Go find Goth and tell her I need to see her."

"Ellie's not talking to me either."

"You're a big fucking help. What do you know about vampires?"

"I read Dracula a couple of years ago."

"Great. Purdy knows more than you do. I need you to do me a favor. I need you to go to the library and find out what it takes to kill them."

"Duh... silver bullets, wooden stakes to the heart. What were you and Tara doing at the midnight horror movie the last long weekend?"

"Not watching the fucking movie." He thought about Tom's question. "Okay, so you and Jacey actually watched it. Maybe that's good. Maybe Jacey does have a clue."

"Jacey's not stupid, Ryan."

"Has she given it up to you yet?"

Tom glanced down at the floor.

"I rest my case."

The sound of the front door opening silenced their conversation. Purdy subconsciously picked some wax from his ear as he came back inside. He was quiet as he took his jacket off, sat down in his chair and put his feet up on his desk. Ryan was in his direct line of sight.

"Exactly what did you ever do to Michael McMann to make him hate you so much, Lachey? I'm just curious. I get the whole Ralph/Tara Wildman thing, but McMann's got a son. Something I should know about?"

"It's not my fault his kid can't throw a football worth a shit and didn't make the team for the third year in a row. Why? What did the old coot say?"

"He says he saw you with the girl on Halloween. He's going to make a statement to the Chief when he gets here."

"He's full of shit."

"Lucky for you, I know that." He pointed at his own head. "Internal bullshit radar."

"Then quit wasting your time with him."

"Yes boss," Purdy said sarcastically.

"No disrespect intended," Ryan began, "but Purd, the dude you asked me to describe before Tom got here has threatened my brother's life. You know, the kid you're supposed to be protecting. Maybe you should be spending more time worrying about him, than reading my love notes that come crashing through the window."

"Stan does not need protection. He needs a babysitter. I found him one."

"Are ya sure? Remember the long, dark haired, skinny dude... about Tom's height, minus the hair gel?"

"Hey, leave my hair out of it," Tom interjected.

"What does your bullshit radar say about that, Officer Purdy?" Ryan continued. "Or does it fade in and out like the cellular signals in this hellhole town?"

Before Purdy could answer, their attention turned to the sound of a police siren getting closer and closer. Another cruiser had arrived outside.

"You're lucky. Colin Dayton's here," Purdy said, pulling his own car keys from his pant pocket as he looked out the window. "I've had enough of your lip today. I'm done here." He put his heavy winter coat back on. "Is there anything you want me to say to your mom when I see her?"

Ryan was quiet.

"I didn't think so," Purdy said as he left the building.

Tom noticed a grin forming across Ryan's face. "What are you smiling about? He just totally silenced you."

"The dude's starting to believe me," Ryan said, as he sat back down on the bed.

"Does this mean I don't have to go get Jacey and Ellie now?"

"Remember that time when you were ten and I covered for you when you broke Old Man Wagner's front window with the baseball?"

"Yeah, why?"

"When I got out of jail for that, Betty made me pay for it out of my paper route money. It took me another six months to save up enough for a new bike, but I took it like a man because we were friends. You said you owed me one. It's time. I'm calling in the biggest favor of our lives. I need you to help me deal with some demons."

Tom thought about it. "If my dad had found out it was me; I never would have got to go to Disneyland that summer. I never would have got kissed by that totally hot twelve-year-old they made me ride with in the teacup. My entire sex life might have been delayed. That was pretty decent of you."

"Too true." He made a gesture like he was putting a microphone in front of Tom. "Tom Williams, now that we haven't won the Varsity Cup because the best damned player is stuck in jail, are you going to go to back to Disneyland?"

"Hell no. I'm going to the library to get us some books on how to kick-ass kill vampires, baby!"

Ryan stuck his hand out the between the cell bars so that Tom could high-five him.

"And that, dude, is why we're still friends even though your hair is totally over-processed."

Tom laughed. "I've got to get up early and re-stock the shelves over at the store before my Dad opens up tomorrow, so I have to go. I'll catch you later." He flashed a peace sign at Ryan before heading out the door.

"He is going to be absolutely no fucking help," Ryan sighed to himself. He watched as Officer Colin Dayton came into the police station, ignored him, and immediately headed into the washroom.

"Yo, hi to you too," Ryan scoffed.

It was ten minutes before the grumpier half of the Dayton twin patrol came out of the bathroom with a wet cloth over his eyes.

"Did you party hard last night or something?" Ryan asked. "What happened to your eye?"

"What's it to you?" the officer said. "I got hit with some debris out on the highway. But for the record, what I do or don't do in this shitty little town is no concern of yours."

"Just trying to make conversation," Ryan mumbled to himself.

The office phone rang. Colin Dayton answered it.

"Yeah, I'm here. Sorry about that Chief. I've still got a bit of the flu." He took the cloth from his eyes just long enough to look at Ryan. "He's fine. The side window is smashed, though. The mob outside probably did it. It was a gong show when I first got here. I had to use the horn of my truck to clear them from the driveway so I could park. I don't know what the hell Purdy was doing, letting them all go crazy like that." He paused and glanced outside through the broken glass. "It's quiet all of a sudden. I think they went over to the Topaz now that it's open, to get organized. As organized as a bunch of pitchfork-toting farmers can get. I'll call the glass guys, and see if I can get them over here today. It'll probably be overtime for them, being Sunday and all. I'll let you explain that one to the town council. The bright side is, those bars on the windows have paid for themselves today."

He glanced over at Ryan who had moved to the toilet in his cell.

"Lachey, do you think you could take your dump after I finish this phone call?"

"Nature calls, dude."

"Listen Chief," Colin continued. "I've got to go lock myself in our bathroom until the broken window lets some air in to take out Lachey's breakfast stench. I'll call you back later."

"Well, if you guys would bring me a salad every once and a while, it might help," Ryan said loudly.

Colin took the cloth from his head and used it to cover his nose as he headed into the bathroom.

"Drama Queen," Ryan taunted.

Once inside the tiny station bathroom, Colin uncovered his nose and looked into the mirror. His skin was white, his eyes were puffy and he felt like throwing up. He reached into his pocket and pulled out his cell phone. It was flashing. He opened his directory and saw that it was a text message from his brother Cody.

"PARTY-ON"

"Shit," Colin said. "There's just no rest for the wicked."

Chapter 16

Helena poured Roy a cup of coffee while he finished his first phone call of the morning from the comfort of her kitchen. He had already showered and dressed, and only had a few minutes for a quick Helena-style breakfast of java and toast before he would have to make his way to the police station for what was promising to be a long day.

"You sit down," she instructed. "Let the pumpernickel digest. You don't want your acid reflux acting up on you again."

"This coffee will kill the acid reflux," Roy insisted. "This coffee will kill anything."

"Well, I wasn't really paying attention when I measured. Or didn't measure," she muttered as she glanced out the window. "It's a dreary day. I think we're in for some snow."

"How can you tell? It's only seven o'clock. It's winter. It's still dark."

"My fingers ache and I feel restless," Helena replied, squeezing some hand cream from the bottle she kept by the sink and massaging it into her hands. "And besides, there's an eerie haze around that full moon outside. It gives me the willies."

The phrase had an ironic meaning to her that Roy would never understand.

"Great. Just what I needed. More lunatics in Troy. He saw his remark didn't improve her mood, so he motioned for her to come nearer. "As long as we're only weathering a meteorological storm, we'll get through it," he smiled at her, placing her hand in his own. "I just don't want any other kind of storms around here, okay? I've got enough on my plate right now."

She wished she could assure him that the worst was over, but every nerve in her body was telling her it wasn't.

"Did one of the Dayton's make it in?" she asked, moving the ceramic sugar bowl towards his oversized coffee mug. She had managed to get Roy to cut down on his salt over the past six months, but sugar was a whole other issue. She watched as he dumped three heaping spoonfuls into his cup.

"Finally," Roy answered, blowing on the coffee before taking a big sip. Bitter as it was, he knew he wouldn't find time for another before noon. "Colin. He says he came down with the flu yesterday and was too sick to call in. I haven't heard from Cody yet."

"I know it's none of my business," Helena began, "I don't know them from Adam, but maybe you should think about training a few new recruits. Back-up cops."

"Back-up cops? Why, are you offering?" he laughed, playfully grabbing her waist. "I know you're good with the cuffs, but..."

"Never you mind. I could run circles around those two if I had half a mind to. They might be in their thirties, but they'd be begging for mercy before we got to the end of the block. I saw them chasing after Ronnie Thornton when he broke out of the Shady Acres rest home last Easter. It was like they were running in slow motion compared to Ronnie, and he's in his seventies."

Roy laughed. "You're probably right. They're not the quickest on their feet. Though the dirty work doesn't seem to faze them. There'll be no trauma counseling for those two, guaranteed. That's why I wish they had been around the past couple of days. Purdy's putting up a good front, but I can see the pressure is getting to him. So if you don't mind, I'd like to keep the twins around for a while. We all get sick from time to time, they just picked an inconvenient time."

"I'm just saying they just seem to have their own agenda."

"Who doesn't have their own agenda in this town?" Roy laughed. "When you figure out what theirs is Sherlock, you let me know. I'll send a memo to human resources."

Helena punched him playfully on the shoulder. "I know when you're sassing me, Roy Cohen."

Roy often talked about the Dayton twins, but Helena never really had a chance to get to know them. Most of what she knew about them she knew from the women in the hair salon who gossiped about them from time to time. They all seemed to agree the Dayton's were good looking men who never seemed interested in any of the women from Troy.

"Are they gay?" Helena asked.

"No, they're not gay," Roy sighed.

"Then they need to meet some good women," Helena announced. "I would have thought they'd have settled down by now. I can't be the only single woman in this town insane enough to carry on with a man on the force."

"They'll get around to it someday," Roy said. "They just like to blow off some steam by getting out of Troy and heading down to the casino off the highway. The head of security down there tries to keep an eye on them for me, so I won't have to read about them in the local paper. He tells me they do quite well at the ladies, and roulette. So there goes your gay theory."

"Well, then maybe Helen..."

"Oh-ho-no," Roy stammered. "I know there are two of them, but they wouldn't stand a chance against her. Speaking of chances, is Hurricane Helen normally a late sleeper? Because if she is, is there any chance I could get another piece of that excellent toast before I have to head out?"

"Ouch," Helena sighed. "How is your head?"

"Sore as hell. I've got a bump the size of an egg right at the back," he replied, rubbing it gingerly. He stopped sipping his coffee as he heard the sound of footsteps coming down the stairs. "Tell you what," he said, finishing the rest of it in one long gulp and quickly getting up from the chair. "Hold the toast."

"Relax," Helena laughed. "That is only one hundred and ten pounds of energy coming down the stairs. It's Tropical Storm Ellie. You're safe."

"Should I leave?" Roy asked.

"No. Sit down," Helena commanded. "You have every right to be here. Besides, I've already started your toast."

Ellie entered the kitchen wearing her standard T-shirt and pajama bottoms. If she was surprised by Roy's presence, she didn't let on. She walked over to the fridge, poured herself some juice and headed towards the table. Noticing that Roy's gun holster was hanging on the right side of his body, she made a sudden swerve and sat down in the chair on his left. Guns, she concluded, were not a part of a healthy breakfast.

"Ellie, I want you to know that Roy..." Helena began, but Ellie raised her hand, signaling for her grandmother to stop talking.

"I figured it all out last night," she said between sips of her juice. "It was kind of hard not to. The moaning, the doors banging..."

Roy became flustered. "Well, Helena and I have been friends for quite some time, and um, uh..."

Helena looked at him with amusement and handed him his second plate of toast.

"Save it," Ellie pleaded. "As long as you keep the toilet seat down so I don't fall in if I sleepwalk, I'm a happy camper. Just don't make me call you 'uncle'."

"You've got a deal. Call me Roy," he said, feeling like he had dodged a bullet. "So," he said between bites of bread, "you're a sleepwalker?" He tried to make the question sound casual, but he did find it unusual that someone Ellie's age was having an issue like that.

Helena walked behind Ellie and lovingly pulled her granddaughter's hair behind her shoulders. "She's just going through a phase," Helena assured him.

"We hope so," Ellie sighed. "Just keep your pants on, okay Roy?"

"Another deal. Do you have any idea when your mother will be through her phase?" Roy asked.

Ellie unexpectedly laughed so hard that the juice she was drinking started to come out of her nose. She quickly grabbed a napkin from the table. "You're hilarious. And your powers of observation are bang-on." She noticed a bruise on the side of Roy's face. "Whoa, looks like Mom gave you a knockdown punch last night! It's good to know your screams were real and I wasn't having another creepy nightmare."

Helena shook her head at Ellie and motioned for her to zip it, but it was too late. Her granddaughter had just opened the door for Roy to attempt to validate a piece of Ryan's story, and Helena knew he wasn't going to let it go.

"I've been meaning to ask you about a dream you had, Ellie." Roy touched the injured area on his face gingerly. Sometime between now and the time he got to work, he was going to have to come up with a cover story about how he got that bruise or he'd never hear the end of it.

"Roy, let's not bring up the nightmare thing again," Helena interrupted. "We're all under a lot of stress right now with the murders going on. Why don't we just talk about something normal, like the weather?"

"Murder...s?" Ellie questioned. "Forget the weather. What's up with the murders?"

"I'm under the impression you had a dream about Brooke Quinlan," Roy stated, continuing his line of questioning.

"Roy, stop interrogating my granddaughter. This is our home, and I don't seem to recall you reading her the Miranda rights."

"I did dream about her," Ellie acknowledged. She saw Helena looking at her as if she was going to reach over and physically gag her. "What, Nan? Don't look at me like that. I'm not Sylvia Browne or anything. It was just one big co-incidence."

"Sylvia Browne?" Roy questioned.

"She was a psychic and frequent guest of Montel Williams," Helena explained.

"But you dreamt about a little girl being carried off, correct? Supposedly to an area with water running under a bridge? You told Ryan about it, didn't you?" the Chief challenged.

"Roy, do you want me to pour the rest of the hot coffee over your head? I told you to leave Ellie alone," Helena said angrily.

Ellie looked at Roy and shrugged. She hadn't done anything wrong. It was just a dream. So what was the big deal?

"Well yeah, I did have this weird dream the first night we got here. There was a girl in it that looked just like the girl that everyone is looking for. I mean, I didn't know at the time that was who she was. She was just a girl in my dream, wearing a Dorothy costume." She glanced at Helena. "Okay, I guess it's turned out to be a little bit like an episode of *Paranormal State*, but it's not like I wanted her in my dream." She twitched uncomfortably in her chair. "Maybe we should talk about the weather. Do you think it's going to snow today?"

"*Now* you want to listen to your Nan?" Helena said indignantly. "It's a bit late for that. You might as well go on with your story."

"In my dream, she was by some old bridge," Ellie continued. "Then the next day, when the little girl really had gone missing, I began to wonder where it was, if it even existed. I told Tom and Ryan about it on the way home from the search party and they laughed at me. They thought I was crazy and made fun of me. Tom came over later to apologize but he turned out to be the ultimate jerk. I hate him," Ellie insisted, subconsciously kicking the bottom of Roy's chair with her foot.

Helena looked at Roy and shook her head. "She doesn't hate him," she whispered.

"You knew about this, Helena?" Roy asked. "Didn't you think that perhaps I would find it interesting?"

Helena threw her arms in the air. "What? Teenagers come up with the craziest dreams. One minute they're dreaming about a where to find a great pair of boots and the next thing you know..."

"Helena, this is no joke."

"As if a judge would accept a dream as evidence," Helena retorted. "Really, Roy. You're going too far."

"Why? What happened?" Ellie asked. "How come you're so interested in my stupid dream?"

"You might as well tell her," Roy said, looking at Helena for some direction. "She'll hear about it anyway."

"You tell her. You're the one who was there," Helena said, still annoyed. "But be careful you don't lead your witness." She took his plate and cup away from him before he had a chance to ask for more.

Roy looked at Ellie. He wanted to study her reaction carefully. "Brooke's body was found out at Stillman's Creek last night. Out by the old covered bridge."

"Nan!" Ellie gasped. "Get out! Does Mom know?"

"I don't know," Helena answered. "I don't think so. It didn't come up in our conversation last night."

"She's going to freak, you know that," Ellie said. "She goes mental when stuff like that happens."

"Never mind your mother. How are you?" Helena asked. "This news must come as bit of a shock."

"A shock of a co-incidence," Ellie said defensively.

Their conversation abruptly ended as the sound of a loud set of footsteps was heard coming down the old wooden staircase in the hall.

"Okay," Roy said, knowing there was only one person left in the house that it could be, and he wasn't in the mood to face her right now. "That's my cue. I'm out of here."

"I'll deal with her," Helena sighed. "You don't have to rush off."

"Ellie, we'll continue our chat later," he said as he hurriedly grabbed his jacket from the back of his chair. "Nice try, Helena. But I really think it's time for me to get going. She might want a re-match."

He rubbed the goose bump on the back of his head, gave Helena a quick kiss and left quickly out the back door.

"Sweet," Ellie said, rising from the table. "But if the man with the gun is afraid of Mom, I'm out of here too."

"Where do you think you're going, Ellie LaRose?" Helena said sternly, placing her hands on her hips. "You sit back down. I'll get you some frozen waffles. I picked them up at the grocery store on Thursday. You're eating them in one of the few pictures I have of you. You were a toddler, so I'm hoping you still like them."

"I'm really not that hungry," Ellie lied. "And I really don't want to be in the room with you and Mom right now. I think you need some alone time. And I know I need some time to shake off the heebie-jeebies I'm getting from this whole dream thing."

"Do I have to remind you I saved you from a rabid dog?" Helena asked.

"Why is there always a payback time?" Ellie sighed, sitting back down into the chair just in time to get the full effect of Helen storming through the dining room door and into the kitchen.

Ellie and Helena stared at her in disbelief. The normally precision-groomed Helen hadn't so much as ran her fingers through her hair. It was squished against her head on one side and full of static on the other, making her look like a were-wolf having a really bad hair day.

Ellie figured that wasn't a good sign. "I'll owe you one, Nan," she said, as she started to stand back up.

Helena grabbed her by her shoulder and pushed her back down into her chair.

"Tell me about the man. Tell me about the boy," Helen yelled at them without stopping to say good morning.

"Mom?" Ellie asked.

"Hellsbelles, Helen. Do you need some meds?" Helena asked sarcastically.

Helen snarled in anger. It was an air-through-the-nose, wide-awake snore of a snarl, that surprised her almost as much as it did Ellie and Helena when it happened.

Ellie started to laugh.

Helen raised her hand threateningly and moved towards her daughter.

Helena reached across and grabbed Helen's arm.

"What do you think you're doing? So help me, Helen. I'll take a knife from the butcher block if I have to," she warned her daughter. "Step away from Ellie. What the hell is wrong with you?"

"I want to know all about the man of your dreams," Helen said to her mother sarcastically. "And I want to know all about the boy in yours," she said to Ellie.

"Seriously, Helen. Have you been drinking?" Helena asked. She had seen her daughter angry before, but this was borderline psychotic. "It's a little early in the morning for mad cow cocktails."

"I asked you a question, Mother," Helen said, ignoring the sarcasm.

"Helen, you have no right to ask me anything of the sort. I'm a grown woman. This is my house. Your daughter is not five. She's old enough to know that from time to time we all need a little push in the bush."

"Do you have to be so vulgar?" Helen screamed. "That's what I am talking about. I am trying to teach Ellie that sex does not equal love, so that she doesn't get hurt and you're having a boudoir party a floor beneath her. What kind of an example is that?"

"It was hardly a party, Helen. You didn't have to crash it."

"Do you love this guy... Roy? Do you?" Helen stammered.

Helena thought for a moment. "Well, not that it's any of your business, but yes, I do happen to love Roy Cohen. I have for quite some time. And I think you owe me an apology for beating him to a pulp last night. You can make up for it by hopping in that bug van of yours and going to get me a new bedroom door from the renovation store in the city. A metal one if you're feeling inclined to break it down again." She picked up Roy's coffee cup and threw it against the wall. "And pick up a new mug set for me while you're at it. You want crazy? I'll show you crazy."

"Whoa," Ellie gasped. "Now I know where Mom gets it from."

"Shut up, Ellie," Helen snapped. "Or I'll ground you until you're twenty."

Ellie slunk back in her chair.

"Then I'll un-ground her," Helena yelled back. "My house. My rules. Why is that so hard for you to comprehend?"

Helen's face was so red so looked like she was going to pass out. She breathed in and out deeply, trying to calm herself down. "Who is the boy in your dream, Ellie?" she asked again, this time trying to be calmer.

"Enough with the dream already, okay Mom?" Ellie pleaded.

Helena moved towards Ellie's chair and put her arm around her grand-daughter. "That really might be best, Helen."

"Don't you start being all protective of Ellie. She's hiding something. She told us about the dream. But she left out one major detail."

"I didn't know I had to tell it to you scene by scene," Ellie protested. "Are you talking about the vampire? Is that what you're going on about?"

"Whoa," Helena gasped.

"Yes! I mean the vampire!" Helen said, throwing her arms into the air. "Why haven't you told us about him? Rewind. You said there was a missing girl. You said there was a bridge. You even said there was a creepy cowboy cutout guy. But you said nothing about a vampire. Did you?"

"I guess it slipped my mind," Ellie said quietly. "But... how did you know about him?"

"Just like that?" Helen questioned, snapping her fingers and ignoring Ellie's question. "You forgot about him just like that?"

Ellie began tapping the arms of the chair with her fingers. "Um, okay, so maybe there was a vampire in my dream. And maybe he had the girl in his arms. And maybe she was still alive then..."

"What do you mean she was still alive *then?*" Helen asked, pretending to know nothing about the discovery of the body. "What are you talking about?"

"They found Brooke Quinlan's body last night," Helena told her.

"This is not good," Helen said, suddenly feeling weak. She grabbed the back of a chair and spun it around so she could sit down. Deep down inside, she had hoped that her visions, and Willie's side of the night-ride tale, had just been a crazy ghost story. "Ellie, what did the vampire look like?"

"A vampire," Ellie shrugged.

"Ellie, this is no time to frustrate the hell out of me," her mother said lowering her head into her hands.

Helena moved another chair between Helen and Ellie and sat down. She looked at her girls, one clearly distraught, the other clearly confused. She was at a loss how to help one of them, let alone both.

"Sweetheart," she said gently to Ellie, "not that it matters, because you're right, a vampire is a vampire, but... do you remember anything at all about him?"

"Of course I remember," Ellie said. "I'll never forget him as long as I live. He was a teenager, like me. He had dark hair, like me. And he was very scary. Even more scary than Mom." She blew Helen a kiss in a feeble attempt to lighten the mood. It used to make her mother smile. Not this time.

"Ellie, I'm not in the mood," Helen cautioned.

They were interrupted by a knock at the back door. There was a tall blonde teenaged girl standing outside on the landing, attempting to peek through the kitchen window.

"Don't answer that door," Helen demanded. "We need to finish this."

"Helen, don't be ridiculous," her mother said, thankful for the distraction. She needed time to figure out what was really going on, and she couldn't do it with her girls hovering around her. She needed to get them out of the house. "Ellie's friends are always welcome here."

"She's not exactly my friend," Ellie said, recognizing the girl. "You don't have to open the door."

"Nonsense," Helena insisted, reaching for the doorknob. "Neither of you are in the position to be picky. I don't hear any BFF reality show producers banging our door down."

"BFF?" Helen asked, looking at Ellie for an answer.

"Best friend forever," Ellie answered. "Nan's been watching too much MTV. It must run in the family."

Jacey Sumner, bundled up in a matching navy pea coat and hat, brushed some snowflakes from her shoulder and turned to face Helena at the door.

"I knew it," Helena said to herself with satisfaction. "I told Roy it was going to snow."

"Erm, is Ellie home?" Jacey asked when Helena opened the door. "I don't have the wrong house or anything, do I?"

"Yes, darling. I mean no. Yes, Ellie is home. No you don't have the wrong house. Oh, you know what I mean." Helena said, motioning Jacey into the kitchen.

Jacey paused at the threshold. Under the circumstances, that made Helen overly cautious. Was the girl waiting to be invited in?

"There aren't any cockroaches in here are there?" Jacey asked awkwardly. "Only I saw a van out front…"

"Great," all three LaRoses said in unison.

"Get it out of here," Ellie and Helena both said to Helen.

"All right, already," Helen said alone, feeling foolish on a few fronts.

"The house is vermin free," Helena assured Jacey. "It's safe to come in. Don't worry about taking your boots off," she said glancing at Jacey's feet. "I have to do the floors later anyway." She paused. "Hellsbelles, are those Jimmy Choo's?"

"Uh-huh," Jacey said proudly. "I bought them myself after I got paid from a modeling job."

Ellie rolled her eyes.

Helen was impressed that the girl had a job.

Helena wanted a pair of boots just like them.

Jacey stepped into the house and suddenly felt an uncomfortable shiver run through her body. It was cold in the house and it wasn't just the temperature. "Should I come back another time?" she asked. "I get a sense things are a little crazy right now."

"She's sensitive," Helena whispered in Helen's ear.

Helen forced a smile. It wouldn't take a genius to sense there was tension in the room. All three LaRose women were standing with their hands folded defiantly over their chests.

"I didn't mean to interrupt anything, but I just wondered if Ellie would like to come to church with me this morning?" Jacey asked.

"Church?" Helen questioned.

"Yes, that's right," Jacey answered. "I'm headed over to St. Mary's for the early mass. I thought maybe we could go and then grab a bite together afterwards down at the Topaz."

"I'm in," Ellie said suddenly. Right now, any excuse to get out of the house was looking pretty good, even if it meant spending an hour or two with Jacey and a priest.

"What?" Helen replied.

"I said I was in," she answered back. "You guys don't mind if I go out with Jacey for a while? I mean, you didn't make any plans for us or anything?" she asked, knowing damn well that the re-arranging of the front porch furniture could wait.

"Jacey, stay here," Ellie said running from the room. "I'll be five minutes, I swear. I've just got to get dressed."

"Wonders never cease," Helen said under her breath.

"Hello," Jacey said, extending her hand to her. "I'm Jacey Sumner. You must be Ellie's mother."

"I am," Helen said, somewhat taken aback by the handshake.

"And you must be Helena LaRose," Jacey said, turning her attention to the matriarch. "You really helped David Kim's psoriasis. He's my guardian. He thinks you're awesome." She offered her hand to Helena as well.

"It's nice to meet you, Jacey. Tell him I've ordered in more of the salve to get him through the winter," Helena said, holding onto Jacey's hand for a moment longer than one normally does. She looked into the girl's green eyes and smiled.

"I will, Mrs. LaRose," Jacey said, nodding and taking her hand back.

"Church... is that a regular thing for you, Jacey? I don't think it's a priority for most teenaged girls," Helen asked suspiciously. For all she knew, this girl could be whisking Ellie off to God knows where.

Jacey shrugged. "I do like to sleep in most Sundays but with all the craziness in town right now, it's kind of hard. I don't mean to be disrespectful, but who can't use a few angels on your side to cover your ass, erm, I mean bases? You never know, right?"

"Well, we can't argue with that, can we Helen?" Helena said, pulling her daughter closer to her side. She tugged at Helen's sleeve. "Seriously. Sensitive."

"Seriously fruity-loopy," Helen whispered back.

"Don't worry about Ellie, I'll make sure she's fine," Jacey promised.

"I feel better already," Helen said sarcastically, not certain herself if the tone was directed at Helena or Jacey or both.

Helena gave her daughter a quick jab to the ribs.

"Thank you, Jacey. We'd appreciate that." Helena said. "Ellie doesn't know much of the town yet. It's very nice of you to offer to show her around."

Ellie re-appeared in the kitchen. She had thrown on her jeans and under her jacket was a sweater she had found in her grandmother's closet. Helena could see a hint of black lace below Ellie's coat collar.

Helena tilted her head. "Is that my Lacroix sweater under your coat?"

"Smart girl. She's up against the Choo's," Helen reminded her mother.

"Bye," Ellie said, running from the house before anyone had a chance to tell her to go back upstairs and change.

"It was nice meeting you," Jacey said cheerily as the door slammed behind the teenagers.

"If she wrecks that sweater, you're paying for it," Helena remarked, taking her finger and poking Helen on her left shoulder.

"Good luck with that. I'm an unemployed gravedigger, remember?"

"I could kill her. That would solve both our problems."

"Now you know what I go through every day," Helen sighed. "I'm going upstairs. I have a headache."

Helena let her go. She needed time to think. Although she wasn't about to let on, she too, was troubled by the revelation that Ellie's dream had involved a young vampire.

"I warned you," she said icily.

Chapter 17

"Okay, where are we really going?" Ellie asked before she even got to the driveway. "Are you driving us to the city to go shopping? Because I could really use some new gloves." She held up her left hand and showed Jacey where her fingers were poking out from the holes in the tips of the ones she was wearing.

"I told you," Jacey said. "You're going to church."

"Why?" Ellie asked. "I mean, I don't mean to insult you or anything, but I thought you were just saying that so I could get out of the house."

Jacey looked at her with a puzzled expression. "Do you have to lie to get out of the house?"

"No," Ellie said honestly. "Let's just say that you came over at a really good time. We were having a family discussion that I didn't want to be a part of."

"They seemed nice to me," Jacey shrugged. She looked at the heavy cloud cover in the sky. "I don't like to drive when the weather gets crazy like this, so I left my car at home. The walk will do you good."

"Me good?" Ellie wondered what she meant by that? It wasn't like she was overweight or anything. Maybe a pound or two by Jacey standards, but not from the viewpoint of the rest of society. "What do you mean by that?" she questioned.

"Well…" Jacey hesitated.

The snow was really starting to come down, making the thought of going for a walk even less attractive to Ellie. "Maybe this isn't such a good idea after all, Jacey. Do you want to go back inside and watch a video or something? Nan had Ryan put a DVD player in my room. I don't know how good her collection is, but there has to be something we could watch."

Jacey pulled some balm out of her pocket and applied it to her lips. "Right. Listen El, we have a little problem. This is how it is. I'm the one who had to lie. I'm stuck next door, looking after Stan, but I really need you to go to church for me." She reached back into the pocket, pulled out a piece of paper and handed it to Ellie. "Here's a list of things I want you to bring back to me."

"What?" Ellie asked, looking at the list. "Are you serious?"

Jacey's expression said she was. "Is there a problem?"

"Uh, yeah there's a problem. Do you really want me to go to church alone and get these... things? I distinctly remember you saying 'come-with-me'. I don't even know where the church is. That would be the first problem."

Ellie watched Jacey scowl. The fact that those flawless features could even form a scowl indicated to Ellie that for whatever reason, Jacey was bound and determined to make this happen. Ellie decided to humor her and look at the list again.

"Incense," she noted, her eyes scanning down the paper. "I'm pretty sure Helena's got some in her office. It's probably like a stethoscope to a naturopath. But the second thing, the consecrated ground, that might be a toughie. And is there anything in particular I need to put the third item, the holy water, into? Or can I just put it in an empty water bottle? I don't know if that will wreck it. Like, what do I do if a plastic number five container breaks it down into cancerous Satan particles?"

"Brilliant. You're mocking me," Jacey sighed.

"Well, it's not like you want to borrow a pair of earrings," Ellie tried to reason. "What do you need these things for anyway? Are you and Stan planning on playing voodoo warrior or something?"

"Very funny," Jacey said, her head shaking with disapproval. She grabbed Ellie by her coat collar and pulled her within inches of her face. Suddenly, Jacey's perfect hair, perfect smile and perfect voice distorted, as if she were possessed. "Listen to me, Ellie LaRose. Evil lurks. It lurks here in Troy. We need to take precautions to protect ourselves," Jacey insisted, taking her hands off Ellie and placing her fingers on the silver cross around her own neck instead.

"Jacey?" Ellie questioned, taking a step back from her.

"Sorry about that," Jacey replied, tilting her head in a '*look at me, I'm a cheerleader*' fashion that told Ellie that Jacey was her annoying perky self once again. "Hormones."

"Jacey, what's going on?" Ellie asked. "You just did a total banshee on me."

"I'm sorry," she said. "It's just that with all these murders, I'm a little on edge."

That's right, Ellie remembered. Nan had said murders, plural. Only they never got around to telling her about the other one... or ones. But Jacey seemed to know all about them. Interesting, she thought. "But... the incense, consecrated ground and holy water? What's up with that? Is your necklace not doing it for you anymore?"

"It's like I told your mom, I just feel better with a few religious things around me. They keep me grounded," Jacey replied, fingering her silver cross necklace lovingly. "My mother gave this to me before she went away. It's the last thing she ever gave me, and pretty much all I have left from my life back in England with her and my father. That's why I always wear it."

"Sorry," Ellie offered. "I thought..."

"What?" Jacey laughed. "Did you think I was a devout little Catholic schoolgirl or summat? All knee socks and hail Mary's?"

"Kind of," Ellie admitted, taking a closer look at Jacey's necklace. It was a heavy piece that looked a little out of place on Jacey's delicate neck. The ornate edges of the cross hinted that it might have been an antique passed down through the generations. It looked like it was pure sterling silver, as it had begun to tarnish a bit on the bottom. "It's very pretty, really."

"I know Ryan thinks I'm a religious freak for wearing it, but when Tom starts to pressure me about sex, I just dangle it in front of him and he backs off pretty quick. Subject closed." She looked Ellie straight in the eye. "That's our little secret, okay?"

"Okay," Ellie said. "Do you love Tom?"

The words were out of her mouth before she realized what she had been pondering in her head the past few minutes had been verbalized. If Jacey hadn't picked up that she had feelings for Tom before, she probably would now.

The question didn't seem to faze Jacey. Or if it did, she wasn't letting it show.

"I don't know. I'm kind of messed up about him," Jacey replied. "Sometimes I think I do and sometimes I want to strangle him. He can be a right PBP."

"PBP?" Ellie asked.

"Pretty-boy prat," Jacey explained. "Why? Does our Tommy make you want to girlie wank?" It was her turn to be blunt.

"Girlie wank?"

"Girlie jerk-off, as Ryan would say."

"Oh," Ellie said, now getting the reference. "He's pretty cute. But I don't know either. You're probably not supposed to love someone you've known for less than a week." She smiled at Jacey. "Wank, maybe though."

"Too true." Jacey laughed.

"Unless Tom is your boyfriend... because then, you know, I wouldn't do that to you," Ellie attested.

"You wouldn't admit it."

"No, really," Ellie insisted. "I wouldn't do it." That would be the ultimate betrayal, Ellie thought. She had watched enough movies to know that no good ever came out of stealing your girlfriend's boyfriend. Friends were supposed to be loyal. That's why you called them friends.

"Ellie," Jacey began to explain, "there's summat you should know. Tom is every girl's boyfriend. At least he thinks he is. And tries to be. So, the official answer from me, is no. He is not my boyfriend. So feel free to do whatever you want with him."

Ellie smiled her own perfect smile and giggled in her own '*look at me, I'm a cheerleader*' fashion that she would never admit she had. "Thanks for that. I'm kind of messed up myself. I want a boyfriend, but I don't. Do you know what I mean?"

"Totally," Jacey agreed. "You should be able to rent them for a while. Maybe they could come with a video and popcorn."

"And no late fees," Ellie added.

"And you return them after a week."

"But you'd never buy a used one," Ellie laughed.

"Ew!" Jacey giggled.

The bonding effort was not lost on Ellie. It made her feel a little bit better about moving to Troy. If Jacey could make an effort to be friendly, she thought, maybe it wouldn't hurt to try to do the same. Maybe she could cut this fashion doll standing before her some slack. Maybe Jacey would be able to help her maneuver through the dating minefield. She seemed to have some experience at it.

"What's up with the groping?" Ellie asked. "Why do they always want to grope you? I'm almost sorry I have boobs. I wouldn't mind so much if there was a little conversation first."

"Did Tom try to grope you? He did, didn't he? That is so his move." Jacey laughed harder. "Did you like groping him?"

"I didn't," Ellie protested. "I mean, I didn't grope him." Seriously, Ellie wondered, what wasn't Jacey getting about the betrayal business? How many times was she going to have to tell her?

"Why not?" Jacey asked. She saw Ellie's face begin to redden. "I've hit a nerve there, haven't I, El?"

"What do you think about Ryan?" Ellie asked, changing the subject. She wasn't ready to share all her intimate secrets about boys with Jacey. In Ellie's mind, you shared those kinds of things with people you had known for a long time and trusted. Right now, Jacey was neither of those things.

"I don't really think about Ryan," Jacey admitted honestly. "He's not my type. He's too much of an action man for my liking. Besides, he always calls me names. Like Jace-o-matic."

"I've never heard him call you that," Ellie offered.

"Have you heard him call me Spacey-Jacey?"

Ellie suddenly felt a little guilty.

"Do *you* think about Ryan?" Jacey asked. "You know, in that kind of way?"

"He was nice to me, when we walked home from the game the other night. Nicer than Tom. But he's not really my type either," Ellie replied. "I mean, I like him but... I think he might be in love with my grandmother."

Jacey laughed. "That sounds like Ryan. Do you think he did it?"

"Did what?" Ellie asked.

Jacey's smile vanished from her face. It was evident that Ellie was the only person in Troy who hadn't heard the news. "They didn't tell you, did they? He's in jail. He was caught last night with Brooke Quinlan's body in his arms. He was down at Stillman's Creek, by Tara's place. His mother Betty's in the psyche ward. That's why I'm watching Stan."

Ellie threw her hands up over her mouth. "Oh my God, no. I guess they forgot to tell me that part."

Tears began to well up in Ellie's eyes. If Ryan had been found with the body of the little girl down by the creek, it could only mean one thing. He had believed her about her dream and he had gone there to check out her story. Part of her felt vindicated and part of her was horrified. Whatever had happened to him was partially her fault. "Why didn't they tell me?" she wondered aloud.

Jacey reached out for Ellie's gloved hand. "I don't know, Ellie. Maybe they were trying to protect you."

"My Mom and Nan, they were mad at me for not telling them about the vampire that was in my stupid dream, and then they go and not tell me about Ryan. I hate them right now. I hate the Helens." She turned and pulled Jacey by her pea-coat collar to within inches of her own face. "Ryan did not do this. I know it."

"Ellie, let go!"

She released Jacey. "Sorry. Hormones."

"Did they tell you about Kevin Clark?" Jacey asked, taking her own step back from Ellie.

"Who?"

"He hangs around with Stan Lachey. The one who's had a few too many bacon butties." She translated by using her hand to indicate a large belly.

Ellie remembered the tubby kid who was with them on Halloween night. His name was Kevin. "I think I know who you mean. What about him?"

"He was found at Tara's place," Jacey told her. "I gave her a ride home last night, but I left her at the end of the driveway, thank God. When she went around to the back of her house she found her dad under an old fridge and there was Kevin, stuffed inside it."

"What?" Ellie asked, unable to fully comprehend what Jacey had just told her.

"I know. It's horrid," Jacey shuddered. Her eyes were like saucers as she told Ellie the rest of the story she had heard from Tara. "I don't know whether Ryan is innocent, or if he killed one of them or both of them or what. He might be a mass murderer," she concluded.

"I can't believe Kevin is dead too," Ellie replied, shaking her head in disbelief. "Ryan didn't do it. He couldn't have."

"How can you be so sure?" Jacey asked her. "He gets pretty rough out there on the football field. Maybe he finally snapped."

"I just know it in my heart," Ellie tried to explain without going into great detail.

"But isn't that like the love thing?" Jacey asked. "Can you really know it in your heart if you've only known him less than a week?"

Ellie remained silent. If Jacey had known Ryan a lot longer than a week, and she had doubts, could she really be Ryan's judge and jury based on what she saw in her own crazy nightmare?

"Did you say you dreamt about a vampire?" Jacey asked.

"Just forget it," Ellie said. "Can we just forget the whole thing... Ryan and Tom and the dream and the church, and go inside? I'll help you watch Stan. I'm freezing out here."

"Look, if you don't want to talk about it right now, that's okay, but I won't forget it," Jacey said. "I'll help you with your little problem if you want me to."

"How can you help me, Jacey?" Ellie said with exasperation. "I don't even know what the hell I'm dealing with."

Jacey put her arm around Ellie's shoulder and looked directly into her eyes. "I can help you because I had a weird dream myself last night. I dreamt I had to go to church today and get three things..."

Chapter 18

Helena went up to the third floor and knocked gently on Helen's closed bedroom door. She needed to try and smooth things over to keep peace in her household. She knew full well that Helen's stubbornness would prevent her from being the one to initiate the healing process herself.

"Come in," she heard Helen answer from behind the door.

"Were you sleeping?" Helena asked, poking her head around to try to get a feel for Helen's mood before she entered the room.

"It's hard to sleep in the day with these damn flowers on the wall," Helen answered. She knew it was only in her imagination, but when she had a headache, the six-inch peonies seemed to grow bigger with every throb of her head. "Would you be terribly upset if, while I'm at the home renovation store getting you a new door and a set of coffee mugs, I took a look at their wallpaper selection as well?"

"Does that mean you're planning on staying for a while?" Helena asked, noting that Helen was out of bed and busy unpacking her suitcase.

"It means I might be thinking about it," Helen replied. She took some socks and placed them in the top drawer of the big oak dresser in the room. Ever since she was a child, Helen had reserved the top drawer for her socks. Helen liked routine.

Helena stood by the edge of the bed and adjusted her robe. "It's draughty in here. I never noticed that before. I suppose you should pick up some window sealer while you're out. If you think you can carry a tube of silicone, wallpaper, mugs... and a door, that is."

Helen forced a shy smile. "Does this mean we're good?"

"I'll let you know after you answer one more question," Helena replied. "You never did answer Ellie. How did you know about the vampire in her dream? Spill the beans, Helen. I can always hit you up with truth serum when you're sleeping tonight. I keep hypodermics in my office for just such an emergency."

Helen turned and looked out the window. She could see Ellie and Jacey standing in the driveway, just talking. It was nothing more than a typical afternoon for a couple of teenaged girls, but somehow Helen found their actions unsettling. What if Ellie really was in danger? She decided to tell Helena about her own visitor last night. Just to get a second opinion. "Willie told me."

Helena was shocked. "Willie? You were talking to Willie? You? When?"

"He came into the bathroom when I was taking a bath and you were otherwise occupied, thank you very much. He told me about the vampire, and he told me there had been a second murder."

"Kevin Clark," Helena nodded. "Such a tragedy. The town is going to be in mourning for quite a while, I'm afraid. What else did Willie tell you?"

"He told me Ellie was in danger. That's why I went storming into your room last night. I heard a moan and I thought maybe he had changed his mind and went after you instead. Seriously, I thought you were in pain."

"Well, I'm not as flexible as I once was," Helena sighed. "And for future reference, I can handle Willie just fine on my own. Did he tell you why Ellie was in danger?"

"He said he couldn't tell me. I'm supposed to just figure that out, I guess."

"You guess? You can do more than guess."

"No I can't."

Helena stared obstinately at her daughter. Helen was incredibly stubborn, and had learned to turn her back on her calling no matter how loudly she was beckoned. But this time, it involved her own flesh and blood, and Helena found Helen's reluctance to get involved more than a little disturbing. "You mean that you won't," Helena argued. "My God, Helen. If Willie has come here twice in one week, something is definitely up. It's not like he just drops in for dinner. Did he tell you that Ryan Lachey is in jail?"

"Oh, that's a shame," she answered sarcastically.

"He's in jail for murdering Brooke Quinlan. Have you ever heard of anything so ridiculous? It's all because Tara Wildman's father found him with the little girl's dead body in his arms. If you ask me, it's nothing more than circumstantial evidence. I haven't killed every dead body that I've held in my arms."

"You're maybe not the best example," Helen replied. "Wildman… he was that farmer at the search party gathering, right? He said that Ryan was a pervert, and probably had something to do with the little girl's disappearance. Probably, allegedly, the meanings are strikingly similar. Did you notice at the football game that Ryan is twice the size of the other players? Who knows what chemicals he's taking to bulk up? It's a well-documented fact that steroids lead to aggressive behavior. I think it's a bonus that he's behind bars. At least now I won't have to worry about that testosterone-fueled maniac coming after Ellie."

"Did Willie tell you that? Because if Willie knows Ryan is in jail, then he also knows Ryan is no danger to Ellie."

"It's not just murder I think the 'boy next door' is capable of," she said, sitting back down on the bed. "I'd recognize that sex-crazed look in his eyes anywhere."

"I'm going to have to get you laid, Helen."

"There you go again. Did you have to say that? Just when we were getting good?"

"I apologize. That was uncalled for," Helena admitted. "My life is an open book, and I need to be reminded from time to time that other people aren't so inclined."

"Then tell me about Mrs. Harbinger," Helen replied, "if you've got nothing to hide between your covers."

"Not now," Helena said tersely.

Helen put her hands defiantly on her hips. "I'm waiting…"

"Oh all right," Helena sighed, and sat down on the edge of the bed beside her daughter. "About a year ago, Marita Harbinger, your former babysitter, rented the house on the other side of the Lachey's. She hadn't changed much from the sweet young thing that appeared on my doorstep years ago, when Ellie was younger. Did I ever tell you the story of how she came to arrive on your own doorstep?"

"Not that I recall," Helen answered. "She just kind of showed up."

"Exactly. She showed up at my old house one day telling a tale of woe about how some man had a lengthy affair with her but ended it all rather abruptly. He kicked Marita and her son out of the house they were living in and took up with an even younger woman. This just goes to show you there is always someone younger. Anyway, she had no job and no place to live. Sound familiar? I felt sorry for her, so I hired her as a nanny for you. You were struggling yourself at the time, trying to raise a toddler on your own. I was as surprised as you were when she suddenly up and vanished. Easy come, easy go, I guess. You had a new man on the scene shortly after that so you managed."

Helena paused, hoping that would be enough of a story to appease Helen. Mrs. Harbinger was better left dead and buried. The less anyone remembered about that day the better.

"And..."

"And nothing," Helena sighed, standing up and making an effort to leave the room. "I never thought about her again until she turned up in Troy the summer before last. Imagine that, after all these years."

"Okay, so it wouldn't be the first place I'd move to," Helen began to say then realized it was exactly what she had done.

"I thought it was a little strange too," Helena admitted. "Obviously we didn't need a babysitter anymore. I told her that. End of story."

"Hang on," Helen insisted, "if that's all that happened, why was Betty Lachey going on about her the other day?"

Helena turned around and dropped her butt back down on the bed. There would be no deflecting the Mrs. Harbinger story, no matter how badly she wanted to. Helen was in one of her poke, poke, poke moods and wasn't about to stop.

"Well... it was the Fourth of July and I was having a quiet neighborhood party out in the backyard. I thought it would be a good chance for people to get to know Marita. But you know how it goes, there's always one uninvited guest who gets drunk and decides to perform an exorcism. It happens every time they have an occult marathon on cable."

"An exorcism?"

"We tried to humor him and it was all fine and dandy until Marita imploded. I swear, we thought we had all her pieces cleaned up, but Betty found some pretty big chunks of her in the lawn the next morning. I think that's when she really started to hate me."

"So… this uninvited guest of yours watches a few hours of cable, attempts a centuries old religious rite and something actually happens?"

"I know! I was as surprised as you are. His Latin wasn't very good. Maybe that's why she didn't just turn to ash like she was supposed to. You get one thing wrong with one of those spells… call it what you want, but that's what they are… and all hell breaks loose." She fiddled with the bottom of her robe, picking at an imaginary piece of fluff. It was easier not to have to look at Helen right now.

"You mean she really was possessed? That surprises me. I mean, she was a little loud and cranky when I knew her, but I there was no sign of any head spinning or anything."

"Noooo," Helena hesitated. "She would have had to have been taken over bodily to be possessed." She made the sign of the cross across her chest. "Our little Marita was the real deal from day one."

"You mean you sent a full-fledged demon over to take care of my child?"

"I didn't know she was a demon then," Helena insisted. "They're getting better at assimilating here on earth all the time."

"Tell me more," Helen said, leaning in closer towards her mother. "I'm intrigued. Obviously Ellie and I survived her employment despite the lack of resume research you did."

Helena thought back. They had been in the middle of a heat wave, and the temperature had been almost unbearable. The air conditioner had decided to quit working earlier in the day, probably due to over exertion, making an indoor celebration impossible. As the Fourth of July wasn't one of those occasions you could postpone, she had tried to make the best of it by moving the festivities outside.

"It was crazy. Roy was just putting the finishing touches on my guest cottage, but it was so hot that we were seriously thinking of opening up the fire hydrant out front and running through it like a bunch of kids."

"You have a guest cottage?"

"You've seen it out back. It's my office now. Don't look so excited, you can't move in there."

Helen pouted momentarily. "So... did Roy see the exorcism happen?"

"Unfortunately, yes. Marita was heading back to her house to refill her punchbowl... she made a killer margarita, let me tell you... when the idiot guest started chanting. So unfortunately, Marita blew apart in front of Roy. And Betty. And Mr. Wagner."

"Betty saw the whole thing? Not just the aftermath?"

Helena nodded her head. "I've never seen anything quite like it, and I'm certain Betty Lachey hadn't either. It was an ugly night."

"What about Roy?"

"Roy had seen bodies blowup before, in the war," Helena answered. "But I don't think he was expecting it to happen here, in the middle of Mr. Wagner's banjo tribute to Buck Owens and Roy Clark."

"And Mr. Wagner?"

"Mr. Wagner was a big horror film fan. I think he secretly enjoyed it."

Helen slapped her hand to her head. This was the most ridiculous story that had come out of her mother's mouth in quite some time.

"That's when I had to tell Roy about our little family secret. It put him in an awful position. In order to get Betty off our scent, he was forced to come up with a story that Marita was really a terrorist and had strapped a bomb to herself. Luckily for us, Betty likes her booze and doesn't always have a sober sense of reality to begin with."

"Roy's story is a bit far-fetched, even for this weird little town."

"I know," Helena shrugged. "But his story worked. At least it did for Betty. Mr. Wagner, not so much. That's when I fell in love with him. Roy, I mean. Any man who can come up with a plausible explanation for something supernatural is a keeper."

"I wouldn't know."

"Someday you will Helen," she said, patting her daughter's knee. "Trust me on that one. And before you ask, Roy is single. He was married once, but has been divorced for several years. And I'm not expecting any more explosions, in case you were wondering."

Helen let out a deep sigh. About sixteen years ago, she thought she had found her own special someone, Ellie's father.

"You're lucky you found Roy," Helen told her mother. "I don't know if I can ever love like that again. I dabble in affairs from time to time, thinking it's love, but ever since..."

She couldn't finish the sentence. Tears welled up in her eyes and before she knew it, she was sobbing uncontrollably.

Helena placed her arms around her daughter. "You have to let go of the past, Helen."

"But, I killed the only man I ever loved."

"Are you ready to tell me about it?" Helena asked, handing her a tissue from the nightstand. "I'll just sit quiet and listen."

"We were in St. Paul de Vence. I was called in as an historical consultant on a small excavation of a site built during the Renaissance period. The building had been damaged by a car missing a left hand turn on the narrow roadway and it had to be completely torn down. It had historical significance, but they couldn't save it structurally. While I was there, I unearthed a tiny clay pot, no bigger than a pill box. It suddenly got really heavy, like it was trying to get me to drop it back into the ground. But you know me, stubborn has hell, I refused to do what it wanted."

Helena smiled. There was no way in hell Helen could have left it alone. When she was a child, the presents could never go under the tree until Christmas Eve for the same reason.

"I opened the little lid. Big mistake. It unleashed a wraith rider who said he would spare my life, if I gave up something I loved. Well, you know I wasn't crazy about this vision thing to begin with, so that's what I gave up. Or so I thought. Until later that evening when I had a vision about Ellie's father's death. Two days later, it happened just like the vision said it would. So you see, I still had the visions, but I no longer had Ellie's father. The wraith knew my true love and took it. That's why I'm so afraid to dabble in that power again. I can't bear the thought of losing someone else."

"I'm sorry. I have to interrupt. You didn't try to kill it, did you?" Helena asked. "The wraith rider? Because if you do it wrong they split in two and then you have bigger problems. I hope you'll call me if you ever have to do that."

Helen nodded. "Don't worry, I have learned my lesson with wraith riders. I can still see their image to this day. They are nasty beasts, even if they do look human."

"It's another job best left to the professionals."

"Maybe that's why I felt the need to leave Tony. I don't like to kill things. He kills things every day. I try to live my life like I'm normal. What's so wrong with that?"

"We may not have a choice." Helena said, hugging her daughter tightly. "We've all done things we're not proud of. Conscience is an unfortunate part of the human side of us. It can weigh heavily on our minds."

As she attempted to release Helen she felt her daughter shake in her arms. The tremble strengthened, and for a moment Helena thought her daughter was having petit-mal seizure.

"Take a deep breath, Helen. It's over now," she said reassuringly, as Helen's body began to calm.

"It's far from over," Helen mumbled as she tried to regain her composure. Beads of sweat were forming on her brow even though she felt her internal temperature drop by about ten degrees.

"Just be quiet for a few moments," Helena instructed.

"If I don't tell you now," Helen sobbed, "I'll never have the courage to tell you. I need you to call Roy."

"Seriously Helen, you can apologize later," her mother assured her.

"No, I just had a vision. I couldn't stop it. There's been an accident. About six miles out of town. The section where there's the S-curve atop the first ridge by the ski hill. Tell him to go there and to look down to the right."

"What did you see?" Helena asked patiently.

"A woman," Helen whispered. "She's in the front passenger seat of the vehicle next to a man. He didn't have his seat-belt on. He's gone through the front windshield," she paused. "Tell Roy there's no point rushing to get to them."

Helena's face grew grim.

"Is it a white truck, Helen? Is it the Clark's? Roy said they were having trouble locating Kevin's parents."

Helen nodded. "I think so."

"Hellsbelles," Helena said. "You just had a pretty strong premonition attack for something that doesn't involve our own family." She paused. "Maybe it does. Maybe it's all connected to this situation of Ellie's."

"I don't know," Helen answered honestly. "But since we're not keeping secrets, there's something else you need to know about Ellie's situation. Willie says it's going to happen whether I like it or not. He said that you were going to have to help me stop it, and even then we might not be able to."

"Willie's on crack," Helena said emphatically. "Is that why you were so crazy this morning? Because of him?"

"You don't understand. He said I had to watch Ellie. Carefully. And what did I just do? I let her go out the door with a future Ms. Plaything-of-the-Month, who wears expensive designer boots in the middle of a snowstorm."

"You really have been tuning it out," Helena said. "I wasn't kidding when I said Jacey was sensitive. A sensitive. As in, someone who is perceptive without being psychic. That's why she shook our hands. I felt her tapping into my sensory nerves. Well, attempting to anyway. She didn't quite have the technique down, but she sure as hell was trying."

"I thought she wanted to steal my ring," Helen admitted, spinning her old engagement ring around so the diamond faced her palm. She'd need a ring to replace it when she divorced Tony. She couldn't stand the feeling of her finger without the weight of a ring.

"Well, unless you know something I don't," Helena began, "Ellie is safe enough for the time being. Nightfall might be a whole other story."

"So what are we supposed to do?" Helen asked.

"You go do what you have to do, and I'll do what I have to do," she said rising from the bed. "I'm glad we had a chance to sit down and talk about this, Helen. I'm not here to judge you. I'm here to help. I'm very sorry about what happened between you and the ring wraith and Ellie's dad. But please consider giving your talents another chance. For Ellie's sake."

"I will," Helen said as her mother left the room. "And thanks."

"That woman is so gullible," Helena thought to herself as she left the room. "It's like shooting fish from a barrel."

Behind the closed door, Helen was smiling smugly to herself.

"Nice try, Mother. I've got you hook, line and sinker," she laughed.

Chapter 19

*T*om looked at the stack of winter supplies that had come in over the weekend and grimaced. This was going to take forever, and today he didn't have forever to spend at the hardware store.

"Nobody's ever prepared for the first big snowfall of the year," his father said, and as Tom looked out the storefront window he could see that his father was right with his weather prediction. The snow was no longer melting as it hit the ground. It was sticking, and cars were beginning to slide uncontrollably down the hill.

"Tom," his father yelled as he watched his son drag the last salt bag across the floor, "I told you half an hour ago to use the handcart."

Tom shrugged. "Sorry, Dad. Do you want me to bring the shovels up from the basement?"

"I told you to do that first," his father sighed. "Look, obviously you've got something else on your mind today. Just go and take care of it. I'll finish up here."

"Do I still get paid for four hours?" Tom asked.

"Get out of here," his father answered.

While this had seemed like the answer to Tom's prayers at the time, he soon realized that it meant he had no excuse not to go over to Ryan's house. The walk, a walk he had taken countless times in his life, seemed endless, his feet seemingly heavier with each step he took. Dread. To anticipate with alarm, distaste or reluctance. That pretty much summed it up.

He stopped at the foot of the first driveway past the corner of Maple and Elm, and sighed. Ellie and Jacey were outside, standing on separate ends of the "y" formation the shared driveway divided into, just past the two house structures. Ellie was on the right and Jacey was on the left. Neither of them looked particularly happy to see him.

He was dead meat and he knew it.

"I'm going to have to sweet them," he said to himself. "Give them a little of the Tom-boy mojo."

He took his time strolling up the driveway, with a calculated swagger that he knew would say "I am the man and I am in control." At least that was the plan before he hit a slippery patch of wet snow on the driveway and fell flat on his ass.

"What the hell is he doing?" Ellie asked, moving closer towards Jacey. Part of her wanted to rush down the driveway to see if Tom was all right, but a bigger part of her wanted to clap her hands in delight and laugh herself silly. She settled for a self-serving smirk.

"He's trying to convince us that we want him," Jacey replied. "Watch, about half way up the driveway he'll stop, put his hands on his hips like this, smile, drop his voice down an octave and say, 'uh, Ladies'."

"For real?"

"Sha..." Jacey insisted, as she reached down to the ground and took some of the wet snow that had fallen on the ground into her gloved hand, where she easily pressed it into a compact, hard ball.

Tom studied the girls from his new vantage point on the ground. They were like two alien robo-babes. They displayed no facial emotion, but their bodies were poised to kill at the slightest hint of his vulnerability.

He stood up and smiled warily.

"Uh, ladies?" he asked, his voice rising, as he tried to shake the snow from his lower extremities. He was surprised that he had fallen. His white cross-trainers normally had good traction in wet snow, but they were no match for his legs, quivering with anxiety having seen the girls.

Ellie smiled at Jacey. "You were right."

"Erm, technically no," Jacey admitted, tossing the snowball from one hand to another. "I went for a statement. He gave us a question. And the voice went up. Two marks off for the British contestant." She made certain the snowball was as packed as hard as she could.

"Was it just me, or did he sound a little pre-pubescent?" Ellie asked rhetorically. She tried not to notice the imprint the wet snow had left on his ass as he turned briefly to wipe it off. As wet asses go, Tom's was pretty good.

"Right then, Mr. Williams," Jacey began, tossing the snowball directly towards Tom's head, missing him by a mile. "What have you got to say for yourself? I hear you've been putting the moves on my bezzie here." She brushed the traces of snow from the palm of her gloves and sunk her hands deep into the pockets of her coat to keep them warm.

"Well," Tom pleaded. "You can't blame a guy for trying."

"Don't be so sure," Ellie answered back, forcing her voice to sound as ominous as she could possibly make it. He did look sincere though, and for a moment she wondered if she was being too harsh with him.

"Look, I'm sorry," Tom sighed. "I'd like to try to make it up to you two lovely ladies. Just tell me what it'll take."

"Actually, Tommy-luv," Jacey began. "If you really mean it, and you're not just saying that to try to wiggle your way back into our hearts, you can do us a huge favor and watch Stan. Ellie and I need to go run a little errand downtown and Betty isn't home yet. I'm supposed to be babysitting, but like I said, there's summat we just have to do. We'd be ever so grateful if you could take care of him for me, just for a little while."

Tom smiled. Jacey's idea didn't seem like such a bad one to him. He could take Stan out of the house and down to the jail where Ryan and the cops could deal with the situation themselves. That would allow him to wash his hands of the whole mind-numbing problem. Sure, jail wasn't the best place for Stan, but the kid had to learn the cruel facts of life sometime, and now was as good a time as any. Once Stan was out of the house, it would then give him time to be alone with Jacey or Ellie, whoever caved first. The plan made for a perfect afternoon if it weren't for that one nagging thing he had promised Ryan he would do.

"Did you hear me?" Jacey asked. "Because you're staring at us like a deer in a headlight or summat."

"No, I heard you," Tom nodded, still scheming. "Maybe we can make a deal. I don't suppose you gals know anything about the art of... vampire killing? I don't have my laptop with me, and I'm thinking that maybe you could do me a favor and hit the library along the way and pick up some resource materials for me? I need something like 'How to Kill Immortals in Five Easy Steps'. It could be either a DVD or book, I'm not that picky. You would really be helping me out. I need them, and it's not like I can drag Stan along with me into the occult section."

"Vampire killing?" Ellie said incredulously, his words piercing her like the tip of a sharp needle. "Is that supposed to be funny? Do you know what you can do, Tom Williams? You can go straight to hell."

"It doesn't have to be the occult section," Tom offered feebly. "You could find Stoker in the classics."

Ellie turned her back to the two of them, trying to hold back the tears she felt welling in her eyes. There was nothing Ellie wanted more right now than for her mother to poke her head out the window and demand she come back inside to pack because they were going back to the city to live with Tony. He might have been god-awful hairy, but he wasn't crazy. This whole town on the other hand, no matter how athletic, or cute, or beautiful it appeared upon first glance... was totally freaking crazy.

"Okay, okay," Tom tried to explain, "Ellie, Ryan told me to tell you he saw your vampire."

"Really?" Ellie asked, not certain whether Tom was just trying to appease her.

"Yes," Tom continued, "and I know it sounds totally bogus, but he thinks that the dude is out to get Stan and the only thing that will save the twerp is if Ryan figures out how to kill the vampire before it kills Stan. So, I was thinking maybe you, Ellie, could kind of lead me in the right direction, having had some experience in close encounters of the fangtastic kind."

"You're a right plonker, Tom Williams!" Jacey retorted indignantly. "How can you mock Ellie when she's standing right here?"

"I'm not," Tom insisted. "Ryan really wants to know how to do it, and he can't exactly look it up himself right now." He jerked his head to the left a couple of times, motioning for Jacey to shut-up.

"Oh, and why is that?" Ellie demanded, turning back to face Tom. "Can't Mr. Superstar navigate his way through an ISBN catalogue?"

Tom clasped his hands together, raised them and placed them momentarily on top of his head, a mannerism he often did when he was verbally frustrated.

"Ellie, I swear to you," he said, releasing his head grip and crossing his heart with his right hand, "I am not making fun of you. You know Ryan's in jail, right?"

"Yes, we know all about it." Jacey said. "The girl. The pond. We know. It's all part of why we need you to stay here while we go and do a little shopping," she sighed. She was getting impatient and Tom's reluctance to shut up and co-operate was taking its toll on her. A feeling deep within her was telling her she needed to finish her scavenger hunt before nightfall, and nightfall came early this time of year.

"You know what? Forget that." Tom pleaded, clearly frustrated. "Why don't we all just stay here? We'll get Stan to fire up the Lachey's computer and we can go online and figure this out together. Jacey, you could go online and buy whatever you need and Ellie... you can do whatever you want to do so long as you stop being mad at me."

"So, it's okay if *I'm* still mad at you?" Jacey retorted.

"No. I that's not what I meant," Tom pleaded. "Ladies, please. You're doing my head in."

Jacey shook her head and started to move towards him. "Sorry, sweetie. Ellie and I need to go right now because," she sighed, moving close enough to Tom that he could smell her sweet scented cologne in the crisp winter air, "when we get through with our little errand, we will have what we need to come back and make you... one... happy... man."

"You will?" Tom questioned. Although the thought of Jacey and Ellie making him happy more than appealed to him, he was doubtful that Jacey really meant what his brain told him she was suggesting.

"We will?" Ellie echoed, moving closer towards the two of them. Like Tom, she wished she knew what Jacey was up to. Ellie liked to flirt as much as the next girl, but Jacey seemed to be going beyond flirting on the proposition meter.

"Let Stan sleep," Jacey continued. "Ellie and I will be gone for about an hour or so, but when we come back, we will rock ... your ... world."

She smiled with confidence.

Ellie smiled with uncertainty.

Tom smiled through his pants.

"Okay, girls," he grinned. "I'll watch the little Lachey for you. You just remember your part of the deal. I will not be happy if you come back empty-handed and suddenly have no memory of this whole conversation."

"Oh we will," Jacey said, tugging on the black scarf hanging haphazardly around Tom's neck. "Remember, I mean. Don't you worry your pretty little head about that."

She licked the lip-gloss off her lips slowly and pursed her lips together, sending Tom an untouchable kiss.

He swallowed hard.

Raising her eyebrow teasingly at him, Jacey then turned and grabbed Ellie by the hand. "Come on, girlfriend. We have to go get our toys," she said saucily knowing it would warp Tom's mind.

Ellie swallowed hard.

Tom thought he was going to explode right then and there merely from the innuendoes in the air. The two girls promising togetherness, or even just suggesting togetherness, was like throwing two candy breath mints into a full soda bottle and letting it ejaculate itself into the next block.

"Babes," he breathed softly, "I really have to leave you now, but promise me, promise me, that you're not just jerking me around."

Waiting for an answer and not getting one, he tugged on the handle of the steel screen door at the side of the Lachey house, nearly hitting himself in the head when the door easily opened. "Don't know my own strength," he mumbled, quickly opening the wooden door and heading inside, away from the two robo-vixens in his own private hell.

"He's going totally barmy, I swear," Jacey laughed.

"Was that fair?" Ellie asked, as Tom disappeared inside the house, locking the door behind him. "What you said to him. It *so* puts us on his level."

"It's all in his interpretation," Jacey shrugged. "Not much we can do about that."

"We're not really going to… you know… together with Tom are we?" Ellie asked timidly. She was surprised that the thought both excited and turned her off at the same time. Particularly since Jacey still hadn't let go of her hand. She hadn't had another girl hold her hand since she was in grade school and it felt strangely uncomfortable.

"I'm a bit surprised you're contemplating it, Ellie. And a bit flattered," Jacey said, biting her lip and giving Ellie a glance that simmered with erotic bemusement.

"That's not what I meant," Ellie insisted, unsure if Jacey was actually trying to pick her up, or whether she was just imagining it. "I mean, you're gorgeous and everything but..."

Jacey laughed as she started to slide purposefully down the slippery driveway, pulling Ellie along with her.

"Come on, El. We're not going to have to worry about our sexuality at all if we don't get done what we need to do. When we get back, remind me to tell Tom he's going to have to get us some bullets from his dad's hardware store."

"Jacey?"

"Silver ones."

"Jacey! You're really freaking me out," Ellie said, pulling her hand back to her own side. The afternoon was getting more uncomfortable by the moment.

"Well, we can't get those from St. Mary's," Jacey shrugged.

"But they're not on your list," Ellie noted. She didn't dare ask where they were going to get a gun. On the one hand she hoped that Jacey hadn't got that far in her thought process. On the other, she wondered whether Jacey already had a loaded Sig-Sauer in the seemingly endless pocket of her coat.

"Are you okay, El?" Jacey asked.

"Stellar," Ellie replied. Her mind ran through the past twenty minutes she had spent with Jacey. First she had hated her, then she liked her, then it got a bit weird, and now, now she was thinking that maybe Ryan was right and this beautiful, quasi-religious, possibly bi-sexual temptress was really all of those things and none of those things at the same time. "Spacey-Jacey," she thought to herself.

But it was nice to have made a friend.

Maybe.

Chapter 20

Walking into the Lachey home was like walking into a stranger's house.
Tom walked up the landing steps and into the kitchen without Betty
yelling at him to get his dirty wet shoes off her nice clean floor. Stan wasn't
parked in the living room recliner chair, slurping pop from a straw while he
drew yet another picture to hang on the fridge with the other fifty thousand pictures he had drawn the week before. And Ryan wasn't locked in the bathroom
doing whatever the hell it was that Ryan did in the bathroom.

It was like he was in an alternate Lachey universe, and it was downright
creepy.

He retraced his steps and glanced at something that had caught his eye as he
walked by Stan's colorings. There was a calendar hanging beside them that had
a big red circle around today's date. It was Betty's birthday.

"Happy freaking birthday, Betster," he said aloud.

There wasn't going to be any celebrating today, that was for damn sure.
Betty was more likely to have a sedative than her usual nightcap of orange
brandy that she poured for herself at precisely eleven o'clock. She had done it
every night since Ryan's dad had left, he knew. Tonight being a special occasion
she would have started a little early, had one too many and offered a wee drink
to Ryan and himself so she wouldn't have to toast the occasion alone. It happened like that every holiday at the Lachey's.

Feeling a pang of guilt, Tom took his runners off out of respect before he
continued on up the carpeted hallway stairs that led to the bedrooms on the
second floor.

The first room he passed was Betty's. The door was open and he could see
that the bed was still made from the day before. That was a bit unusual. Betty's

neat-freak tendencies normally stopped at the staircase. If company wouldn't see the mess, she wasn't as concerned.

The second room was Ryan's. The door was open and he could see it looked like a bomb had gone off in it. Nothing unusual there. The room was waiting for Ryan to come back, kick his clothes into a pile by the cupboard, and spend the next hour or so lifting weights. That wasn't going to happen today either.

The third room was Stan's. The door was closed. That was a bad sign. Stan's door was never closed. He was afraid of the dark. They kept a night light on in the hallway for him most nights. But apparently not last night. Tom reached down and flicked the switch. The bulb had burned out.

"Poor bastard," Tom thought. "He's probably been stuck in his room since he went to bed."

He knocked on Stan's door.

"Stan, it's Tom. Are you awake? Can I come in?"

He waited a few moments, and after getting no answer, he slowly turned the doorknob. He knew there was no chance of it being locked because Betty had removed all the bedroom locks when she had caught Ryan up in his room with Tara. Ryan had bitched to Tom about it for days. Betty had opened the door at a really inopportune moment. Ryan said his mother probably hadn't seen him that erect since she had last changed his diaper and he took a surprise whiz. It was summer, and Betty grounded Ryan for a month, after a stern lecture about condoms. Betty wouldn't have grounded Ryan if he had done something during football season. Betty had seasonal priorities.

"Stan?" Tom whispered, poking his head through the doorframe.

The young Lachey was sitting straight up in his bed with the covers pulled close to his body, his watery eyes staring off into space as a steady stream of tears ran down his cheeks.

"And they called me a deer in a headlight," Tom thought to himself. He tried to put himself in Stan's shoes, but quite frankly, nothing like this had ever happened to him when he was that young. "Stan-man, get a grip. Ryan would smack you one if he saw you like this."

"Ryan's not here," Stan sniffed. "My mom's not here, or my dad either. I've just got the loaner." He wiped his nose on the sleeve of his thermal pajama top.

Tom laughed. "You could do worse, Stan." The 'loaner' term had come from Ryan, who thought the word 'babysitter' left nobody with any respect.

Tom came into the room and sat down on Stan's bed. He didn't have any brothers or sisters, so relating to someone Stan's age wasn't exactly easy for him to do. But he had known Stan almost since the day the little Lachey kid was born, and right now, he knew he was all Stan had. One look at his sad little face and any plans Tom had of running him down to the cop shop disappeared. He had to try to help him. He'd stay with Stan until the girls got back. Or until Betty got back. The cruel facts of life Stan needed to learn could wait another twenty-four hours or so.

"I'm not really a loaner," Tom told him. "I've been around here way more than Jacey, or your dad for that matter, so it kind of moves me up a notch. I'm kind of like a stepbrother once removed."

"What's that?" Stan asked.

"I'm kind of like your big friend," Tom explained gently. He reached over to the tissue box on Stan's study desk and handed him a handful. "I know everything sucks right now, so I got rid of the girls, thinking maybe we could hang out together for a little while. Just you and me."

Sure, it was a lie, but given the situation, a little lying wasn't going to hurt anyone.

Stan tried to smile. "It sucks the big one," he admitted.

Tom laughed. Ryan's influence was all over that statement, and Stan was lucky Betty wasn't around to hear him say it. Betty kept a special bar of soap in the bathroom for just such an occasion.

"Too true," Tom admitted. "Your powers of observation are always impressive, Stan-man."

"Tom, we're in big trouble," Stan said, wiping the tears from his face. His sobs had quieted to the odd sniffle. "Ryan's in jail and they took my mom to the nutter."

"Yeah," Tom replied. "I know that. But Stan, your brother has been in trouble before and he's always got out of it, right? This time's no different. And your mom's not exactly in the nutter, she's just in the hospital getting a little rest."

"I guess so."

"You can't keep Ryan down, you know that. And Betty..." Tom paused, trying to think of something comforting to say, "...well, that's probably where Ryan gets his toughness from. But don't tell him I said that."

"What did Ryan do?" Stan asked. "Nobody will tell me what's happening. It has something to do with T.H.E.M. in Mrs. LaRose's backyard, right? He said he was going to get me."

Tom thought back to the conversation about the "corpse-o-matic 500 styling comb" on Halloween night. Ryan had told Stan at the time he was only joking, but in hindsight it had been a really stupid thing to say. Or ironic. Or insightful. Or maybe all the above. Only time would tell.

"I really don't know what's going on, Stan-man," Tom admitted. "But when I figure it out, you'll be the first to know, I promise."

"You're smart, right?" Stan asked, pointing his index finger defiantly at him. All the Lachey's did that when they wanted to make a point, Tom had noticed.

"Uh-huh," Tom nodded cautiously. "Where are you going with this?"

"Then you should be able to figure something out to help me kill it."

Tom could have lied to Stan, he could have told him that everything was going to be fine, and no one was going to do any killing, but he sensed that Stan wouldn't believe him even if he tried to cushion it.

"I think we should let Ryan kill it," Tom answered honestly.

"From jail? How's he supposed to do that? We're gonners."

Tom sighed. "That is a bit of a problem, but that's where you can help me. Go start up the computer in the basement so that I can do a bit of web surfing."

"I'm not supposed to be on the computer when Ma's not around."

"Dude," Tom said, trying to keep a straight face, "you've got to learn to live a little. Look, if it will make you feel better, just turn it on and log in for me. I'll do everything else. She'll never know, I swear."

"Are you going to Google 'jail breakouts'?" he asked excitedly. "I can get the nail file from the bathroom if we're going to bake a cake."

"Wrong kind of file, buddy. There will be no cake baking. And no peeking at what I'm looking at on the computer. That way if Betty starts to interrogate you later, you can honestly be in complete denial."

"I could help. Whatever the plan is. I'm a minor. They can't put me in jail."

"True," Tom said slowly, "even though I don't know how you know that."

"You're sixteen. They'll toss you in the slammer."

"I won't go to jail," Tom assured him. "Stop watching old movies so your vocabulary has a chance to meet this century, okay?"

"They put Ryan in jail."

"Okay," Tom sighed. "See here's the thing, Stan. Ryan is in jail because he was in the wrong place at the wrong time. That's all. It will sort itself out without us having to break him out of jail, trust me. I've just got to do... a little homework on a project we're doing together. So he keeps caught up at school. We don't want his marks to drop, do we?"

The explanation seemed to satisfy Stan. "Okay. Can I watch TV with you while you're down there? I don't want to stay up here all by myself."

Tom smiled. Betty never let Stan watch television in the mornings, especially Sunday mornings. In the Lachey household, Sunday mornings were strictly for sleeping in. No noise was allowed.

"Sure, Stan. But no puppets. Or anything that resembles a puppet. Or a sponge."

"Can I watch wrestling?"

Tom laughed. "Only if you promise learn a few gob-smacking moves."

Finally, a full smile crossed Stan's face. "Where'd Jacey go? I can practice putting the moves on her when she gets back. I think I can take her."

"No way, little man," Tom said, patting Stan on the leg. "I'll be the one putting the moves on the ladies when they get back... and they will be back."

Their conversation stopped when the side doorbell rang.

"I told you," Tom smiled. "The girls couldn't stay away from us. We're like liquid attraction. They could put us in a bottle and call us perfume."

Stan smiled too; glad to be a part of Tom's plans, if only for a few minutes.

"Liquid attraction," he echoed.

"Come on in," Tom yelled towards the hallway, playfully giving Stan an easy one-two punch to his shoulders. "Your love-buddies are upstairs."

Stan stopped smiling. He could smell a musty aroma coming through the heating ducts in the floor. "You shouldn't have done that, Tom. Jacey would have come in by herself if the door was open. Something's wrong."

"I locked the door, Stan. I promised Ryan I'd take care of you. Jacey has a key. She came in on her own."

"No she doesn't," Stan insisted. "Officer Purdy used the hidden key from under the flowerpot. He put the key in his pocket when he left. I watched him do it."

"Stan, I hear her coming up the stairs."

Stan started to wheeze. "Does smelling b.o. count as a power of observation?" he gasped. "Jacey doesn't smell like that. She smells good. I don't think it was Jacey at the door, Tom."

Tom began to notice the smell himself. "It's probably just a dead mouse. It most likely died between the walls and when the heat came on, the fan circulated the smell through air-ducts. Just hold your nose for a bit until it shuts off." He noticed Stan was looking a little pasty. "Where's your puffer big-guy?"

Stan plugged his nose with his left hand and pointed to the dresser by the door.

Or at least Tom thought he was pointing towards the bureau by the door.

"I'll grab it for you," he offered, turning halfway around.

He never knew what hit him.

"Hello, love-buddies," the vampire said, as he spun his left leg in the air and landed a drop kick to Tom's head. "So much for you being the smart one. We vampires don't need keys, so there's not really much point locking the door. You should have listened to the kid and checked who was there before inviting me in." He turned to Stan. "He must have missed 'don't open the door to strangers' day at pre-school."

"What do you want?" Stan asked breathlessly.

"I want you to want me," he sneered.

Stan started to hyperventilate.

The vampire took no pity on the youngster. "If you keep that up, this is going to be way too easy. Why don't you make me work for it, Stan-man? Stan-man. Is that like your super-hero name?"

Stan continued to hyperventilate until he lost consciousness.

"I guess not," the vampire said. He looked around the room. "You know, I've seen you staring at me from this upstairs window for months now, Stan.

You never even had the courtesy to invite me in to read comic books with you. Some kind of neighbor you turned out to be."

He crossed over to the bedroom window and opened it wide. The cold air immediately began to fill the room, but no one, apart from himself, was conscious enough to notice.

"You, Mr. Liquid Attraction," he sneered, going over to Tom and giving him a swift kick in the ribs to ensure he was still out cold, "maybe you should spend more time watching wrestling yourself."

He walked back to the bed and hovered over Stan. "Decisions, decisions. How do I remove you from this den of nerdiness? We could take the stairs, but that would be so anti-climactic," he sneered. He heaved Stan's limp body over his left shoulder and moved towards the window. A moment later he carried Stan effortlessly up onto the snowy roof.

"You're turning into a human freezie," he laughed as he felt Stan start to involuntarily shiver. He leaned him up against the slope of the roof. "Should I lick you till you're done, or crush you up and pull your juices out slowly between my teeth? Which way gives me the migraine brain freeze? I can never remember."

There was no answer from the human life form.

The wind and snow were picking up considerably, hiding the sun behind a deep cloud cover. It didn't look like mid-afternoon. It looked like dusk.

"How does that song go? Da da da beautiful morning, da da da beautiful day," the vampire began to sing to himself. "Da da da beautiful feeling...everything's going my way."

Chapter 21

*I*t had been nearly three hours before Ellie and Jacey returned to the neighborhood, having succeeded in their mission to obtain incense, holy water, consecrated ground and two low-fat, non-dairy lattés to go.

Ellie was definitely looking forward to warming up inside. The heat from the latté wasn't making it past her inner core. To add to her discomfort, the outer layer of skin beneath her jeans was beginning to tingle. The tingle before the numbness. Winter was a drag.

"I still disagree with you about the sermon," Jacey commented as she munched on an apple she had purchased from the diner. It had quickly become apparent to her that Ellie's view of religion was contradictory to her own. "If you want to be a doubting Thomas, go right ahead."

Ellie had tried to turn their conversation to safer territories; movies, bands, and whether or not it was really necessary to pay hundreds of dollars for a purse. Again, a split decision. But Ellie was quickly learning that Jacey never really let any subject drop for long. "Says the girl eating the forbidden fruit," Ellie pointed out.

Jacey held the core of the Royal Gala away from her body and examined it. "It's not the same kind of apple. It's all in the interpretation, remember?" She tossed it into an empty garbage can at the end of a nearby driveway.

"That's my point exactly," Ellie reminded her. "It's all open to interpretation."

"Father Franklin seems like an okay guy though, right? Do you think he plays poker at night with the nuns?" Jacey asked.

"Uh... I don't know," Ellie stammered. "I wasn't listening to him. I was too busy freaking out about the dirt you put in the offering envelope, remember?"

"Consecrated ground. We needed it. Don't worry, I put some money in the plate. By the way, you owe me five bucks."

"That's not the point. I think there were more than flowers planted in that little garden we raided. Unless the brass markers were really garden stakes, but the names didn't look very biological to me."

"There was an Ivy Rose," Jacey pointed out.

"You know what I mean. People were buried there. There's probably a whole group of church elders mad at us for disturbing their eternal resting place," she sighed. "Maybe we should have brought a coffee back for Tom. We *have* been gone a while."

"Look, if I got a little of Sister Michaelangeline's ashes in with the soil, it can't hurt. It's like using a top-coat over your nail polish or summat. Think of it as extra protection. She scared the hell out of me before she died. She can scare the hell out of anything."

Ellie raised her palm to her forehead. It had been a difficult afternoon so far. She watched as Jacey put the holy water in a little Buddha bottle she found in the dollar store. The same store that sold her a box of incense complete with Hare Krishna's likeness on the box. Jacey was definitely pushing the limits of karma in her search for religious artifacts.

"Give me your phone," Jacey said to Ellie. "I'm going to put my number in it for you. Do you tweet? I've got a great texting plan, so feel free to keep me totally updated on your status."

"I'm not hooked up with Twitter. I already lose too much of my life to facebook."

"You must tweet. We'll set you up later when we get back to Ryan's. Tara and I do it all the time."

"I thought you hated Tara," Ellie said, handing Jacey her phone.

"Why do you think that?" Jacey asked.

"Just something Ryan said."

"Ryan probably said he doesn't like her either, but we all know that's not true," she said as she typed her contact info into the memory of Ellie's phone. "She's not my favorite person in the world, but sometimes I have to hang around with her because Tom and Ryan are inseparable. Where Ryan goes, Tara tends to turn up."

"You didn't want to sit with her at the game," Ellie reminded her.

"Tara's easier to take when Ryan is with her. She's on her best behavior around him."

"Aren't you guys kind of being two-faced about her? You like her, you don't like her. Just so we're clear, I have no problem disliking her after what she said to me at the football game. She was rude."

"She *is* rude. She doesn't really like me either, but we try to fake it," Jacey shrugged. She handed the phone back to Ellie. "There. All done."

"You put Tara's number in there too?" Ellie said, glancing at the contact list, and then putting the phone back in the front pocket of her jeans. "Have you not been listening to a word I said?"

"You might as well get used to her. That's all I'm saying. I wish I hadn't been with her last night, though." Jacey shuddered at the memory of dropping Tara off at the murder scene.

"Where was Tom then?"

"Tom and I had gone to the Topaz for a bite to eat when Tara came in all in a tizzy because she had a row with Ryan. Tom wasn't in the mood to listen to her, and she wasn't offering to leave us alone, so Tom bailed and I wound up with Tara. I thought he went home."

"That must have been when he came over to my place."

"Sod. He's still so in trouble over that. Thank God they had an all-nighter of flicks at the theatre, or I wouldn't have known what to do with Tara. We saw you at the nine o'clock show, you and your mom and grandmother. We stayed for the next one too. We finally left after that one and I drove her home. Talk about scary. What if we had arrived earlier, when the murderer was still there?"

Ellie had wanted to talk to her about the second murder, but didn't know how to broach the subject. This seemed like the opportune moment.

"Did you see anyone hanging around Tara's place?" Ellie asked hesitantly, not sure how much she wanted to divulge to Jacey about why she wanted to know. She had to make the question sound like a routine one. "I mean, were there any strange looking guys hanging around the street corner or anything?"

"Hardly," Jacey replied. "Tara lives out the highway, on a farm near Stillman's Creek. It's not too far from the old abandoned Amish school. You don't get many blokes hanging around way out there. There is no way Kevin Clark should have been out there. Not with Ralph and his stupid mutts roaming around. I dropped Tara off at the laneway because I didn't want to deal with either of them."

"When did you find out what happened?"

"Tara called me from the hospital. They took Ralph there."

"How much do you know about the dream I had?" Ellie asked her. She wondered how far the gossip had spread.

"Tara told me you knew where they would find Brooke's body. I know that much. But you didn't know anything about the murder at her place before it happened, did you?"

"No." Ellie thought for a moment and shook her head. "I only dreamt about the little girl."

"Maybe you have a closer connection to her or summat," Jacey shrugged.

"Why? I never met her before. I met Kevin on Halloween, when he was out with Ryan, Tom and Stan, but I swear, I didn't lose any sleep over him. He was not in my dream that night or any night since."

"Maybe the dream wasn't really about Brooke. Maybe she just happened along into it, and it was really all about summat else."

Ellie hadn't considered this. It was possible that the dream, if it had any hidden meaning at all, was about something less obvious. But what?

"You said there was an abandoned school out by Tara's?"

Jacey nodded. "It's across the bridge from her place. If you hang a left at Emerson's Feed Mill and go for about a mile, you can't miss it."

A bridge, a creek and an old school. Ellie tucked the information into the back of her brain. More pieces of the puzzle were slowly coming together. If the shadowman hadn't taken her from her room to save the little girl, what was he really trying to tell her? What was it he had said?

"*Do something, Ellie. You're the only one who can. It's your problem.*" The words began to echo in her head.

As they reached the front of the Lachey house, Jacey stopped dead in her tracks. "Okay, that's not right."

"What?" Ellie asked, clearly missing something.

"Look at the side of the house. Stan's window is open. Stan never opens his window. Ryan said he kept it closed even during the heat wave last August." She took a few steps up the driveway to examine the second story window further.

"Why?" Ellie asked. "I get why he wouldn't want it open while it's freezing outside, but what's wrong with having it open in the summer?"

Jacey took a sip of her now chilled drink. "Don't take this the wrong way El, but Stan thinks the bogeyman lives in your grandmother's backyard."

"There's no such thing as a bogeyman, Jacey."

"Maybe not. But there is a darkness over his house," Jacey said solemnly. "I'm sure of that."

"What do you mean? What darkness?" Ellie asked. The wind had really picked up, but it wasn't as if the area was experiencing any power failures. She could see the Lachey's kitchen light shining through the window.

Jacey slowly moved her head from side to side. "Can't put my finger on it," she sighed. I get these crazy ideas in my head and then they disappear."

"Then it's probably nothing," Ellie reasoned.

"Erm… maybe we should go get your mom and your grandmother, just to be safe," Jacey hesitated. "To be honest, I'm a little afraid of the non-existent bogeyman myself."

"Are you crazy? Why would we want to involve the Helens?"

"Re-enforcements?"

"Let's not," Jacey insisted. "You weren't there this morning when they freaked over the mere mention of a vampire. Bogeyman is not going to go over any better, trust me. Do you know what we're supposed to do with all these things we collected?"

"No." Jacey shrugged. "My clock radio went off and I woke up."

Ellie wanted to slap Jacey.

"Great," Ellie sighed. "Maybe we'll be really lucky and we'll get in the house and find Stan and Tom are playing Texas hold 'em with your priest and the nuns. Sister Michaelangeline included. Maybe they're our re-enforcements and maybe they'll know what to do with all this crap."

Jacey opened the side door to the Lachey house. "Tom? Stan?" she called, and waited for an answer.

"That's weird," Ellie said, when no one replied.

"Oh, I so have the creeps," Jacey remarked, as they kicked their boots off and went up the landing into the kitchen. "It is way too quiet in this house."

Jacey motioned for Ellie to follow her through the empty living room and up the stairs to the bedroom areas. "Maybe Betty got home early and they've gone for all-you can-eat pancakes."

"It's a little late in the day for that," Ellie reminded her, as they briefly peeked inside Betty and Ryan's rooms.

"Geez, he's got a lot of trophies," Ellie noted.

"Half of them are for piano," Jacey smiled. "Betcha wouldn't have guessed that in a million years."

"He told me he played guitar," Ellie said softly.

"He plays both," Jacey sighed, wondering if he'd ever get to play either again.

The girls turned into Stan's room next and found Tom lying unconscious on the floor.

"Oh my God," Jacey gasped, running over to him. She wanted to pick his limp body up and hold him in her arms, but she was afraid to move him.

"Did he faint again?" Ellie asked. "He passed out the other night on my Nan's porch."

"No. He's been totally rag-dolled," Jacey said in disbelief. "Look at the welt on the side of his face." She brushed the blond hair from the side of his face to see if he was bleeding. She couldn't see any open wounds. "My poor, perfect, Tommy."

"Is he breathing?" Ellie asked.

Jacey nodded. "He's just out cold."

"He's probably got a concussion. Stay here with him," Ellie said. "Call 911. Don't move him, just in case."

"Where are you going?" Jacey yelled.

"I have to find Stan."

Jacey pulled her phone from her pocket and began to dial. "Directory assistance, please."

"Jacey," Ellie said in frustration. "You don't need them to dial 9-1-1."

Jacey ignored her.

"Fine," Ellie said, "I don't have time to argue with you." She began to frantically move through the unfamiliar territory of the Lachey home, searching the rest of the rooms upstairs then running down to the basement to check it out as well. There was no one down there.

"Stan!" she yelled. "Where the hell are you?"

She ran back upstairs, pulled on her boots and ran outside to the garage.

"Kid," she pleaded, "I've counted to one hundred. It's time to come out now, I give up."

Off in the distance, she could hear the church bells of St. Mary's begin to chime. Mass was over, and while she supposed they could have been tolling for an afternoon funeral, in her heart she knew they weren't. The notes were unmistakably for her, F-G-A-F, F-G-A-F, A-B-C, A-B-C.

"Frère Jacques," Ellie gasped. "The bastard's got him."

Chapter 22

"Stop. Right. There," Helen demanded, raising her left palm. The woman coming down the stairs sort of looked like her mother, but one never could tell. It wouldn't be the first time an entity had tried to take over a human body. It was the subtle signs that gave them away.

"Now what?" Helena asked.

"You're wearing a turtleneck."

"So?"

"So... you don't do turtlenecks. You do French bodices, but you don't do Irish wool." Helen walked around her mother, eyeing her up and down. Her mother had put on a few pounds since the last time she had seen her. It was nothing an acquaintance would notice, but to the eagle eye of a daughter, about ten pounds, give or take.

"Don't read too much into that, Helen. It's cold outside, that's all," Helena replied, squirming in her jeans that were a size too small. "Stop that twirling around me. You're making me dizzy."

"And?"

"And I think my thong is stuck up my butt crack."

"That's better," Helen smiled, and gave her mother a hug. "You had me worried there for a second. I just wanted to make sure you were still in that body I know so well. The one that gave birth to me."

"This body is getting harder to maintain, let me tell you. If my ass gets any bigger, I'll be able to rent it out for advertising." Helena pulled her sweater out from beneath the waistline of her pants, loosening the fit. "Damn dryer. It shrinks everything."

"Uh-huh," Helen smiled.

"What do you feel like doing?" Helena asked. "We have the house to ourselves. I could hook up the Karaoke machine." She raised her fist near her mouth, like a microphone and threatened to sing. "That'll kill a few hours. We could start with KC and the Sunshine Band… 'shake, shake, shake'…"

"Or not. Maybe we should start cleaning up the porch?" Helen offered. She was already dressed in her winter coat and boots in preparation for the task. "It's probably time to take the Halloween decorations down," she noted, looking out the window. The wind had already made a mess of the cotton cob-webs.

"I guess so," Helena sighed. "I hate the taking them down part. It's the same at Christmas, only at least at Christmas they get to stay up longer. Sometimes I wonder why I put so much effort into Halloween." She took her own jacket from the closet and slipped it on. "Remind me to call Forest Lawn tomorrow. I need to find out when Mr. Wagner's funeral is. I think I'll have a little party back here after the service."

"A party?"

"Well, you know what I mean. A gathering. With food. And alcohol."

"So, a party…"

"Pretty much," Helena agreed. "I doubt anyone else is doing anything for him. He was a bit of a loner." She paused. "Helen, when I die, make sure there's plenty of wine, okay? Spring for the good stuff. I'll leave you the money."

"You're never going to die, Mother. You'll annoy me forever."

"I can still do that after I'm dead, but I'd rather do it now," she smiled. "And I don't want any lilies. Lilies make me sneeze. Even when I'm dead, they'll make me sneeze. I just know it."

"A wake would be a nice gesture," Helen agreed. "For Mr. Wagner," she clarified. "I'm sure you were a good friend to him."

"Well, he was a good friend to me," Helena assured her.

"How good a friend?"

"Helen!"

"I'm just teasing. I think. What religion was he? Do we have to do anything special?"

"I don't know," Helena admitted. "We never talked about that. He liked cheese and lettuce sandwiches, so I guess that's what I'll serve."

"That sounds pretty easy," Helen agreed. Although she was sure she would have to lay out a much bigger spread when Helena did eventually kick the bucket. "Have you heard from Dad lately?" she asked. "Dad likes cheese and lettuce sandwiches."

Helena opened the front door and motioned for Helen to go through. "Define lately."

"This decade," Helen answered, putting her gloves on as she walked outside. The snow was not looking like it was going to let up any time soon. "Maybe this isn't such a good idea. Maybe this can wait until tomorrow. Your new door is going to wait until tomorrow, let me tell you."

"The snow might make it easier for us to slide the swing to the other side of the porch. It's a bit heavy," Helena speculated. She grasped the frame with both hands and tried to give it a shove. "I can't budge it. I'm going to need your help with this."

Helen went around to the other side of the swing and tried to give it a push. It moved, but only a few inches. "It's stuck on something," she said, pointing towards the base. "So, how is he?"

Helena glanced at the wooden floorboard. Kevin Clark's ghost sheet costume had gotten knotted up behind the swing and was preventing it from sliding freely. He had taken it off while Roy was investigating the death of Mr. Wagner. She tugged at it until it came loose. "It's definitely time to clean this porch, poor thing," she sighed, touching the fabric softly. "I heard from your father a while back, Helen. Alexander's the same as he always is."

"And that would be?"

"A royal pain in the ass." She grabbed the broom from the corner of the railing and began to sweep some of the snow away. If the snowplows didn't make it out tonight, it was going to be a tough commute for everyone in the morning. "I see Roy's cruiser coming down the street. Are you ready to tell him about what you saw in your vision?"

"As ready as I ever will be, I suppose," Helen admitted. "I guess it helps that you have this understanding with him. You know, the whole Fourth of July thing." Helen hoped it would save a lot of time and frustration, not having to convince him that her visions were real.

"Maybe after this is all over he'll introduce you to the Dayton boys."

"Mother, I don't think I'm ready for a new relationship right now, thanks anyway."

"You never know, Helen. The best ones come when you're not looking. And like I told you, being a police officer predisposes them to the fragility of human nature. I find that comes in handy."

"You would."

"They're good looking. They have a steady job. You can take your pick between them."

"I'll think about it," Helen said, in an effort to end the conversation.

Roy parked the car behind Helena's Mustang and walked towards the LaRose women. "Do I need pepper spray?" he asked Helen.

"Look, I'm sorry about that whole you, me, the punch to the head thing. I promise not to do it again," she said sheepishly. Secretly, she was still pretty amazed at the beating she was able to lay on him.

"That would be a good thing," he replied, rubbing his neck. "So what's up? Your mother said you had some information for me in regards to the where-abouts of the Clarks?"

"I don't really know where to begin," Helen admitted. "I know you might think this is a little crazy…"

"She's had a vision," Helena said calmly.

"A vision?" He leaned on the porch railing and eyed Helena suspiciously. "Like mother, like daughter. Expect the unexpected."

"Hear her out, Roy. It's not easy for her."

"Okay," Roy sighed. "Let's just assume for the moment that I buy the whole 'vision' thing. I don't need to know your whole back history, Helen. Just get to the point you want to make, then I'll decide if I want to hear more."

"I saw a white truck, with two dead people in it. The truck had been run off the road and it's lying overturned in a ditch."

"It does sound like the Clark's," Helena insisted. "She's trying to describe the cliff out by the ski hill."

"How do you know, Helena? Did you have a vision too?" He wished she would let her daughter tell the story on her own.

"No, she just did a better job explaining it to me earlier. Before you got here. She's nervous now."

Roy wondered how anyone who had managed to knock him unconscious could suddenly have a case of the nerves. "Okay," he sighed. "Maybe you'd better start at the beginning, Helen."

Helen subconsciously twisted her pony tail around her fingers. It hung in a loose curl when she released it. "Roy, I know this sounds crazy. It all started with a terrible migraine that I had earlier. It happens when I get a vision."

"It does," Helena interrupted. "You have to see her to believe it. Her forehead goes all wrinkly."

"Go on…" he replied, his voice indicating suspicion. He raised his hand to Helena. "I mean, go on *Helen*."

"I could see the white truck travelling back towards town," Helen continued. "A man was driving, and there was a woman in the front with him. I think they'd been out shopping because the rear seat was full of groceries. He was a stocky guy with red hair and she… she was just… plain," Helen shrugged. There was nothing particularly outstanding about the woman's features.

"Tell me more," Roy said, now with interest. It did sound like the Clarks.

"This car came up from behind them and smashed into them. The red haired guy in the truck tried to steer back onto the highway, but the car hit him again. They were deliberate hits. The white truck had nowhere to go. It went over the embankment."

"The car that hit the white truck, can you describe it? Roy asked.

"It was a Hummer. Black. Not a fully decked out one or anything," she said, trying to focus in on the vehicle in her subconscious. "An older model. I don't think it's worth a lot anymore."

"What about the truck?" Roy asked. "Anything about it stick out in your memory?"

"I can see the license plate on the truck, it says ACEMAN1."

"Yeah, that's the Clarks," Roy sighed, clearly disturbed. "He's a big poker player." He studied Helen's face. Whether her story was true or not he didn't know. But he believed, that she believed, that it was.

"I think I've seen a Hummer just like that around town," Helena remembered. "Or maybe I'm thinking of a Jeep. I don't know. I used to be able to tell them apart, but now they're making the Jeeps bigger and the Hummer's smaller. It's confusing the hell out of me."

Roy took his phone from his pocket, began to call Purdy, and then reconsidered. If he didn't have to involve any of the officers with Helen's information, it might be the best thing for all concerned. Roy knew there was a Hummer like that in town. And he knew who it belonged to. "Okay, Helen," he said. "I'll head out on the highway to take a look. But if you're wrong about this, you owe your mother and I dinner at Delphine's. I eat a lot. You should know that."

"All right," Helen conceded. "Thanks, Roy... for at least hearing me out."

"No problem," he replied. "That's what I do. But if you don't mind, before I go, I just need to talk to your mother about... about... about the upcoming tea party for the senior's center next Wednesday. There's a problem with the seating arrangements, and she knows better than anyone who to put with whom."

"That sounds too thrilling for me," Helen replied, happy for the excuse to leave. "I'm cold anyway. I'll go inside and start some laundry."

"Don't you dare put my white peek-a-boo blouse in with Ellie's mud soaked jeans," Helena begged. She looked at Roy. "I'll tell you about the angora sweater incident some other time."

"Who said I was doing *your* laundry?" Helen laughed as she headed inside. The door stuck as she tried to close it. "We should get some new weather stripping at the hardware store tomorrow while we're at it," she noted.

"Good plan," Helena acknowledged, pulling the door firmly shut.

"Okay, Helena. What's going on around here?" Roy asked when they were finally alone.

"What do you mean?" Helena asked, feigning innocence.

"First, there was Brooke Quinlan. It was the darndest thing. I got a call from the coroner saying she had no blood in that tiny little body of hers beyond what clung to her body tissues when they did the autopsy. Then Kevin Clark gets murdered. And you know what? The coroner calls me again, and guess what he says?"

"What?" Helena winced.

"He can't figure out why Kevin Clark is down a half a body of blood! He said he found two puncture wounds on his ankle. Wounds that under normal circumstances would bleed a like a paper cut and then stop."

"Well, not if he was dead."

"Or, if there was some other force that had time to suck some of the blood out of him."

"Like what? Really, Roy. Aren't you jumping to conclusions that are pretty far out there?" she said sheepishly.

"You tell me. It's your daughter having the visions. And your granddaughter who had the weird dream. What does that all mean? Do we need to re-visit your infamous Fourth of July party, Helena?"

"Let's not."

"Oh, I think we will. Purdy and I had an incident with Stan Lachey the other night. We left him alone in the back seat of the cruiser when we were dealing with the situation out at the Wildman's farm. When we finally got to leave, we found a teenager by the car, giving Stan some serious grief. When we approached him, the teenager laughed at us. And I couldn't help thinking I had heard that laugh before. But where? It's been driving me crazy the past few hours. And then I remembered. Your party."

Helena rested the broom between her arms, took her fingers to her head and began to rub her temples. "I have had enough of that day to last a lifetime."

"I remember turning around in your backyard, to see who was laughing manically at us from across the lawn. I knew I was going to have to do a thorough job of covering your tracks that day, and obviously someone else besides you, Mr. Wagner, Betty Lachey, Marita Harbinger, and myself, had seen the whole thing happen. And I'm not referring to the brief appearance of the exorcist. There was a teenaged boy standing there as well, taking it all in. I went to approach him, but he vanished. In the blink of an eye, he was gone. I went looking for him, but he never turned up again. You know me, Helena. I don't like leaving loose ends around."

"It was a hot, crazy, July day," Helena offered. "But it's over now."

"I don't think it is, Helena. The laugh I heard last night was the same. The boy was the same. And he was at the scene of Kevin Clark's murder. I need to find that boy, Helena. Where is he?"

"I don't know," Helena said honestly.

"Well, you think about that," Roy said knowingly. "And when you do know, you call me." He turned his back on Helena and walked slowly to his car.

"This is all getting very complicated," Helena admitted to herself. "There is a tornado spinning around my house, and I don't know how to make it stop." She put the broom back in its spot on the corner of the verandah and went inside her home. Maybe it was time to start to come clean with Helen about what was really going on. She had to figure out a way to delicately broach the subject. It might be best to get Helen mad about something else and then divert her to the conversation she really wanted to have. Blindside her. She went down to the laundry room in the basement to find her and give it a try. Helen was sitting on top of the vibrating washer.

"Um, what are you doing?" Helena asked.

Helen was red-faced. "Nothing."

"You are more like me than you are willing to admit," her mother laughed.

"Change the subject please," Helen begged.

"About Ellie's father..." Helena began.

"Change it back please," Helen wished. "I'm getting my jollies from the spin cycle, okay? Let's talk about how wrong that is."

"Too late. Tell me about him."

"Julian? You want to know about Julian?"

"Julian?" Helena questioned, tilting her head ever so slightly. "I thought his name was Jules."

"You're losing it, Mother."

"I don't think so, Helen. If you don't remember her father's name, or if you don't know her father's name, you should just admit it."

"His name was Julian," Helen said adamantly. "What about him?"

"I'm just very sorry about everything you went through at the time of his death. I'm sorry I didn't get to know him. What was he like?"

"He was tall, dark and handsome. And smart. And funny. He was everything I ever wanted."

"He sounds perfect."

"No," Helen said softly. "He was far from that. But he was mine. At least for a little while."

"It takes a long time to get over the loss of someone you love," Helena admitted. There had been times in her life when she had felt just like she assumed Helen must have then. More so when she was younger, when love's betrayal somehow meant so much more.

"It takes forever," Helen replied solemnly.

"You moved on," her mother reminded her.

"I did," Helen agreed. "But it wasn't easy. I still keep comparing every man I'm with to him. Maybe that's why it never works out."

"It's hard for a man to compete with a memory," Helena said. "You need to let go."

"It's not that easy. I feel like he's always around."

"Helen?" her mother said, noticing her daughter had drifted off somewhere.

Helen realized she might have said too much. "You're right. I need to let go. It's just hard, that's all." She reminded herself that she was going to have to be more careful around the subject if she didn't want to raise suspicions.

"So what's next in the life of Helen?" her mother asked. Something in Helen's demeanor indicated she was being unusually coy about the whole issue. She hoped it wasn't because her daughter wanted to return to Tony.

"The Daytons," Helen laughed. "Would that make you happy?"

"Yes, actually. It just might. You should see them. I think there's a picture of them in last week's paper, I'll go get it." Helena said with satisfaction.

"God give me strength," Helen whispered. "It hasn't even been a week and she's taking over my social calendar."

"Yes, here it is," Helena said, coming back into the room. "They gave a talk to the grade threes about winter safety this week. You can read all about it." She started to hand the paper to Helen, and then remembered the sordid front-page story of the missing animals in Troy. "Here, Helen. Let me take that front page. I spilled some coffee on it earlier, it's all crinkled." She removed the page and opened the newspaper to the article. "Personally I think Cody is the better looking of the two, but they're really quite similar."

Helen glanced at the picture. "Yeah, they're kind of cute," she had to admit. She handed the paper back to her mother. They reminded her of Davey Weiss from her own third grade class. Blond and blue-eyed, a total one-eighty from the men she was usually attracted to. That might be a good thing.

"I know. You'd think they'd be off the market by now, but they're not," Helena said, tucking the issue under her arm. "I can't imagine why."

Helen grabbed the paper back from Helena. "Oh, my God. Let me see that picture again." She quickly flipped through the pages until she found the right one.

"What is it, Helen?"

"I know them," she gasped. "He was one, now he's two. St. Paul de Vence. They're the wraith riders I unleashed from that box."

"You mean you weren't lying about that?" Helena exclaimed in disbelief.

"No, I wasn't lying about that. Not that part anyway." Helen grabbed her mother's arm. "Oh no, it's happening again."

"What is it, Helen?" She looked at her daughter's face. "You're going all wrinkly."

"The accident. It's replaying in my mind. I can see the man in the Hummer. He's blonde. He has a badge. He's one of them. A Dayton."

"Are you sure?" Helena gasped

"Yes, I'm sure."

"Hellsbelles! Can this day get any worse? I mean, really..."

The upstairs phone began to ring.

"Answer it, Mother," Helen said. "My head is killing me."

"Let it go to the answering machine," Helena replied. She wanted to stay by her daughter until this latest vision subsided.

"ANSWER IT!" Helen screamed.

"Okay, okay," Helena replied, running upstairs to answer the phone. She was out of breath by the time she picked up the receiver. "Hello? Oh, hello

Jacey…" she answered, "…of course we can come right over. What's wrong?" She listened intently to the hysterical girl on the other end of the line.

"Helen," Helena yelled. "You put that migraine on hold and get your boots on." She flew up staircase, taking the stairs two at a time.

"What's wrong?" Helen asked upon her return. "I'm feeling kind of woozy."

"I'll woozy you to hell and back, if you don't hurry up," Helena warned. "Can you hear that church bell ringing in the distance? It's summoning us, but not to mass."

"Mother?"

Helena threw her jacket haphazardly over her arm and headed out the door, grabbing Helen by the hand. Helen nearly slipped on the wet snow-covered pavement as Helena pulled her along to the Lachey's side door.

"Helen," she began earnestly, "I need you to focus. I mean really focus. Willie was right. Ellie's life is in danger."

"What?" Helen replied, wide-eyed. "But you said…"

"I didn't know then what I know now. Well, I knew part of what I know now, but that's beside the point. We have some very nasty people to take care of, Helen.

"You mean take care of as in… bringing them to your clinic, right?" Helen hoped.

"I mean," Helena clarified. "We have some very nasty people that we have to kill. And for the record, I don't do that at my clinic."

Chapter 23

Colin Dayton sat in the Chief's black leather chair with his feet upon the desk. He was flipping casually through a paperback edition of "Big Poker for Big Winners" that his brother Cody had lent him. The tattered corners of the pages indicated that he wasn't the first "Big Winner" to have read the book.

"Need help with that?" Ryan joked. He was sitting on the floor of the jail cell, watching the officer try to concentrate on an instructional manual that was unfortunately beyond his comprehension.

"Cody gave this to me." Colin said nonchalantly. "He found it. He thinks it'll improve my game." His brother had been dragging him into high stakes games at the casino lately, and the cards had not been in his favor. Cody thought he just wasn't paying attention, which might have been the case. He was more of a roulette man himself. Less work. Spin the wheel and gravity does the rest.

"Why don't you sit on the bed?" he asked Ryan. "The floor's got to be cold."

"I'm sick of sitting on the bed," Ryan replied. He wondered if he was entitled to an hour of exercise a day. He would have to ask his lawyer that, if he ever got one.

"Don't blame me if you get hemorrhoids," Colin shrugged.

Ryan rolled his eyes. "So where is the Code-ster, anyway? Did he pull a bender in Vegas? Is that why I haven't seen your brother's sorry ass around here?"

Colin took his feet off the desk and wheeled the chair slowly over towards the cell. "What's it to you, you a cop?" he laughed, dropping the book through the bars. "Here. You might as well get an education, courtesy of Troy's finest. I'm better off losing anyway. Cody'd have a snit fit if I ever beat him at his game. Peace in the family and all that."

Ryan glanced at the book. "It's from the library. With my luck it's overdue and I'll be fined on top of the rest of the shit happening to me in this nightmare." He flipped to the back page, and found a card tucked in the library pocket. "It's totally overdue," he said to himself, noting the book had been checked out in 1970. They didn't even use this type of library card anymore. He glanced at the name on it and grimaced. Quickly taking the card and tucking it into his shirt pocket, he then closed the book and tried to throw the paperback directly on the Chief's desk. It landed on the floor, beside the waste paper basket.

"I expected more from you," Colin said.

It was then Ryan noticed the face of the vampire in the window, watching he and Colin with a look of amusement on his face. "Shit. Not again."

Colin turned around to see what Ryan was looking at, and noticed the teenager outside.

The vampire tapped on the window and waved at them.

"Come on in," Colin indicated to the teenager at the window.

"Are you crazy?" Ryan asked. "Don't let him in unless you're going to arrest him. He's the bad guy. Tell him he's not welcome."

"The Chief won't get re-elected if we do things like that, will he?" Colin smirked. "Every vote counts. This citizen of Troy is as welcome in here as you are."

"I don't think he's a registered voter," Ryan tried to argue. "Seriously, tell him to take a hike."

"It's not always about you," Colin offered. "Maybe he wants to see me for something, did you ever think of that?" His cell phone began to vibrate in its holder. He reached to his belt and pulled it out, "Troy Police. Officer Colin Dayton here. He listened intently to the voice on the other end of the line. "Okay, I'll be right there."

"I don't believe this," Ryan sighed.

"What?" the vampire smirked as he entered the room. "Do you think you're the only one with friends?"

"You," Colin said to the vampire, "whatever it is that you want, is it urgent? Or can I talk to you later? I have to go deal with a... situation." He put his phone back. "Never a dull moment in this town lately."

"I guess it can wait," the vampire sighed. "I'll just stay here and keep Ryan company."

"Can I trust you two to play nice?" Colin asked, grabbing his coat from the back of the chair.

"Don't lock the door," the vampire requested, "I'm expecting another visitor."

Colin nodded. "Just lock it up when you're done. And if you kill anyone, clean it up, will ya?"

"Wha...t?" Ryan cringed.

"That's *your* job," the vampire said to the officer.

"I've been kind of busy lately," Colin sneered.

"You've been busy doing a shitty job," the vampire countered.

Ryan listened intently to their banter. While he had to agree with the assessment of Colin's work ethic, for two people who had no reason to know each other, it sure sounded to him like they did. "Do you two need some alone time?" he asked.

"None of your business," the two said in unison.

"You're not seriously going to leave me here with him?" Ryan asked Colin. "You didn't even frisk him or anything. He might be carrying a syringe or something." Geez, Stan would make a better police officer, he thought to himself.

Colin looked at the teenager. "I doubt he's got a needle. He doesn't look the type. Besides, you need all the friends you can get right now. Talk about the weather or something. I'll be back in an hour," he said as he headed out the door.

"Whadaya mean?" Ryan protested. "He's white and pasty and looks half-dead. That sounds exactly like a guy who's got a needle." He made a mental note to have a long chat with Chief Cohen about the hired hands he was entrusting with his precinct.

"So, how's it going there, buddy?" the vampire asked him. "Getting a little stuffy in here?"

Ryan tried to avoid his gaze. He wasn't in a mood to make friends.

"Stop trying to ignore me," the vampire told him. "If you ever want to see your brother alive again, you will listen, and you will do exactly what I want."

"What did you do with Stan?" Ryan demanded, his neck muscles beginning to tense up as he spoke. It was a natural reflex action his subconscious used to prepare him for a potential blow to the head.

"I stuffed him like cannoli," the vampire said. He could intuitively feel the pulse of Ryan's carotid artery expanding as the adrenaline in him began to take hold. "Try not to give yourself an aneurism," he chided.

"What?" Ryan asked incredulously, moving menacingly towards his adversary.

"Uh-uh," the vampire cautioned. "Save it. The orange flag is already down on this play. You're in no condition to try to out-wit me." He paused. "Stan doesn't like the cold much, does he? Those red pajamas he wears are getting a little thin."

"Okay, I'm listening," Ryan said, sitting back down on the bed, feeling defeated. The vampire was right. There was little Ryan could do in his current situation. His lack of sleep was beginning to take its toll on him. Attempting to kill the vampire, even if he knew how to do it, would be a tough task to do alone. "If you've hurt him I'll kill you," he said weakly.

"Yeah, yeah," the vampire taunted. "Whatever."

"If you don't tell me what you've done with him, I'll find a way to erase you from this earth," Ryan promised.

"Maybe when you wake up you will. Besides, we had a deal," the vampire reminded Ryan. "I'll give you Mini-You when you bring me the girl."

"I don't remember agreeing to that."

"I don't remember you not agreeing to that. Here's how it's going to work, Ryan. Lucky for you, she's on her way over here, the girl you call Goth-Chic. Kismet has arranged it so she's coming to see you. That's not the smartest thing she could do, but she's totally messed up in the head right now, thank you very much, and she needs to talk to you because she thinks you'll understand. You can thank me later. I'm going to be nice and count that as you bringing me the girl. See, I'm not all bad."

"What are you going to do with her?" Ryan asked. If he could only tap into the vampire's psyche, he told himself, he might be able to stop his crazy plan to capture Ellie. A plan that he was unwillingly a part of. Before he could even attempt to help her, he had to somehow find out what had happened to Stan. Blood was thicker than neighbors. Even Goth-Chic.

"I'm going to go into the washroom and I'm going to stay there, until the time is right for me to come out," the vampire said. "You are going to say nothing about me being there, because if you do, if I get any indication that she knows I'm here, I'll just vanish. For as long as you live. They'll find Stan's body next summer, after it has cured like rawhide."

Ryan stared blankly at him.

"Nod if you understand," the vampire said sarcastically.

Ryan raised and lowered his head in agreement, and let out a long sigh. He stumbled back to the bed and collapsed upon it.

What a mess he was in. Less than a week ago he had been a happy-go lucky high school student with a pro scout dogging him for an easy scholarship. Betty had been over the moon with that news. A free college education courtesy of the 30-yard line. What could be sweeter? And now, now he was locked in jail with a serious case of fright night taking control of his life. It was getting to be too much for him to handle. He reckoned he knew how Betty must be feeling right now. He felt the same, without the benefit of medication.

He watched as the vampire entered the washroom, leaving the door open just a crack so he could see and hear whatever he wanted to. Ryan knew the vampire was in control, and although every bone in his body wanted to fight him, every nerve ending in his brain was shutting down. He succumbed to exhaustion for almost an hour before the sound of the door opening brought him back to semi-consciousness. He hoped upon hope that it was Chief Cohen, or even Purdy, coming back to check up on him. But it wasn't. It was Ellie, just like the vampire had predicted. He slowly sat up and turned towards her.

"Ryan, oh my God," Ellie gasped, seeing him behind bars. The boy before her was almost unrecognizable. His hair was beginning to grow back, both on his face and atop his head, and she knew he was unlikely to see a razor anytime soon. The corners of his mouth were turned down in anguish and dark circles were forming under his eyes. "I am so sorry," was all she could say.

"Then get me out of here," Ryan pleaded. "Help me, Ellie."

The tone in his voice was eerily similar to the sounds little Brooke had made, begging for help in the dream that started all this. "I'm trying," Ellie said softly. "I told the Chief about the dream. And Jacey and I went on an artifact hunt for all kinds of crazy stuff that she thinks is going to help. Tom was supposed to find a way to get rid of the vampire by doing some research on the computer while we were gone, but..." she looked at Ryan with tears in her eyes, "when we came back, Tom was unconscious and Stan was gone."

"I knew Tom would be the dead man fainting. When will you chicks learn to count on the brawn before the brain? It's the number one rule of cavemanism for a reason. Survival of the fittest. Since you hardly know Jacey, let me fill you in. Whatever she's doing, it's going to be half-baked."

"Don't be so ungrateful," Ellie responded. "She's trying to help you. I don't see many other people doing that. And as for Tom, let's just say you don't look so superhuman yourself right now."

"And you..." Ryan continued, looking away from her, trying to hide the tears forming in the corners of his own eyes, "...Goth, I'm spent. I don't even know if I have the words available to adequately express how I feel about you right now."

Ellie walked to within inches of the bars separating her from Ryan. "Don't you dare blame this whole mess on me," she said calmly. "You don't scare me, Ryan Lachey. You can say whatever you want about me. Let me fill you in. If you had invited me, or Tom, or even Jacey along with you that night, this whole thing probably wouldn't have happened. At least not this way. But you had to be the big star and do it all yourself. Happy now? Your brother is missing, and I think the vampire has him. Don't pretend to not know what I'm talking about, because I know you do."

"Shh," he whispered, putting his finger to his lips and pointing at the door.

"I don't care if Roy's in there," she said. "I told you. Roy already knows about my crazy dream."

"It's not Roy," he frantically mouthed in silence. Chicks, he thought. Even when you want them to understand, even if their life depends on it, sometimes there's just no getting through to them.

The vampire emerged from the washroom with the toilet plunger in his hand. He sped towards Ellie, swinging his arms like a baseball bat. The rubber bottom of the cleaning utensil hit her hard in the head. It stunned her, throwing her body off balance.

"That's dirty, you asshole!" Ryan exclaimed.

The vampire smiled slyly at Ryan, then turned and pushed the already dizzy Ellie to the concrete floor. Her head smacked the brick wall on the way down, knocking her out.

"Sometime can I meet a human that actually gives me a challenge?" the vampire asked rhetorically, squatting down next to her. He placed his thumb and forefinger together and flicked twice at Ellie's cheek. She didn't respond. "Out cold," he acknowledged.

"Dude, you don't hit girls," Ryan said angrily.

"That's not hitting her," he said. "This is hitting her..." He smacked Ellie across the face. She still didn't stir. "I hate this bitch," he said. He leaned towards her neck, opened his mouth wide, exposing his overgrown incisors.

"What the fuck are you doing?" Ryan screamed.

The vampire stopped. He looked at Ryan. "You're probably right," he admitted. "I shouldn't kill her here. Colin's not around."

"You can't kill her," Ryan argued. Internally, he was digesting what the vampire had said... 'Colin's not around.' There was something going on between the two of them. That made his predicament all the more sinister.

"Of course I can kill her," the vampire reminded him. "That's what I do for a living. It's my job."

"You said it was Colin's job. It'll just be easier, you know, if you wait until both of the twins are around," he guessed.

"Why Ryan Lachey," the vampire chuckled. "There *is* a light on in that brain of yours." He moved Ellie's body away from the wall and struggled to take her in his arms. "She's a lot heavier than she looks," he said to Ryan, "just so you know."

"Why don't you get me out of here?" Ryan offered. "So I can carry her for you."

"Well, that light bulb moment of yours ended pretty quickly, didn't it?" he laughed. "Nice try. But we've got a party to go to and you're not invited." He threw Ellie over his shoulder and waved good-bye to Ryan.

"Wait!" Ryan shrieked. "What about Stan? You said you'd let him go. Where is he? Are you going to bring him here to me or are you taking him back to the house?"

The vampire turned and laughed at Ryan hysterically. "You know, as I think back, you're right, Ryan. We never really did have a deal. I mean, we didn't cut our palms and become blood brothers or anything." He shrugged. "So unfortunate."

"You son-of-a-bitch," Ryan screamed. "I am going to get out of here, and I am going to hunt you down. I am going to pluck every hair from your head one by one, and I am going to enjoy doing it. Then I'm going to sit back and watch my palm prints fade from around your neck after you've taken your last breath, you fucking piece of shit."

"Wow! That's a couple of run-on sentences," the vampire laughed, kicking Ryan the TV channel changer that had fallen on the floor. "Entertain yourself, mortal. Maybe there's a Supernatural all-nighter on that'll get you inspired." He adjusted Ellie's weight, spun their bodies around like a centrifugal top, and dematerialized before Ryan's eyes.

"How the fuck does he do that?" Ryan wondered, as he sat on the bed with his back to the wall "Okay Lachey," he said to himself, "let's evaluate the other team. We've got a deranged psycho-sucker playing center, and a duffus cop guarding him on the right." He pulled the library card out of his pocket and took a closer look at the signature. "Shit," he said, reading through the scrawl. "It's Kevin's dad's. And if Cody gave Colin the book, that pretty much means the no-show brother is guarding his twin on the left of the field. The question is, is anyone running interference?"

Before Ryan could think this thought through further, he felt his eyelids becoming increasingly heavy. It was only a few minutes before his body toppled sideways on the bed, and he began to snore.

His slumber was far from peaceful. Ryan instinctively curled up on the bed with his back to the wall, much like a dog would for protection. The grey blanket stamped 'Property of Troy Police' was lying at the bottom of the steel framed bed, and despite the fact that he lay there shivering, he did not have enough awareness about himself to pull the cover over his body.

He fell into a fragmented dream of no particular significance. One moment he was on the football field, hitting the ball with his six string guitar, the next he was arguing with Betty whether Stan could drive the Toyota. Throughout it all his shoulder throbbed and his legs became cramped, but he refused to change position.

"Jacey's my best friend," he cried out in delusion.

He broke into a cold sweat, and eventually the dampness against his shirt woke him from his REM stage. "Fuck," he said, finally reaching for the blanket. "I'm seriously going mental in here and it's only been a few days. There's no way I could do this for the rest of my life."

He sat up in the corner, draping the wool around him. "Somebody's going to slip up somewhere, and I'm going to have to be ready. I just need some time to think clearly and write the playbook." He continued the thought process he was going through earlier, placing the vampire and the two Dayton's on one side of the field, and himself, Ellie, Tom and Jacey on the other. "We're doomed," he acknowledged as the outside door to the police station began to open once more.

Chapter 24

As soon as the Lachey's side door opened, Jacey threw her arms around the first person she saw. It happened to be Helen, who didn't like to be touched by people she hardly knew in the first place, let alone locked in a fright squeeze by one.

"Help us," Jacey begged.

"I will if you let me go," Helen replied.

"Give her to me," Helena said, putting her arms around Jacey's shoulder, pulling her away from Helen as she did so. "What on earth happened?" she asked the frightened girl.

As they went up the stairs, Jacey briefly told them that she and Ellie had gone out shopping after church, leaving Stan with Tom, and when they returned home, they had found Tom lying unconscious on the floor.

"Ellie went to look for Stan," she explained. "I dialed directory assistance to get your number. She thought I needed it to dial 911. Sha... like I'm an airhead or summat."

"Have you called an ambulance?" Helen asked.

"What for? I don't think this is an ambulance type of thing. I don't think paramedics take paranormal classes even though they kind of sound the same. You know, para-whatsits." She paused, fingering the cross around her neck. "I could be wrong I guess, but I don't know... my spooky senses are tingling. I think Tom was knocked senseless by a vampire. And I think the vampire might have Stan."

"Oh dear," Helena sighed.

"Good God," Helen said, looking at her mother. "I want to laugh, but somehow... somehow I get the feeling nobody is joking around here."

Tom was sitting on the bed, rubbing his head, when the ladies walked into Stan's bedroom. The encounter had left him somewhat dazed and confused. "Where am I?" he asked.

"You're at the Lachey's. Let me see that eye," Helena demanded, grabbing Tom's head in her hands. A welt stretched from the side of his head to his nose. It looked like he had run into the proverbial brick wall. "You're going to have a beauty of a black eye," she noted, checking the rest of his head for contusions.

"A shiner?" Tom winced. "I never had a shiner before. How's it going to look?"

"In less than a week," Helena predicted, "you will be up to your leading man antics. But you might want to lay low for a while. Tell your parents you got in the way of Stan's baseball bat."

"Stan," Tom remembered. "I forgot about Stan. Where is he?"

The ladies looked at each other helplessly.

"Goth-Chic's gone to find him," Jacey offered.

"Goth-Chic?" Helen questioned.

"I'll explain later," Helena replied.

"Seriously? They're calling her Goth-Chic?" Helen continued. "I was afraid something like this would happen if I didn't get her to the Biggie-Mart." She looked sternly at Jacey. "What do they call you?"

"Hot," Jacey offered with a big smile on her face.

"Never mind, Helen," her mother interrupted. "We have bigger things to worry about."

"Oh really?" Helen agreed sarcastically. "Those vampires have a way of slipping your mind, don't they?"

"Shit, I forgot about him too," Tom remembered. "He must have hit me harder than I thought. My brain's not working right."

"You'll be fine, Tom," Helena assured him.

"So let me get this straight," Helen said, trying to put the pieces of the puzzle together. "You, Tom... you think you were kicked in the head by a vampire?"

"I know I was," he answered.

"And you, Jacey... you believe him?"

"Well, I've never actually seen him," she began, "but Stan talks about him all the time."

"All the time?" Helena asked.

Tom and Jacey nodded in unison.

"And you, Mother… you believe what they are saying to be true?"

"Uh-oh," Helena grimaced. Maybe it was too late for the Colorado blue lawn seed after all. Maybe the whole neighborhood knew about her backyard guest. "Think, Helena, think," she thought to herself. "How do I get out of this one?"

"You can't," Helen said aloud.

"Now?" Helena said, shocked. "Now you decide to read people's minds?"

"Not people's," Helen said. "Yours. You are not people. You are my mother. You are an entirely different sub-genre. I had this argument with Ellie a few days ago."

Helena folded her arms across her chest and looked disapprovingly at her daughter.

"Don't try to block me out," Helen warned. "It's too late for that. I want to know all about the vampire. So you can tell me, or…"

"Or what, Helen?"

"Or I'll break down that wall you're trying to put up and discover all kinds of secrets about you that I probably don't really want to know."

"Is anyone else in here freezing?" Helena asked, ignoring her for the moment. She'd rather get into it with Helen at home later, without other people's children listening to the whole conversation.

She walked around the bed to the open window, and was about to close it when something drew her attention away from that thought. She noticed a tiny footprint on the windowsill. She looked down at the ground hoping for a clue as to where the vampire had taken Stan, but there were too many footprints already in the snow to tell for sure. "Let's get downstairs, start a fire and think this thing through," she said to them.

She had never been in Betty's house before, and doubted she ever would again. "Shame," she thought to herself. The pictures on the walls, and the collection of antiques she was discovering throughout the house, gave Helena a whole new sense of Betty. A Betty she might actually get to like, should she have the chance. "Not going to happen," she sighed.

"What's that, Mother?" Helen asked, following the three others down to the Lachey's living room. "You know, we could just turn up the heat."

"That's strange," Helena commented, noticing something peculiar in the otherwise orderly room. "Why is there ash on Betty's Persian rug?" She bent down, took a little of the soot into the palm of her hand and sniffed. "Hmm, white oak. I have a heck of a time with the hardwoods. I usually opt for spruce. She must get Ryan to split it for her."

The fresh trail of soot led directly into the fireplace. Helena felt the grate. It was cold. "Weird. This mess looks fresh; like it's just been blown out of the chimney."

"Maybe it's the wind," Jacey offered. "It's kind of nasty out there."

"Do you want me to grab the vacuum and clean it up?" Tom asked. "Betty will freak, and… well… maybe Betty doesn't really need to freak out again right now."

"Tom, find me a flashlight, will you?" Helena asked. "I want to look up the flue."

"Sure thing," he said. "Stan has flashlights all over the house." He opened up the drawer on the coffee table and took one out. "Would you like me to check it out for you, Mrs. LaRose? I'm looking kind of shabby now anyway."

"Okay Tom," she said apprehensively. Tom had a point, the vampire had left him rather rumpled, and her turtleneck was brand new. No sense wrecking a perfectly good sweater, she reckoned.

Tom sunk to the floor and leaned on the base of the fireplace. He turned on the flashlight and contorted his body into a position that allowed him to look up inside the chimney. "I think there's something stuck up there," he said. "I can't see any daylight."

"Maybe it's just really dirty," Helen offered.

"No," Tom said. "Betty had it swept out at the beginning of the month. I remember her coming into the hardware store looking for a self-cleaning log. My dad said she was better off to have it professionally done for insurance purposes. The chimney sweep came on a Saturday, the day after the Trojans beat the Argonauts. Ryan told me the guy woke him up by walking on the roof."

"I guess we can rule neglect out," Helena agreed. "I wonder what the problem is?"

"Maybe a there's a raccoon in there," Tom said. "I hear something whimpering." He shoved his head as far as he could into the brick structure to take a better look.

Like the whispering walls of St. Paul's Cathedral, the soft cries coming from the animal caught in the brick and mortar stack worked their way down to Tom. "I think it's talking to me," he said bewilderedly. "I could have sworn it called my name."

"Oh, no…" Helena said, clamping her hand over her mouth.

"My head, my head…" Helen cried. "It's starting again." She pressed her hands to her skull. Her forehead began to wrinkle.

"Helen, do you see what I think you see?" Helena asked. She feared now that the reason she had not seen extra footprints in the snow was because the vampire had not gone to the ground. He had gone up.

"Yes, I do." Helen squeaked, jumping up and down nervously on the spot. "Oh my God, call the fire department."

"We can't call the fire department," Helena said calmly.

"What's wrong?" Jacey asked. "Do you want me to call the police?"

"No! No police," the LaRoses cried. It was not going to be good if the Dayton's answered the call.

"Tom, come out from there," Helena instructed. "Let me talk to him."

Tom didn't move.

"Helen, keep focused," she demanded. "Jacey, help me pull Tom out of there. He's fainted again."

Helena crouched down and grabbed one of Tom's legs, indicating to Jacey that she should do the same with the other. They pulled hard, moving Tom's limp body out from inside the hearth as fast as they could.

"Why would Tom faint again?" Jacey asked. "I thought he was okay now. If it's just a stupid raccoon…" Then it dawned on her. "Stan," she whispered. "He's in the chimney?"

The LaRoses looked at her gravely and nodded.

"I'm afraid so," Helena admitted.

255

"We have to call Roy," Helen insisted.

"We can't call Roy either," Helena said. "This is something we're going to have to handle ourselves." She raised the finger of her left hand to her lips and tapped gently upon them. "Think, Helena, think. How on earth do we get Stan out of this alive?" There was no simple answer. "So help me, Hannah," she said under her breath, "when I get my hands on that undead little beggar, he's going to wish he was dead." She turned and pulled a crocheted afghan from the sofa. "And no, I was not talking about little Stan."

"Where are you going?" Helen asked her. She could see the determination in her mother's pursed lips.

"I'm going up on the roof," Helena answered.

"You can't go up on the roof," Helen protested "You'll kill yourself."

"No such luck," Helena reasoned. "Jacey, go throw some water on Tom's face. I need him to find me some rope. He seems to know where everything is in this house. Helen, go back to my basement and get me my rock climbing shoes. I keep them under the stairs."

"You have rock climbing shoes?" Jacey asked in wonderment. "I didn't know Jimmy Choo made those."

"He doesn't," Helena said. "But he never spent a god-forsaken honeymoon in the Himalayas with Helen's father."

Less than five minutes later, the four regrouped themselves back on the driveway. Helen, Jacey and the now revived Tom watched in wonder as Helena took the rope Tom had found and began to form a lariat. She quickly tied a honda knot, leaving enough room in the loop to go over the top of the chimney.

"Where were you and Dad when you learned that?" Helen asked. She had never seen Helena pull this particular trick out of her sleeve before.

"Mexico," Helena answered. "And I wasn't with your father, I was with Jesse James."

"Whoa," Tom said. "I didn't know you went in for tattooed guys. Ryan will be stoked."

"I don't think we're talking about the same Jesse James," Helen said.

Helena began her windup. The first attempt landed short of the target, but luckily fell back to the ground without snagging on anything else. Her second effort was better, but only caught the corner of the chimney. "Third time's the charm," she said, swinging harder and aiming higher than the two previous attempts. This time the rope landed over the stack. "Voila!" she said, pleased with herself.

"I am in awe," Tom admitted.

"Wish me luck," she said, tying the crocheted afghan around her neck. She pulled the rope taught and began to climb, the blanket flowing down her back like a cape.

"I'm beginning to see what Ryan sees in your mother," Tom said, perhaps inappropriately.

"What?" Helen asked.

"She's Batman," he confirmed.

"Batgirl," Jacey corrected him.

As Helena swung her leg over the side of the eaves, she collided with the drainpipe. Already heavily laden with wet soggy leaves, it didn't take much for it to give way. It came crashing to the ground, missing Jacey's head by about an inch.

"Kerpow!" Tom said, looking at the damage. "Good thing my dad has them in stock this time of year."

"Sorry!" Helena yelled. "Foot slipped."

"Mother please be careful," Helen begged.

Helena pulled herself the rest of the way onto the roof, where the wet snow and the slope of the timbers made her every move all the more perilous. She stood up cautiously. "Tom, the guy who did the chimney cleaning for Betty, will he do the eaves as well? My own don't look any better from up here."

"Mother, pay attention please!" Helen begged.

Helena had almost reached the chimney when she hit a patch of ice and began to slide backward from the slope. "Uh-oh," she exclaimed, hanging onto the rope for dear life. "I should have tied a safety."

Helen and the teenagers watched breathlessly as Helena came within inches of the end of the roof and then stopped.

"Mother! You are out of your ever-loving mind. Get back down here and let me call Roy."

Helena knew that was not an option. Roy was going to have his hands full dealing with the Daytons when this was all over. He didn't need to have to explain to the taxpayers of Troy how little Stan Lachey, while his brother was in jail and his mother was in the hospital, got stuck in a chimney on the first winter storm of the year. She pulled herself back up onto her feet and moved very slowly back towards the stack.

"Stan," she said, when she was close enough that she thought he might hear her. "Stan, it's Helena. I'm here."

Much to her surprise, a tiny hand poked its way out of the chimney. Helena heaved a sigh of relief. He was still alive. "Stan, listen to me. I'm going to get you out of there, but I need you to stay really still. Wave your hand if you understand."

There was no motion.

"It's okay to move your hand if you can, Stan" she corrected. "I didn't mean you had to stay that still."

She saw his palm move from left to right and back again.

Tom looked up at the activity on the roof. "What's she going to do now?" he asked.

"I don't know," Helen admitted.

Jacey cocked her head. "It looks like she's going to karate chop the chimney."

"That would just be stupid," Helen said.

"I think she's right," Tom offered. "She's sizing it up, like you would a stack of planks. Look, she's turning her hand to the grain of the brick. She's done this before."

On the roof, Helena took a huge breath. She knew she had to calculate just how much force it would take to smash the bricks yet leave Stan unscathed. She could do it, she knew, but it had been a few years since she had to summon this kind of strength from her forearm, and she needed to prepare mentally for it. She wasn't just fighting the technical engineering of the contractors who had built the house in the late sixties. She was also fighting a force of the undead. That took extra prep time.

"Hi-yaaaa!" she screamed, raising her left arm to chest level and plowing through the clay mass like it was a bale of hay.

"Look out!" Helen screamed, as pieces of the structure began to fall to the ground.

"She is just…" Tom searched for the words, "…totally bitchin'."

Enough of the bricks had fallen away from the side of the chimney for Helena to be able to reach for the child. "Stan," Helena said, looking him directly in the eye, "you are a star. I need you to just stay calm for a few minutes more." She lifted his body from the confines of the chimney. He was amazingly warm. The tightness of his body to the chimney walls had acted as an insulator while he was stuck inside them.

She draped the afghan around both of their bodies and pulled him closer. She wanted to keep him from going into shock now that he was free. "Bet you never thought you'd be doing this today, did you Stan?" she said, trying to break the tension. She reached for the rope. It might have been a good way for her to get up on the roof, but it wasn't the easiest way for them to get off it.

"Don't just stand there like a bunch of reporters waiting for the fall," she said to the three people below, gaping at her with their mouths wide open. "Tom, go get the trampoline from the end of the yard and move it closer." She gave Stan a light squeeze. "Stan, we're going to do this together, okay? We're going to go for a little bouncy ride."

"Mrs. LaRose," Stan asked wearily, "can you do me a favor?"

"What is it, Stan?"

"Can you not tell Ryan that I peed my pants?"

Helena smiled. "I think that can be our little secret."

"Good," Stan sighed. "And Mrs. LaRose… when I wake up… can you give me some medicine so I don't dream about the vampire in your backyard anymore?"

"I'll see what I can do Stan," she said, putting his arms around her neck and hers around his waist before jumping off the roof onto the trampoline beneath. The two of them took more than a few bounces before coming to a halt. The canvas almost touched the ground with the weight of them falling from such a height. When the motion finally stopped, Helena still had Stan in her arms. She pulled their bodies from the trampoline.

"Where are you going?" Helen asked. "Shouldn't we take him to a doctor?"

"I am a doctor," her mother reminded her. "I'm taking him to my office. I'm going to give him a little something to help him sleep, and hopefully not remember any of this. Ix-nay on the vampire-ay, okay you guys? Not a word to anyone about this. Ever."

They nodded in agreement.

Alone in her office, Helena sat Stan on her couch and covered him with the crocheted blanket. She prepared some valerian tea to rehydrate him. He drank it thirstily. She could tell he was drowsy from his ordeal, but his adrenaline was most likely stopping him from falling asleep. She needed him asleep.

"Stan, let's read," she said, pulling a book randomly from her bookcase. It happened to be a copy of Grey's Anatomy. She opened the book in the middle and began to read in a low, monotonous tone. It was enough to make Stan close his eyes.

"Finally," she whispered, and reached for another book. It was a small, black, tattered and torn book with a cover that had 'Book of Spells' embossed on it. She gently thumbed through the weathered pages until she found what she was looking for.

"Somnus quod alieno," she sang over and over again, in a lullaby, until Stan began to snore. "Sleep and forget, my child," she whispered softly in his ear. She looked up to see Helen's face peering at her through the window. She motioned for her to come in, indicating for her to be quiet.

"Where are Tom and Jacey?" Helen asked, looking around the room. Her mother had done a marvelous job turning the cottage in the backyard into an office. She saw the doctorate proudly displayed in a frame beside the door.

"They've gone to visit Ryan," Helen answered. "And to try to find Ellie."

Helena turned and looked out the window. Her garden was completely covered in snow, and she hadn't had a chance to plant the spring bulbs yet. Just another thing left undone, she acknowledged to herself.

"Is he okay?" Helen asked her, noticing Stan curled up on the couch.

"He's fine. I've used a memory spell on him. When he wakes up, he's not going to remember a thing." She reached over the child and stroked his sweaty hair. "I guess I'd better get him back to his room. I lifted him once, I can lift him again. It'll be easier than explaining why he's here when he wakes up." She looked at Helen. "We'll have to stay with him until the kids get back."

Helen nodded in agreement. "You know," she said, "you were really brave this afternoon."

"Thank you," Helena replied.

"I didn't know you still had it in you."

"Why? Is it because you think I'm not exactly young? I'm not exactly old either. Not in our lives. Not in anyone's life, actually. You should go see your grandmother some time."

"Elaine?"

"Yes, Elaine. She's still living in the castle in England. She's not one to leave her home for long, my mother."

"How old is she now?" Helen asked.

"I don't know... one century, seven centuries... she hides her age well. She's walking with a bit of a limp though, from that last battle with Beelzebub. He's her own personal stalker. How'd you like to have to shoulder that?"

"No thanks," Helen admitted. "What does this all mean, anyway?" she asked her mother. "If a vampire did really take Stan, why would he stuff him in the chimney? Why didn't he finish him off like he presumably did to Brooke and Kevin?"

"Stan's just the bait," Helena said sadly. "It means he's really after Ellie."

Chapter 25

The teenager stepped on the round ring attached to the base of the old hand-washing fountain in the boys' washroom. Tiny streams of water shot out from the top of the birdbath-like apparatus and landed in the large granite sink below. That had surprised him when he first moved in. He would have thought someone would have turned the water off long ago. He doubted the old schoolhouse had been used in years.

People in Troy were undeniably stupid, he reckoned. He couldn't deny though, that their little oversight would come in handy. He did like to freshen up every once in a while. The stench on his hands of recently eaten rodent burger offended him, and he needed to cleanse it off before he could do anything else. Someone had stolen the copper piping from the shower room, so the makeshift basin would have to do. It had been hard to keep clean since SHE kicked him out of the house. That was just one more reason to hate HER.

He looked at himself through the cracked mirror. "Gaspar BonVillaine, you are one scary dude. You used to be so handsome." Funny how he could see his own reflection in the mirror, although no human would ever be able to do so. "I guess they see what they want to see," he shrugged, lowering his sweaty black hair into the sink as best he could. The water was cold, but he preferred it that way.

He had found the empty building his first night away from HER. What did she really expect? Did she think he was going to be able to change his ways when those other people arrived? He was enjoying a symbiotic relationship with HER before she had answered the phone that night. Then everything changed. SHE suddenly didn't care about him. SHE suddenly mistrusted him. As if it was his fault. Was he supposed to just flip a switch and erase everything that had happened to him and what he had become? SHE knew better than that.

"You're like family to me," SHE had once said.

"So much for that," he said to himself. SHE had told him he had to get out. Well, maybe that wasn't really what had happened. SHE had told him he couldn't come in. Small difference, and yet a big one. He physically couldn't come in anymore. He wondered why that rule came in to play. Was there some union somewhere that negotiated the right to trespass out of the vampire/human contract? He didn't know. He could only accept that SHE had warned him it would be like that, and he had very recently found it to be true.

So he had searched for a new place to rest and came upon the deserted schoolhouse. Since no one lived there, technically he didn't have to be invited in. Score one for the bloodsucker. And it really wasn't so bad. There was plenty of room. He had his choice of several rooms to call his own, although he did find the furnishings a little sparse. The desks were all gone now, but a bed was still in what had been the sick room. The sick room that had no windows. It was like it had been designed to his particular taste. "Queer Eye for the Dead Guy," he laughed.

Taste. That was the bonus. There was no one around to care whether he was eating properly or not. Eating properly bothered the humans, he knew. Here, he wasn't going to have to remember to bury the bones. He could stockpile them like little trophies. Humans found that to be incredibly rude. They looked upon it with the same scorn they did when someone drank milk straight out of the carton. They had an odd sense of the uncouth, humans. T-bones were all fine and dandy, but leave a little rabbit head around and all hell breaks loose.

Why things like this would suddenly bother HER, did not make any sense to him. SHE had been the one who initially taught him how to feed. True, SHE didn't participate herself, but SHE had gone to all that trouble to find him that book. The feeding book. It wasn't something you could order over the internet through Barnes and Noble. SHE had taken a trip to Louisiana to get it for him. SHE had aided and abetted him.

The book had been a godsend. Ironic, that. It taught him the kinds of animals that you could take without people noticing... crows, seagulls, and squirrels. It also taught him the kinds of animal that you could take but needed to be quick about… dogs, cats, and rabbits. And it had pictures. Lots of graphic, how-to pictures of quick and easy dissections.

It also stated very clearly, that when eventually those dietary choices weren't enough, one would have to expand the food groups to humans. SHE knew this. SHE said it was like going from strained peas to solids. He would have to cut his teeth all over again, SHE said, but this time the bleeding gums wouldn't bother him.

So it wasn't like SHE didn't know it would happen sometime. Had SHE figured out that this was the time?

He couldn't fully explain what had happened to him when he saw the little girl go running around the corner that night. He hadn't planned on snatching her. Something had come over him. It had been fine until the little girl fell and scraped her knee. Then the aroma hit him. He could taste her just by the smell of that tiny trickle of hemoglobin. It whiffed through his nostrils and sent his saliva glands into hyper drive. He couldn't control the drool. The child became his fix, and he moved silently and stealthy towards her until the girl had no choice but to surrender, Dorothy.

He had started to take her back to the schoolhouse, but that had been problematic. A shadowman and a teenaged girl, half hidden under the cover of an old bridge had come across him in his travels. He tried to run by them, but his prey had summoned some inner strength and called out to them. He had no choice but to disappear under the bridge with the girl and take the life from her.

He started to feed.

It hadn't been like he had expected, tasting human flesh for the first time. He bowed his head above her carotid artery and threw any sense of right and wrong to the wind. His incisors ached as he tore through the young girl's flesh. He found it sweet, but tougher than he would have imagined. It was strangely sinewy like a cheaper cut of meat, pre-seasoned with the salt from her own sweat. Her blood didn't taste much different than his own had, when he was human. She was like sucking on one big rib-eye, he told himself.

He should have been repulsed. He knew that. But it was a lot like when he used to crave salt and found himself eating far more potato chips than he should of. He just couldn't help himself. His throat filled with her rich red syrup, and he found himself choking in his vigor, forgetting to take time to swallow.

But the girl was bigger than anything he had fed on before, and he couldn't finish her off. Not then and there. He was going to have to find a place to store her, temporarily. He opted to use the cold murky water of the creek as a make-shift refrigerator, planning to return and feed on her later.

Except that then, the bald headed giant decided to join the party uninvited. The big boy had stumbled upon his water pantry. He lived next door to HER, with his nerdy little brother and his big, fat mama. There was a score to settle with their whole frickin' family, but now was hardly the time.

Now he was going to have to fight for the girl. The earlier feast had left him a little tired and a little intoxicated, making it difficult to fend off the boy he had watched play football almost every Friday night for the past year. True, the jock had conveniently wound up going to jail for the crime, taking the heat off for a while, but it wasn't a particularly proud moment for his vampire legacy.

So, the next time he prepared. He had located a proper refrigerator to store his dinner in, and he had picked a little porker boy to gnaw on. But that hadn't worked out as planned either.

Damn that old farmer. He wasn't supposed to have come out of the house to see the old beer fridge walking away. He wasn't supposed to give chase. That had turned the whole thing into a messy situation that ended with the cops coming to take away his kill for a second time.

He had been depressed for a moment until he got a whiff of the Lachey kid, who was conveniently all alone in the cop car. If only the police had stayed away from the cruiser for a few more moments, he could have caught the kid on the first go round, saving everyone so much frickin' time.

He laughed. He had more frickin' time than any of them, when you thought about it.

The monster he was becoming was not lost on him. It seemed like yester-day, he had been minding his own business, playing a little basketball in the driveway, when the fight had begun. And he knew he should be grateful that he was given another chance at life... or a reasonable facsimile of one... but darn it all to hell, he just wasn't feeling very appreciative today.

He was feeling particularly unloved. SHE didn't miss him. No one missed him. He had only lived in the stupid town a short time before his humanity ended. It had been a truly bad move, landing in that neighborhood. His mother was dead. No one had offered her another life. And come to think of it, SHE could have.

"Things could have been so different," he lamented. He might have even been a friend of the leviathan, Ryan. He could see himself riding around in that beat-up car with him and the guy with the perfect hair. He might have been able to make things right for the British girl, the one with all the secrets. But none of that was going to happen now.

"You bet your Mrs. Harbinger it's not," he sighed. He glanced over to the spot his eyes had been avoiding for the past few hours… the corner where his latest prey was lying limp like a wet doormat. Just before he had knocked her out earlier, he had felt something he hadn't felt for a long time. Emotion.

"It makes me want to throw up," he said, heading towards the bathroom stall. He went through the motions of retching, even though he knew damn well it wasn't going to happen. He had always had a solid constitution.

He sat on the cold toilet and hung his head, trying not to think about the girl. He wasn't ready for her, but she mustn't stumble upon that tidbit of information.

Ellie lay semi-conscious on the cold, hard, cement floor. She opened her eyes and waited for her sight to adjust to the dim light around her.

Her head was pounding from the blow she had taken earlier, and just opening her eyes gave her migraine-like pain. But being awake and hurting, she knew, was better than being dead. She tried to stop her world from spinning. "Earth to Ellie," she told herself. "Come in, Ellie."

There was no one in her direct line of sight, but she had the sense she was not alone. "Where did that rat bastard go?" she wondered, peering into the unknown surroundings. Slowly, her eyes adjusted to the dimly lit room and she was able to see things more clearly.

The walls surrounding her were painted an industrial shade of green that was starting to flake off in spots. There was graffiti on the wall beside her.

Whoever Mary Ann Martin was, she was evidently a girl of many talents, as noted by the likes of "Bad Bobby Braun" and someone named "The Whip."

"Why can they never spell?" she commented, wondering how anyone could get the word penis wrong.

She turned her head and noticed the large wash basin beside her. Behind that, was a y-shaped pipe leading down to a low, ten-foot long trough. "Good God," she surmised. "I'm in the boys' washroom in St. Mary's Shrine of the Little Hellhole High." The only thing missing was a crucifix.

She tried to sit up, and was startled by the sound of a chain dragging across the floor. A chain that was attached to her right leg and then to the ring pedestal of the fountain.

"What the hell?" she wondered.

"Poppet," she heard the voice sneer, "you've come to your senses. I've been waiting for you."

"I am not your PUPPET," she snarled at him, turning her body towards the voice. She recognized her captor as the vampire in her dream and the thug that had hit her at the police station.

"I said Poppet," he insisted. "But really it means almost the same thing. It's my pet name for you. I heard that English girl call your little next door neighbor that once. I like it. Makes my lips pop when I say it. Pop-pet," he mouthed.

"Then learn to ENUNCIATE through those drooling fangs of yours."

"Now, now, Poppet," he sighed. "Why can't you just sit chained in the corner like a good little girl and leave me alone to think?"

She struggled to her feet. "Maybe because I'm not a little girl, you sorry excuse for a freak of nature. Come out where I can see you." She gritted her teeth and looked for him in the shadows.

The vampire was amused by her bravado. He emerged from behind one of the stalls and crept towards her, licking his lips as he did so. "Look at the little girl trying to be all big and scary," he laughed. "Oooh, I'm shaking."

"Try this little one on for size," she said, making a fist and daring him to come nearer. "Look at the vampire trying to be all big and scary," she said, throwing a punch towards his face. "Shake this."

"Nice try," he said, catching her wrist with his left hand and pulling it behind her back before she had time to think twice. "No more wrestling channel for you, unless of course you'd like a cage match." He gave her a good look. "That would probably be more fun when you're older."

"Ow!" she cried.

"Hurts, huh?" he taunted. "And they say wrestling is fake. Say uncle, Poppet."

"Uncle," she said reluctantly. "Uncle Poppet."

The vampire released her. "Always with the sarcasm. Now you see why I don't need to tie down all of your extremities. Only the one. But I will, if you keep it up. Your choice."

He took his long, bony finger and gave her shoulder a little push, causing her to fall back to the floor. "Amateur," he said.

She defied him and stood back up, this time a little quicker. "Leech."

He smiled. "Synonym for a dark blood-sucking creature. I like it. You've got spunk, I'll give you that." He pushed her back to the floor "You don't really want to play teeter-totter all day, do you? It gets kind of boring. The heavy kid always wins in the end."

"I'm getting the hell out of here," Ellie said, getting up once more.

"Noohoo you're not. You're getting maybe three feet away from that wall. That's where the chain ends. And if you don't shut up and be quiet, it'll be shortened the next time you have the nerve to doze off in front of your host. Bad manners, girlfriend."

"You knock me out, kidnap me, and chain me to an ancient form of water torture, and you have the nerve to question my politeness? And I am *so* not your girlfriend, sister."

Gaspar smacked her hard in the face, his fingers stinging her in the eye.

"What did you do that for?" she asked.

"Because I can, little girl cry-baby," he taunted, noticing she was tearing up. "I didn't ask you to enter my world. But you did. Three times. First with Willie and then with HER, and then with your pro-ball friend."

"You hit me again, and you'll be sorry."

"Why? What are you going to do to me?" Gaspar laughed at her. "Seriously, what exactly do I have to be afraid of?"

Ellie mulled this over. He had a point. Hurting his feelings wouldn't work. Pain probably wasn't an issue with him, but there had to be another way to get to him. She only hoped she had enough time to figure out his weakness. "Who's Willie?" she asked, stalling for time. "One of your sabre-tooth pals?"

"The man you were with on the bridge."

"Shadowman? You know the shadowman?"

"His name's Willie. Trust HER not to tell you."

"Who's HER? I mean, who is SHE?"

"Don't play stupid with me."

"I'm not playing anything."

"You're pretty bitchy for someone in chains, Alice."

"Look. I don't know who these people are that you're talking about," Ellie said, exasperated. "Are they your stand-ins for some 'Spawn of the Dead' play you're rehearsing?"

"Liar. You came to live with HER. You and that other woman."

"HER is my grandmother?" she asked. "Helena?"

"Your grandmother? Well then, that's even better. SHE's really going to miss you, now that I've got you. You're not just some stray she took in from the street. SHE does have a habit of doing that, you know. Waif adoptions. The orphanage on Maple Street, a.k.a. the LaRose Naturopathic Clinic." He sighed. "A rose by any other name..."

"You took me and you don't even know who I am? Thanks for making me feel special."

"Get over yourself. The 'you' wasn't important. I just wanted to re-stock my pantry for the winter with someone SHE'd chase. I didn't know you were related to HER."

"Look, I don't know what your problem is, but I'm sure there's a self-help book out there that covers this. Why don't we just go to the local bookstore and find one for you?" she quipped. "I'll buy."

"SHUT UP!" he demanded.

He studied her face. It was young and it was pretty, and oddly familiar. "You know I should have figured it out earlier. You look like HER. Those same green eyes that try to look right through you. I knew I had seen eyes like that before.

That same coal colored hair that would grow back even longer if one were to rip it from your head by the roots."

Ellie felt around her scalp. Thankfully, all of her locks seemed to be in place. "You're still into tugging girls' hair? Isn't that kind of grade three?"

"I love HER and I hate HER. How can that be possible, Poppet?" he asked, a hint of despair in his voice.

Ellie paused. His face was inches from her own, and yet he had held back from further confrontation, preferring to wait for her to answer. Did he really expect her to offer advice under these circumstances? "You suffer from hetero-chromia," she finally said.

"I don't suffer from anything," he told her, but she could see he was troubled by her remark. "That's a pretty big word for someone your age. What's my eye color got to do with it?"

"Colors. Plural." She glanced again at his irises. It was odd enough that they were different colors, but if she wasn't mistaken, they were the same two colors the mangy dog's had been. The dog that had trapped her in the van her first night in Troy. "Woof," she said, expecting a reaction from him. "You're geneti-cally mixed up."

The vampire remained ominously quiet.

"You're a deranged sociopath, you know that? "Why did you kill those two kids? What did they ever do to you?" she asked.

"They didn't have to do anything to me. I'm a vampire. Why don't you humans get that we are not nice people? We're not people at all."

Ellie stared at him blankly. For her, it was one of those moments when there really was nothing you could say to make things better.

"What? I'm not all bad. I let one get away. That Lachey kid. I could have kept you both, but I didn't. That should count for something, shouldn't it?"

"Ryan?"

The vampire laughed. "Ryan? What the hell would I want with Ryan? I had the nerdy one. And just to make you happy, I left him where they'll find him. I think. If it's not too late."

"What's wrong with Ryan? What's wrong with Stan for that matter? He's not nerdy. He's just a kid."

"Let me explain this to you," The vampire began. "You know how some-times you open a bottle of wine and it's corked? Of course you don't. You're just a child. Well, take my word for it. Stan's corked. It was pour him down the drain or let him go," he shrugged. "You should be happy I chose the second option. I poured him down something."

Ellie's hand grabbed near her heart. "I'm truly touched. Not."

"I broke his seal, took a couple of sips, and something wasn't quite right. He went all melanoma on me. I had to spit him out. I hate it when that happens."

"I think you mean malolactic, you idiot," Ellie challenged. "I've seen those wine shows on PBS. And it's not always considered a bad thing."

"Whatever," the vampire replied. "I thought he was going to be a bottle I could keep in the cellar to age for a few months. But I was wrong. He started to coagulate. I HATE THAT." He paused and studied his prey. "You really don't know what happened, do you?"

"No."

"Your friends. They betrayed you," he whispered vindictively, mimicking her and clutching his hands to his own heart. "How does that make you feel?"

"What are you talking about?"

"Pro-boy wanted to trade your life for his brother's. Pretty-boy's two-tim-ing you, and the one with the perfect lips? Well, she's got the biggest mouth on the planet... 'don't tell the Helens, don't tell the Helens'... and as for your grandmother..."

"Let me try to explain this to you," Ellie snarled. "SHE never has loved you. SHE never will love you. SHE will always hate you, because you have no redeeming qualities." She rose the middle finger of her right hand and gave him an F-salute.

"That's where you're wrong, Poppet," he said sincerely. "I have one big redeeming quality. No one will feel the need to cry for me when I'm dead, dead. It's too bad we can't say the same about you."

He stormed out of the washroom, leaving Ellie to imagine all kinds of atrocities that might become of her. She broke down and wept.

Chapter 26

*H*e said he'd let him go.

Ryan pounded his fist against the cement walls of his cell. He couldn't believe he had been so naive as to think he had an honor bound agreement with a member of the dark side. He winced as the rough edges of the brick wall tore the skin from his knuckles upon contact.

"Cut that out," Roy Cohen said. "I don't want to have to take you to the hospital. Or repair the wall. The last repair bill I got from Mike Webster was ridiculous, and it was just to insulate the window. I hate to imagine what he charges for grouting."

"How's Betty?" Ryan asked. He hadn't had an update on his mother since he last saw her. Sometimes no news was good news. Other times it was just no news. "Have you heard anything?"

"She's still under observation. By the doctors and us. I have Colin Dayton guarding her hospital door." The Chief checked the answering service for messages as he was talking, but there were none.

"Do you think that's a good idea?" Ryan asked, pacing nervously back and forth in his cell. Did he dare tell the Chief what he thought he knew about the Daytons?

"Why wouldn't it be?" Roy asked the teenager. "I did it as a precaution. I thought you'd like that." He took his pistol out of his holster, intent on cleaning it, but then decided that perhaps now was not the time. The way things were going, he might have the need to fire his weapon at any time.

"A precaution for who? Betty doesn't need a guard. The vampire's not after her."

272

"Did it ever occur to you that you might not be the only person in Troy who needs a bodyguard?" the Chief asked, sliding the gun back into its holster on his utility belt. "Betty doesn't need a bunch of gossiping church ladies appearing by her bedside reminding her that her number one son is behind bars."

"Betty doesn't go to church."

"And you're not a serial killer. Enquiring minds still want to know."

"I'm thinking you put Colin there so you'd know where he was." Ryan stated, immune to the Chief's attempted dig. "He's in on it, you know."

The Chief sat in his chair and gave Ryan a steady stare. "Really? How is it you keep finding all these things out before I do?" he asked. He noticed the poker book lying on the floor. He picked it up and read the description on the back cover. "How did this get in here?"

"Colin brought it in," Ryan said, pulling the library card from his pocket. "He gave me the book and I pulled this out from it before I tossed it back at him. I'm more of a comic reader myself." He twirled the card between his fingers. "He said Cody gave the book to him. I don't know how he got it. I thought you weren't supposed to lend library books to other people. Red Clark's going to have some hefty dues to pay, just sayin'. Do me a favor, don't arrest him for it. It'd be a little crowded in here."

The Chief made no indication to Ryan that he had found the Clark's bodies in their white truck, over the cliff, just like Helen had told him he would. There were black paint scrapes on the crushed driver-side door panel of the vehicle that had done more than one rollover on its journey down the embankment. In all likelihood, the foreign paint came from the Hummer that Helen also had seen in her dream. There was only one Hummer in town, the Chief knew, and most days it was parked out back of his police station. It belonged to Cody Dayton. So Ryan was right. Unless Cody Dayton was lying in a hospital somewhere, and all indications were that he wasn't, he was in on it. Whether it was a hit and run, or whether his officer had intentionally murdered the Clarks was yet to be determined. Roy had posted Colin at the hospital to keep him under surveillance for the time being. The hospital had security cameras through the corridors, and he had alerted their security team to call him if for some reason Colin Dayton left his post.

"Why are you pacing, Ryan?" the Chief asked. Ryan had been walking a steady path back and forth in the cell since the Chief had arrived back and it was beginning to irritate him. "If you're missing any medication, I really need to know that."

"I'm not missing any fucking medication," Ryan yelled. "I'm locked up, I can't sleep, and…"

"And what, Ryan?" The Chief asked when Ryan ended the conversation abruptly. "Spill it."

"He was here again. The vampire. Dayton invited him in! It's like they're best buds or something. You need to fire his ass. He fucking left me alone with him, and I gotta tell ya, that's happening way too often around here. He left the damn door open like y'all are doing, and Ellie walked right on in. She didn't know he was here. The vampire hit her over the head with the plunger." He pointed to the weapon that was still lying on the floor. "Fucking gross, man."

The Chief got out of his chair and walked over for a closer look. This definitely wasn't where they normally kept the plunger. "What exactly are you trying to tell me?" he asked his prisoner.

"He took the plunger and swung at her like he was practicing for softball. Ellie hit her head on the wall on her way down. She's lucky she didn't crack her skull open. She was out cold, and he hit her again. The bastard hit her across the face."

"Where is she now?" the concerned Chief asked.

"Finally," Ryan said excitedly. "Finally someone fucking believes me."

"Ryan…"

"He took her. He picked her up, put her on his back and they disappeared. I know it sounds crazy, but swear to God, that's what happened. I wanted to tell you when you first walked through the door, but let's just say nobody's been taking what I say very seriously around here."

The Chief turned to him. He was about to say something to the teenager that would get him laughed out of the legal community. "I believe you, Ryan.

I'll perjure myself if I ever have to testify to the fact, but I do believe you." He reached for the heavy winter coat he had hung on the coat rack and put it on.

"Wait!" Ryan said. "Where are you going? You're not going to leave me alone again, are you?"

"I have to," the Chief admitted. "I need to go tell Helena what's happened. Purdy will be in soon. You can trust Purdy."

"Are you sure?" Ryan asked as the Chief turned to leave. "Will you tell him to bring me a sub? I'm fucking starving." He sat back down on the bed and watched the door close, leaving him by himself once more. "I give it five minutes before someone else walks through that stupid door," he said to himself. With the luck he had been having, he knew it wasn't going to be Purdy, but he prayed it wasn't the vampire. This time, he got lucky.

"Right then," Jacey said, stomping the snow off her boots, as she walked into the police station, holding the door open as she did so. "Come on, Tom," she moaned. "We've got some work to do. Hurry up." She nodded to Ryan. "He's not much of a runner, our Tommy." She had easily outpaced Tom in their dash to the jail.

"You two," Ryan said angrily as the winded Tom entered the room, "could you screw things up any more if you tried? Did you wake up thinking 'what else can I do to mess with Lachey?' No. Because that would take some thought." He took a closer look at Tom. "Nice eye, dude."

"A big hello to you too, Ryan," Jacey said sarcastically. Having never been in the jail before, she surveyed the surroundings. "A bit shabby, innit? Where's your orange jumpy?" She took her gloves off and put them on the Chief's desk.

"I don't do orange," Ryan sighed.

"Listen, Ry…we've got some news for you," Tom said slowly. He tried to find the words to begin to tell Ryan about his brother. "Stan is…"

"Save it, you knobs," Ryan protested. "I already know the vampire has Stan."

"Erm, no. He doesn't actually have Stan," Jaccy updated him. "Mrs. LaRose has Stan."

"Really?" Ryan asked hopefully, his mouth forming a slight smile. It was the best news he had heard in hours. He could feel some proverbial weight finally being lifted off his ailing shoulder. He subconsciously rotated it, the motion making him wince. It still hurt like hell, but his chances of having a doctor look at it were currently slim and none.

"She got him out of the chimney," Jacey said, like it was an everyday occurrence. "She's says he's going to be fine." She glanced at her fingernails. "All this running about has made my fingers all sweaty. I knew I should have waited longer for the topcoat to dry."

"What?" Ryan said unbelievingly.

"I've got the fuzzies from the inside of my gloves stuck to my nails," she said. "I'm going to have to do them all over again."

"Not your nails, Jacey," he said with exasperation. "What's this about Stan and the chimney?"

"Mrs. Larose climbed up on the roof and got Stan out of your whatsits," Jacey told him.

"Are you kidding me?" Ryan asked.

"Let's just say I wouldn't light a fire in your living room anytime soon," Jacey told him.

Ryan looked to Tom for help. "What the hell is she talking about?"

"It's true," Tom confirmed. "You should have seen her. I think she's an X-Man. She totally destroyed your stack."

"Woman," Jacey corrected him. "And what you said sounded rude."

"Whatever," Tom replied, annoyed.

"Actually it's 'X-Men'," Ryan added. "The chicks are still men. Don't look at me like that Jacey, I don't know why they are, but they are." He momentarily imagined Helena in a spandex suit. He smiled and shook his head, trying to remove the image from his brain. "Quit steering me away from reality. The bastard never should have got Stan in the first place. What we have here people," he said "is a fucking failure to fucking…"

"Communicate?" Tom asked.

"Launch?" Jacey said weakly.

"I was thinking 'plan'," Ryan said sarcastically. "But execute might be the right word under the circumstances. Weren't you listening, Tom? Didn't I try to tell you the vampire was after Stan? Didn't I tell you not to leave him alone? Because I'm thinking I did."

"I didn't leave him alone," Tom stammered, "I was with him the whole time."

"Except for when you were lying unconscious on the floor," Jacey reminded him.

Tom shrugged his shoulders. "A technicality. I'm lucky my neck wasn't broken during the battle."

Jacey rolled her eyes. "Battle?" The empathy she had initially felt for Tom's earlier ordeal had clearly worn off. "You could learn a thing or two about battle from Lord Nelson's statue."

"That dude," Tom continued, ignoring her, "he came out of nowhere."

"Yeah," Ryan admitted. "He does that. One minute he's there, and then poof."

Tom nodded. "We were way too hard on Ellie the day we walked back from the gravel pit. It turns out 'poof' and 'vampire' actually can happen."

"Here's the sit-u-ation…" Ryan began, as he told them what had happened to Ellie earlier in the police station.

"Oh, poor Ellie," Jacey said, shocked.

"Harsh," Ryan agreed.

"So what are we going to do now?" Tom asked. "How do we find her?"

"You need to go to Stillman's Creek," Ryan replied. "I'd say that's ground zero in vampireville."

Jacey nodded. "Ellie was pretty intent on going there herself. She was asking me earlier how to get to the old schoolhouse. She must have been asking about it for a reason."

"Yeah," Ryan nodded in agreement. "She told us it was in her dream. She said she saw an old schoolhouse, and I remember thinking about the one out by Tara's. It's been abandoned for a while."

"Then we need to borrow your car, Ryan. So we can get there," Tom added. "We'll hide out there until he leaves and then grab her."

"Take Jacey's car," Ryan said quickly. Tom driving the Toyota was not a good idea, even to save a girl. "The Toyota won't help you. I left the beast on the bridge."

"They had it towed. It's sitting at the back of the station in the fenced-off area. I saw it when we came around the corner," Tom told him.

"It's got to be getting low on gas," Ryan added. "Take Jacey's will you?"

"I haven't got my snow tires on yet," Jacey pouted. "We might get stuck."

"Okay, okay," Ryan relented. "You can take the Toyota, but Jacey drives."

With that settled, he thought again about the plan Tom had come up with. On the surface it sounded like a good one, except for the fact that it would just be Tom and Jacey trying to save Ellie. That wouldn't work. They needed more muscle. Cleary they hadn't thought this through.

"What are you going to do if she's hurt? Drag her to the car?" he sighed. Sore shoulder or not, he was worth two of them. "You guys have to get me out of here somehow."

"Way ahead of you, dude," Tom smiled. "We've got the formula."

"Spell," Jacey corrected him, "dude, we've got the spell." She reached into her pocket and brought out the three items that had been tucked deep inside.

Ryan eyed the goods with suspicion. "You brought a candle, a fat-boy bottle and some dirt? That's supposed to get me out?"

Jacey sighed. "Who's the knob now? What you see before you are incense, holy water and consecrated ground. Singularly, they're just stuff, but together they are like dynamite for a vampire killing spree." She pulled her phone from her pocket. "I'm just going to surf the web, enter those words and hit search," she smiled. "Then all your troubles will be over."

Ryan looked at Tom. "You're not seriously buying this?"

Tom shrugged. "I don't know if we need a spree, exactly."

"Here we go," Jacey said. "A perfect spell to set you free, courtesy of Google. Just give me a moment." She placed the items on the ground. "Does anyone have any matches?"

Ryan shook his head. So much for Jacey's preparation. "You didn't think of that? Like wouldn't that have been the easiest of the things to get?"

She ignored him and walked over to the emergency kit hanging on the wall. Inside the cabinet, she found what she needed. "Fire!" she said excitedly.

"What are you doing, Jaccy?" Ryan asked nervously. He didn't want the jail to catch on fire while he was locked inside the cell. He instinctively backed up from the bars.

"Ryan, come closer," Jacey said, lighting the incense.

"I'm okay where I am thanks," he replied.

"I said COME CLOSER TO THE BARS," she screeched. "Everybody do what I say. I'm going to stretch my arm, with the palm down, like this," she demonstrated. "Now Tom, I want you to place your hand the same way, over mine without touching it."

"Okay," he said, following her directions.

"Now Ryan," I need you to do the same thing. Get over here and put your hand over Tom's."

"Jacey," Ryan said with false patience, "we don't have time to play séance."

"No séance involved, I promise," she said. "I had this dream. It told me to go get specific items... that's why Ellie and I left you and Stan alone, Tom."

"No dreams!" Ryan yelled at her. "I've had enough of other people's dreams for like, FOREVER!"

"Just DO IT!" Jacey yelled back.

"Okay, okay," Ryan caved, and followed her orders.

"Good," she sighed with satisfaction. "Now we do the same thing with our other hand," she said, placing her left hand above Ryan's and waiting for them to follow her lead. "Now repeat with me... attero parietis, attero parietis, attero parietis."

"Jacey," Ryan sighed, "this idea is baked."

"I said REPEAT WITH ME," she shrieked, her facial features distorting grotesquely as she did so.

"I've never seen this poltergeist side of her before," Ryan said to Tom. "You're okay with this?"

"Let's just do what she says," Tom said, more than a little frightened. "It'll be easier that way."

"Attero parietis, attero parietis, attero parietis," they chanted.

Nothing happened.

Ryan looked at Tom. Tom looked at Jacey. Jacey got nervous and her foot hit the Buddha bottle. It tipped over, taking the incense to the floor with it. The holy water spilled onto the ground, and the flame that should have been extinguished, intensified.

"Holy shit," Ryan said. "This is no time for a miracle of water turning to oil. Jacey, what are you doing?"

"Attero parietis, attero parietis, attero parietis," Jacey continued. "Keep going…"

"Jacey!" Ryan begged. "You *do* realize I can't get out of here?"

"Just a little more… attero parietis, attero parietis, attero parietis!" she said, pushing the burning water bottle away from Ryan with her boot. The liquid splashed up the side of the prison wall.

"Will you please be careful, Spacey?" Ryan begged. He detected a smell in the air that reminded him of spent firecrackers. "This is not going to be good," he said nervously, staring at the liquid that had turned from clear to a red-hot.

The flickering flames used the liquid like a fuse, running from the bottom of the concrete floor, through the brick mortar, finally reaching the ceiling where they could move upward no more. Instead they turned the corner, fanned out, and ran across the back wall of Ryan's cell.

"Jacey!" Tom screamed in terror.

"Uh-oh," Jacey said. "Attero parietis!"

"Jacey," Ryan pleaded, "for the love of God, shut up!"

What happened next would leave the town of Troy whispering for years. An explosion blew up two walls of the Troy jail, leaving Ryan, Tom and Jacey standing debris covered, in a pile of rubble that once was the prison.

"Holy fuck," Ryan stammered, his mind having a tough time understanding what had just happened. "Did you throw a little gunpowder in that dirt?"

"What did you make us say?" Tom asked.

"Tear down the walls," Jacey said softly, looking at the damage that had been done. "Are you guys okay?" Tom had bits of concrete stuck to the gel in his hair.

"Yeah," Ryan nodded. "But next time Jacey, next time maybe you could try chanting 'open the door'. Just sayin'." He wondered what the Chief was going to say when he saw his non-existent jail. "Mike Webster's next invoice is going to be totally insane," he chuckled.

The sound of the explosion had woken up half the town, and it wasn't long before they heard the sound of fire trucks in the distance.

"What do we do now?" Tom asked.

"We run," Ryan answered, making a path through the pile of rubble that had once been his cell. "Jacey, I've got to hand it to you. This may go down as the greatest Trojan escape of all time." He took her hand to help her maneuver through the debris. "But if there's a mark on the Toyota because of this, I'll kill you," he said, squeezing her hand harder than he needed to.

The three of them ran to the back of the police station parking lot, where like Tom had said, Ryan's Toyota was waiting for them. The fence surrounding the impound lot had come down in the explosion.

"We need a gun. Tom, I forgot to tell you to get a gun. And some silver bullets," Jacey said while running towards the vehicle. "Do you have the keys to the hardware store?"

"I stocked the shelves this morning and we were all out of silver bullets," Tom replied, taken aback by Jacey's request. "Couldn't you ask for something a little easier to get? Like sulfur?"

"She just had sulfur," Ryan said, trying to open the car door. It was locked. "Look what happened. Kaboom! No sulfur." He reached under the car's frame for a magnetic key holder he had hidden beneath it." He took the spare key and unlocked the doors. "Get in," he ordered.

"Well, let me Google…" Jacey offered, jumping into the back seat as Tom took his place beside Ryan.

"No!" the boys cried out, turning around to look at her. "No Google!"

They tore out of the parking lot, just as Purdy's police car was arriving on the scene, the lights flashing as he brought the car to a stop.

"What the hell?" the officer yelled to them. He couldn't believe his own eyes. The police station was a smoldering mess.

"Purdy," Ryan yelled back at him through his open window. "We're okay, but we've got to go, dude."

Purdy shook his head in confusion. Part of him knew he should chase after them, and part of him needed to control the scene in front of him. "Fuck it," he said. "I didn't see anything."

Tom noticed Jacey reaching into her pocket. "What are you doing, Jacey?" he asked nervously.

"I'm going to try to call Ellie," she said, reaching for her phone.

"Tom," Ryan said sheepishly, "do you have any gas money?"

"She's not answering," Jacey said, reaching back into her pocket and pulling out a platinum credit card. "I have this for emergencies," she offered. "I'm thinking this counts."

"Jacey," Ryan began, "when this is all over I'm going to give you a big fat kiss."

Chapter 27

*H*elena took a key from her pocket and opened the door to her office. She had slipped away from Helen and Stan under the auspices that she had left the cottage door unlocked.

"Sure, that door you lock," Helen had noted. But she remembered her mother had not used a key to secure it when they had left. "Maybe you'd better check to make sure. Just hurry back. This house is giving me the creeps."

Helena knew damn well that the door had automatically locked behind them when they took Stan back home. She had thousands of dollars of non-prescription medicine locked away in her cupboards, so there was no way in hell she was going to leave it open. That would be irresponsible and she could lose her naturopath license as a result. No, there was something she needed to do alone, and she knew that her alone time was all but gone.

She opened the door, stepped inside and took a deep breath. She had always tried to keep negative energy out of her office, but she knew that this time she might not be able to help it. It would need a good smudging of sweet grass and a prayer to the spirits of the earth before she could ever bring a patient back into the room. That was the least of her worries at the moment.

Slowly, she began to rock her body back and forth. At first there was no rhyme or reason to the tempo, but after a few moments, a steady rhythm began to take over. She started to hum a melody, Beethoven's ninth symphony, more commonly recognized as Ode to Joy. It was a particular favorite of hers. She took a deep breath and tried to whistle the tune, but she had never been very good at whistling, even though the tune needed neither sharps nor flats. She took a tissue from her desk and wiped away the spittle that involuntarily appeared upon her lips as she impatiently tried to get to the end of the song.

"Oh, to hell with it," she cried out loud. "Willie, get your ass on in here. I'm going to count to three. One... two..."

The Shadowman instantly appeared before her.

"Hells," he smiled. "How've you been?" He tipped his cowboy hat to her in a formal gesture of greeting.

It was hard for Helena to tell whether he was happy to see her, or whether he was being sarcastic. She opted for the latter. "Cut the crap, Willie," Helena snapped. "What the hell's going on?"

Willie walked over to the leather couch and casually lay down on it, his well-worn Fry boots upon the far armrest, his hands propping his head up against the other. He turned and looked at her with a look of smug satisfaction on his face. "Aren't you going to offer me some tea? I'm all cotton-mouthed."

"You have not begun to know the meaning of the word," Helena threatened.

"I'm dead thirsty," he bantered.

"That's because you're dead."

"Humor me. It's been ages since I've had anything warm run through my veins."

"Fine. But if you find anything isn't working in that life form of yours, don't say I didn't warn you. And I want something in return."

"Hells," he explained with no sense of urgency, "you know the rules. I'm not supposed to interfere. The man in charge frowns upon that. I want to get out of purgatory sometime this century. I'm not getting any younger you know."

He looked at her and sighed. Their relationship had gone back more years than he cared to remember. Perhaps that was why, even though the woman was his polar opposite, she was somehow bewitching to him at the same time. "You called me, but you're not looking too happy to see me. What's the matter? Did Helen tell you about our little rendezvous in your bathroom? I love the tile, by the way. It just screams Mediterranean blue. Did you get it on sale at the end of the Greek Mycenaean period? Or was it that big Roman fire-sale?"

"Let's cut the small talk, shall we? You are interfering with my family," Helena scolded him. "You are well aware how much we LaRose's despise that. Do I have to remind you of the time you tried to double-cross my mother?"

Willie sat up. "God no," he shuddered. "How is Elaine, anyway? Still alive and kicking in jolly old England?"

"Of course," Helena replied. "I take it you're not sending her a Christmas card this year?" She walked over to the little sink, ran some water into the electric kettle and plugged it in. Willie wasn't the only one who was thirsty.

"You know; I think I lost her address." He paused for a moment, taking time to choose his next words carefully. "I can say this," he offered. "That dead spot in your lawn has to go."

"I know," Helena sighed. Willie clearly knew about the vampire that up until a few days ago had lived on her property. She reached for a couple of mugs at the end of the counter. "I have a pineapple/coconut herbal tea blend that I'd like to use up. Is that okay?"

"That sounds good. I like piña coladas. You don't have anything stronger to put in it, do you?"

Helena put a few loose leaves into the cup and poured the boiling water over them. "No," she said adamantly.

"You can't blame a guy for trying. I just thought if anyone had any well aged rum lying around, it would be you. No offense."

"None taken," she lamented, unplugging the appliance. "I'm pretty sure I know what's going on, so that'll get you off the hook as far as the "thou shalt not blab" rule goes. Helen is a problem right now. She's starting to come around, but I don't think I can afford to wait until she remembers how to be a clairvoyant. Right now her focus is sporadic at best. I had the same problem getting her to practice the piano."

"I know!" Willie agreed. "You'd think that being as anal as she is, she'd be one of those practice makes perfect types. But no."

Helena looked at him suspiciously. Just how long had he been hanging around her family she wondered? "I fear that Ellie is in danger," she continued, walking back over to the seating area.

"She *is* in danger. I told Helen that. Seriously, sometimes that daughter of yours is thick as a brick. You know what you're going to have to do, Helena," Willie responded, sitting up on the couch. "I really don't understand why you are delaying the inevitable."

"Gaspar has become like family to me," Helena acknowledged, handing Willie a cup of the herbal tea. She sat down in a chair across from him. "I know I'm going to have to deal with him, but I can't help but wonder where I went wrong."

Willie gagged on his tea.

"Well he has," she insisted. "What's wrong? Is the tea too hot or was that your reflex opinion of my child rearing abilities?"

"The tea is fine. As for the other… didn't you teach him about the Black Veil?" Willie asked, taking another sip of the brew. "The thirteen rules of House Sahjaza are said to pretty much govern modern vampire communities."

"I'm surprised you know about that," Helena commented.

"That vampire woman, Michelle Belanger, you know the one… she keeps popping up across the cable networks… she was on a reality show and I googled her. I like that woman's revision of the doctrine. She's kind of the David Suzuki of their kind. You could have just sat Gaspar down in front of that flat screen of yours and said 'learn something from her.' Kind of like the way you taught Helen sex-ed with all those medical books you have. Say what you will about the t.v. genre, it keeps people like me informed. I love it."

"That is not how I taught Helen the facts of life. Not that it's any of your business," Helena insisted. "And I did teach Gaspar the rules. Although I might have also said that personally I thought they were hardly better than the Boy Scout's oath. It doesn't look like it did any good. I'm pretty sure he's broken all of them, despite my insistence that he toe the line."

"Regardless," Willie said flatly. "It's clear that your young man did not grasp the meaning of the decree. Don't take it to heart. It's never easy to raise children. Or so they tell me. It's not like I've had a lot of experience with it. I can't imagine raising somebody else's."

"It's not all his fault," Helena protested. "The rules don't cover the mentally ill. He is ill, Willie. That child has had issues since his birth."

"Helena, that philosophy doesn't wash any better with vampires than it does with humans. Not every entity with a disorder in their chemical makeup is a natural born killer. On the other hand, some very sane people are. We all have free choice, even the non-dead."

"I suppose…" Helena said with sorrow in her voice.

"Ultimately, he's not your responsibility, Helena," Willie offered. "Your backyard is not zoned for half-way houses for the demonically disturbed." A smile crossed his face. "Despite that kick-ass fourth of July party."

"Shut up, Willie."

"Alexander made a right mess of things, didn't he?"

"We've all made a right mess of things."

"Have you told Helen yet? You know, that her father crashed your party and started a supernatural scandal that they're still talking about at the spirit bar? Did you hear the one about Alexander and the exorcism?" he laughed. "I know you haven't told her. Please let me be around for that one. Just name your price."

"That man," Helena said angrily. "This whole thing is his doing, and once again I'm stuck here cleaning it up. That is *so* Alexander. I don't know what possessed him to try it in the first place. He's never been a man of the cloth. And he never could hold his booze." She looked sternly at Willie. "If you say one word about this to Helen, I'll… I'll…"

"You'll what?" he smiled.

"I won't be very happy," she screamed. "And I'm not a very nice person when I'm not very happy." She picked up his coffee cup and threw it against the wall just inches above his head. "I'm going through a lot of these lately, just for the record."

"Calm down, Helena," he cautioned. "I'm not the bad guy this time."

"What the hell am I supposed to do?" she shouted at him. "That stupid, immature, blood-sucking kid I gave refuge to, is terrorizing this town, making my boyfriend's job a living hell. Now Gaspar wants to take on the rest of my family." She paced back and forth in the limited space her office gave her. "This is really pissing me off."

"You're going to have to do what you should have done in the first place," Willie said to her. "That vampire has pushed all of your family ties to the max. He's fully cognoscente of what he is doing. He's going to have to suffer the consequences."

"Sometimes, Willie," Helena responded, her anger starting to subside as she took deep breaths, "you are such a downer."

She knew Willie was right. Gaspar was a vampire after all, and with all vampires it was only a matter of time before they couldn't help themselves. She had hoped that the recently human part of Gaspar's DNA would have knocked some sense into him. That was her first mistake.

"Kill him before he kills again," Willie told her.

"It's not that simple," she replied.

"It really is," he responded.

Helena started to say something then reconsidered. She was, after all, a natural born killer herself. Not the kind that randomly killed innocent people, but she doubted most people could make the distinction between the two. She had been called upon to kill before, and she would be called upon to kill again. It never got any easier.

"The truth hurts, Helena," he added. "No one knows that more than you and I. I get that you have an emotional connection to him, but sometimes…" he struggled for words, "…sometimes you have to walk away from children you love."

His words moved Helena. She looked at him, and for a moment, saw a side of him she had never seen before. A kinder, gentler, Willie.

She took the last sip of tea from her own cup and looked at the tea leaves left behind in the bottom of the porcelain. She swirled the dregs three times clockwise, then touched the edge of the cup to its saucer, turning it upside down carefully as she did so. The last of the moisture in the cup trickled onto the plate, leaving the tea leaves stuck to the side of the cup. She looked at the pattern they made, her face turning grim as she did so.

"What's wrong, Helena?" Willie asked. "What do you see?"

"I need a favor," Helena said solemnly.

"A favor from me?" Willie asked, shocked by her request.

"I need you to babysit Stan for a bit," she explained.

"Uh, I'm not much of a babysitter, Helena," he stammered, "I thought that would have been a given. I don't know how to play with them. Let's go for a walk has a whole different meaning with me."

"I'll lay it out for you, Willie. The tea leaves in my cup indicate all is not as it appears," she explained. "I see a cat. That tells me I should be wary of a false friend. We know who that is. There are also two daggers pointed towards a cross pattern. They're telling me that two of us have a difficult task to perform. I know that they represent Helen and myself and the job we're going to have to do. But we can't leave Stan alone. He's suffered enough. His mother is in the hospital; his brother is in jail. We can't leave him with just anybody. It's too dangerous."

"Uh…" Willie hesitated. He was already far more involved in the situation than he should have been.

"No uh's," Helena instructed. "I respect that you have helped us all you can by alerting us to this situation we find ourselves in. You can't come with us, I know that."

"The kid will freak if he sees me, if he can see me at all," Willie countered. "I don't have a fuzzy sweater like Mr. Rogers."

"He'll be asleep. This whole ordeal will be over by dawn. It has to be. I need to do this before he has a chance to rest and recharge." She leaned closer to the Shadowman and looked him directly in the eye. "Willie, I'm begging you. Help us out here. It may not count as a soul for you, but it will count for something, I promise. I'll owe you one."

Willie considered her offer. "Suppose I do, Helena. Suppose I take care of this little situation while you take care of the bigger one. Will you give me your soul?"

Helena looked at him defiantly. "You can have it," she said, "when I'm good and ready. And I'm not good and ready. And I won't be for quite some time."

"What about Helen?" he asked.

"You can't have her soul either. And don't even ask about Ellie."

"It's not Helen's soul I want. Never has been. And I have a certain fondness for your granddaughter."

"I beg your pardon?" Helena said, incredulously.

"Don't look at me like that. Why does everyone always look at me like that? I just happen to like both of them, okay?" he said sincerely.

"Then will you help us and watch Stan?" Helena asked softly.

"Okay," Willie sighed. "But be back by dawn because I heard rumor there's going to be a plane crash tomorrow, and you know how I love those!"

"Thank you, Willie," Helena smiled. "Give me about fifteen minutes. Let me get Helen out of the Lachey's house before you go there. That'll be best for all of us. I'll make up some story so she doesn't get suspicious. She's been really gullible lately, thank God."

"Okay," Willie agreed.

"I *will* owe you one," Helena thanked him, as she left the cottage. She paused at the window and waved at him as if she were saying goodbye to a friend. "A big one."

"Helena," Willie said when she was no longer in sight. "You don't owe me a thing. This one's a freebie."

Chapter 28

Through the tiny opaque windows at the top of the washroom ceiling, Ellie could see that the storm had worsened against the night sky. The whiteness illuminating from the pile of snow against the pane of glass was almost brilliant. The precipitation would make rescuing her next to impossible, if anyone had even thought to try to do that.

She imagined her mother and her grandmother would be at home right now, arguing about something silly, like, is it better to use sugar, get fat and die from a massive heart attack, or endure a slow, painful death from chemical substitutes? It would probably be her grandmother's boyfriend, the Chief, who would finally put two and two together and say something like "that's why I like my coffee black. How does Ellie take hers? And by the way, isn't it kind of late for her to be out?" The Helens would then stare blankly at each other, and eventually come to the conclusion that something was terribly amiss.

Then again, they could also think she had just left the house to escape them, like she had the past few mornings, and not even bother looking for her until she didn't show up for breakfast.

"What the hell is wrong with them?" she asked herself. "Why isn't anyone coming to save me?"

She reached around to the side pocket of her jeans, wondering whether her cell phone was still there. Had the vampire frisked her while she lay unconscious on the floor? That was a creepy thought. He could have touched her everywhere and she wouldn't even have known. She was only slightly comforted to feel a vibration against her leg. Someone was trying to call her, but she had thankfully switched her ringtone off the other night at the movie. She pressed her thigh into the floor to drown out the slight buzzing sound, glancing at the vampire as she did so. If he had heard anything, he wasn't letting on.

"I've got to get a message to my mother," she thought to herself. She put her fingers to her temple and tried to send a telepathic message. She didn't know if she really believed the Helens the other morning when they said they were witches/not witches, but it right now it sure as hell was better than thinking they weren't. She did know her mother had an uncanny ability to play hide and seek with her when she was younger. Helen always found her no matter what size of hole she had crawled into.

"Mom, come find me in this hellhole," she whispered.

"What's that?" the vampire asked, suddenly taking an interest in her again.

"Don't you have to go crawl back under a rock, or the earth or something?" Ellie asked.

"Why? Does that turn you on?"

"Hardly."

"That's not very nice, Poppet."

"Will you quit calling me that?" she protested. "I hate that. My name is..."

"Don't say it!" he ordered. "I don't want to know. If you insist on telling me, I'll kill you right now." He stomped his foot to the ground, like a three-year old throwing a tantrum.

"Why? Is it easier for you when you don't know our names? You called Brooke 'Dorothy', what did you call Kevin?" Ellie taunted. She had been analyzing the vampire for what seemed like hours now, and she knew that the more she annoyed him, the more he walked around in circles and seemed to forget she was there. "Maybe it's time you took your nap."

"Shut up, Poppet. You are really beginning to get on my nerves," he yelled, starting to pace the floor. His right arm moved across his chest, he held his left arm by the elbow, and he cupped his chin in his left palm while pondering God knows what.

"I have to go to the bathroom," Ellie interrupted.

"So go to the bathroom," he said, not looking at her but continuing his steady cantor. "I won't look, I'm busy thinking."

"Can't you chain me up in the girls' bathroom?" she yelled loud enough to break his train of thought.

"Use the stall."

"No."

"You can make it, the chain is long enough," he sighed, stopping dead in his tracks. She was looking at him like he was out of his mind. "You are one bitchy broad, do you know that? What difference does it make?"

"If you must know, I'm PMS-ing. It's only going to get worse. I need the GIRLS' bathroom."

Gaspar looked at her, horrified. "That can't be possible. How old are you?"

"I'm fifteen, asshole."

He crept closer towards her. "You are not," he replied, shaking his head in disbelief. "Fifteen-year-old girls are more... mature than you are."

"Nice. I swear to God... or whatever pagan idol that works for you... that I will be sweet sixteen in a matter of months. Why do you find that so shocking?" she asked, as she watched his gaze go from her eyes to her chest and stay there. Great. Another boob guy. She was stuck in a hellhole with a teenaged blood sucking murder/tit gawker, and there wasn't anything she could do about it.

"Because it's a problem. A huge problem," he said, waving his arms over his head in an overly dramatic fashion. "It's like a lactose intolerant thing. It means I can't use you for food."

"That's tragic," Ellie said cynically. "And hello, I'd appreciate it if you would look me in the face when you talked to me." She self-consciously tugged at the sweater she had borrowed to make it cling less to her body.

Gaspar sighed and slowly sat down beside her. This was not part of his plan. Now what was he going to do with her? He only killed for food, he wasn't a murderer-murderer, despite what they all thought. But the feeding book had clearly stated that until his second set of canine teeth came through, signaling his maturation as a vampire, he would be unable to handle the blood of an adult. The adult blood would be too hard for him to digest. It would tire him, making it almost impossible for him to hunt at all, and he would eventually starve himself into oblivion. Not death, oblivion. That would be tragic. One didn't come back from oblivion.

"But you look so young," he said, wondering to himself why the book had not said anything about drinking teenaged blood. Child. Adult. It had been specific. Nothing about pubescent pixies of the Goth kind. Or maybe it had. Even as a child he had always been one to skip over pages and read the ending first. Would it be worth the risk to try to feed on her? Would the hormone crazy blood of a girl his own age be more than he could handle? He found himself salivating at the thought.

"Looks can be deceiving," Ellie retorted. "You should know. You saw me the other night. You trapped me in the van. You were foaming at the mouth, looking like a wolf from a black velvet "howl at the moon" poster, but I know it was you."

"How?" he asked. Perhaps this girl knew more than he initially thought. Perhaps she already knew and accepted the fact that he was different. SHE had told him that one day he would meet a girl that would truly understand. Could this be the girl?

"Your eyes. One blue, one brown. Same as the damn dog," Ellie said. "A little too much of a co-incidence, don'tcha think?"

"Sorry," he shrugged. That hadn't been the answer he was hoping for. Maybe it wasn't going to be love at first capture. He chuckled to himself. "I guess I wasn't paying all that much attention to your face then either."

"You're giving the term 'one sick puppy' a whole new meaning, do you know that?" Ellie pointed out.

"Was that some sort of compliment?" he asked.

"Whatever works for you," Ellie answered.

"I wasn't being a pervert," he protested. "I did notice you, but I was keeping an eye on the rake your grandmother was threatening to lobotomize me with. We wolves are funny that way."

"Was that some kind of an apology?" she asked.

"Whatever works for you," he mocked.

"I take it you're some sort of shape-shifter?" she bantered. "I'm sorry, were you aiming for wolf? Because you got mutt."

"I can transform, yes," he said indignantly. Poor little Poppet. She would never understand what it was like to be able to take on another life form. She'd never know what it was like to soar through the air like an eagle, with eyesight that could spy your prey from above the clouds. She'd never know what it was like to be a canine, and follow the scent of your meal in fresh made tracks. Unless of course, she became like him.

"Why don't you just turn yourself back into a human?" she asked innocently.

"It doesn't work that way," he answered with a note of regret in his voice.

"I'm not trying to be a bitch or anything," she said softly, offering him some sympathy. "I was just thinking that this whole vampire thing must be a lot to deal with."

"Like your fresh scrubbed cherubic face isn't a bit of an issue for you?" he asked sarcastically.

Ellie was taken aback.

"I get issues, girlie. I have a few of them myself."

He took a deep breath, his nostrils flaring as he unconsciously let out a snort. He wanted to turn around and slap her silly, like she was an annoying little sister. But she wasn't his sister, she was someone his own age as it turned out. And she was really quite… pretty. Those green eyes that alternately flashed with anger and clouded with tears. He could feel himself getting an erection just thinking about her. It was the first one he had since his transformation and it felt pretty darn good, he had to admit. Aside from the obvious sexual arousal, it made him feel… warm… and perhaps even borderline fuzzy.

"Hit me with your best shot," she stammered, fighting back emotions that she knew would end in tears.

"You're very intuitive," he sighed, taking a strand of her hair into his fingers. "I do feel like knocking you senseless again, but that's starting to get old. You look different now, that's all I meant. You were less put together both then and when I saw you at the bridge. You looked girlier." He paused. "But today's look. I get that as well. The dark eye shadow and the heavy mascara. Make-up hides the imperfections. You use it to transform yourself into an enchanting little vixen." He put the strand of hair between his lips and tossed it lightly with his tongue before releasing it. "Maybe sometime you can give me a lesson or two."

"Okay," Ellie thought, not sure which was more uncomfortable, the hair thing, or him secretly wanting to be a goth-vamp in disguise. That was pointless, really. Either you were the real thing or you weren't. It made her wonder… was his demonic look really just some sort of male teenaged fetish?

"That would be nice," he said softly, bowing his head before her. "Sometimes I feel all alone. But now I have you."

She hadn't noticed it before, when he was standing up, but as he bent his face forward she saw that he had white spots on a patch of hair towards the back of his head. At the roots.

"Since we're besties, sharing make-up secrets and all, do you dye your hair?" she asked.

"I don't have heterochromia," he said quietly, refusing to look at her. "You're wrong about that."

"Uh, what do you mean?" she asked, not knowing whether she really wanted to hear the answer. Anything either hetero or non-hetero in this conversation was making her even more nervous.

"Give me a break, Poppet."

Her curiosity got the better of her and she continued to stare at his hair. There was more than a slight variance in the color tone closer to his head. She smiled to herself, knowing she was right. He may fancy himself as a creature of the night, but really he was someone who needed another trip to the salon.

"I know you think I'm pale because I'm a vampire, but that's not really why I look this way. I've always been pale. When I was mortal I had stage two Waardenburg syndrome."

"And that would be…?"

"A rare condition, characterized by one blue eye and one…"

"Brown," Ellie said softly, becoming aware that at least a part of his condition was still human.

"Among other traits."

"You know," Ellie offered, feeling a slight guilt pang for even having brought the subject up at all. "It's not all that rare. I remember I had a nanny once whose son had eyes like yours. We used to play together. He must have had Worden…"

"Waardenburg," he corrected.

"Right. He must have had it too. But he had other problems. He was deaf, and he wore leg braces to help himself walk." She laughed. "I know that's not funny, but he'd kick me with them every once and a while and it hurt like hell."

"You must have been mean to him," he snapped.

"It was just kid stuff. I took one of his dump trucks once and smashed his sandcastle. He kicked me, then he stomped his heavy shoes on the ground and waived his arms in the air like a crazy kid until I gave it back to him. Much like... you did... a few moments ago."

The teenagers turned and stared at each other. For two people so different it was becoming abundantly clear that there was an uncanny connection between them.

"Gaspar?" Ellie whispered, as she wondered whether this prick who was holding her captive was once the little boy she played with in a sandbox.

He looked at her, trying to place the tiny face tucked deep in his memory upon the body in front of him. She knew his name. How could that be?

He looked into her eyes again. They were like HERS, yes... but that wasn't why they were familiar.

He took her hand in his and held it for a moment. Just to touch someone again was in indescribable thrill to him. When his soul... perhaps not the right word given his circumstance... when his being connected her with his past, the feeling within him was almost orgasmic.

He began to use her fingers to sign a name, as he had been taught as a deaf child. He struggled with the first letter 'E', but the sequence came back to him quickly and he easily added 'L-L.'

She put her hand over his. It was cold to her touch, but not as cold as she remembered when she had touched him in her nightmare. It was seasonably cool. A little uncomfortable maybe, but nothing a pair of fingerless gloves couldn't help with. She reached for his fingers and finished the word for him, signing "I.E." with her hand.

"I remember," she said softly.

"Ellie. The pretty girl with the pretty mother," he sighed. "This is an unexpected crossroad in our lives."

"I can't believe it," she said, not knowing whether to laugh or cry. "What happened to you? Are you really a vampire?"

"I don't want to talk about it."

"But listen to you... you are talking. You can obviously hear. And you can run faster than anyone I know. Is it..." she hesitated, "...better?"

"Sometimes," he answered. He sniffed her. The scent she was emitting aroused him but not like the blood of the children had. It aroused him in a way he found both sensual and dangerous. "You're so confusing, Ellie. You're driving me wild."

"Is that a bad thing?" she asked. She could see a look of lust in his eyes. She knew the look. Tom had looked at her that same way the night he was in Helena's kitchen. She had found it exciting then, until things went awry. This time the awry had come first.

"I don't know whether to eat you or not," he said.

"You're still considering it?" she gasped. "Even though we were friends when we were younger?"

"Yes," he answered honestly. He felt he owed her that much. She had been one of the few children who would play with him. The others had found him too unusual. Or their parents had. Same difference. "I don't know if we were friends. Playmates maybe. We were sometimes horrible to each other."

"We were toddlers. That's how we expressed ourselves. There wasn't a whole lot of premeditation involved."

"Are you a virgin, Ellie?" he asked.

"Whoa. How did you segue to that?" Ellie answered. "Are you inferring a different meaning to the verb 'eat'? Because I am definitely not in the mood right now, thanks. And that has nothing to do with whether I'm a virgin or not. Who are you? My mother?"

He smiled and ran his fingers through her hair again. "See, that's what I mean. How old are you Ellie? One minute you're risking your life to get a stuffed animal out of a van and the next you're talking like a dick magnet. You've crossed the line from coy to cock teaser, and I don't know if it's intentional. Do you?"

"Go write about it on the wall over there, since you know how to spell my name. And leave Beastie Boy out of it."

"You haven't answered my question."

"You never answered mine."

Gaspar picked at the flaking paint on the wall. He hadn't allowed himself to spend much time thinking about whether his life had been better as a human. It hadn't been normal in any sense of the word, so it was rather hard to judge. "It's better than being dead," he shrugged.

"Being a vampire?" Ellie said softly.

"Yes," he nodded. "You were right. I can shape-shift whenever I want to. It makes it easier to feed. People get anxious when they see a wild animal feeding on prey, but they usually keep their distance. It's better that way. I've learned that now. That's why I do it."

"So, how old does all this make you? Not that you look ancient or anything, but with vampires, you never know, right? Like, when I thought you were three, you weren't really three hundred or anything?"

A slow grin came across Gaspar's face. "I'm one vampire year of age. I was fifteen human years, just like you, when it happened."

"So this just happened, this change in you?"

"It was a dark and stormy night."

"If you don't want to tell me, just say so. You don't have to be a smart-ass about it. I'm just curious."

"Don't believe all that 'knowledge is power' crap." Gaspar said. "The less you know about me, the better. Ignorance is bliss, as they say."

"Who? Who says that? They're wrong. I don't know anything about my dad, but that doesn't make the pain any less. The more I try to forget him, the more I want to know about him. It's a whole new definition of reverse osmosis."

Gaspar took an interest. "You don't know who your dad is?"

"No. He was gone by the time I was born and my mother refuses to talk about him."

"Interesting. My dad was around when I was born, but my mother tired of him and married a French Count named Henri BonVillaine. That's where my surname comes from… some rich guy my mother married for a year. It's not a bad name, I guess. Gaspar BonVillaine. Sometimes I have this nightmare where I learn my real name is Gaspar Gomez. Talk about a letdown. I wake up in a cold sweat. Maybe that's why I never ask. Who my real father is, I mean."

"Try Ellie Bocelli…"

"What?"

"Never mind. What happened after that? After your mother left the Count?"

"She eventually tired of him as well and we moved here, to Troy. Somewhere in all that, we met you and your mother. Now history is repeating itself. I guess we were always meant to cross paths again."

"Cross paths? You talk like you're from the eighteenth century. How many dog years is one vampire year?" she laughed. "Just curious." She could see it hit a nerve in him.

"See, there's that mean streak in you again. You forget I couldn't hear properly as a child. Speech, just like hearing, is relatively new to me. I've been reading some historical romances just to get the hang of it."

Ellie laughed harder. "Now I know two people who actually read them."

"Well, you read what is around. Bookstores don't keep my hours."

"I'm just kidding. Don't you need a light to read? Doesn't that bother your kind? Nothing personal, a friend of mine said that to me the other night."

"Audio books," Gaspar answered.

"Gotcha," Ellie nodded.

"Now I'm kidding," Gaspar laughed. "Don't believe everything you've read about us. I can handle light. Just not for long. It burns me, much like a sunburn does you, but it burns me beneath the skin. I try to stay out of it. Sunscreen's not much help."

"Even the pink lights?"

Gaspar looked at her oddly.

"Never mind. You had to be there."

"Would you like me to bring you a pillow and a blanket?"

Ellie weighed his statement. Why would he bring her that if he was going to kill her? On the other hand, if he was offering to bring her bedding, it meant he wasn't going to let her go anytime soon. He was getting comfortable. Or horny.

Neither of which was appealing to her. She contemplated her chances of both life and escape.

She could feel tears forming in her eyes again, and blinked them back. This was no time to be a cry-baby. She had to keep her wits about her as much as any teenager could when faced with this situation. If he didn't like mature, mature she would be.

"What are you wondering, Ellie?" he asked, as if reading her mind. "Are you wondering whether it's better for me to kill you now or later?"

"I was, yes."

"And what did you decide?"

"I was thinking later would be good."

"Me too."

"So, you're going to let me go?" Ellie asked hopefully. "We can still be friends. Maybe even go to a movie sometime."

"Go?" he laughed. "Whatever gave you that stupid idea? I'm still going to kill you. Someday. We're just going to take a little detour. I'm going to take you to hell and back, and then it's off to grandmother's house we go."

He pulled a switchblade from his pocket.

"What are you doing?" she asked, terrified to hear the answer.

"You're too perfect, Ellie."

"What's that supposed to mean?"

"They'd never believe it. The rest of them. They'd never believe that girl like you would want a boy like me."

"Then they'd be right."

He grabbed her arm and pushed up her sleeve. The edge of the knife was cold as he very lightly drew the blade across her wrist. No blood flowed, but it scared the shit out of her, he could tell.

"There's this thing that happens," he began to explain, "when one of us wants one of you. Forever. We make a nice little slice in an artery, like this vein hidden so delicately under your skin. Then we suck the consciousness from you, almost to the bitter end. But just before you take your last breath, we give you back one."

He saw the terror in her eyes.

"Which means?" she asked, her voice barely audible.

"Which means I bring you back to life. And then you are my slave."

He took the edge of the knife and gave her skin a poke. Droplets of ruby red blood rose to the surface. He raised her arm to his lips, his tongue darting to the blood in a slow, deliberate lick.

She felt a warm uneasiness run through her. The initial unpleasantness was replaced by something she could only describe as anesthetic-like. She felt euphoric. Her senses were going into hyper drive. She could see the miniscule pores on his skin. She could smell his perspiration. She could hear his heartbeat. She found none of it unpleasant.

"Does that give you some idea, Ellie?" he asked. "Of how magical it all could be?"

Chapter 29

Helena went back into the neighbor's house and found her daughter sitting at the kitchen table, flipping through an older issue of National Geographic. The pages were crinkly and sticking together, indicating it had most likely fallen into the dishwater at some recent point during the magazine's life.

"Brushing up on the 'Wraith Riders of St. Paul de Vence' issue?" Helena chided. As much as she tried to forget that Helen told her she had dealt with some nasty demons, she couldn't.

Helen had the pages open to the centerfold. It had her totally transfixed. "Take a look at this photo," Helen said, sliding the magazine towards her mother.

"You want me to look at a group of naked women in Papua New Guinea?" Helena asked, sliding it back.

"No," I want you to take a closer look at the tribal chief who is standing there with the naked women from Papua New Guinea. Is it just me, or does he look familiar?" The magazine made another trip across the wooden table.

Helena looked at the picture and sighed. "Trust National Geo to take a magnificent photo of your father." She looked at the date on the issue. "I guess I now know where he was that time he missed your elementary school Christmas pageant. His loss, you were an excellent sugarplum fairy." She turned the magazine over and looked at the cover. "Yup, this goes back a few decades. Betty must have been cleaning out the attic recently."

"Aren't those tribes cannibalistic?" Helen shuddered. "I hate to think of Dad being offered up as a human burger."

The idea was not nearly as distasteful to Helena. "We should be so lucky," she sighed.

"I beg your pardon?"

"I said we should look so plucky," Helena covered. "Forget about the cannibals. I need you to try and focus on Gaspar."

"Who?" Helen asked. She rocked her chair backwards, tipping it precariously against the wainscoting on the wall.

"The vampire. He has a name." Helena stood her ground on the other side of the table. The chair-tipping maneuver was something Helen had always done when she wanted to get into an argument. It had started when she was four and didn't want to eat her peas and progressed through to her teens when she didn't want to do anything.

"How do you know this?" Helen asked suspiciously. Her mother was avoiding her gaze, a certain sign that something was amiss. "You know," Helen added mischievously, "I had some time to think while you were back at your office locking up."

"Oh really?" Helena replied.

"Do you know what's bugging me?" Helen asked. "When you told me the whole 'Marita blows up on the Fourth of July' story, you never mentioned what happened to her son. That's kind of ironic now, because I seem to recall her son's name was…"

Helena tapped her fingers nervously on her other arm. "Gaspar. So? Don't look at me like that, Helen. Gaspar is a common name."

"Where? In Portugal? Come on, how many other Gaspars do you know?" she waited for her mother to come up with a number, but Helena was too slow. "I thought so," she smirked with satisfaction.

"Yes, Marita's son was named Gaspar," Helena admitted. "However, I remember she was Spanish, not Portuguese."

"Do you know what I remember? I remember that he had a lot of issues," Helen continued. "What happened to him? Did he die?"

"Sort of," Helena replied. "I still see him around from time to time."

"What?" Helen asked, moving forward so that her chair legs touched the ground again. "What do you mean, sort of? Is he dead or isn't he?"

Helena glanced at her wrist watch and sighed. "Okay, Helen. I've got something to tell you, but we need to make it fast. We'll just wrap everything up in one shot, okay? We'll talk about your father, that rat-bastard, and how he always has to make a scene wherever he goes. And we'll talk about Gaspar, Marita's son, and why, up until you and Ellie came here a few nights ago, he lived with me. Sort of. And we'll talk about how we LaRose women have to stick together, come hell or high water."

Helen sighed. "I'm not going to like this, am I?"

"Not much," Helena admitted. "Let's start with your father, Alexander."

Helen raised her hand. "Mother, I know he's not your favorite person. You've made that clear over the years, and it's unnecessarily clouded my opinion of him to some extent. That's another reason I don't talk to Ellie about her father. I want her to have her own imaginary version of Jules. It's easier that way."

"You called him Julian earlier," Helena reminded her.

"No I didn't," Helen protested weakly.

"Yes, you did. You told me I was crazy for suggesting his name was Jules." Helena noticed Helen's lower lip start to tremble.

"I did, didn't I?" Helen winced. It was her turn to be slow with a suitable cover story.

"Fine, Helen. I don't really care who Ellie's father is or isn't. One thing's for certain though, your J-man whoever he is, might have been perfect, but Alexander is at the other end of the scale, let me tell you. You are old enough now, Helen, to know the bitter truth."

"You know I've got this line from '*A Few Good Men*' going through my head right now..." Helen admitted. "I'm not so sure I want to hear this."

"He was an animal," Helena declared, sitting down in the chair across from Helen. "Handsome as hell, but an animal all the same. I couldn't satisfy that man if I tried. And try I did. ALL THE TIME. Morning, noon, and night. Hellsbelles, that man was driving me crazy. Come here, Helena. Bend over, Helena..."

"Mother, please!" Helen said, putting her hand over her ears. "Some things should just be left in the closet." She had always imagined her mother as the sexpot in the family, and she wasn't ready for another family myth to come crashing down.

"Stop being childish," Helena insisted, waiting for her daughter to listen to what she was saying. "As much as I enjoy a good physical release to this day..."

"I figured that out the other night," Helen reminded her.

"Helen, let me finish. Alexander was sleeping with every woman that he could within a five-mile radius of the house. I was mortified when I found out. I was a clichéd woman. I was a Betty Lachey, for God's sake. So I tossed him out."

"To tell you the truth, I figured it was something like that," Helen admitted. She had seen her father sneaking out of her best friend's house one grade ten afternoon. She had never told Helena about it. "After you two had divorced, he came with someone new every time he came to see me." Helen admitted. "He came to visit a lot after Ellie was first born, but then he just stopped. Good Lord, I hope one of the ladies he brought with him wasn't from his cannibal-fetish days."

"Forget the cannibals, will you? There's something I need to get off my chest." She stood up again and walked over to the kitchen counter, where she stood facing Helen, putting some distance between the two of them in case the fur started to fly. "It was Alexander who messed up the exorcism," Helena said, watching for Helen's reaction. Willie would have been disappointed. Helen barely flinched at the news.

"It was Alexander who accidentally killed Marita Harbinger," Helena continued. "Seriously, I wish people would just leave the supernatural problems to the experts."

"Experts like us?" Helen asked. The tone of her voice was sarcastic in nature.

"Yes. Whether we like it or not," Helena replied, sincerely.

"So, Dad just popped in to say hello and wound up killing your neighbor, my ex-nanny?"

"She wasn't just your ex-Nanny," Helena started to explain.

"I know. You told me. She was a demon," Helen screamed at her. "Why can't anything be simple with you?"

"Me? It was your father who had the affair with Marita Harbinger. It was your father who tossed her out, when she became pregnant. Marita knew where I lived because he had flaunted her in front of me the summer before. You count your lucky stars that at least he continues to acknowledge you. He ignores the rest of them. Anyway, that's why I felt sorry for Marita, and why I inadvertently sent a demon over to your house to babysit Ellie. I swear I just thought she was your father's ex-floozy who needed some help, not an escapee from hell."

"Back up," Helen said angrily. She got out of her chair and approached her mother. "The rest of them?"

"The rest of his illegitimate children. I guess he makes an attempt to stay in touch with you every so often because I'm the only woman he married."

"Exactly how many children does he have?" she asked hesitantly. She had grown up thinking she was an only child, so the news that she had other siblings opened a flood of emotions for her. Her father had told her he was a government spy who had to change his identity and whereabouts from time to time for their protection, and she had chosen to believe him. Their rendezvous were always clandestine. She knew now it was probably to avoid her mother, but it had given her father an air of mystery and intrigue, and a reason for forgiveness, all the same.

"A few. I know at least one of them, or I thought I did. Marita's son, Gaspar. He's your half-brother."

"Gaspar? That sickly little boy? Are you sure? It sounds like Marita slept around a lot too." She certainly hadn't noticed any family resemblance between herself and the young child.

"I'm sure, Helen. I've gotten to know him over the past year, and let me tell you, you are two peas in a pod."

"What do you mean you've gotten to know him? Where is he?"

"He lives at my house. Or he used to. And he's not sickly anymore. Not that type of sickly, anyway."

"What did you do with him? Did you send him on vacation or something because we were coming?" She presumed that was possible. She had initially told her mother she and Ellie were just staying for a short visit.

"Of course not. He's kind of on his own journey right now," Helen offered.

"Where does he sleep? You don't have any other bedrooms in this house, and let's face it, our rooms are definitely feminine. I didn't see him in the basement when I was doing laundry. Does he sleep in the cottage?" She stood up and faced her mother. "Is your Naturopathy Clinic just one big cover-up?"

"My office?" Helen laughed nervously. "I'm almost offended by that remark, but we don't exactly have a history of being honest with one another, so I'm willing to let it slide. Sit back down, will you? We really need to talk."

"I'd rather keep standing, thanks."

"He sleeps in the garden. Below the dirt. Usually."

"Okay, maybe I will sit back down," Helen said, grabbing the closest chair. Her body fell effortlessly to the seat. She raised her hand towards her mother. "Wait," she said, taking a deep breath and exhaling slowly. "Okay, I think I'm ready now."

"He used to come into the house, but I don't let him in anymore. You shouldn't invite him in either, if he comes back."

"Why shouldn't I invite him in? Oh, no. Don't tell me you were serious about him being a vampire?"

"You know, if you'd just believe me the first time I told you these things, it would be a whole lot easier on all of us," her mother insisted.

Helen slapped herself in the head. "Of course he is."

"It was the only way to save him. He was so shaken by the death of his mother that he tried to kill himself later that night. I had to work fast, let me tell you. Roy only knows half of what really happened at that stupid party. The night was still young when they took Marita's parts away in a body bag." She took both of Helen's hands into her own. "I'm sorry I held the truth from you all these years, Helen. You had a right to know about your father. He's a bit of an egotistical nutcase, but it was easier to just let you think that I was the unfair one, never giving him a chance. He does love you, I know that in my heart. It's the only reason we keep in touch from time to time. I have to warn you though; I'm not inviting him here for Christmas. You can beg me to all you like."

Helen hung her head and remained silent.

"We really should get ready, Helen," her mother said. "We've got a job to do. I've asked Willie to babysit Stan."

"Willie?" Helen questioned.

"Don't freak, Helen. It's going to be all right. I know he's a handful, but I think he'll be okay with the boy. He'll never admit it, but while we were talking back at my office…"

"You were just talking to him at your office?" Helen said in disbelief.

"Yes," Helena admitted. "We were talking about other people's children and he seemed... I don't know... somewhat sad that he didn't have any of his own."

"Um, mother..." Helen flinched. "I wouldn't be so sure about that."

"No, I think he was sincere."

"Oh, I'm sure he was. It's just that..." she looked for words she didn't want to say. "Oh, good God." Helen sighed, putting her head into her hands. "There is no Jules. There is no Julian. There's just...Willie."

"Willie?" Helena screeched uncontrollably. "Are you trying to tell me that Willie is Ellie's father? Willie's dead, Helen. What were you thinking? That's one step short of necrophilia in my books."

"Nooo," Helen replied delicately. "He still has some life in him, let me tell you."

"Seriously, Helen? Our Willie? Not some other Willie? Like Willie Wonka or even Willie Nelson?"

Helen shrugged. "Like I said, I've never really gotten over Ellie's father. Willie is Ellie's father."

"Talk about your long distance relationships," Helena sighed.

"When we're apart I miss him," Helen continued, "but whenever we're together I just want to ring his bloody neck. That man is impossible. He was never home and he was always sneaking around. I couldn't get a straight answer out of him if I tried." She tried to mimic his voice. "*I can't tell you, Helen.* That's all he ever said."

"Well, technically he can't tell you."

"You're not helping, Mother."

"Did you elope with him or anything?"

"No."

"Well that's good. 'Till death do us part' would have a whole new meaning with him." She paused and thought for a moment. "I thought you hated Willie. You were furious with him the other night."

"I was furious with him because I thought the whole night walk was a ploy to take Ellie away from me. But I see now that he only had her best interests at heart." Her voice softened. "I guess I owe him an apology."

"Well that takes the cake," Helena exploded. "We are one messed up family, let me tell you. Who exactly split the wraiths, Helen? It was Willie, wasn't it?"

Helena nodded sheepishly. "Well, he did kind of help."

"You should have called me," Helena insisted. "I would have come in a flash."

"There comes a time when you just don't want to call your Mommy."

"There is never a time you can't call your Mommy. Not while I'm alive... or after I'm dead for that matter. No wonder Willie's so paranoid about helping us now. St. Peter must have had a field day with that one, let me tell you."

"We just thought maybe it would help with his body count. Bonus points or something."

"Let me tell you something, Helen. When it comes to opening the pearly gates, our testosterone fueled next-door neighbor has a better chance of springing them than Willie ever will. Ryan will be out of jail long before Willie gets out of purgatory." She put her hands on her hips and tilted her head towards her daughter, pausing a moment before she spoke. "I see now, why you're so dead set against Ryan and Ellie becoming friends. You don't hate the bad boys; you love the bad boys."

"Busted," Helen admitted. "Ryan has those qualities... bad boy/good heart... you said yourself that Willie isn't all bad."

"For the record, I think Ellie likes Tom better anyway."

"Right now, I'd be happy if she was in love with either of them. Because I'm afraid someone else has entered the picture. Someone who might not have that 'good heart' attribute. Someone who's bad through and through."

"Helen, Gaspar is Ellie's half-uncle."

"She doesn't know that."

"She's a sensible girl..."

"She's still a teenager. A teenager who thinks her mother is wrong, wrong, wrong."

"Hmm," Helena pondered. In her mind she pictured Tom and Gaspar side by side. "I still think she's pick Tom," Helena said. "I think Gaspar's going to remind her too much of someone else she knows."

"I just wish she was sitting in front of us right now, so I could say, 'Ellie, you're a great kid. Dress any way you want. Hang out with anyone you want.

Just don't be in such a hurry to grow up. I'll miss you." She wiped away the tear that had trickled down her cheek. "I am so afraid that's going to happen before I'm ready."

"You don't have to miss her. If you're open to it, you can become good friends. She won't stop needing you just because she's a woman." She looked Helen in the eyes. "Right?"

Helen gave her mother a hug. "You are more right than you will ever know."

"Do you know what I'm afraid of?" Helena began, shaking ever so slightly with the words. "With Willie being Ellie's father, what does this means Ellie is? Part human, part gatekeeper, part…"

"Dead?" Helen questioned, and then quickly regretted her words. "I mean loved. She is very fully and wholly loved."

"You are sounding patronizingly like your father now and I don't appreciate it. What the hell are we supposed to do?"

Helen put her fingers to her temple. "Is there time for a massage before Willie gets here? Because that would help." She moved her fingers to her ears and rubbed her lobes. "Did you hear that?" she asked her mother nervously.

"Hear what?" Helena asked. "I didn't hear anything."

"Ellie," she said with terror in her voice. "She just called to me. She said 'Mom, come find me in this hellhole.' Helen's eyes began to well up uncontrollably. "What do we do now, Mom?"

"We get ready to kill your half-brother," Helena said matter-of-factly.

"But he's…"

"He's what? Family? I made that mistake too, Helen. Now look at what's happened." She rubbed Helen's back to try to comfort her. "Are you sure you can handle this? I know killing is never easy, and it's worse when it's someone you know."

"I have another confession to make," Helen replied.

"Now?"

"I killed cousin Frankie. Out by the lake. Full moon, werewolf. That's the condensed version. I thought I had sunk his body out in the deep blue water well enough, but the next day Ellie and I were out canoeing and up he came. The body part, anyway. She saw the whole thing."

"You killed cousin Frankie? Your aunt Joan has been blaming me for years. I kept telling her I didn't do it."

"I'm sorry," Helen offered.

"It's okay," Helena sighed. "He had it coming. His father was a werewolf. I did kill *him*. What did you do with Frankie's head? They never found it as far as I know."

"I toasted it with the marshmallows," Helen confessed. "Willie got rid of the skull. He does come in handy from time to time."

"Well, experience is good, I guess. I'm sorry but there's really no choice with Gaspar and Ellie," Helena said solemnly. "I know in my heart that only one of them is going to come out of this situation alive. I think we're in agreement which one it has to be."

Helen placed her fingertips on the table.

"What's wrong?" Helena asked.

"Nothing," Helen replied. "For a second there I felt the ground shake a bit. I guess it was nothing."

Helen stood up bravely from the table and did up her coat. "Where do you think Betty hides her whiskey?" she asked.

Helena opened the cupboard above the stove. "I took a guess," she said removing the cap from the bottle and taking a swig. "It's so 1970 to hide it there." She passed the bottle to Helen. "One for courage?"

"One to ease the pain," she said, taking a big swallow. "I've got to enter a trance and find out where Ellie is. I'm going to have one hell of a migraine."

"That's my girl," Helena said, her face turning fierce. "Heaven has no rage like love to hatred turned / Nor hell a fury like a woman scorned, - William Congreve. Well, let me tell you this, Mr. Congreve. Gaspar has just royally pissed-off two women. The wrong two."

Chapter 30

Gaspar held Ellie in his arms as her body went limp. He watched her eyelids flutter, trying to re-open from the effects of the drug-like sensation palpating through her veins. He felt no need to slap her this time. He would let her awaken when she was good and ready. Instead, he pushed back her black hair from her shoulders and smelled her neck. The combination of the scent of her hair and the aroma of her skin aroused him.

"What have I done?" he asked himself. Unfortunately, as fleetingly as the question entered his mind, it left. He was more curious than apologetic.

His hands started to move up her body, his testosterone wanting to know what lay beneath that sweater she wore. He wanted to reach across her back, and undo her bra, like he had seen many a man do on those soap operas Helena PVR'd. His fingers moved slowly to the middle of her back, his mind a mixture of eagerness and panic. In the end, he did nothing. He knew she had no free will at the moment, and while that was beneficial for killing, it crossed the line for anything so instinctively human. So much for being a monster.

"What am I doing?" he reflected, and this time his ego allowed him time to ponder the question.

SHE had told him to try to avoid romantic entanglements. SHE had said there would come a time when he would find women who would offer themselves up freely, both sexually and food wise to him, with no strings attached. Ladies of the night, SHE called them, a new twist on an old moniker. SHE hadn't said how long it would take before he found such a slut, or how he would recognize the signals from one, but he knew the scenario would not be like the one before him now.

Ellie began to stir. She let out a steady stream of garbled expletives and random thoughts under her breath before she started to make any sense to Gaspar. "Hate me, why?" she eventually uttered, still somewhat delirious.

"I don't hate you, Ellie," he said, kissing the top of her head lightly. She didn't seem to notice. He gave her a light squeeze, almost a hug, and tried to get her to sit upright on her own. That failing, he propped her up in the corner of the wall and sat beside her, his arms around her protectively. "I think I feel exactly the opposite."

"Then why," she asked groggily, her head flopping softly onto his shoulder, "are you doing this to me?"

"Your grandmother," Gaspar said icily, "killed my mother."

"My Nan is not a killer," Ellie insisted, becoming more alert. "You can't just go around accusing people of being murderers. You're one to talk."

"How much do you really know about your grandmother, Ellie?" he asked, gently stroking her hair.

This time, she was aware of Gaspar showing affection. It startled her, but at the same time if felt somewhat reassuring. At least he wasn't trying to kill her.

"Not a lot, you've got me there," she admitted, thinking back to the few times she had spent with her Nan. She couldn't for the life of her remember any moments of Helena being anything but kind. Except for that night in Troy, when Helena had gone after the dog. The dog that turned out to be Gaspar. And maybe that time when she had thrown a cup at Helen when their argument got heated at breakfast. The memories made reconsider her opinion of Helena. "Okay, just suppose my Nan has some anger issues. Wouldn't they have locked her up if she killed your mother? Especially in front of witnesses?" Ellie asked, finally regaining the strength to sit up on her own. "I mean; she sleeps with the Chief of Police for crying out loud. You'd think he would have dumped her if that happened."

"Your grandmother invited my mother to a party where Momsey ultimately met her untimely death," Gaspar told her.

"That doesn't make Nan a killer. A bad hostess maybe, but not a killer."

"One degree of separation," Gaspar shrugged. "There was another man there. A rather well put together man, who reminded me of that Victor guy on the 'Young and the Restless'. What accent does that actor have, anyway? Sometimes I think it's Southern, sometimes I think it's British. Beats me. Helena says he's really of German descent. Anyway, this man, he did something very evil and I had to stand there and watch helplessly as his actions made my mother explode into a million pieces. Can you imagine that, Ellie? Someone you love not only dying before you, but being physically burst apart like a cheap dollar-store firework? It wasn't pretty."

"You watch the Y&R?" Ellie questioned.

"Is that all you have to say?" Gaspar asked, clearly hurt. "I just poured my heart out to you."

"What do you want me to say? Of course I'm very sorry for your loss, Gaspar. Whoever this man was at Nan's house, and whatever he did, I'm sure it was an accident."

"An accident?"

"Well, I'm thinking he wasn't arrested either. You're not showing a whole lot of closure here."

"I've seen this man before, Ellie. In photo albums that my mother had tucked away under her bed. He was my father. The father I never knew."

"So, your father killed your mother. I'm sorry to seem so cold-blooded, Gaspar but I've kind of had a lot to deal with lately. What does this have to do with my Nan? Why are you so mad at her?"

"Your grandmother didn't care. Just like you don't care. There was no panic from HER when it happened. There were no tears. SHE just began picking up the pieces of my mother as if Marita was confetti thrown at a wedding. SHE used a shovel, as I recall. SHE scooped the remnants of my mother up with a hardware store winter sale item. My mother deserved better."

Ellie thought back to that first morning in Troy. She remembered asking her mother how Helena had wrecked her shovel over... Mrs. Harbinger. A look of horror came over Ellie's face. Could it be true? Was Gaspar telling the truth about her Nan?

Flashing back to the trip to Troy in Tony's van, Ellie remembered even her own mother having reservations about Helena. She remembered clearly that her mother referred to Helena as 'people' and that Helen was reluctant to call

Helena 'nice'. Maybe it was because of the whole slutty schoolgirl/popstar persona her mother associated with Helena, or maybe it was really something else, something so sinister even Helen didn't want to talk about it.

"Believe it, Ellie," he cautioned. "It's not just your grandmother. Your mother doesn't care when people lose their life either. She just pretends to."

"You're a liar."

"Am I? Was she terribly broken up about that old guy dying on your porch? Did she lose any sleep over little Brooke? Did she weep with despair when the fat kid was discovered dead as a doornail in the utility fridge?"

"No," Ellie whispered, adding her personal recall of the canoeing incident into the mix.

"What makes you think you're any different? You can't fool me. You're one of them. A LaRose by any other name..."

"I'm not like them," Ellie insisted. "I can't even kill a spider."

Gaspar put his finger to her lips. "Hush, Ellie. Don't speak. Just let me look at you."

"What's wrong?" Ellie asked, turning her head ever so slightly away from him.

"Nothing," Gaspar whispered, taking her chin in his fingertips and turning her face towards his. "You're beautiful." He leaned in closer and kissed her lightly on the lips.

Her heart began to race. To her surprise, she wasn't finding the caress the least bit repulsive. A bit of a shocker, but exciting at the same time. "What did you do that for?" she asked breathlessly.

"I don't know," he admitted. "It just felt like the right thing to do. Isn't that what sixteen-year-old boys do to fifteen-year-old girls? Are you mad at me?"

"Not about that," Ellie found herself admitting. The kiss had unleashed a flood of new feelings. Oddly, every evil atrocity she knew he had done in the past was suddenly of less significance. Beneath the long dark hair and brooding demeanor lurked a sadly misunderstood guy trying his best to live in a world in which he didn't belong. A world that chose him, not the other way around. If she were in his position, she probably would have had to become a feeder herself. What other choice did he really have? It all was so clear to her now.

"It's okay, Gaspar," she said, softly licking her lips with her tongue not knowing whether he was going to try to kiss her again. She waited, feeling the hot flashes of teenage angst passing between them through stolen glances.

"It wasn't my choice, Ellie," he said, as if reading her mind.

"How can you be so bad, and so beautiful at the same time?" she asked him, touching his face softly. She closed her eyes and explored blindly the soft, cool texture of his skin. It was baby-like, with no sign of stubble forming around his jaw line. Perhaps he too, was waiting for his body to grow into his chronological age. Then again, maybe not. She opened her eyes and inhaled deeply as the face that had earlier represented such evil took on a new guise. Gaspar was cute. Maybe even cuter than Tom, in a Goth-Dude kind of way. She leaned in closer and offered her lips to him.

He took her head in his hands and kissed her again, longer and harder this time, and she didn't pull back from him. It was the first time in a long time that he had felt any kind of physical love, and he found himself thinking that perhaps killing her was not the best thing he could do. Not today, anyway.

"So, you don't think I'm twelve anymore?"

"No," he answered, "I can see that you're not. I'm sorry I was such an asshole about that. It's not easy being different, is it Ellie?" he asked sincerely.

Ellie nodded in agreement. "All we want is to be accepted, to be treated like adults. I don't get why that is so hard. I can't help the way I look."

"You're gorgeous," Gaspar responded. "I see through it now, the innocence that your naked face portrays. You're much more mature than you let on."

Ellie took his hand in hers. "How strange," she commented. "A few hours ago, I absolutely hated you, and now…"

"And now?" Gaspar asked breathlessly.

"And now I find you… intoxicating," she smiled. "I didn't think I'd ever use that word in my life, but really, it's the only word that fits."

"It might be the effect of my saliva, from when I tasted your blood. The potion-like attribute in it makes it slightly easier for …" he paused, not wanting to say 'easier for those about to die'.

"I don't think that's it," Ellie said softly, stroking his fingers. His hands were larger than hers, yet somehow delicate. It was almost impossible to believe they had carried out the atrocities that they had.

"My hunger," he tried to explain, "isn't about the feeding, no matter what you think. My hunger is my loneliness. Do you think I like being like this? A freak? I just want to be accepted like everyone else. I hunger for love. Does that really make me any different than you?"

"What's it like?"

"It sucks. Sorry."

"No, I mean, what does it feel like. Physically."

"It's kind of hard to explain. Remember the night by the bridge?"

"My dream?"

"If you want to call it that. Wasn't it the wildest dream you ever had? Didn't you feel and smell things so vividly, even though you were in a trance?"

Ellie nodded in agreement.

"That's what it's like. Only for me, it's no dream. I'm awake and everything is totally pumped up. I don't dream anymore. I rest, but I don't dream."

"Did it hurt?"

"Becoming a vampire?

"Yes."

"Yes."

He stood up and walked over to the fountain sprinkler, cupped his hands, stepped on the water release, and gave his face a rinse. This conversation was draining on him, and the water made him feel slightly refreshed.

"SHE made me the man I am today."

"How?" Ellie said, her green eyes showing empathy for him for perhaps the first time. "I thought you had to be a vampire, to change someone into one."

"You do," Gaspar nodded, turning back towards Ellie. "Trust HER to have the local vampire on speed dial."

"Just like that?" Ellie asked.

Gaspar sat back down on the floor beside her. "I'm sorry about the cold floor, Ellie. I just don't notice these things anymore."

"Well, the blanket helps," Ellie said, offering him a portion of it.

He smiled weakly and spread part of it across his legs. His left foot was twitched nervously as he began to talk. "You have to understand how upset I was that night, Ellie. I wanted to die. I had no one to turn to. My mother was dead. I couldn't trust my father. The Chief was busy with my mother's bits and pieces. The old guy from down the street just kept on strumming his guitar like nothing happened. Betty Lachey was hysterical, and SHE, as I said before, was calm. Dead calm."

"It must have been horrible. What did you do?"

"I went back home into our kitchen and took out a carving knife from the butcher block. At first I just tried to carve my mother's initials into my arm, a self-inflicted DIY tattoo." He pulled up his sleeve to show Ellie where he had done exactly that. "Do you like it? I'm surprised I can still make out the letters. Every other trace of what I did that night has vanished."

Ellie grimaced. The knife had carved the initials jaggedly into his upper arm. "And then?" she asked apprehensively.

"I downed a half a bottle of my mother's pain killers, and took the knife to my wrist," he said calmly. "Actually, sliced might be a better word. It almost did the trick."

"You tried to kill yourself?" Ellie whispered in non-belief.

"I did better than try. I felt my heart stop beating."

"Oh my God!" Ellie gasped. "Did Nan find you and get you to a hospital?"

"No! That Naturo-Nan of yours put me into stasis. I must have been like that for a while, because when I woke up the painkillers had worn off and I was dealing with the worst pain I have ever felt in my life. I remember looking at HER, and begging HER to kill me, just to make the pain stop. But SHE just smiled. And then SHE was gone."

"I can't believe my Nan would leave you alone like that."

"SHE didn't. Not for long. My concept of time is a bit shaky because I was drifting in and out of consciousness, but in a little while there was a man hovering over my body. At first I thought it might be that Tom guy, but I realized that this man's hair was longer and more strawberry colored than gel-boy's. When he talked to me, he sounded messed up. He spoke Latin with an Irish accent. He was leaning over me like he wanted to kiss me, and I remember thinking, 'how am I supposed to stop this?' But instead, he sank his teeth into my shoulder, and he began to feed off me. Just like you read in novels. The blood began to leave my body and enter his. I kept thinking that the whole experience couldn't be real. But it was."

"Freaky," Ellie commented, enthralled in his story.

"SHE was telling him to slow down.

"Ciaran," SHE said. "Watch what you're doing. You need to get a better sense of Gaspar's life force before you finish turning him."

"But this Ciaran guy, he kept saying it was too late for that. I was too far gone. He told HER he had to work quickly to save my life. Save my life. That's a joke."

"How long did it take? Did he drink all of your blood?"

"I'm not sure. I know I felt pleasure and pain for what seemed like an eternity, then he was gone. I haven't seen him since. He didn't even stick around to teach me anything. I woke up in your grandmother's office, no longer who I once was."

"Was SHE there? I mean, was *she* there... when you woke up?"

"Yes. Hovering over me like a pathetic nursemaid. SHE was crying and blubbering out excuse after excuse. It's the only time I've ever seen HER a total train wreck."

"See, she didn't really abandon you."

"Not then."

"Then there must be some good in her."

"There's good and bad in everyone, Ellie. It's the balance of the two that determines which side of the fence you're on." He shrugged. "I've found that need overshadows will on that trait. It's too late for me to be one of those vampires who quietly blend into society, although SHE assures me they are out there."

"It's never too late, Gaspar."

"Yeah, it is. As the months go by, I need more and more blood. Different kinds of blood. A varied menu as recommended by the national food guide. I guess I can shape-shift back to a wolf and start attacking pigs and cattle, but I think even the dumbest human will eventually catch on."

"Maybe I could get a part-time job at the animal hospital. I need money anyway. I could bring you the animals that, you know..." Her voice trailed off sadly.

"Maybe you could be a farmer," Gaspar said without a hint of sarcasm. "But not today, not tomorrow, and certainly not forever. Thanks anyway, Ellie."

"Maybe," Ellie hesitated. "Maybe you could feed from me. You kind of did before, right? You had a taste of my blood. It didn't make you go berserk or anything."

"If I had more it would," he explained. "You're too old for me," he laughed sarcastically.

"You said yourself it was a matter of time before my age wouldn't bother you. Maybe I'm like an anti-depressant and you have to take a little every day before it begins to work. We could try it. You never know, it might become... normal for us."

"But what if I couldn't control myself and I went too far?"

"I guess that gives 'going too far' a whole new meaning," Ellie pondered.

"I don't know enough about how this whole thing works to know for certain," he admitted. "Would you be willing to risk your life? Would you risk becoming like me?"

Ellie was silent.

"Well, at least you're honest," Gaspar offered.

"Maybe we could run away and find him," Ellie offered. "The man who turned you. He must have it figured out."

"You'd do that for me?" Gaspar asked. "You'd leave your safe little world to journey with me to the unknown?"

"Well, a girl's got to leave home sometime," Ellie shrugged. "If you could hang on until the summer, that might be easier."

"But what do I do with you until then?" he asked.

"You learn to trust," Ellie shrugged. "Without trust, there is no relationship."

"Should I be updating my faceplant page?" he smirked, kissing her softly on the forehead.

"I think we still have to leave it as 'it's complicated'," Ellie smiled.

Gaspar's ears perked up. "I think I heard something outside. I'll be back in a minute," he said to her. "Don't go anywhere," he smirked.

Ellie waited for him to leave the washroom, and then quickly pulled the cell phone from her pocket.

"Come on, come on," she said, as she frantically texted a message. She barely had time to push send to the last number entered before Gaspar was back in the room.

"What was it?" Ellie asked nervously, sliding the phone back into her jeans.

"Things that go bump in the night," he replied.

Chapter 31

The drive out to Stillman's Creek was an ominous one for the three teenagers. They knew that the road ahead was full of danger, but they knew they could handle it. What they didn't know, was that their false sense of bravado was about to get them into a whole lot of trouble.

"Kill the engine," Tom instructed Ryan as the Toyota approached the bridge.

"Don't say kill please," Jacey answered. "It gives me the jeebies."

"I don't care how horny I get, I'm not coming back to this place once this day is over," Ryan said, as he opened the car door. The smell of the swampy water was a sensation he'd just as soon forget.

"What's that smell?" Jacey asked. "It makes me want to throw up."

"Stay in the car, Jacey," Ryan instructed. He contemplated whether bringing her along was a good idea in the first place.

"Why? I can run faster than Tom," she said, as if reading his mind. "We already established that." She got out from the backseat and stood on the snow covered ground beside Ryan.

"Good point," Ryan conceded. "Tom, stay in the car."

"Why me? She blew up the jail." He got out of the Toyota and leaned across the trunk.

"Also a valid point," he said as he watched Jacey pull her cell phone from her coat. "What are you doing, Jacey? This is no time to take a call unless it's from 1-800-BITEME."

"Dude, I think you need another digit," Tom noted.

"It's Ellie," Jacey said excitedly. "She's sent me a message. It says 'bloo'." She looked questioningly at Ryan. "What does bloo mean?"

"Gimme that," he said, pulling the phone from her hand. He glanced at the screen. "It says b.loo." He paused for a moment. "I thought you were British."

"I am."

"She's in the old schoolhouse all right. She's trying to tell us she's in the boy's washroom.

"Oh I get it," Jacey laughed, tilting her head in the perky manner that drove Ryan insane. "That's cute," she continued. "b.loo, g.loo". She smiled at Tom, and whether he found it funny, or whether it was just the nervous tension in the air, he found himself giggling too.

Ryan exhaled in exasperation. "Look, both of you girls, stay here. I'll just have to do it myself." He turned to leave.

Jacey unexpectedly grabbed Ryan by the scruff of his neck and pulled him within inches of her face. "You listen to me, Ryan Lachey. You might be the big football star at school, but you didn't get there all by yourself, no matter what you think. You had teammates that helped you. I might not be as fast with my hands as Tommy, but we're all wearing the same jersey here."

"The jersey of the damned," Tom said flippantly. "Why don't we just call the cops?"

"No cops," Ryan insisted. His level of trust for Troy's men in blue had fallen to an all-time low.

"We *all* had a part in this," Jacey continued, stomping her right foot to emphasize the point. "We all have to help her."

"You've wrecked your boots, Jacey," Ryan noticed, looking at her feet. The Jimmy Choo's were wet and torn and stained with a combination of soot and snow. He didn't know whether the world had finally beaten him down or not, but he actually felt bad for her. Her boots were like a cornerstone in an old building. They held the key to the past and they needed to be deconstructed. They might make a good chew toy for Ralph's dogs.

"I don't care," Jacey said, and the honesty in her voice surprised all three of them.

"Okay then. You're in," Ryan agreed." He looked at Tom. "Well?"

"I don't have the big locker room speech to give you," Tom replied. "But I never said I wanted to stay in the car, so quit looking at me like that. I never said I wanted to bail out on you."

Ryan reflected this for a moment until a more urgent issue came over him. "Nature calls. I gotta take a leak. Alone," Ryan told them. "Unless we're all in that together, too?" He waited for Jacey or Tom to comment. "No? So I'm good to go. Thanks for that." He walked off into the trees and proceeded to unzip his fly. "I will never underestimate the freedom of whizzin' in the wild again," he told himself. He was grateful to be out of jail, albeit illegally. He re-adjusted himself in the wilds of the woods and turned when he heard Jacey scream.

"What the fuck?" he wondered, turning around towards his friends. Subconsciously knowing it was time to hide, he ducked down behind the nearest bush. Its leafless limbs didn't offer much camouflage, but it was better than nothing.

Before him were two hulking creatures in what was left of their police uniforms, standing in front of Tom and Jacey. They were big, and they were blond, but their similarity with anything human stopped there. They were the Daytons, but then again, not the Daytons. The twins were "Hulk-ified."

"Again, what the fuck?" Ryan said to himself. He crept as far to the edge of the thicket as he could without revealing himself. He watched as Cody... at least he thought it was Cody... pushed Tom effortlessly to the ground. The officer shoved his boot firmly on Tom's back, holding him down as he reached around for his handcuffs. Tom's brief attempt to struggle was met with a swift kick to the ribs by Cody's other foot. Ryan heard his friend scream in pain, an audible reflex that resulted in another boot to his side.

Colin had Jacey pinned to the ground as well. He was straddling her, his legs pressed against her thighs like a vice. "Look at the pretty girl," Ryan could hear him snarl, in a demonic voice. "Pretty little missy, makes me want to kissy."

Ryan instinctively wanted to rush to help them, but if he had learned anything over the past few days, it was that the old saying 'fools rush in', was sage advice. There was no way he could get to his friends without being seen in advance of any attempted attack. The cop/wraiths had guns and handcuffs and quite possibly supernatural powers, and he had nothing. He had never felt more helpless in his life.

Held to the ground, Jacey froze in terror, as the wraith took his sopping tongue and licked her cheek in a slow, lingering motion. "Why are you crying, pretty girl?" he taunted, his sour breath making her flinch. "I'll give you something to cry about."

The wraith moved his tongue above his top gum line, where something lay hidden in his upper right cheek pocket. He maneuvered the object down to between his front teeth, glowering menacingly in her line of sight as he revealed the disposable razor blade he had deftly kept hidden. He tore it across the surface of his own bottom lip, making it bleed before the girl's eyes, eliminating any possible doubt as to whether it was sharp or not. He moved closer towards her, projecting the edge of the blade within inches of her cheek, and sadistically watched as she began to sob uncontrollably.

"You should have accepted my affection, you stuck-up bitch," he screeched, as he swiftly moved the blade across her left cheek tearing her flesh in a straight slice.

"Leave her alone, you fucking bastard," Tom screamed at him.

Cody Dayton looked at him and laughed. "I visited your daddy's hardware store today," he said. "I needed a new razor too," he said, pulling a pack of disposable razors from his pocket. He grabbed Tom by the hair and began to hack away at his blonde locks in a haphazard fashion. When he had shorn most of it, he pulled Tom's head back so he could admire his handiwork. "This looks like crap, pretty-boy," he said, and began to shave away what was left of Tom's streaked tresses. "Get up," he instructed him, "and show your girlfriend your new hairdo."

"Go to hell," Tom shouted.

"I said get up," Cody repeated, pulling his pistol from his holster and pointing it at Tom's head.

Colin made the same request of Jacey, putting the gun next to her temple so she would be certain to hear the safety being released. "Let's go for a little walk," he said to her, pulling her up from the ground by her elbow. He shoved her in front of him and hit her head with the side of the gun, indicating to her to take the path on the right. She had no choice but to do so. Tom and Cody followed behind them.

Ryan's viewpoint from the thicket indicated that the four were headed towards the old schoolhouse. If he stayed calm, and moved quietly through the edge of the woods, he could most likely get there undetected. "They're big," he muttered to himself, sizing up the wraiths. "But they're still butt-ass half-deaf morons." As he watched the four enter through the nearest side entrance, Ryan made his way around to the far end of the school, to an area big enough to be a gymnasium. The doors were chained together. "Fuck," Ryan cursed, looking around for another point of entry. "Where are the vandals when you need them?" He noticed a curtain blowing through a classroom window. "Looks like Bubba forgot to close the window during the fire drill." He grabbed the window ledge with the palm of his hands and proceeded to pull himself up and over the sill and into the classroom. "And Betty told me nothing good would come out of my detentions. Thank the fuck for the million pull-ups Coach Skinner made me do."

He listened at the door. He could hear voices down in one direction. He took the other. "There's got to be a fucking weapon in here somewhere," he surmised, as he entered the gym. The room was dark, making it next to impossible to find anything. He got down on his hands and knees and crept along the wall until he found what he believed to be a storage locker. He tugged at the mesh door, but it didn't give. "For cryin' out loud," he muttered, "can't I catch a fucking break?" He slid his hand along the mesh until he found a space where it gave some slack. He used his fingers to grasp it and pulled with all his might, wincing as he did so. His shoulder still hurt like hell. Eventually the mesh gave way, and Ryan was able to make a hole big enough to shove his upper body through. His quick search produced three items: a basketball, a javelin and a baseball bat. "Weapons drop. Lives added," he chuckled, quoting his favorite video game.

In the boys' washroom, both Ellie and Gaspar could hear the commotion coming down the hall. The wraiths and their two prisoners soon entered the room.

"Well, well. Look what the cats dragged in," Gaspar laughed, looking at what the wraiths had done to Jacey and Tom. "It's Scarface and Chrome Dome. Thanks for coming to my party, but it's a little late for Halloween."

"Shut the fuck up," Tom told him.

"Now, now, potty-mouth" Gaspar sneered, "don't go all ballsy on me. You've been spending way too much time around the other one. Speaking of which, where is the foul-mouthed Goliath?"

"Right here, fucker," Ryan announced, standing in the doorway, his arsenal of weaponry in his arms.

"Do we have a problem?" Gaspar asked, looking at him. "You seem rather irritated. Do you need to get in a little exercise before your death sentence?"

"Yes we have a problem," Ryan said, turning towards Colin. "Dude, you're supposed to be at the hospital, guarding my mother." He palmed the basketball and threw it towards the wraith. "Dodge ball," he said, hurling it towards the demon's head hoping to stun him. It made contact, but the impact didn't even make Colin flinch.

Tom positioned himself for the rebound, hoping to get a chance to take the other one out. The ball wound up hitting him in face, sending him down to the ground.

"Now?" Ryan asked him. "After all these years, *now* you want to get in the game? You're not Samson. You need your hair, dude." He looked over at Jacey and noticed the gash on her face. He was going to kill the sons-of-bitches that did that to her, if it was the last thing he did. His eyes searched the room frantically for Goth-Chic, and he was momentarily relieved to see that she appeared to be unharmed, despite being chained to an over-sized sink. He winked at her, in an effort to let her know he was going to do everything possible to get them all out of this horror show.

Sensing Ryan's momentary distraction, Gaspar moved towards him and ripped the baseball bat from his left hand. "Let's see how many sports you're good at," he taunted.

The vampire's movements caught Ryan totally off guard, causing him to inadvertently drop the javelin from his right hand as well. So much for being heavily armed.

"Swing low, sweet chariot!" Gaspar sang, swirling the bat first above his head, and then outward from his body like he was a batter warming up at the top of the first. "I know," he sighed, "I never was much good at this. I'm about to strike out," he told Ryan. "Maybe once, maybe twice. But I'll hit something eventually." He took a practice swing in the direction of Ryan's kneecaps. "B-b-b-batter up!"

Ryan's career hopes were a Louisville Slugger away from being taken from him permanently. Jacey's hopes of being a supermodel were all but dashed. Tom's perfect coif was lying in the middle of the forest. Ellie was chained to a monstrous slab of marble, her freedom taken from her before she really had any freedom to speak of. Not exactly a great day for any of them.

The wraiths laughed in unison like a pack of hyenas.

"Goth," Ryan began, "we have made a fuckupery of gothic magnitude. I'm so sorry."

Ellie wasn't listening. Through a broken off pipe in the wall beside her, she heard another version of Sweet Chariot... a hauntingly low, slightly off tempo, whistling of the tune. She began to sing along to it, almost inaudibly at first, then getting louder with each stanza until everyone in the room stopped what they were doing and stared at her like she was crazy. "Tell all my friends, I'm coming too," she sang. "Comin' for to carry me home."

Chapter 32

The Mustang sped down the highway to the county three road and hung a left. It went down past the sign that said "Wildman's Farm", making another immediate left onto the road that led to Stillman's Creek. Helena hit the high beams to illuminate as much of the unfamiliar area as she could. They were almost up to the bridge when Helen noticed Ryan's car, the rear doors still ajar, parked on the side of the road.

"Kill the engine," Helen instructed her mother as they pulled up close to the vehicle.

"Kill. I'm feeling a love for that word right now," Helena admitted. She parked her car next to the Toyota and immediately got out of the vehicle. "What is Ryan's car doing out here?"

"Maybe it's still here from the other night?" Helen offered, joining her mother by the side of her neighbor's car.

"Not a chance. Roy would have had it moved as part of the crime scene. That much I'm certain of."

"Well, we know Ryan's in jail..."

Helena subconsciously tilted her head. "Then why do I get the feeling he isn't?' She stuck her head into the back seat area of Ryan's car and sniffed. "Interesting. I get a mix of Axe cologne and Paris Hilton perfume." She sniffed again. So... I'm thinking Tom and Jacey were here quite recently, in the back seat." She also knew that left someone else driving the car.

"It might smell good in there, but it just reeks out here. What is that smell?" Helen asked, wrinkling her nose. "Skunkweed?"

Helena sniffed the air. "It's coming from the water," she said, turning her head in that direction.

"Phew. It smells like rotten eggs or… sulfur?" She looked at her mother for affirmation. "Burning sulfur?"

"You're right," Helena confirmed. "I think," she said slowly, considering her answer carefully "the creek is covering the fires of hell." She watched for a reaction of her daughter, but Helen had her best poker face on. "Pull your scarf over your nose. It won't block the stench out entirely, but it'll help keep your senses clear," she instructed.

"You have a hellmouth near Troy?" Helen asked, doing her best to keep her cool as she ignored her mother and plugged her nose with her gloved hand.

"I don't think it's so much of a mouth, but it is definitely a crack in the crust," Helena suggested. "It also explains some other things."

"What other things?"

"This is probably not the time to tell you," Helena said softly.

"Great," Helen sighed.

"Where are the kids?" Helena asked, looking around. The full moon was allowing her natural eyesight to scan a good part of the area. She didn't see any sign of the teenagers. "This doesn't look good," she mumbled, walking back towards the rear of her Mustang. "I think we'd better prepare ourselves for the worst."

"You know," Helen began, "the writers of Supernatural gave Dean an Impala for a reason. They were going to give him a Mustang, but the Impala had a bigger trunk. I read that somewhere. It might be something to consider next time you're in line for a new vehicle."

"That may be a valid point for some people," Helena replied. "But I've been doing this quite a bit longer than the Winchester men. It's not the quantity of the ammo, it's the quality," she said, opening the trunk of her car.

Helen's mouth fell open as Helena waved her hand proudly over the arsenal of weaponry she had stashed under a blanket. There were knives made from a variety of metals, guns of varying sizes, bags of salt, a five-gallon bottle of water and a host of other assorted weapons of destruction.

"Whoa," Helen exclaimed.

"Well, the water and the salt help the Mustang's traction in the winter," Helena explained with sincerity. "The rear end fishtails a bit in the snow."

"You always were a good packer," she admitted to her mother, surveying every nook and cranny of the trunk. One item in particular caught her attention. "Where the hell did you get that crossbow?"

"This old thing?" Helena asked, pulling it out so Helen could get a better look at it. The weapon appeared to be handcrafted out of wood and iron. Although it remained rust-free, the wooden surfaces were well worn, and the string had obviously been replaced at some point in time. "I think it's just what we need for the job."

"Well, it's not like you can order it through L.L. Bean..."

"Actually, you *can* get them on line," Helena offered.

"Not like that one you can't," Helen insisted. "C'mon. Spill."

Helena's glove rubbed the metal surface with unusual affection. "This one dates back to the Crusades." She was almost giddy with delight.

"And you came upon it how?"

"Your grandmother gave it to me. She had some nasty business to take care of with Henry Tudor and the Church of England... at least that's how the story goes."

"Oh, that's comforting," Helen replied. "Not."

"Relax. They're used for sport today."

"I'm sure they are," Helen replied sarcastically. "You know, for those situations when a rifle with a scope just won't do the trick."

"Do you have a better suggestion?" Helena paused impatiently for an answer. "I thought not."

"But you've only got one arrow. Is there a spare under the utility wheel?"

"I don't need a spare, Helen. I never miss. Besides, I have another use for that," she said, lifting the spare tire easily from its mount. Hidden beneath the safety device was a pair of hand weapons.

"Of course. It's where you keep the grenades," Helen said sarcastically. "Maybe you should tighten the bolts on that tire lock a little better when you put the wheel back on. Or tell your town council to pave the county roads."

Helena took an explosive and stuffed it into her coat pocket, handing another one to Helen.

"Seriously?" Helen asked. "I'm not big on pineapples."

"Do I look like I'm joking?" Helena asked.

"Okay, okay," Helen said gingerly taking hold of the weapon. "Honestly, the things you make me do," she said, reluctantly putting it into her own pocket.

"When I count to three, you pull the pin and pitch it like you're throwing to the outfield, got it?"

"Sadly, yes. Are you sure you wouldn't rather take a gun? You seem to have more of them in that trunk of yours than the sporting goods section of a Texas Wal-Mart."

"Guns are over-rated," Helena replied, reaching into a bag of road salt she had opened for the use it was intended on the first snowfall of the season. She poured the heaping handful into her other empty pocket before pulling a small plastic department store bag from the trunk as well. "I was going to give this to Ellie for Christmas," she explained, pulling a necklace from a little blue jeweler's box tucked inside. "But I guess I'm going to have to use it."

"Is that a talisman?" Helen asked.

"Some people call it that. I call it a locket," she insisted. "I'm just going to open it and put a few drops of the holy water in it. Holy water is like vanilla. You only need a little."

Helen watched her mother remove the cap from the water bottle and dip her finger into it, allowing a few drops to be transferred to the necklace's chamber.

"That huge jug of water you're lugging around is holy water?" Helen asked.

"It's like premium gas to me," Helena explained. "I like to keep it filled up."

"Why do I get the feeling you've done this before?" Helen asked, watching her mother. "I just hope we're in the right place to find Ellie, and it's not just where Tom and Jacey do what Tom and Jacey probably do, out in a place like this."

"We're in the right place alright. Listen. Can't you hear it?" She put her finger to her lips indicating for Helen to be quiet. "If I'm not mistaken, I can hear the low melodic sound of a gospel hymn."

Helen perked her ears. "Sweet Chariot? Is Willie whistling Sweet Chariot?"

"Well, I'm guessing it's probably not Tom or Jacey doing it. He's doing his best to give us a clue, bless him. This is one time we're actually going to enjoy a Willie tune."

"I love that man," Helen beamed.

"It's probably not the best time for that either, Helen," she cautioned. This was no time for Helen to get any romantic notions in her head. Helena needed her daughter's killer instinct front and center. She reached back into the corners of the trunk and pulled out what appeared to be two elastic bands with lights on them.

"What the hell is this?" Helena asked, as Helen handed her one.

"It's a headlamp. These I do get from L.L. Bean," she replied. "Just put it on, it's going to be dark in there." She sighed. "Just the way they like it."

"Won't it tip them off?"

"They're going to know we're here, Helen. So it doesn't really matter. No sense breaking a leg before we get to them."

The women followed the whistling sound as long as they could, the light on their head leading them down the dark path. The sound became louder as they came nearer, then suddenly stopped as they arrived at the abandoned schoolhouse.

"I guess we're on our own now," Helen sighed.

"He's done what he can for us. Now I need you to concentrate," her mother instructed. "Reach into the back of your mind, Helen. Where is Ellie?"

Helen closed her eyes and took a deep breath, exhaling very slowly. "I've got her on my radar," she whispered. "I know where she is."

"Good. Then let's do this." Helena whispered back, pulling the crossbow closer to her body. "Those burning schoolhouses at the fireworks stores are going to have nothing on this one when we're done. I'm looking forward to this."

"I'll go first," Helen instructed. "You watch my back."

Helena nodded in agreement as Helen began to use her extra sensory perception to lead them into the school, through the dark hallways, past the gym, around the corner and down towards the bathrooms.

They could hear a heated argument from behind the door that read BOYS, and for once, Helen was thankful to hear her next door neighbor dropping a continuum of f-bombs. "How do you want to do this?" She asked her mother, as they stood outside the door.

"I want to make an entrance, of course. Although I know I'm really going to regret it tomorrow," she replied. "Stand back."

She turned her body slightly to the left and raised her leg a few inches higher than her hips. After pausing a moment to take aim with the sole of her boot, Helena pulled her leg back to the ground, took a couple of steps backward, then swung it out again with full force and proceeded to kick the door in.

"Hello, Hell. Meet the hand basket," Helena announced to the stunned occupants of the room.

She evaluated the scene like a triage doctor would. "Four kids, two wraiths and one son-of-a bitch vampire. All living and breathing," she affirmed to Helen. Good news and bad news. The forces of good were a tad more battered than the guardians of evil, it appeared.

Helen followed with a more concentrated overview of the warzone. She saw Ellie huddled in a corner, chained up like a dog, obviously scared out of her mind. Her heart broke at the sight, and she had to remind herself that every move she took had to be a calculated one. This was no time for maternal instinct to take over. She motioned for Ellie to stay put. Ryan was near the sprinkler fountain fully cognizant of what was going on around him. His eyes moved from her to Helena and back again, and she thought she saw him give a sigh of relief. Tom... at least she assumed it was Tom... was rubbing his head in the corner with his other arm around Jacey, who was not looking at all pretty at the moment. That left three others in the room... the twin patrolmen and the teenager she presumed was her half-brother, Gaspar.

"Just answer me one thing," Helena requested of Colin. He was moving towards her with venom in his eyes. "Why did you have to go and kill the Clarks? The parents, I mean. What did they ever do to you? I get that Gaspar did what he did, but what are you and your brother's parts in all this?"

"We're the clean-up crew," Colin replied. He glanced over at Gaspar. "The boss docsn't like loose ends." His contorted mouth let out a screech that sounded like a cat in heat, as his neck tilted backwards. "Party!" he cried out. "Welcome to our new eatery. It's called the Death Zone."

"Yeah, yeah" Helena mocked him, "I've never been very big on Vampire/ Wraith fusion. She turned her attention to Gaspar. "And how exactly did you become the boss?"

"Wouldn't you like to know," Gaspar sneered. He watched Helena raise the crossbow to her own eye-level. "Playing Robin Hood are we? Am I supposed to be afraid?"

"You know, you three look so miserable," Helena taunted him. "Have you ever stopped to consider why the unjust are so much crankier than the just?"

"Not lately, no" Gaspar scoffed. He motioned for his henchmen to take care of Helena. "Go ahead, pretend you're going to shoot me. I know you won't. If you had it in you, you would have let me die this past summer."

"It's not always about you," Helena mocked, spinning her body around towards the wraiths. She closed her eyes and drew the arrow towards her body. "Well here's a big happy, happy, joy, joy to both of you."

"For the love of God, Mother. Open your eyes," Helen screamed. "You're going to miss."

Helena released the iron trigger and the arrow took flight. "I told you. I never miss. I just hate it when it's easy. It's all about the angle of trajectory."

Cody let out a blood-curling screech as he lurched towards Colin from behind. He grabbed him, trying to move his brother away from the approaching quarrel, but the projectile had speed and force on its side, and easily penetrated through the front of Colin's eye socket. Blood began to spurt from the entry wound as the arrow's momentum continued through Colin's head and into the left ear of Cody. When the arrow's flight was finally over, Colin was dead, face-down on the floor with blood oozing from the back of his neck. Cody's body was pinned to the wall, grey matter from his brain seeping out through his ear canal.

"Holy crap," Ryan exclaimed.

"They just don't make weapons like this anymore," Helena said proudly, looking at Helen. "And you wondered why I always made you play pin the tail on the donkey."

"Are you sure they're dead?" Helen asked cautiously. "I'd hate for them to split again. Quadruplet wraiths would be a pain in the ass."

"They're dead," Helena insisted.

"I'm not taking any chances this time," Helen replied, pulling a hidden Ginsu knife from between her leg and her boot. "I took it from your knife drawer back home. I'll get you another one for Christmas," she promised her mother. She grabbed Cody's bloodied hair in her hand to give herself a clear view of his neck. Her cut was swift, and she watched the deputy's body spew even more blood from his once pulsating carotid artery. "That ought to do it," she said icily.

She turned to his twin. "Femora, femora on the wall, who's the fairest one of all?" she said in a guttural voice. She then made two deep incisions, cutting open his upper legs one after the other.

"Still want to do her?" an ashen-faced Tom asked Ryan.

"I just want to stay the fuck out of her way," Ryan replied.

Helena turned to Gaspar. "As for you," she said with bitterness, "shall we make it swift, or shall you suffer a slow, lingering death? Retribution for the pain and suffering you have caused others?"

"Let he who is without sin cast the first stone," Gaspar sneered.

"Baby, the Bible ain't gonna help you now," Helen interjected. "Not even the 'do unto others' part."

"Stop it!" Ellie screamed, finding her voice from beneath her fear. "Leave him alone! He's right. Don't you see? Just because you kill in the name of what you think is good, it doesn't make it just."

"It does!" Ryan tried to tell her. "It makes it okay... really okay."

"Ellie, be quiet," Helen snapped. "This is none of your business."

"It's ALL of my business," Ellie shouted back. "That part isn't complicated at all."

"If you kill me," Gaspar smirked with evil, turning his gaze from Helena to Jacey, "I won't be able to tell little Goldilocks over there where her baby is. Pity."

Jacey's eyes and mouth went wide. "How do you know about that?" she asked nervously.

Tom glared at Jacey. "Baby? What baby? You told me you never did it."

"I never said never, Tom." Jacey answered, afraid to look at her friend. "Think back. I never said never."

Tom removed his arm from around Jacey and looked helplessly at Ryan.

"Chicks," Ryan shrugged. "I tried to tell you."

"Please don't kill him," Jacey begged Helena. "If he knows where my baby is, please don't kill him."

Gaspar walked over to her and kicked at Jacey's once fabulous boots. "You're not the only one who can Google. You're quite the little traveler, aren't you?"

"He's lying, Jacey," Helena insisted. "He knows it, and I know it. He's tugging at your heart strings, buying some time. He's good at that. I should know."

"Maybe he isn't," Jacey said solemnly.

"He likes to play the distraction game," Helena said, emphasizing the adverb. "It's his little ploy for empowerment. Sometimes it works, sometimes it doesn't. Are you feeling particularly lucky now, Gaspar? With your two friends dead?"

Out of the corner of her eye, Helena saw her granddaughter reaching as far as she could across the floor. She kept Gaspar engaged in conversation.

"I thought we had a deal, Gaspar." Helena continued. "I thought we agreed you would come to me when your hunger began to torment you."

"I don't need anything from you," Gaspar sneered.

Ryan was also watching Ellie. She was after something. He extended his right leg and managed to get the fallen javelin to roll towards her.

"Nor I, you," Helena said to the vampire.

Ellie stood up, the javelin in her hands, and pointed it towards Gaspar. "You're not the only one who can be deceitful and manipulative," she told him. "You didn't really think I felt anything for you, did you? You didn't really think I would choose *you* over my own family? You didn't just lose your mother that day."

She hurled the javelin towards Gaspar's torso. It tore through his jacket and into his left ventricle. "Huh," Ellie exclaimed, admiring her own prowess. "What do you know? Sports Day was good for something after all."

Gaspar grabbed his chest and screamed. He screamed for what seemed like an eternity, his body contorting backwards and forwards until it finally collapsed to the ground.

"Dude," Ryan laughed uncontrollably, seeing an end to his nemesis. "I told you not to hit girls. I tried to tell you."

Jacey dropped her head and began to cry uncontrollably. Tom was numb.

Helen's mouth dropped open. Her baby. Her little killer of a baby... she hadn't had a prouder moment in her life. "Will that do it?" she asked Helena, unsure if Ellie's wound would keep him dead.

"It's a start," Helena said. "I'll finish the bastard off myself." She took some salt from her pocket and opened the little locket.

"What are you doing?" Ellie asked.

"Making a Vampire cocktail," her grandmother replied. "A little salt, a little holy water, mixed together in silver... talisman." She shook the contents, then removed her thumb and poured the mixture on Gaspar.

His body turned into a festering pool of rotting flesh, emitting an aroma that had the survivors gagging.

"Peto Abysuss," Helena chanted, waving her arm over Gaspar's remains. She then went to the twins and did the same thing. "Peto Abyssus quod subsisto illic."

Black smoke rose out of the three corpses, removing what was left of their temporarily supernatural life forms.

"See, Jacey," Ryan whispered. "That's how you do it."

"How am I ever going to explain this?" a voice said from behind the activity.

Helena turned around to see Roy standing in the doorway, his pistol drawn. He entered the room, walked around and counted the dead bodies, stopping momentarily to tell the Dayton twins they were officially fired.

"Did you do this?" he asked Helen, as he stood over Gaspar's body.

"Technically?" she replied. "No. The other two..."

"Be quiet, Helen," her mother said sternly.

Roy looked at Helena. "I have no words..." he said. "I asked you time and time again if you knew anything about all this."

"And I told you what I could," Helena told him firmly.

"But not everything," Roy insisted. "So much for the trust in our relationship."

"I'll take care of it, Roy," she told him. "Just like the Fourth of July." She could sense that the bond they between them was now broken, and it saddened her.

Helen could sense it as well. She put her arm across her mother's shoulder. "Let's get out of here," she said, giving Roy a look that may or may not have been deserved.

The seven of them left the building in silence.

Helena glanced around. "Are we all out?" she asked, as they started to head away from the schoolhouse and back towards the bridge.

"Yes," Ellie gasped.

"Helen, we're not done yet," Helena reminded her. "On three…"

"I'm already there, Mother," she informed her, turning around, pulling the pin from the grenade and hurling it through the still opened doorway.

Helena did the same with the device in her pocket, lobbing it through the glass window of the basement washroom. "Hit the deck," she told the others.

Two explosions immediately followed.

"Is everyone okay?" Helena asked once the ensuing smoke and debris had cleared. One by one the six others nodded.

"I suggest you say it was a gas leak," she told Roy tersely.

He walked away from them, shaking his head as he did so. The man in him knew that it was a good thing the three… whatevers… were dead, but the officer in him was having a hard time with the rights and wrongs of the situation.

"Now what? Helen asked. The strength she had summoned from within had been totally exhausted, and she began to tremble.

"Betty's got that bottle of whiskey with our name on it," Helena replied. She gave a sigh of relief and smiled a little, watching the four teenagers head back to Ryan's car, their arms around each other in a formation of love, peace and hope. "I'm thinking that's a start," she laughed, putting her arms around her daughter.

Epilogue

The groundskeeper at Forest Lawn cemetery had placed a canvas canopy over the open grave that would be Mr. Wagner's final resting place. A three-inch layer of snow had formed atop it since the morning. It was now mid-afternoon, and thankfully the precipitation had finally stopped. All the mourners were left to contend with weather-wise was a biting wind coming from the north-west.

Ryan stood at the foot of Old Man Wagner's open grave and tossed a full beer can into it. The crowd of mourners smiled.

"Thanks Old Man... I mean Peter... for giving a guy a break every once and a while. I thought you might get a little thirsty on your journey, so here you go. I know this isn't your favorite brand, but my Ma said under the circumstances I could take one of hers."

From the side of her neighbor's final resting place, Betty Lachey laughed and wiped away a tear from her eye. Peter Wagner had been a cantankerous old coot in her opinion, but the street wasn't going to be the same without him.

She glanced over at the LaRose women, and noted that none of them were dressed in black for the occasion. "Times have changed," she sighed to herself.

Helen seemed to have read her mind. "Nice outfit, Betty," she said sincerely. "Black becomes you."

"Thank you," Betty replied, somewhat rattled by the compliment. People were being inordinately nice to her since she got out of the hospital. Now that Ryan had been cleared of any wrongdoing, she was able to hold her head high once again in the close-knit community. Still, things weren't quite right. She wasn't sure why her living room carpet had come to be cleaned while she was away. Or why she was missing a hell of a lot of whiskey. Or the big one… why she had obtained a soft spot for the women in the house next door. But she had.

She took Helen's hand and patted it. "Stop by for coffee sometime, you lovely woman. And bring that cute daughter of yours along. I think Ryan likes her." She shrugged her shoulders and laughed. "Who knows, we could be related someday."

"Thank you," Helen replied with a smile. "I'll do that sometime." She took a couple of steps away from Betty and joined her mother. "What the hell, Mom? I know you drugged her while Mike Webster was fixing the chimney, but by any chance did you throw a little sugar into the potion to sweeten her up while you were at it?"

"I had her out cold, Helen. A woman has to do what a woman has to do," Helena affirmed mischievously.

Helen sighed.

"Honestly, that man worked so slowly I thought I was going to have to leave her unconscious 'till Christmas. Remind me to take a good look at his invoice when it comes in."

"Shh!" Helen reminded her.

"Mr. Wagner was a cool dude," Ryan continued, ignoring the idle chatter around him. "One summer, Tom and I snuck into his yard and raided his crab apple tree, thinking nobody was home. But he was home alright, and he caught us. He made us pick every fucking apple on the tree." He saw Helen wince, but continued his story. "It took us hours. He wound up making apple sauce with them later that night, and the next day he brought some over to my Ma. She said it was the best she ever had."

"I never heard that part of the story until now," Betty admitted aloud. "Or I would have whooped your ass, Ryan. But the sauce was really good."

Ryan smiled and took a deep breath. Delivering the eulogy was tougher than he thought it was going to be, but deep in his heart he knew he was the man for the job. He collected his thoughts and was about to continue speaking when a short loud wail of a police siren made everyone's head turn towards the parking lot.

"We probably shouldn't have left Stan alone in the front of the car," Purdy confessed to Roy. "Our track record's not that great with him."

"Well, maybe we shouldn't have kept the keys in the ignition," Roy grimaced. "I caught Ryan driving Betty's car before he was legal. I really don't want to have to explain to the town council how Stan took a joyride in the cruiser."

"I didn't want him getting cold," Purdy tried to explain. "He promised me he wouldn't touch anything. He's getting more and more like Ryan every day."

"Maybe that's not such a bad thing after all," Roy acknowledged. Stan had been through a lot and he was worried about the boy. "Have you had a chance to talk to him?" he asked Purdy.

Purdy nodded. "I did when we went to get Betty from the hospital. He seems to have selective recall about the whole ordeal. I can't explain it."

"I bet I can," Roy said, looking disapprovingly at Helena.

Ryan cleared his throat loudly. "Are you done?" Ryan asked the officers. The tone of his voice indicated he harbored some ill-feelings towards the two lawmen despite being off the hook for the murders. "Because I'd like to get through this before supper, unless you've got some toaster pops for me."

The officers turned their eyes to the ground and nodded, feeling a little sheepish.

Ryan started to continue, only to be silenced this time by the sound of a cell phone playing a remixed theme from The Addams Family, thumb clicks and all. Ellie pulled it from her pocket and glanced at the call display before shutting it off.

"Sorry," she offered honestly in response to Ryan's pained look.

"Who was it?" Tom asked, leaning over her shoulder to try and get a peek at the call display.

"Dina," Ellie replied. "A friend from my former life. She can wait," she said, turning her phone off and stuffing it back into her pocket. "Where's Jacey?"

"Jacey doesn't do funerals. I'm confused right now, about what Jacey does and doesn't do, but apparently she doesn't do funerals." He took Ellie's hand and held it.

"People. I know Old-Man Wagner's not goin' anywhere, but I'm getting cold. So shut up, okay?" He waited for silence. "Okay. My mom said he was a fucking sly dude when he was younger," Ryan continued, retelling his favorite story as only Ryan could. "The cops were always hauling his ass off for something. They ripped out his whole garden one summer in the sixties, or so my granny said." He looked at Helen and laughed. "Look, Ms. L., I'm tryin', okay?"

"I know. But just for today, could you say frack?" Helen asked politely. "I mean; it is the man's funeral."

"I can't, Ms. L," he explained. "Especially today, because Old Man...I mean Peter... we used to watch Battlestar Galactica together at his house, and he'd scream at the screen when they kept saying that. 'Say what you mean', he'd yell. 'What's the point? We all know what you're really saying, so just say it.'"

"It's true," Helena agreed. "Mr. Wagner told me that too. It used to drive him crazy when they said frack. Other than that, he was a big fan of the show."

"Ma, can you pass me my guitar?" Ryan asked. "I know I gotta wrap this up, but I wrote a little song about Mr. Wagner, that I'd like to sing for you now." He took the guitar from his mother and strummed a few strings. "Gimme a second," he pleaded, "this cold weather makes it hard for the strings to stay in tune." He adjusted the tension and strummed again. "Okay, like I was saying, this is a song I wrote... well, actually, Helen LaRose and I wrote. She helped me with the lyrics. I know, I know, it's crazy that this foxy mama wanted to spend some alone time with me, but she did," he laughed. He looked over in the direction of Ralph Wildman and Tara, who were standing in the background. "Don't even go there, Wildman. Are we good, Ms. L?"

"We're good," Helen smiled. "But don't push it."

"You did what?" a shocked Helena leaned over and asked her daughter. "When did this happen and should I be worried?"

"Well, I was always liked to write poetry. I just thought I'd help him out a bit. Clean it up a little, if you get my drift. I still know how to sneak out of the house, you know. It's like riding a bike, you never forget."

"You are full of surprises, Helen," her mother laughed. She gave her daughter a hug.

"The apple doesn't fall far from the tree," Helen noted. "Remind me to install an alarm on Ellie's window, will you?"

"If you want to. But it's a waste of time and money. She'll find a way out. It's genetic," Helena protested.

"I know," Helen admitted. "Maybe I want to keep things from coming in. Home sweet home and all that."

"I take it Willie never said good-bye?"

Helen shook her head.

"He'll be back," Helena said, rubbing the back of her daughter's coat. "Whether we want him to or not." Both women pondered the ramifications of that statement for a moment, and then turned to Ryan.

"Okay, here we go," Ryan began, tapping his foot as he sang in a loud baritone voice:

> "You were the last man standing,
> When thy sent you off to war,
> You were the last man standing,
> When your mission was no more.
>
> You were the last man standing,
> When the poker call was made,
> You were the last man standing,
> When the final cards were played.
>
> Now I'm the last man standing,
> Missing you like hell,
> I'll be the last man standing,
> Wishing you farewell."

The crowd clapped quietly as Ryan nodded to the clergyman. "Take it, Padre."

"Ashes to ashes, dust to dust," the preacher began, as Ryan strummed his guitar softly in accompaniment. He waited until the clergyman had given the rites, and then chose the moment to show off some fancy fret work.

"Encore!" Ellie yelled to Ryan.

"You know what Goth?" Ryan responded. "There is a song I can't get out of my head that might just work." He strummed a d-chord, g-chord, d-chord opener and began to sing:

Swing low, sweet chariot,
Comin' for to carry me home;
Swing low, sweet chariot,
Comin' for to carry me home.

I looked over Jordan,
And WHAT did I see,
Comin' for to carry me home,
A band of angels comin' after me,
Comin' for to carry me home.

Swing low, sweet chariot,
Comin' for to carry me home;
Swing low, sweet chariot,
Comin' for to carry me home.

If you get there before I do,
Comin' for to carry me home,
Tell all my friends I'm comin' too,
Comin' for to carry me home.

This time the mourners didn't clap. They coughed, and they cried and they reached for their family members and gave them a hug.

Ryan kissed his guitar pick then tossed it onto the casket. "Godspeed, Old Man Wagner," he whispered, fighting back the tears.

Ellie stepped forward and pulled Beastie Bear from the bag she was carrying. She gave it a kiss and tossed it in as well.

"What are you doing?" Helen shrieked. "That's your bear."

"I don't need it," Ellie sighed. "I offered it to Stan, but he said he didn't want it either. He said he was almost nine," she smiled. "Sometimes you just have to let go."

"Are you sure?" Helen asked. "You don't have to let go of everything. You could let go of just a little…"

"I'm sure," Ellie said, turning to smile at Tom.

"Is there enough room in there to toss in that God-forsaken bug van of yours?" Helena asked. "I mean, while we're giving things away?"

"I'll take it back to Tony tomorrow," Helen offered. "Although it might be good for our family business, if you think about it."

"Get rid of it," Helena insisted. "I'm searching Craig's list for a black Impala for you."

"You know, there's a lot more room in a Beemer than people think," Helen smiled.

"You just keep thinking that," Helena laughed, patting her daughter on the shoulder. "And I'll go see if Forest Lawn's grave digger is looking for an assistant. You still need a job. Unless you feel like becoming a cop. Apparently there's a shortage in town."

Helen grumbled inaudibly to herself.

"What's that?" Helena prodded.

"I guess Roy's heaving a sigh of relief… getting to pin all the murders on the twins you wanted me to date," Helen said sarcastically.

"I think he's got mixed feelings on that one," Helen lamented. "I don't know what this is going to do to our relationship. Maybe it's time to move on."

"From the relationship or from Troy?" Helen asked. "Because I just got here. I'm beginning to settle in. I know where the school is. I know where the movie theatre is. I know where the jail is… or was, and now I know where the cemetery is. Really, what else is there to know?" She glanced over at Ellie, still holding Tom's hand. "And Ellie's making friends."

"And?"

"And that's it. They're a little misguided, but they're good kids. Human kids. That ought to count for something."

"Helen, you sound enlightened," Helena noted. "Are you sure you're okay?"

"Fighting vampires and wraiths can do that to you," she admitted. "I've definitely lost my little girl. But I like the woman she is becoming," she said lovingly. "Sort of. She still wears weird make-up."

"Oh, Helen!" her mother sighed. "What am I going to do with you?"

"Love me like you always do, because you're my mom," she answered. "And learn to lock your doors."

"Deal," Helena agreed, crossing her fingers behind her back.

She needn't have worried. Her promise to her daughter had fallen upon deaf ears. Helen's full attention had turned to a man she had never seen before. A tall man, with reddish blond hair that hung unkemptly over the collar of the long, tan drover coat he wore haphazardly over his left shoulder, despite the weather.

"Who is that incredibly handsome man who just walked up beside Betty?" she asked her mother. "Does Ryan have an older brother I don't know about?"

"Settle down, Helen," Helena replied. "That's Ciaran Quinn."

"Who?"

"An old acquaintance."

"He doesn't look that old to me. He looks positively divine."

"Uh, no. He was a houseguest of Mr. Wagner's. I imagine he's come to say his last respects," her mother informed her.

"I thought you said Mr. Wagner lived alone."

"He did. Ciaran rented his backyard for a month." Helena bobbed her head in contemplation. How much did she really want Helen to know? "Sort of. At the beginning of July."

"No! Don't tell me…"

"Well you didn't think Gaspar was the only vampire in town did you? How did you think I managed to save the boy that night? He tried to kill himself. He had lost a hell of lot of blood by the time I found him. I needed another vampire to bring him back from the dead. If only temporarily," she sighed.

"And Ciaran was…" Helen began, her eyes looking him up and down. She never would have guessed there was anything unnatural about him. "Really?" she sighed.

348

"Listen to me the first time, Helen."

"But he looks so…"

"Human?"

"I was going to say 'fine'."

"Well, I guess he is a step up from your man in purgatory," Helena taunted. "You are incorrigible, you know that, Helen?"

"I get that from you."

"And Ellie gets it from you."

"We're doomed," Helen laughed, putting her arms around her mother. "What do you think happened to Jacey's baby? That must be heartbreaking for her."

"I don't know," Helena replied nervously, taking Helen's arm off her shoulders. "You take the Mustang and drive Ellie home before the guests get there. I think I'm going to go take a little walk. I'm feeling a bit overwhelmed by all this." She caught Ciaran's attention out of the corner of her eye and nodded to him.

"Mother! You get back here," Helena insisted as Helena began to walk away. "You do too know something! Spill it."

Helena stopped in her tracks and was tempted to say something smart back to Helen, then thought the better of it. "I forgot to tell you, darling. Your grandmother has invited us to England for Christmas. Think about it, will you? I'm going to have to let her know our answer soon."

"Let's not. Tell her to come here. We can all be together and celebrate the season in Troy. I'll help you decorate the house."

"I don't know, the whole Santa/Chimney thing…" she hesitated, "…that was a bit of a bummer. Besides, Elaine's not getting any younger."

"Well she sure as hell isn't getting that much older," Helen argued, putting her hands to her temple. Helena watched as her daughter's forehead begin to wrinkle. "Oh crap," Helen said with disappointment. "I have visions of sugar plums fighting in my head."

"I'm so glad you've embraced this power of yours," Helena remarked. "It's going to make life a hell of a lot simpler." Turning, she started to walk off in the direction opposite the parking lot.

At the edge of the cemetery was a sparsely wooded forest that led down to the banks of the river. Helena kept walking until she could no longer hear the sound of the crowd at the funeral ground. She stood alone and breathed in the crisp, cold air. The wind refusing to calm, whipping through the bare branches of the birch tree with little resistance. For Helena, it brought back memories of her childhood in England, where she would walk through old cobblestone streets. When she was young, the wind tried its best to knock her over. She didn't have any of its nonsense then, and she wasn't going to have any of it now. She would dig her heels in as usual.

A tug on her coat sleeve from behind her back brought her back to reality.

"I have eyes in the back of my head, Ryan," she said as he moved in front of her and raised his out-stretched arm towards her face.

"Don't do it," he begged, a look of desperation on his face.

"Do what?" Helen asked, somewhat nervously.

"Don't do to Tom, Jacey and me, what you did to Stan."

"Be quick with this, Ryan. I have an appointment to keep."

"The memory thing. We want to remember all this craziness. This has been the best week of my life. Except for the almost dying part."

"Really, Ryan. I don't know what you're talking about."

"If you say so," he said, sounding eerily like Mr. Wagner.

"I'm sure that Stan will be less nervous now," Helen offered. "He's still Stan, don't worry. He's just been unwound a bit. A good thing, under the circumstances, wouldn't you agree?"

"He punched me in the gut last night," Ryan informed her. "I was just lying there on the couch, calling him a wimp like I usually do, and he up and drove me one," Ryan said with a smile. "I'm thinking he's a cornerback."

"Hmm, interesting," Helena smiled back.

From above their heads, a crow let out an ear-piercing call, then dove downwards towards them from its perch high in the tree. It missed Ryan's head by less than an inch.

"Whoa, that was creepy," Ryan said, clearly shaken. "It's the wrong time of the year for them to be all gonzo. No babies in the nest. Are you okay, Mrs. LaRose?"

"I'm fine, Ryan," Helena assured him. "But maybe it's time you rejoined your friends."

He didn't need to be asked twice. He could see a dozen or so crows heading towards them from the north, all soaring lower than they should be. He turned and ran back towards the crowd as fast as he could.

"Glad to see your shoulder's better," Helena said to herself.

She took the scarf she had wrapped around her neck and placed it over her head, glancing at the sky as she did so. The crows had arrived and formed a circle around her on the ground. She turned around to face the river, and found that once again she was not alone.

"We have unfinished business," the voice said, the Celtic accent being easily understood by Helena.

"I know," she sighed, her boots crunching the frozen snow beneath her feet. "Elaine has called me home. But I'd like to get through Thanksgiving first, Ciaran. No craziness, no voodoo, just homemade turkey and pumpkin pie."

"Good luck with that, Helena," he smiled wryly. "If you bring the girls with you in December, I suggest you book a sightseeing trip for them to keep them occupied. You and I are going to be quite busy, I'm afraid."

"Ciaran," Helena began, "about Gaspar…"

"You did what you had to do," he told her. "Even I understand that. But you owe me one, and I'll be in touch."

He blew a kiss towards her, turned and walked alone down to the riverbank.

She watched him walk along the shoreline until he eventually vanished from her sight. Ciaran's arrival hadn't been happenstance. She was grateful that he had decided to give her some peace. Thanksgiving was just around the corner, and she had a lot to be thankful for. Ellie and Helen wouldn't just be home for the holiday; they were home for good as far as she was concerned. That, more than anything, made her feel like everything was good in her world. At least for now.

The End

About the Author

Author Janine McCaw is known for believable characters being placed in circumstances they'd probably rather not be in, leading to twisting plotlines that keep the reader guessing. While her first novel "Olivia's Mine" is a fictional account of historical events that happened during the early 1900's at Britannia Beach, B.C., McCaw also writes in the general, paranormal, YA, urban fantasy and chick-lit genres. McCaw lives in "Supernatural" Vancouver, British Columbia with her husband Paul. She is not a zombie (twitter) but has been known to roam the streets that way... and not just on Halloween.

www.janinemccaw.com

www.Helens-of-Troy.com

Tweet: @mc_janine

facebook: Helens-of-Troy

facebook: Janine McCaw, Author

Blog: www.supernaturalcentral.blogspot.ca

Made in the USA
Charleston, SC
03 October 2016